Kings of the D...

THE S...
who Claimed Her

Three exotic and thrilling books by
three terrific authors:

Susan Stephens
Teresa Southwick
Barbara McMahon

THE SHEIKH WHO… COLLECTION

On sale 5th July

On sale 2nd August

On sale 6th September

On sale 4th October

On sale 1st November

On sale 6th December

THE SHEIKH
who Claimed Her

Susan
STEPHENS

Teresa
SOUTHWICK

Barbara
McMAHON

Mills & Boon, an imprint of Harlequin (UK) Limited, Eton House, 18-24 Paradise Road, Richmond, Surrey TW9 1SR

THE SHEIKH WHO CLAIMED HER
© Harlequin Enterprises II B.V./S.à.r.l 2013

Master of the Desert © Susan Stephens 2010
The Sheikh's Reluctant Bride © Teresa Ann Southwick 2007
Accidentally the Sheikh's Wife © Barbara McMahon 2010

ISBN: 978 0 263 91009 4

026-0813

Printed and bound in Spain
by Blackprint CPI, Barcelona

MASTER OF THE DESERT

SUSAN STEPHENS

Susan Stephens was a professional singer before meeting her husband on the tiny Mediterranean island of Malta. In true Modern™ romance style they met on Monday, became engaged on Friday and were married three months after that. Almost thirty years and three children later, they are still in love. (Susan does not advise her children to return home one day with a similar story, as she may not take the news with the same fortitude as her own mother!)

Susan had written several non-fiction books when fate took a hand. At a charity costume ball there was an after-dinner auction. One of the lots, 'Spend a Day with an Author', had been donated by Mills & Boon® author Penny Jordan. Susan's husband bought this lot, and Penny was to become not just a great friend but a wonderful mentor, who encouraged Susan to write romance.

Susan loves her family, her pets, her friends and her writing. She enjoys entertaining, travel and going to the theatre. She reads, cooks and plays the piano to relax, and can occasionally be found throwing herself off mountains on a pair of skis or galloping through the countryside. Visit Susan's website: www.susanstephens.net—she loves to hear from her readers all around the world!

CHAPTER ONE

SHE had the figure of a glamour model, the face of an angel—and she was threatening him with a knife.

It wasn't every day his ocean-going yacht was boarded by a barely clothed virago. What few clothes remained on the young girl's bruised and scratched body were ripped and sodden, and the knife she was brandishing looked as if it had come from his galley. In her other hand, she was holding a hunk of bread and cheese, stolen from the same place, he presumed.

Was a French baguette worth killing for?

Probably, he mused, remembering he had persuaded a top French *boulanger* to open a branch in Sinnebar.

As the merciless sun sliced its way through the mist, his first impulse was to get the pirate princess into the shade, but he remained still, not wanting to provoke her into anything more reckless than she had already attempted. She was young, barely out of her teens, but had clearly been through some sort of trauma. He took in the tangled mass of blonde hair and bruised face with slanting blue-green eyes, more wounded than wounding. 'What do you think you're doing?' he said calmly.

'Don't!' she threatened, jabbing the sultry air with her knife.

He held the laugh, relieved she was okay. Mist hung tenaciously, making visibility poor; she must have climbed up on deck while he'd been in the sea checking the hull for storm damage.

'I'm warning you!' she exclaimed, though he hadn't moved.

If she backed away another inch, she'd be over the side.

Her shock at seeing him had forced her into the role of aggressor, he concluded, remaining still so as not to alarm her. She hadn't recognised him or she would have put down her little knife. 'Why don't you give me the knife?' he suggested, knowing if she had meant to attack him she would have done so by now. 'Or, better still, throw it overboard?'

She bared her teeth at that to give him a little warning growl, like a kitten with a toothache. 'Don't you come any closer,' she warned, 'Or I'll—'

'You'll what?' He disarmed her in one absurdly easy move. There was a flash of warm flesh beneath his hands, then it was all shrieking and clawing as she fought him as if to the death. 'Wildcat!' he exclaimed, feeling a sharp thrill of pain as she dug her sharp, white teeth into his hand. Resigned to capture, she couldn't take her eyes off the much bigger knife he wore hanging from his belt. 'I have no intention of harming you,' he reassured her.

She had no intention of listening, which left him dealing with a wriggling desperado, who drummed his deck furiously with her tiny heels as he steered her towards the opening leading to the lower deck and his first-aid kit.

Finally losing patience, he bound her arms to her side and swung her over his shoulder. 'Stop that!' he instructed as she arched her body and pummelled his back. 'Do you want to bang your head?'

She went rigid as he padded sure-footed below deck into what was an all-purpose space on the ocean-going racing yacht. She was still in shock, he registered as he set her down on the one and only seat. All home comforts had been stripped away below deck to make room for necessary equipment, but as he'd been trialling on this voyage rather than racing there was plenty of fresh food on board—hence the bread his pirate wench had stolen. He had brought other supplies and small comforts along to make his time aboard more pleasurable, including the cushions he'd laid out on deck so he could sleep beneath the stars.

When the girl groaned and put her head in her hands, his first thought was to rehydrate her. He reached into the cold box for a glucose drink. 'Here,' he said, loosening the top and offering it to her. Her expression didn't change. She remained stiffly non-responsive, staring ahead with her jaw set in white-faced fright.

'Drink it, or I'll hold your nose and pour it down your throat.' He'd used similar shock tactics years back when his younger brother Razi had refused to take his medicine.

Just like then, she retaliated with a furious, 'You wouldn't dare!'

One look from him was enough to settle that argument. She held out her hand. He gave her the bottle; she gulped down the contents greedily.

'When was the last time you had something to drink?'

She refused to answer. Swiping the back of her hand across her mouth, she raised blue-green eyes to his face. Chips of glacial ice would have held more heat.

No surrender, he concluded. And as for apologising for trespassing on his yacht? Forget it.

Tugging on the first top that came to hand, he began heating water to bathe her wounds. Blocking her escape with his body, he reached into a cupboard for antiseptic, lint and cotton wool. Adding a splash of disinfectant to the water, he stuffed a blanket under his arm and turned around. 'Here—put this round you.'

She flinched and refused to look at him, drawing her legs in defensively, but it was when she crossed her arms over her chest that he finally lost patience. 'I'm not interested in your body,' he assured her, only to be rewarded by a tiny squeak of protest from a girl who was clearly accustomed to being admired. Proving the point, he put the bowl down and tugged the blanket tightly round her slender shoulders, trying not to notice that one lush, pert breast was partially exposed.

Seeing his momentary distraction, she snatched the blanket from him, holding it so tightly closed that her knuckles turned white.

'Don't flatter yourself.'

She was safe from him—too young, too reckless, plus he resented the intrusion. Any other time or place and he would have had her removed from his presence.

But she was tougher than she looked or she would have been reduced to a hysterical mess by now. She was an irritation, but she was also courageous, he concluded, and a breath of fresh air after the painted harpies who regularly served themselves up at court for his perusal.

There was only one thing wrong with the girl: she reminded him of someone else. Those tangled locks and slanting eyes held an echo of his father's mistress, a woman who had destroyed his mother's life and who had referred to Razi—the step-brother he couldn't have loved more if they had shared the same blood—as the worst mistake she had ever made. That woman might be dead now, but she had left disaster in her wake, and as far as he was concerned she had defined his father's weakness. It had been a fatal weakness that had stolen his father's attention away from his country and its people. With that lesson guiding him, things had changed for the better since he had assumed control. There was no longer chaos in Sinnebar, and his people knew that he would never repeat his father's mistake and become a slave to his heart.

He refocused as the girl shifted restlessly on the bench. 'I'm going to bathe your scratches before they turn septic,' he informed her crisply.

She recognised a command, but to his astonishment something in her eyes said she would dearly like to strike him. 'I wouldn't do that if I were you,' he warned grimly, at which she scowled and slumped back like the spoiled teen he thought her to be. 'When did you last eat?' he demanded as he assessed her wounds and general condition.

Her stomach answered this question with an imperative growl, and then he remembered the hunk of bread she'd dropped on the deck. 'When I've finished, you can eat.'

She tilted her chin at a defiant angle to stare haughtily past him.

So, let her go hungry—though he was forced to concede he admired her nerve. He liked the electricity between them too, but neither of these things would affect how he dealt with her. He would administer basic first-aid and then turn her over to the authorities. 'Arms,' he prompted brusquely, and then, deciding he would teach her what it meant to risk her life in the Gulf, he demanded, 'Don't you know anything about maritime law?'

Her flickering gaze suggested not.

'If I report your actions to the ruling Sheikh in Sinnebar... You have heard of the man known as the "Sword of Vengeance", I take it?' He had the satisfaction of seeing her pale. 'If I tell him that you came aboard my yacht, stole my food and threatened me with one of my own knives I would imagine the most lenient sentence he could hand out would be life imprisonment.'

'But you wouldn't!'

Even as she protested her eyes were narrowing in defiance. He liked her fire. He liked her voice. He liked... 'Report you?' he rapped, calling his wayward thoughts back to order. 'That depends on you telling me exactly how you got here. And be completely honest with me; I shall know at once if you lie.'

Hearing the menace in his voice, she slowly unfurled her legs as if deciding a temporary truce was her only option. 'You were moored up, and so I thought...'

She'd take her chances, he silently supplied, feeling a beat of lust as she held his gaze. She spoke English well, but with the faintest of Italian accents. 'You don't look Italian,' he said, dropping it in casually.

'I had an English mother,' she explained, before her mouth clamped shut, as if she felt she'd said too much.

'Start by telling me what brought you to the Gulf and how you arrived on my yacht.'

'I jumped overboard and swam.'

'You swam?' He weighed up her guarded expression. 'You're telling me you jumped overboard and swam through these seas?' His tone of voice reflected his disbelief.

'For what felt like hours.' She blurted this, and then fell silent.

'Go on,' he prompted, continuing to bathe her wounds.

'Before the mist closed in, the boat we were on was hugging the coastline.'

'"We"?'

She shook her head as if it was important to concentrate. 'I could see this island and was confident I could make it to the shore.'

'You must swim well,' he commented.

'I do.'

She spoke without pride, and, taking in her lithe strength, he was tempted to believe her. But she must have swum like an athlete to survive the storm, and however capable she believed herself to be she was no match for the dangerous currents and unpredictable weather conditions in the waters of the Gulf.

The girl had stirred some instinct in him, he realised. It was the instinct to protect and defend, and he hadn't felt that so strongly since his brother Razi had been young. 'What made you jump overboard?' He had his own suspicions, but wanted to hear it from the girl.

Her face grew strained as she remembered. 'Our boat was attacked.'

'I'll need more than that.' If his suspicions were correct, his security forces would need all the information he could glean from her. 'Was your boat attacked by pirates?'

'How do you know that?' The terror in her eyes suggested she thought he was one of them. In fairness, she had had quite an experience, and he was tempted to comfort her. It was an impulse he resisted.

'I suspected as much, and you just confirmed it. And I'm not a criminal,' he added when she continued to stare at him as if he had just grown horns. 'Quite the contrary—I bring people to justice.'

'So you're a law-enforcement officer?'

'Something like that,' he agreed.

Partially reassured, she settled back. 'I was lucky to escape with my life,' she said, echoing his thoughts exactly. 'I escaped.'

And now she was over-doing it with a dramatic hitch in her voice. As she looked at him, as if trying to gauge his reaction, he suspected she was used to playing someone— an older brother, perhaps? She was out of luck with him. He wasn't so easily won over. 'You are lucky to have escaped with your life—and I'm not talking about the pirates now. You boarded my yacht without permission. I carry arms on board and wouldn't hesitate to use them. What use would your little knife have been to you then?'

Colour rushed to her cheeks while her intelligent eyes sparkled like aquamarines. He didn't need a further reminder to put some distance between them. He picked up the radio, to call the officer on duty and let him know the girl had been found and was safe—and when he turned to look at her he felt another bolt of lust.

She couldn't stop shaking and the man didn't help. She had never imagined such a combination of brutal strength and keen intelligence existed, let alone in such a perfectly sculpted form. His manner was proud—disdainful, even. He was magnificent. He only had to touch her for her body to react as if he was caressing her intimately. There was just one thing wrong. She could be as bold and determined as she liked, but she was way out of her depth here, and he frightened her. She was a flirt, a tease, and was used to getting her own way, but she had never met a man so hard—so hard on *her*. She wasn't used to indifference. She was spoiled—she was the first to admit it—spoiled, both by a brother who adored her and by the attention of half the world's men. If anything, there were times when she wished herself invisible. This was not one of those times.

But why should the man be interested in her? He was out of her league—older, tougher, better looking and more experienced in every way. She had left her comfortable cocoon back in Rome to learn about life, but never had she anticipated learning quite so much quite so fast. She didn't even know if this man was more trustworthy than the pirates, and only had the fact that he had bathed her wounds to go on. Would he have done that if he had intended to harm her?

However caring that might make him seem, she refused to be reassured, or to relax her guard. There was something dangerous about him. At least when the pirates had attacked she'd had the chance to jump overboard, but she suspected this man had lightning reflexes and slept with one eye open. Right now he was talking on the radio in a husky tongue she guessed must be Sinnebalese. She had studied the language before setting out on her journey, and could pick up a word or two, but frustratingly not enough. She could learn more from his manner, Antonia decided, which was brisk, to the point and carried an air of authority. He was someone important—someone people listened to—but who?

He made no allowances for the fact that she was young and vulnerable, and she couldn't decide if she liked that or not. Her brother smothered her, believing she required his constant supervision, whereas this man was more like a warrior from one of her fantasies, and had no time to waste on indulging her. Tall, dark and formidably built, in her dreams she would think of him as a dark master of the night, intense and ruthless, the ultimate prize—in reality, he made her wish she had never left home.

She continued to watch him furtively through a curtain of hair. She'd had no alternative but to board his yacht. She had swum to the point of exhaustion, and when she'd seen his boat looming out of the mist she hadn't thought twice about seizing her chance.

As soon as he finished the call, she quickly drew up her feet and locked her arms around her knees, burying her head to avoid his penetrating stare. But he was ignoring her again, she realised, peeping at him.

She studied him some more as he moved about the cabin. He was spectacularly good-looking, with deeply bronzed skin and wild, black hair that caught on his stubble. The firm, expressive mouth, the earring, the look in his eyes, his menacing form all contributed to the air of danger surrounding him. He might look like her ideal man, but this was not one of her fantasies, and she was so far out of her comfort zone she was having to make up the rules as she went along. But there was no question he could melt hearts from Hollywood to Hindustan, and would certainly make a great Hollywood pirate, with those sweeping, ebony brows and that aquiline nose.

Then she remembered that real pirates were scrawny, smelly, ugly and mean.

As she whimpered at the memory of them, he whirled around. 'What's wrong with you now?'

'Nothing,' she protested. She'd get no sympathy here.

CHAPTER TWO

'YOU must never put yourself in such a vulnerable position again,' he told the girl sternly.

She looked at him in mute surprise, but he cut her no slack. If he eased up she'd think taking chances in the wilderness was acceptable, whereas he knew that if the visibility had been better, and helicopter gun-ships from his air force had been flying over the yacht when she boarded, his snipers might have shot her.

'My boat was attacked by pirates,' she protested. 'I jumped overboard and swam for my life. What else was I supposed to do?'

He couldn't remember the last time anyone had challenged him. In a world of bowed heads and whispering obedience, it was almost a refreshing change. But the girl's safety came first, and for the pirates to be captured he had to warn her off ever doing anything similar again, and find out everything she could tell him. 'Save the attitude,' he barked, 'And stick to the facts.'

She blinked and rallied determinedly, and as her story unfolded his admiration for her grew. It also made him doubly determined that she must learn from the experience.

'You seem to have confused some romantic notion with reality,' he observed acidly when she paused for breath. 'This part of the Gulf is no holiday resort, and you're lucky these are only scratches.'

It had been a relief to find that none of her injuries was serious and was what he might have expected after hearing she'd jumped overboard. 'This will sting,' he warned, loosening the top on a bottle of iodine. To her credit, she barely flinched as he painted it on. The only sign that it hurt her was a sharp intake of breath. She had beautiful legs, coltish and long, and her skin was lightly tanned, as if she had only recently landed in the Gulf. 'What brought you to these shores—a gap year?'

'Sort of.'

She winced—from fear of discovery that she was doing something she shouldn't, he guessed—but before he could question her she hit him with, 'What brought *you* here?'

No one questioned him. He had to forcefully remind himself that here on this desert island they were anonymous strangers and she couldn't know who he was. He shrugged. 'The storm.'

That was the simple answer. Sailing grounded him; it reminded him he was not only a king but a man, and that the man owed it to his country and his people to go hunting for his humanity from time to time. Whether he would ever be successful in that quest, only history would judge. 'And where did you say you were heading?' he prompted.

'I didn't say, but I'm heading for Sinnebar,' she admitted grudgingly when he held her stare.

She was hiding something, he concluded when her gaze flickered away.

'Do we have to talk now?' she muttered, playing the hard-done-by card.

'If you want the pirates to escape…'

'No, of course I don't,' she declared, staring him full in the face.

'Good. So tell me where the attack took place. Did you get a fix—coordinates?' he pressed when she didn't answer right away.

'I know what you mean,' she flared, but for the first time he thought she seemed disappointed in herself because she couldn't give him the detail he required.

He gathered from what she went on to tell him that the pirates had taken advantage of the poor visibility to target an unsophisticated boat that lacked the latest radar equipment and alarm systems. 'So you weren't sailing your own boat when the pirates attacked?' he guessed.

'No.'

Burying her head in her knees, she tensed, but with the criminals still on the loose this was no time to go easy on her. 'Sit up,' he barked.

She snapped upright, and the look in her eyes suggested she was only now realising she might have jumped from the frying pan into the fire. He felt some sympathy for her. Dressed in cut-off shorts and faded top with a shark knife hanging from his belt, he was hardly a reassuring sight. 'Come on,' he pressed impatiently. 'I need this information now, not sometime next week.'

She bit her lip and then admitted in a voice that was barely audible, 'I hitched a lift on a fishing boat.'

'You hitched?' Words failed him. The girl's naivety

appalled him; the danger she had put herself in defied reason. 'What were you trying to prove?'

'Nothing.'

He doubted that. There would be someone back home she wanted to impress. 'Couldn't you have caught the ferry? Or was that too easy for you?'

'I thought the fishing boat would give me a more authentic experience.'

'More authentic?' he demanded cuttingly. 'So, you're another tourist who thinks you can visit a foreign country with nothing more than your thirst for adventure and a bleeding heart in your survival kit?'

Her face paled. 'It wasn't like that at all.'

'It was exactly like that. And then you wonder why you find yourself in danger? Keep your arms outstretched,' he reminded her when she flinched.

His pulse was thundering with outrage at the thought of pirates in the sea off the shores of Sinnebar, though the girl had his attention too. He looked at her tiny hand and thought her courage all the more remarkable, given her petite frame. She was barely half his size, her skin-tone pale against his bronze. Her quick thinking had saved her, he concluded, and because her boldness was at odds with her fragile appearance the pirates had underestimated her. He would not make the same mistake.

Now she was speaking more, she went on to talk with passion of punishment for the pirates and compensation for the fishermen, which launched another unwelcome surge of arousal which he quickly stamped on. However soft and yielding she felt beneath his hands, her mind was not half so compliant, and he had no room in his life for complications. 'What type of boat did they have? Never mind,' he rapped, impatient to gather as much information as he could before placing a second call to the commander of his naval forces. 'Just tell me the colour.'

'It was a skiff,' she said with mild affront. 'Powerful engine; peeling white paint above the water-line; black below. And the interior was painted a vivid shade of aquamarine.'

'A vivid shade of aquamarine?' he murmured dryly. 'Are you sure?'

'Perfectly sure,' she said, holding his gaze with curiosity, as if surprised to see the humour there. 'Have I told you enough?' she asked as he turned to use the radio.

'More than I expected,' he conceded as he prepared to place the call. 'You did well.'

He could feel the heat of her gaze on his back as he fired off orders. He had become part of her desert fantasy, he guessed. Too bad; he wasn't interested. There were plenty of women who knew the score, and this girl wasn't one of them. Breaking radio connection, he turned to face her again.

'Okay?' she said hopefully.

'Okay,' he confirmed. 'So now it's all about you.' He ran a cool stare over her. 'Let's start with your name and what you're doing here.'

No name. She could have no name. Signorina Antonia Ruggiero *must* have no name. Whoever he was, this man was successful; successful people knew other people. And people talked. How good would it look for her to be branded a thief? Or, worse still, a demented creature with a knife? Before she'd even begun the work she'd set out to do.

'You're European,' the man observed in a voice that

strummed something deep inside her. 'Although, like me, I suspect you were educated in England. Am I right?'

She took in the fact that his husky, confident baritone was barely accented even though he had spoken Sinnebalese fluently. 'Yes, that's right.' Her own voice sounded hoarse.

'Where in England were you educated?' His keen eyes watched her closely, and the intensity of expression in those eyes warned her not to lie to him.

'I went to school in Ascot.'

'Ascot?' There was a faint note of mockery in his voice. He'd heard of the very expensive girls' school there. 'So you're a very proper young lady?'

Not in her head. One flash of this man's muscular back when he changed his top confirmed she was anything but proper. 'I try,' she said primly.

'What is such a well-brought-up young lady doing on my yacht, stealing my food and threatening me with a knife?'

His relentless stare sent ribbons of sensation flooding through her, making it hard to concentrate—but this was her best, maybe her only, chance to get to the mainland and it was crucial to forge a relationship with him. She also had to persuade him not to report her to the authorities to avoid being arrested the moment she landed. 'I was hungry— thirsty. Your yacht was here; I took my chances.'

She flinched when he laughed. Short and sharp, it held no hint of humour.

'You certainly did,' he agreed. 'Didn't you think to call out when you came on board? You could have made some attempt to locate the owner before you stole his food.'

'I did call out, but no one answered.'

His lips curved as he propped his hip against the bench

where she was sitting. 'So you helped yourself to whatever you felt like?'

'I didn't touch anything outside the galley.' Must he move so close and tower over her?

'And that makes it right?'

'I'm sorry.' She sounded childlike—plaintive, even—but was lost for something else to say.

'Next time I'm in Ascot, I'll wander into your house and see what I fancy taking, shall I?'

'I don't live in Ascot.' The angry words shot from her mouth without any assistance from her brain and her reward was an ironic grin.

'So, we've ruled out Ascot,' he said.

Before he could delve any further, she swayed and clutched her throat.

'Feeling faint?' he demanded caustically, refusing to be fooled by her amateur dramatics for a single moment.

'I'm fine,' she assured him, matching him stare for stare. Whatever it took, she wasn't about to let him see how badly he affected her.

'You're not fine,' he argued, narrowing his eyes. 'You've had a shock and need time to get over it.'

She hoped that meant a reprieve, and shrank instinctively from his intense maleness as he eased away from the bench.

'Relax.' His lips tugged with very masculine amusement. 'You're safe with me.'

Did he mean that to be reassuring, or was he insulting her? And *was* she safe? Could he be trusted? For once, she didn't know what to think. The man's manner was dismissive and abrupt, and his appearance… Well, that was rather more intimidating than the pirates.

There could be no guarantees, Antonia concluded, even if he had bathed her wounds. So was the flutter inside her chest a warning to be on her guard, or awareness of his sexuality?

'Are you travelling alone?'

A shiver of apprehension coursed through her as she stared into his eyes. Why would he ask that? 'Yes,' she admitted cautiously. 'I'm travelling alone—but people know where I am.'

'Of course they do,' he said sarcastically. 'So your family allows you to wander the world without their protection?'

This time she couldn't hold back. 'They trust me.' She was not defending herself now, but Rigo, the older brother who had cared for her since her mother had died six months after giving birth to her, her father having passed away shortly after that.

But the man pursued her relentlessly. 'And breaking the law is how you repay your family for their care?'

'I've already apologised to you for coming on board,' she fired back. 'I explained I had no option but to board your yacht.'

His hands signalled calm as her voice rose. 'Lucky for you I was moored up here.'

She balled her hands into fists as a last-ditch attempt to keep her temper under control, but all it gained her was another mocking stare. But *what* a stare… She couldn't help wondering how it would feel to have that stare fire with interest, or darken with desire.

'I hope you've learned your lesson,' he snapped, shattering that particular illusion.

'Oh, I have,' she assured him meekly. It was time to stop dreaming and accept the facts. She was far too young and inexperienced to interest a man like this. He thought her fragile and foolish, and couldn't know her determination. She wasn't fragile, and this trip was her chance to prove she wasn't foolish. To prove to the brother she adored—who protected her, perhaps a little too much—that she could survive without his supervision. Not that she'd made the best of starts, Antonia conceded as the man held her gaze.

'Tell me more about your family,' he prompted.

Being the object of such an intense stare was both alarming and seductive, but she wouldn't tell him anything that might risk her mission. She hadn't come to Sinnebar on her own behalf, or as part of some ill-thought-out adventure, but to persuade the authorities in the country to open a branch of her brother's children's charity. Rigo's work had already helped so many sick and disadvantaged children, and she had pledged to help him expand the reach of his charity across the world.

And there was a second reason, Antonia conceded silently. Coming to Sinnebar would give her the opportunity to track down information about the mother it broke her heart to think she couldn't remember—not her voice, her touch, what she looked like or even the scent of her hair. She knew nothing at all about the woman who had given birth to her, beyond the fact that her mother had been very young when she'd died, and that before marrying Antonia's father and moving to Rome she had apparently spent some time at the royal court in Sinnebar.

'I'm waiting to hear about your family,' the man said, slicing through her thoughts.

Antonia composed herself before replying, knowing it was important not to let anything slip. Rigo had drummed it into her from an early age that the truth was non-negotiable, though she might have to get used to twisting it where this man was concerned. 'My family don't know I'm here,' she admitted, which was true in part, at least.

'Your family don't know you're here?' The man picked up the radio phone and held it out to her. 'Don't you think you'd better call them?'

No. Men like this, men like her brother Rigo, shared a common understanding. They would demand she return home immediately. Rigo might even insist on coming to fetch her, so once again she would be no more effective than a balloon, weightless and directionless as they batted her between them.

'I'll ring them if you don't,' he threatened.

'No, please don't.' She reached out and then withdrew her hand, thinking better of touching him. 'I don't want to worry them.' She mustered a steady stare. 'Better to call them when I'm safely in Sinnebar and settled in a hotel, don't you think?'

Worry them? Rigo would be down on her like a ton of bricks. Her brother only had to file a flight plan and he'd be over here. And what would that prove—that she was as headstrong and reckless as Rigo believed her to be? Her brother would never let her work for his charity then. And she had begged him for this chance to do a real job instead of accepting her brother's generous allowance. It was a chance to do something for others instead of for herself. 'The moment I'm safe on the mainland, I'll ring them—I promise.' She was taking a lot for granted by assuming the man would take her anywhere, but she had no option when there was everything to play for.

His eyes remained narrowed with suspicion, and then to her relief he shrugged. 'You know your family better than I do.'

Yes, she knew Rigo. He could be a pain sometimes, but it was thanks to her brother she had enjoyed such a privileged childhood, which in Rigo's language meant she could ride, ski, sail, fence and swim. More importantly, living with him had taught her how to survive a man like this.

As she watched him clear up the debris from the recent triage session, she offered to help. He ignored her. Closing the cupboard on his supplies, he turned to face her. 'So all you wanted when you came on board was my food?'

'What else?' she said in bewilderment.

'You weren't thinking of stealing my yacht, for instance?'

Antonia's cheeks flushed red. She *had* considered it.

He made a contemptuous sound, as if he already knew this, and then barked, 'We'll continue this conversation when you have no more excuses left.'

'But, I—'

'Not now,' he snarled.

His tone only confirmed what she already knew—this was not a man to bend to her will, or to anyone's will.

'You will rest now,' he said as if anything he commanded would happen immediately. 'I'm prepared to give you time to get over the shock—but not much time. And don't play me,' he warned.

A shiver of awareness rippled down her spine. When he turned away, it was another opportunity to watch him again. Resting her chin on her knees, she realised that against all the odds she had grown calmer around him. Calmer and yet more unsettled, Antonia concluded, realising her libido had received an unusual boost. The man moved around the confined space with the confidence of someone who knew every inch of his territory intimately, and some of the openings were so small he had to raise his arms and coax his body through. He looked amazing at full stretch, like an athlete in the peak of condition. His air of command went with being super-fit, she supposed, though she found trying to pigeon-hole him in the outside world impossible. His frayed and faded shorts looked as if he'd hacked the legs off an old pair of jeans with the lethal-looking knife hanging from his belt, and his top had definitely seen better days.

She gave up trying to work him out. He could be crew or he could own the boat—either way, she had to build bridges and hope they stretched to the mainland. She waited until the next time he squeezed past to attempt to make her peace. 'I apologise for trespassing on your yacht and for stealing your food and the knife. Please believe me when I say I would never have used the knife. And please don't report me to the Sheikh.'

'I thought I told you to rest,' he said, showing no sign of having accepted her apology.

There was no chance of 'playing him', as he seemed to think, Antonia concluded, and he'd done nothing more than care for her as he would care for a stray dog, so she could forget the fantasies. Using her so-called womanly wiles had got her nowhere. And there was something more, something that made her shudder to think about it. While he was helping her, she was safe, but should he ever turn against her...

'What happens next is up to you,' he snapped as if he

had read these troubled thoughts. 'All you have to do is answer my questions promptly and honestly.'

And that was all? Did he know how intimidating and fierce he looked? 'I will,' she promised on a dry throat. *If all your questions are connected to the attack*, she hedged silently.

CHAPTER THREE

THE man might terrify her, but she was determined to hold her nerve; so much depended on getting to the mainland. If only she knew who he was it might be easier to talk to him, but she had searched for clues to his identity and found none on the yacht. There was plenty of food and drink in the tiny galley and all sorts of fancy technical equipment—and, now she put her shopping head on, she realised the blanket around her shoulder was cashmere. But the man remained a mystery. Apart from his working clothes, he wore a strap around his wrist formed of black twine, and the gold hoop in his ear which she found sexy, but neither item was unique.

It wasn't much to go on. She should have noticed the name of his yacht, but she had been so traumatised when she'd clambered on board her thoughts had been solely concerned with survival. She hadn't even paused to think who the yacht might belong to. Food, drink and a fast ticket back to the mainland had been her only concern. And if she had to steal a sleek, sexy racing yacht to get there, so be it.

'I don't have all day,' he warned. 'The least you can do is tell me why you're here.'

Even if she had been prepared to tell him the truth it was hard to think straight with his sexuality overwhelming her. Command was instinctive for him, while she was a girl used to getting her own way; theirs could be an explosive partnership.

In the realms of fantasy only, Antonia cautioned herself firmly. She had been so absorbed in sleuthing it took her a moment to realise that he was holding out the most delicious-looking baguette. Slathered in butter, it had a wedge of cheese inside it so thick it would normally have fed her for a week. And she hadn't eaten for... She couldn't remember.

'Is that for me?' She granted him the first smile of the day as she reached for it.

He held it out of reach. 'Talk first,' he said brusquely. 'You've had enough time to collect your thoughts. And if you can't remember your own name...' A quirk of his eyebrow was all it took to call her a liar. 'Why don't you start with your parents' names?'

'Both my parents are dead.'

'And they had no name either, I suppose?'

Had she expected sympathy? Antonia's skin prickled at this evidence of a man who was cold and remote. It under-scored what she had already sensed about him, that you wouldn't want him as an enemy, and as she stared into his eyes she wondered if she had never met anyone so removed from human feeling. He unnerved her to the point that she felt like voicing her mother's name, almost as if it were a talisman that could protect her. But her mother's name was too precious for that, and so she attempted a little sob instead. 'Please, let me eat first. I'm s-so hungry...'

There was a moment of silence between them, and

then, as if she had planned it, her stomach growled in anguish. 'Please…'

She must have paled or swayed, or gasped for breath; all three were possible when the man was so close to her. 'Eat, then talk,' he conceded brusquely, handing over the baguette.

She dropped her gaze to hide her relief as she crammed the delicious roll into her mouth, going to heaven and back in the space of a couple of gargantuan bites.

'Steady—drink something.'

He took the top off a bottle of water, which she grabbed from him gracelessly and gulped down.

'Take a few minutes to let the food settle.'

His words might have seemed considerate, but the look on his face was not. He was telling her she had better not take longer than he expected to pull herself round. Brusque or not, his manner thrilled her. Why did it always have to be the pretty boys who wanted her, when what she wanted was a real man who could stare her in the eyes—a man like this man, who made her body tremble?

Clearly, his thoughts were not running in tandem with her. Far from returning her interest, he simply dumped another blanket on top of her in passing. He couldn't have been more unromantic if he'd tried, while her head was full of him touching her in quite a different way.

'You need to sleep,' he said brusquely. 'You're still in shock. We'll talk later.'

Sleep? Was he serious? He obviously thought he only had to issue a command and her eyes would close immediately. 'Sleep here?' She stared dubiously at the narrow bunk.

'Yes, of course here,' he rapped with a frown that would have sent grown men scurrying for cover.

'I'm not sure I can sleep,' she said honestly.

'You can try,' he insisted.

She reluctantly dragged the blanket close. Like the man, it held the fresh tang of the ocean, and like him it felt wonderful against her skin. But as she curled up on the bunk all her bravado fell away, leaving just longing and loneliness. However formidable he seemed, and however much of a threat he posed, he had made her feel safe. And that was such a good feeling, Antonia reflected, biting back tears.

She was physically and mentally exhausted, Antonia reasoned, impatient with herself for the weakness. Her emotions were in tatters, and no wonder, when in the short space of time she'd known him this brute of a man had turned her life plan on its head. She'd carried a mental image with her of returning to Rome in triumph after opening branches of Rigo's charity across the Middle East. Eventually, she would return home and settle down—probably with some nice, safe man her brother had chosen for her. After which, life would go on pretty much as it always had, with lots of pats on the head for Antonia and not too many problems to worry her. And of course, her husband, like her brother, would adore her.

But now…

How was she supposed to lose her innocence to some lesser man now? The man had ruined her prospects of a nice, cosy future. And as for sex…

'Relax,' he insisted as she squirmed beneath the blanket. 'No one's going to touch you while I'm around.'

Especially not him, she gathered.

Throwing herself down on the bunk, she stretched out. Why had fate chosen to bring her to the attention of a man who had turned her world upside down with one contemptuous stare when he wasn't even interested in her?

Tugging the blanket over her head, she determined that out of sight would mean out of mind—but how was that supposed to happen when she could hear him moving about, and when even the sound of his steady pacing was starting to soothe her? Then incredibly, thanks to the man's strangely reassuring presence and the gentle rocking of the boat, her eyes drifted shut and she fell asleep.

His voice was muted, so he didn't wake her as he issued orders to his Chief of Staff. The girl was sleeping soundly now, her blonde hair drifting in a curtain of gold to the floor. He turned away from that distraction to relay every detail his unexpected guest had been able to recall. When he ended the call, he went up on deck where a technicolour sky would soon darken to the impenetrable mantle of a desert night.

Time had passed rapidly since the girl's arrival, and as he paced the deck he realised that just the thought of her was enough to unsettle him. It was as if the two of them had created some unusual energy, almost as if together they possessed the power to forge some new force. Having been only too glad to turn his back on her, he now found he was impatient for her to wake up. He wanted to test that energy to see if she would be like all the rest—outwardly intriguing, but ultimately shallow.

He remained alert while he paced, and realised now he was listening for her soft footfall, but all he could hear was the sigh of a restless sea and the rhythmical chirrup of the cicadas on shore. Leaning back against the mast, he allowed his thoughts to drift. They returned at once to the mystery girl—her clear, blue-green eyes hazed over with passion and the sight of her begging him for more…

He pulled away from the mast, shaking his head like an angry wolf, as if that could dislodge her from his thoughts. He had already decided she was too young for him.

But she was intriguing.

The trill of the satellite phone provided a welcome distraction, until he learned the purpose of the call. He had ordered that all his late father's palaces be aired and cleaned before being redecorated and opened to the public, and it appeared they had found a locked room today. When his comptroller of palaces went on to advise him that they hadn't been able to locate a key to the room, a thought occurred to him. Was it possible the room had belonged to his father's mistress? There were so many secrets where that woman was concerned.

He commanded that they remove the door from its hinges—or break it down if they had to. Once they had gained access, if it proved to have been her lair, everything she had owned must be taken out and destroyed.

She must have cat-napped; when she woke there was no sign of the man. She guessed he was up on deck and, though sleeping under the stars sounded idyllic to her, she was beginning to feel guilty at the thought that she was taking up his one and only bunk. Sitting up and stretching, she realised it was still relatively early, and that he was unlikely to be asleep.

She wanted to see him again. She wanted to make a fresh start. She wanted him to see her differently. She had been so shocked at their first encounter she had acted foolishly, and hadn't seen anything from his point of view, but now she had slept and felt refreshed she could understand his brusque manner. She was the trespasser, and yet he'd fed her and bathed her wounds. What had she done for him? She must earn her passage back to the mainland as cook, crew, anything he wanted—within reason, of course. The least she could do now was to take him a cooling drink.

The *very* least, Antonia concluded, her heart hammering with anticipation as she padded silently across the deck with a cooling lemonade she had decorated with a slice of lemon, an ice cube and even a sprig of mint she had found in the man's supplies.

The dark shape loomed out of nowhere. She screamed and the drink went flying. The man yanked her in front of him and, dipping his head, demanded, 'Do you never learn?'

She was trembling so much it took her a moment to speak, and then fury and shock turned her intended apology on its head. '"Are you all right?" might be nice,' she raged back at him.

The man was already blazing with affront, which only increased at her outburst. Bringing his face close to hers in the most intimidating way imaginable, he snarled, 'Do yourself a favour and learn how dangerous it is to creep up on me.'

'Well, I'm sorry if I frightened you.'

'Frightened me?' He seemed surprised for a moment, and then, throwing back his head, he laughed, strong white teeth flashing in the moonlight.

She couldn't even bring him a drink without making a mess of things, Antonia seethed inwardly. She could cope in her brother's sophisticated circles in Rome without any trouble at all, but she couldn't seem to get a single thing right where this man was concerned. And now she was in danger of ruining everything and losing her lift to the mainland. 'Look, I'm sorry.'

'Cloth,' he snapped without sparing her a glance.

She bit back an angry retort, accepting he was right on this occasion. She shouldn't have shouted at him or spilled lemonade on his deck. She should have remembered this wasn't some pleasure cruiser and that she was here under sufferance. 'I'll get you a cloth.'

'You bet you will. You made the mess, you clear it up!'

So much for her kind gesture! She should have saved some of the lemonade to toss over him. 'I thought you might want a drink. Was it my fault you leapt out at me? And now you expect me to follow orders like a dog. You'll be whistling for me next.'

'Have you finished?'

His quiet way of speaking drew her attention to his lips. Taking herself out of danger range, she headed below deck at speed. She was going to stick with her original plan, which was to be useful to him so he would be more likely to give her a lift to the mainland.

She returned moments later with a fresh drink, a clean cloth and a new sense of purpose in her step. 'Here,' she said, hanging on to the cloth as she offered him the freshly prepared drink. She was bowed, but not defeated. If she had a hope of reaching Sinnebar, pride was not an option.

'Where are you going?' the man demanded as she carried on walking.

She waved the cloth at him. 'To clean up.'

'Sit down over there,' he ordered, indicating a bulkhead well out of his way. 'And please try not to fall overboard while I make a proper job of clearing up the mess you made.'

So she couldn't even be trusted with a cloth? She hung on to it, expecting every moment he would snatch it from her. 'I'd like to help,' she said bluntly, amazed by the steadiness of her voice. 'I've made a mistake—I know that, I'm pretty clumsy—but I'd like to put it right.'

There was a moment of silence, and then he saluted her with the plastic tumbler. 'Do your worst.'

She saw the glint in his eyes. He was laughing at her, but she kept her temper under control. Apart from the lift she so badly needed, she was playing a very dangerous game with a man she didn't know. There could be no mixing up of dreams and reality here. Placating him was her best, her only, option.

Once she'd cleared up the mess, she faced him again. 'I realise I haven't exactly got off on the best foot.'

She waited for him to contradict her. Any gentleman would. But this man wasn't a gentleman, he was a barbarian, who angled his chin to stare at her with derision as if he were wondering how deep she would care to dig the hole before jumping into it. 'Can we start again?' she suggested, somehow remaining calm.

The sight of one inky eyebrow peaking made her cheeks flame red, but with her lift in serious jeopardy she wasn't about to take any chances. 'I'm prepared to work my passage back to the mainland, if you'll just tell me what you'd like me to do.'

'You could leave me in peace?' he suggested.

Antonia's jaw dropped. She was welcome everywhere.

Except here, she concluded as the man directed a pointed glance at the companionway leading below deck.

'Can I do anything more for you?' he said pointedly.

'Absolutely not,' she assured him, spinning on her heels. She paused at the top of the steps to deliver her exit line: 'You've done quite enough for me already.'

But as she spoke she glimpsed the island behind him. It looked so desolate in the fading light. Did she really want to be stranded there? 'Just for the record, I really am sorry I made such a mess of things and spilled a drink, but you shouldn't have leapt out at me.'

The man's eyes narrowed threateningly.

She tensed and went on, 'I only brought you a drink because—'

'You felt guilty?' He suggested. 'And I'm guessing that's a first for you.'

'You don't know anything about me.'

'I know all I want to know.'

'How can you say that?' Because he didn't want to know any more about her, Antonia realised, heating up with embarrassment. 'What have I ever done to you? Why do you hate me so much?'

'I don't hate you,' he said. 'I don't feel anything that requires that much energy. Let me spell it out for you,' he offered. 'I have neither the time nor the inclination to deal with spoiled brats who march into danger with their eyes wide open, expecting other people to bail them out.'

'It wasn't like that.'

'How would you describe it?'

For once she was lost for words. 'I'm going below.'

'You do that.'

She had never been dismissed by anyone before, and the thought that it was so unjust forced her to turn one last time and confront him. 'Why should I sleep below deck where it's hot and stuffy, while you're up here enjoying the breeze?'

'Have you never been told "thank you, we'll call you" after one of your dramatic performances? No, I guess not,' he said wearily. 'Well, there's a first time for everything, I guess. Off you go,' he prompted with a dismissive gesture.

'I'm staying right here.'

He shrugged, turned his back and walked away.

CHAPTER FOUR

HE WATCHED her out of the corner of his eye. She sat well away from him, glancing at him when she thought he wasn't looking. She reminded him of a newly caged animal taking account of its changed circumstances before making any rash moves. When she realised he was watching her, she quickly looked away.

The light had begun to fade, cloaking them in shadows. The yacht was barely moving, and even the waves had grown lazy as they lapped against the side of the boat, as if the ocean was preparing itself for sleep. Night fell quickly in the desert, and he guessed she would want to freshen up before she had something to eat. Although she had annoyed him intensely, he had no intention of starving her. 'Are you hungry?'

She pretended not to hear him.

She stirred, but refused to look at him. Instead, she stretched out on her back, staring up at the sky, her sun-bleached hair dusting the deck. 'What time is it?' she said as if they were the best of friends.

'Time for you to swim and freshen up, and then we'll eat,' he told her in a tone of voice that gave her no encouragement.

Putting conditions on her chance to eat grabbed her attention. She sat bolt upright, still pretending unconcern as she twisted her hair into an expert knot, which she then secured with a band she wore around her wrist.

Her delicate bone-structure held his interest momentarily. 'Up,' he commanded, shaking the sight of her long, naked limbs out of his head. 'You've been lazing around long enough. What you need now is exercise.'

'To get over the shock?' she challenged him with a glare.

'To stretch your limbs,' he countered, refusing to be sucked in by her 'poor little victim' act. She had been through a trauma, but it wouldn't help her to dwell on it— and he suspected she wasn't as badly affected as she made out, if only because acting was something she could turn on and off at will.

She stood up and stretched. 'A swim?' she said, slanting a blue-green gaze at him. 'I could handle that.'

Shaking his head, he turned away. What was it about this girl that drew him to her? She was a feisty bundle of trouble, and he should know better than to lead her on when he went for mature, gracious women—usually with a title, and always with a keen sense of what was and wasn't correct. Something told him there was nothing remotely correct about this girl.

He should not have suggested she go for a swim. He could count the mistakes he'd made in his adult life on the fingers of one hand and this was up there with the best. Did he need reminding that the girl who had insisted on scrubbing the whole of his deck after mopping up the original spill, and polishing every surface until it gleamed, had the frame of a young gazelle and the bosom of a centrefold, or that plastic surgery had played no part in her good fortune?

He was on shore, preparing a cooking fire, when she walked out of the sea and strolled towards him looking like a nubile film-star in her too-short shorts and ripped top. He steeled himself not to look, but it was already too late when the image was branded on his mind.

Apparently unaware of the effect she was having on him, she came to stand within splashing distance, and, twisting her hair to get rid of the water before flinging it carelessly back, she demanded, 'What are you cooking?'

He gave her a look. 'What does it look like?'

'Fish?'

'Well done.'

'Not too well done, I hope?' she chipped in cheekily, clearly refreshed by her swim. 'You don't like anything about me, do you?' she protested when he slanted an ironic stare in her direction.

She would wait a long time for him to play along with that line. But, actually, she was growing on him. Apart from her obvious attractions, or perhaps in spite of them, beneath her adolescent quirkiness there was real grit and determination. She was uncompromising, he had concluded, like him, and now he sat back to enjoy the show he was sure was about to begin. He didn't have to wait long.

Seeing that she had failed to provoke him, she upped the ante. 'I'm just in the way.' She pulled a broken face. 'You'd far rather be here on your own.'

'Without the cabaret?' He stirred the fire. 'You've got that right.'

While he spoke she was circling him like a young gazelle not quite sure what she was dealing with, until finally curiosity overcame her and she came to peer over his shoulder at the food he was preparing. 'It's got its head on!' she exclaimed as he impaled on a spit the fish he'd just caught.

'They grow that way in the Gulf.'

'Is that the only choice for supper?'

'Did I forget to give you the menu?'

'Stop teasing me,' she protested.

Without any effort on his part a new sense of ease was developing between them. She'd made a bad start, but she had worked really hard since then to make up for it. 'You don't have to eat the fish,' he said, playing along. 'You don't have to eat at all. Or, if you want something off the menu, I'm sure there's plenty more bread in the galley that could do with eating up.'

She scowled at this, but then an uncertain smile lit her face when their glances connected.

They were beginning to get the measure of each other, and both of them liked what they saw, he concluded. He was more relaxed than usual; this was luxury for him, eating simply, cooking the fresh fish he'd caught over an open fire. It gave him a chance to kick back and experience a very different life.

The fish did smell good. And she was ravenous. 'Can we start over?' Antonia suggested, knowing there was more at stake than her first proper meal of the day—her voyage to the mainland, for instance, not to mention sharing a meal with a frighteningly attractive man she dared to believe was starting to warm to her.

'That all depends.'

'I've told you that I'd like to help, and I mean it,' she said. 'I can sail—I can help you sail to the mainland.'

'Help me sail?' he murmured, skimming a gaze over her tiny frame.

'Seriously—let me prove it to you. I'm not as useless as I look.'

He stared into the fire to hide his smile.

'If I knew your name, it would be a start,' she persisted. 'Maybe we could relax around each other more if we knew what to call each other.'

'Wasn't that my question to you?'

Antonia's cheeks blazed. How could she be so careless? Wasn't that the one question she wouldn't answer? 'I have to call you something,' she pressed, getting her question in first.

She had almost given up when he answered, 'You can call me Saif.'

'Saif?' she exclaimed, seizing on the word. 'Doesn't that mean sword in Sinnebalese?' And, without giving him a chance to answer, she rattled on, 'When I first planned to travel to Sinnebar I studied the language.'

Instead of turning things around as she had hoped, this only provoked one of his dismissive gestures. 'The name Saif is very popular in Sinnebar,' he explained, stoking the fire with a very big stick.

'But it isn't your real name?' she said, tearing her gaze away. 'Saif is just a name you've adopted for while you're here,' she guessed.

Please, please say something, she urged him silently. 'If you don't want to tell me your real name, that's all right by me.'

Nothing.

'We could have a name truce,' she pressed as another idea occurred to her.

'What do you mean by that?'

Her confidence grew; imagination was her speciality. 'Our outside lives can't touch us here—you can be Saif, and I can be—'

'I shall call you Tuesday.'

'Tuesday?' She frowned.

'I take it you've heard of Man Friday?'

'Of course I have, but—'

He shrugged. 'You came on board on a Tuesday.'

They were really communicating, and for the first time since she'd come aboard his yacht she could see the light at the end of the tunnel.

Or at least the lighthouse guarding the entrance to the harbour of Sinnebar.

'Tuesday it is, then,' she agreed eagerly. 'Would you like me to fillet the fish for you?' She wanted to prove she could be helpful in so many ways.

Saif paused, knife suspended. His expression reflected his doubt in her abilities. 'All right, go ahead,' he said reluctantly.

And make a mess of it if you dare, Antonia silently translated.

She swallowed as Saif drew his knife, and took it gingerly from him with the thick, beautifully carved pommel facing towards her hand. 'This is very nice,' she said, struggling to wrap her hand around it. 'Is it an heirloom?'

'There's nothing special about it,' Saif said as he removed the fish from the spit he'd made out of twigs and a piece of twine. 'It's a utility item and nothing more.'

'Well, it's a very nice utility item.'

Nothing *special*? Apart from the knife's size, and the fact that it could slice the gizzard out of a shark at a single stroke, it was the most fearsome weapon she had ever seen. And one she would put to good use. Her juices ran as Saif waved the fish on the stick to cool it, sending mouth-watering aromas her way.

It was a relief to discover that all the trips to fabulous restaurants with her brother Rigo hadn't been wasted. Positioning the fish on the large, clean leaf that would act as a plate, she removed the head, skin and bones with a few skilful passes of Saif's razor-sharp blade. 'You first,' she insisted, passing the succulent white morsels of fish to him on their bed of lush emerald-green leaf.

She breathed a sigh of relief when Saif's lips pressed down with approval and he murmured, 'Good work.'

'Thank you.'

'This is delicious,' she observed, tucking in with gusto. 'We make a good team, you and I.'

Careless words, Antonia realised when one arrogant ebony eyebrow peaked. She ate in silence after that, and when they were finished went to rinse her hands in the sea. Sitting down on the sand a safe distance from Saif, she leaned back on her hands to stare at the moon. It wasn't long before she was longing for things she couldn't have—a sexy Arabian lover with a body made for non-stop sin, for instance.

Saif turned when she sighed, but what could she do? It was such a romantic evening. There was a smudge of luminous orange at the horizon, and overhead a candy-striped canvas of pink and aquamarine remained stub-bornly in place as the sky darkened into night. 'You don't know how lucky you are living here,' she murmured. 'Though they say the ruling Sheikh is—'

'What?' Saif demanded sharply. 'What do they say about the ruling sheikh?'

From the look on his face, she had over-stepped some unseen boundary. Rolling onto her stomach, she laced her hands beneath her chin, sensing diplomacy was urgently required. 'Surely you know him better than I do?'

'Maybe,' he admitted.

'Aren't you allowed to be rude about him?'

'I can be as rude as I like—but I don't like,' Saif said pointedly, flashing a warning glance her way.

'I'm sorry; I didn't mean to offend you. I just heard he was fierce, that's all.'

Rolling onto her back, she hoped she'd done enough to placate him. She really hadn't meant to offend him. 'Shall we have pudding now?' she suggested, hoping to break the sudden tense silence.

'Pudding?'

She only needed the smallest encouragement. 'Yes— then it will be like a proper picnic.' She sprang up and ran back to the boat, emerging minutes later with more blankets under her arm, determinedly swinging the cool box. Smoothing out rugs well clear of the water's edge, she lifted the lid on her treasure trove—ice-cold drinks, together with fat green olives and the sweet dates she'd found in Saif's galley. 'I told you I could be useful,' she said when he complimented her on the spread.

They ate in silence, but at least it wasn't a hostile silence. It was more of a rebalancing exercise, Antonia concluded.

'What are you doing now?' he demanded as she stared up at the moon.

His voice made her tingle, made her want to stretch out

her hands to feel the cooling surf on her racing pulse. She concluded it was best to tell him the truth—or at least an edited version of it. 'I was just thinking I've had quite a day, what with the pirate attack, swimming through a storm and now you.'

'I see your point,' he agreed dryly, but just when she'd been sure they were making real progress he sprang up and walked away.

He had to put distance between them. It had been a long time since he had wanted a woman so badly. In fact, he couldn't remember wanting anyone as much as this girl. It was the ambience, he reasoned, pausing at the water's edge. There was nothing like a desert night to stir the senses.

He shook his head with amusement when she called, 'Wait for me!'

Nothing fazed her. And he wanted to wait for her, which prompted the question: when was the last time he had waited for anyone? 'I'm going for a swim, Tuesday—you stay here.' He dipped into the traditional Sinnebalese salutation before wheeling away. But the image of her nibbling dates with her small white teeth was still with him.

She was still feasting on the dates when she caught up with him. There was no artifice about her. She was hungry; they were on a beach, and she was eating to fill her stomach and not to impress him with finicky ways. She had a healthy appetite. He refused to dwell on that thought any longer than was necessary.

'Sorry,' she gulped, wiping her mouth with the back of her hand. 'You really shouldn't swim so soon after eating, Saif.'

She was giving him advice now? 'Is that so? And what

do you think you are doing now?' She was staring at the sky and waving her arms around, doing some sort of dance he found both innocent and seductive.

'I'm invoking the moon.'

'Of course you are,' he agreed wryly. 'And why are you doing that?'

'Don't laugh at me, Saif. For all you know, I'm a hand-maiden of the moon.'

'And I'm a camel. *Man jadda wajad wa man zara'a hasad.*'

'Oh, that's lovely!' she exclaimed. 'What does it mean?'

His gaze slipped to her lips as she repeated the words after him in Sinnebalese. 'He who perseveres finds,' he translated. 'And he who sows harvests—'

'Perfect,' she interrupted dreamily. 'It could have been written for me.'

'Then you'd better remember it, and I'll test you tomorrow.'

'Tomorrow?' Her face lit up and then became carefully expressionless again.

'We won't be sailing any time soon,' he confirmed, glancing at the sky.

'Great!' she exclaimed. 'Lots more time to dance.'

That wasn't exactly what he had in mind. 'You're crazy.'

As was the surge of desire he felt. She might be younger than him, but she warmed him with her *joie de vivre*, and it was hard not to smile at her antics. She drew him to her as no one ever had before, and he wasn't fighting it. Instead of wanting solitary time alone in the sea, he wanted Tuesday. 'Have you ever caught a fish?' he said, guessing that was a challenge she would find hard to refuse.

'I'd go hungry if I had to.'

The closest she had ever come to catching a fish was lifting one out of the freezer, Antonia realised.

'Would you like me to show you how to catch one?' Saif suggested.

She was so surprised by his offer she made the mistake of holding his gaze, only to feel her hormones riot in response. 'I'd like that.' The chance to do anything with Saif was an exciting prospect. And if she had to catch a fish…

She had not expected Saif to stand so close behind her in the rock pool, or to place his hand over hers when she plied the line. The fish were plentiful in the shallows, but all she could think about was Saif's warmth infusing her, and it was no time at all before there was a fish on the line and a world of erotic thoughts in her head.

This time Saif wielded the knife while she found fresh wood to make the fire blaze. They both took a hand in the cooking, and when Saif glanced at her and smiled it felt like all her Christmases had come at once. She could get things right if she believed in herself enough, Antonia concluded. A life of pampering didn't mean she lacked fibre— she just hadn't been tested before. Perhaps they were both finding out about themselves, she mused as Saif's glance warmed her. They weren't exactly friends, but they were certainly easier around each other, and there was something else that sprang between them, like electricity—something that made her heart thunder. 'What?' she said, angling her chin when he stared at her.

'I was just wondering about you.'

Wondering what? She blushed. If he was wondering if she was good in bed, he was in for the wrong kind of surprise. She was an amateur, a tease—a virgin, pretty much. It was better they direct their conversations towards harmless things, like business. 'The appointment I told you about?' she said brightly to distract him. 'That's not the only reason I'm travelling to Sinnebar.'

Saif's gaze sharpened.

'I'm here to find out about my mother,' she admitted, careful not to let her feelings show. 'She died when I was a baby and I learned recently that she spent some time in Sinnebar. How about you?' she prompted.

'Me?' He shrugged. 'This is just a break from work for me.'

'That's great. I can't think of anywhere better to relax.'

'I think it's time to swim,' he said, as if he was as keen as she was not to delve too deep. 'Unless you've seen enough water for today?'

'No, I like swimming.' Did she sound too keen? She was already on her feet. 'It must be way past half an hour since we ate,' she agreed, turning serious.

'Way past,' Saif agreed dryly, striding ahead of her into the foam.

CHAPTER FIVE

THEY swam like dolphins, and in spite of everything that had happened that day Antonia wondered if a day had ever ended so well. Saif was a much stronger swimmer than she was, and when a giant wave crashed over her head he was there in moments, drawing her to him where she felt safe. She was intensely aware of the brush of his hard, warm body against her own.

She felt safe and yet at the same time in the worst danger of her life, if only because no one had ever made her feel so aware of her physical self before. Saif made her want to swim better and to tease him all she could. She wanted to show off and flirt with him—with danger. Some small inexperienced part of her hoped he wouldn't notice her attempt to attract him, but the rest of her most definitely hoped that he would.

She would wait a long time for another night like this. They were miles away from anywhere on a desert island, with no one to see them as they stepped out of their normal lives and did whatever they wanted to do; they could be whoever they wanted to be...

And she wanted to be attractive to Saif.

She plunged into the waves at his side and began

powering out to sea, leaving him with no alternative but to go after her. Seizing hold of her, he trod water, demanding, 'What do you think you're doing?'

Her answer was to playfully spray a mouthful of salt water in his face. Astonishment barely covered it. He gave her a look. She dodged out of his grip and started swimming away. 'Last time I was too gentle with you!' he exclaimed, catching up with her again.

Her answer this time was to splash him as she called out, 'If you don't like it, catch me and punish me.'

And, like a sleek young otter she slipped out of his grasp and swam away again.

'Okay, I'm sorry!' She shrieked with excitement when he caught hold of her. She was playing with him as if they were lovers. But this was the Gulf, and he was a king, while she was...wonderful. She felt so warm and supple beneath his hands, and it was impossible not to notice that they fit together perfectly when he struck out for shore.

'You're not a bit sorry,' he accused, rejoicing in her defiance.

'Okay, not that sorry,' she agreed, her lips curving in a mischievous smile as she turned her head to look at him.

'Do you always live so dangerously, Tuesday?' he demanded as he matched his stroke to hers. This was shifting rapidly from surreal to erotic, he realised as he waited for her reply.

'Never as dangerously as this,' she admitted.

He could believe it.

'Anything rather than live a dull life,' she declared, putting her head down and diving into the waves as she used the power of the sea to drive her into shore.

There was nothing dull about her. She had more verve than his entire court put together. In a few short hours she had pointed out what was missing in his council of elders—personality, youth and vigour were just a few of the qualities he could name. And however passionate he was about taking Sinnebar forward he couldn't steer each new initiative himself. It would be good to have someone like her on board, he thought fleetingly, before dismissing the idea as ridiculous. But she was young and vital, and though she made mistakes in many ways Tuesday was a kindred spirit. How could he blame her for getting things wrong, when the only people who never made a mistake were those who never tried anything new?

'Can't you slow down?' she begged him finally. 'I'm exhausted pretending I can keep up with you.'

He laughed and called back some taunting challenge, but slowed his pace and waited for her. He was already standing, well within his depth when she swam past him. Her safety was paramount to him and he rode shotgun behind her as she waded into shore. She was strong in mind and in body, and he could understand how she had escaped the pirates, but did he need the complication of such a high spirited young woman in his life? The answer to that was a firm no.

Building a case against Tuesday was easy, he concluded as she turned to smile at him over her shoulder—another point in her favour, he conceded wryly. She would challenge him. She would prove more than a match for most men.

But most men couldn't have her.

He was suffering a bad case of desert-island fever, he decided, determined to put her out of his mind.

'Where are you going, Saif?' she demanded, catching hold of his arm when he turned to walk away from her.

As she stared into his eyes he felt tugged right in, as if Tuesday's eyes held the secret of life. 'Isn't there enough sand to go round?' He pretended impatience as he stared at the vast stretch of beach turned silver by the moonlight. 'Must we inhabit the same square metre of sand?'

'That's up to you,' she said.

He held her gaze. Her eyelashes were clogged with water and her lips were slightly parted and moist. She was excited at the thought of what might happen next, while he knew only too well he could offer her none of the things she dreamed about.

Nor would he stand by while she heaped more reasons for regret on top of what had already been a traumatic day for her, he determined, pulling away. But then he knew this was the opportunity he had been looking for to ask Tuesday a question that had been nagging at the back of his mind. If she had been assaulted during the attack, he would call ahead and arrange specialist counselling for when she returned to the mainland.

Saif's question should have embarrassed her, but it didn't. They had past that marker some time ago, Antonia realised, and now she owed him the truth. 'The boat was attacked,' she explained, 'But I jumped into the sea before they could touch me.'

'Bad enough,' Saif commented.

And it could have been so much worse; they communed silently in a moment of real contact between them.

Then, incredibly, Saif's eyes warmed as he stared down

at her, and his lips tugged in a slow grin. 'You came out of it well,' he said.

Time stood still as they stared at each other, while her heart pounded louder than the surf. It wasn't that Saif touched her—he didn't need to when she swayed towards him.

They were cool from the sea, but she was hot, hot enough to make the sea boil when he kissed her. He tasted salty and clean and wonderful, and her wildest fantasies could never have conjured up that hot-cold, salty-sweet kiss.

'Am I safe?' she murmured when he released her, without opening her eyes.

'You're as safe as you want to be,' Saif told her.

'Not safe at all, then.' Her lips started to curve in a smile as she looked at him.

'You're not frightened of me?' he said.

'A little,' she admitted.

He shook his head. 'How can the girl who swam through a storm in no visibility and no guarantee of success be frightened now?'

'Because I think you are a very dangerous man,' she told him softly.

'Hmm. Are you cold?' he demanded as she shivered with anticipation.

Her answer was a sigh, and so he nuzzled her neck, and everything inside her melted.

'You can always go back to the yacht and sleep safely in a bunk,' Saif murmured.

'Why would I do that?'

'I've no idea.'

And then he strode across the beach, holding her in his arms as if she weighed nothing, while she linked her hands behind his neck and snuggled her face against his chest. It was the easiest thing in the world to believe they belonged together, and that this was their island with no outside world to complicate things or muddy the water. There was no tomorrow here, no yesterday, there was only now, with the ocean lapping rhythmically on a sugar-sand shore, with a sickle moon and diamond stars to light their way. There was just one man, one woman.

There was only this…

'Still feeling safe?' he said.

She drew a fast breath as he ran the fingertips of one hand very lightly down her arm. This was madness, she registered as her heart beat wildly. She didn't even know Saif. She might have fantasised about such things happening, but had never imagined they would.

Saif continued to tease her with the lightest touch. It was a touch that carried the promise of so much more, and that was all it took to convince her that she was free to do as she liked here.

Free to enjoy sex with a complete stranger?

Why not? Antonia argued stubbornly with her inner voice. 'Do you believe in fate, Saif?'

'Maybe.'

'You do. I know you do,' she insisted. 'Just think about it—why am I here? Why did I swim to this particular island where you were moored up? We were meant to meet,' she said with certainty, holding Saif's brooding gaze.

'It was the closest port in a storm for both of us,' he said, injecting some realism into her thinking.

But she did feel the pull of kismet, and was sure Saif must feel it too. 'I'm not frightened of you,' she said. 'In fact…'

Saif shushed her, and as he looped his arms around her waist her body responded with indecent urgency. This wasn't some soft, office-bound male. Saif was a barbarian, raw and sexual, and there was steel behind that brooding stare.

He would be tuned to every desire she had ever dreamed of. He was the mate nature had chosen for her, she decided, choosing to ignore the voice in her head that said he was ruthless, and that Saif lived his life by very different rules. This would be a night to remember for the rest of her life. Saif wanted sex, and she did too. What was wrong with that? Now his lips were soft and persuasive on her mouth and on her neck.

While his stubble was sharp like a warning.

She was moist and hot. She was ready for him.

But was she ready for sex with a man as experienced and as exciting as Saif? Could she trust him? Could she trust him enough?

She was more frightened of her own inexperience than she was of Saif, Antonia realised; she was frightened she might disappoint him.

The silence deepened as he stared at her. They were both fiercely aroused, and he took pleasure in keeping her waiting. Meanwhile, his strength and heat were washing over her, and his expression said he would exceed every dream she'd ever had.

She softened against him, arching her back to encourage his hands to move lower, and she groaned with satisfaction when he cupped her buttocks. It only took the smallest adjustment to angle herself so she could feel the steel of his erection, to which he responded by pressing and releasing her against him, allowing her a hint of the pleasure to come.

But she wanted more than this. All thoughts of standing hesitantly on the brink, and of decisions yet to be made, had vanished. Her world comprised the throbbing hunger between her legs. There was nothing more. One night, she argued with her inner voice. She had to. She had never known such a primal instinct to mate with one man, or even known that she possessed such hunger. It was as if Saif had made her supremely conscious of her feminine power.

As if he sensed this confidence in her, he swung her into his arms again and carried her on board the yacht. When he laid her on the cushions beneath the stars, she felt one moment of anxiety, because now it seemed Saif was hesitating. 'Don't you want me?'

'I want you.'

His eyes were flecked with gold and amber, and as he stretched out at her side his mouth curved in a lazy smile. 'Do you know what happens when you play with fire?' he murmured, toying with a strand of her hair.

'I get burned?' she said hopefully.

He laughed, and then dragged her close to whisper all sorts of outrageous suggestions in her ear—words that carried such an erotic charge she would reach a conclusion without him if he didn't hurry to put his promises into practice.

Saif wielded an unusual power over her, Antonia realised as his hands warmed and controlled her. She should be aware of that—and be cautious. She didn't know him or what he was capable of, but then she hardly knew herself in this new guise of reckless heat. 'I want you,' she murmured, quickly forgetting her reservations when Saif moved over her.

'You've got me.' Impossibly attractive and indescribably

intimidating, he was experienced and she was not, and she was only now realising he had prepared her to the point where there could be no turning back. To the point where she felt a frantic need to welcome him inside her as nature, and Saif, intended.

'Patience,' he whispered when she moved urgently against him.

Her obedience was partially rewarded when he feathered kisses down her neck, while his hands worked more productively on even more sensitive areas. 'Calm,' he commanded as she fought for breath.

'How…?' She couldn't even speak.

'Easy for me.' His lips curved with amusement.

'That's so unfair,' she complained in a gasp.

'No doubt,' he agreed evenly. 'But everything I do is for your own good.'

She knew what was for her own good—and it wasn't patience!

Saif allowed her no respite from his teasing kisses on her breastbone, the swell of her breasts and on her belly, where her wet top was pushed back. But did he feel *anything*? Antonia wondered. How could anyone be so controlled, when she was composed entirely of sensation?

She strained towards him, wanting him to acknowledge her arousal, and gasped with relief when he made the lightest pass of his thumb against the swollen tip of her nipple before chafing each in turn with the utmost delicacy. 'You're teasing me,' she complained on another shuddering sigh.

'Am I?' he murmured.

'You know you are,' she accused him, feeling more excited than ever at the thought of what else Saif had in store for her. But still he was distanced and unmoved. 'Don't you feel anything?' she demanded, close to breaking point.

'Plenty. Believe me, I feel plenty.'

Then why wouldn't he rush things along?

'I know exactly what you want,' he said. A faint smile curved his mouth. 'Soon,' he murmured, kissing her brow chastely, as if he knew every wicked thought in her head.

'No,' she burst out. 'Now!'

Saif laughed as he brought her into firm contact with the thrust of his erection. 'Is that what you want?'

'You know it is.'

She was lost in an erotic haze, desperately seeking more contact, and hardly aware that Saif was lifting her top over her head. Her bra followed and was tossed aside, and now her breasts gleamed pale in the moonlight, while her nipples were dark, thrusting peaks that called for his attention. 'Take me,' she demanded, thrashing her head about on the cushions.

Saif continued to stare down at her with faint amusement. He refused to be hurried, and so she thrust her breasts towards him in deliberate provocation.

He chose the time, and when he dipped his head to suckle she was nearly delirious with relief. Now the zip on her shorts was undone. She wriggled frantically to be free of them, desperate to be naked against him. And now the smallest scrap of lace divided them. He ripped it off.

'If you stop now...' she warned him.

'Yes?' he said mildly.

'I'll never forgive you.'

Saif's cynical expression was fuel to her fire. 'Don't you dare stop now,' she warned him.

He murmured something provocative in his own language, but then he stilled and, cupping her face in his strong, warm hands, he kissed her so tenderly she felt tears spring to her eyes. 'This is more than sex for you, isn't it?' she said with wonder when he released her.

She wanted to hear Saif say he cared, Antonia realised, feeling a pain in her heart when he remained silent. 'Please say something,' she begged him.

'What's left to say?' he murmured, nudging one hard thigh between her legs.

CHAPTER SIX

HE HAD never met a woman like her. It even occurred to him that he might have met his match. She begged him, ordered him, demanded that he pleasure her, whilst all the time pummelling him when she wasn't scraping her small white teeth against his flesh for emphasis.

'Easy, tiger-woman,' he murmured, taking hold of her. 'This isn't a battleground—we're making love.'

Love?

This was sex, pure and simple, something they both wanted and needed, something that could only happen on a night like this—a night detached from reality, a night when they were both free to throw caution to the wind.

Antonia, meanwhile, was lost to reason. 'Oh, yes,' she gasped as Saif's lean fingers delicately parted her swollen lips. She was on the highest plateau of sensation and greedy for more. 'Please touch me there.' She should be shrinking from this man she hardly knew, not using him for pleasure. But Saif had opened a door and she had walked through, and now he was exposing her to his gaze in a way she could never have imagined feeling easy with—but she did. She'd had torrid thoughts for as long as she could remember, but had never put those thoughts into action. Now all she could say was, 'Please…Please…' when what she really meant was, *oh, yes, that's right…* and, *oh, yes, thank you…thank you…*

Easing her legs over his shoulders, Saif dipped his head to touch her with the tip of his tongue. She shuddered with delight, wondering how she was supposed to hold on—and then he increased the pressure. Was this a test? She had never wanted to fail a test quite so badly. Then he tasted her, and in that moment, that string of moments, she knew she had found the exquisite high point of her life. Saif had taken her to a realm she hadn't even known existed where he could order her pleasure with the skill of a maestro.

Governed entirely by raging hunger, she reached her goal and dissolved into a starburst of pleasure, her shuddering screams slicing through the sultry night. But it wasn't enough. Rather than slaking her hunger, Saif had woken a slumbering tiger, and now all she could think about was having him deep inside her so she could claim him for her own.

Losing control with Saif had laid her bare, Antonia realised when she quietened. He might not have taken her fully yet, but she had given him something that could never be recaptured—her trust. Saif had taken a girl and made her a woman, and now there could be no turning back.

Forgetfulness was one of the most valuable commodities for men who could afford anything, and, briefly, Tuesday would provide that. She was resting, but not for long, he suspected. He anticipated a long and deeply satisfying night, but for now he was content to let Tuesday set the pace, especially with the news from the palace still nagging at the back of his mind. Why, with so many rooms to survey and create inventories for, had they rung him tonight of all nights with the news that the treasure room of his father's concubine had been uncovered?

It certainly killed off Tuesday's romantic notion of some rosy destiny for them. Did he need a reminder of the rapaciousness of women? Did he need a reminder of that other woman on a night like this?

He should forget the past, shut it out of his mind, but when he stared at Tuesday he thought he understood his father's weakness perhaps for the first time. He understood, but could not excuse it. He was a very different man from his father, and had not pledged himself to a country and its people to be distracted by anyone. His father might have squandered his reputation, but, *ma sha'a allah*, there wasn't the remotest possibility that Ra'id al Maktabi would do the same.

'What are you doing?' he demanded as Tuesday, having stretched languorously, came to kneel before him. He wanted her, but not like this—not like a king with his mistress on her knees in front of him, waiting to serve.

'I wanted to repay you,' she said innocently.

He frowned. 'Explain…'

'The pleasure? I would have thought you knew,' she said, blushing.

He knew that she had never looked more beautiful, but the sight of her naked and proud and on her knees in front of him made his head pound. In that one innocent and provocative gesture, Tuesday had thrown him back into a world where sycophants knelt and equals stood at his side.

Springing up, he brought her in front of him. Embracing her, he kissed her hungrily, and by the time he released her she had forgotten the moment that could have gone so badly wrong for her. He knew then that she had been right to say this was more than a sexual encounter, but he would never admit it, because he had nothing to offer her.

But this was…sweet.

Holding Tuesday safe against his chest, he rested his face on her tangled hair and savoured the uncomplicated moment. This could be as straightforward as he wanted it to be, he reasoned. Taking hold of her hand, he kissed her palm, and, closing his eyes, he inhaled her innocent scent, as if the magic of the desert could make everything right.

Saif's touch made her arch against him. Hot flesh on hot flesh inflamed her past reason. 'Pleasure me,' she demanded, drunk on sensation, rubbing herself against him. She was completely lost in the fantasy of the desert and the dark stranger she had always known she would find there. She trembled uncontrollably as the hardness of Saif's muscle bore into her soft flesh, and she was impatient for him to move lower so he could satisfy her needs. 'Oh, please,' she begged him, bucking helplessly beneath his touch. 'I can't wait any longer.'

'You must wait,' he told her in a stern voice.

'I can't—' Her voice wavered.

'Tuesday,' he instructed sharply. 'You will wait.'

She held his gaze, and then he smiled at her as if he was pleased with her. She found his voice hypnotic and seductive, while his eyes carried the promise of pleasure and the certainty of danger. She exhaled shakily as he pressed her down into the cushions, and he held her there with little more than a compelling stare. She moaned in complaint when he held himself aloof, while all she could do was writhe helplessly in time to the insistent beat between her legs. 'I need…'

'I know what you need,' Saif assured her, taking fierce possession of her mouth.

Sensation surged through her. She pressed against him, feeling stronger than she had ever felt. Saif's desire empowered her, just as his planned delays infuriated her. Striking his back in frustration, she wondered how long she was supposed to wait. Her body was ready; he knew this and still he tormented her. But, as he kissed her, something happened. He kissed away the image of an experienced man and a much younger girl and replaced it with two lovers of equal standing, so that now there was only a man and a woman, and a desert moon shining over them like a beacon in the watchful sky.

He had awoken a whirlwind. He would never have believed it of the girl, though he should have known from the moment she boarded his boat that she was wilful, strong, and courageous in all areas—and that their first encounter had only hinted at the fires beneath. When it came to sex, she had stated her needs in the bluntest of language, and appeared utterly without self-consciousness. She had even tried to take hold of him, and, finding her tiny hand would barely encompass half of him, she had exclaimed with impatience and angled herself hungrily—and this before the last of the exquisite tremors had had a chance to subside after her first bout of pleasure at his hands.

Cupping her chin, he made her look at him so he could

be sure she knew what she was doing. Her eyes were still misty with desire and with passion, just as he had imagined them, but there was purpose there too. She had discovered physical love and was elemental in her need. Suddenly struck by a spear of jealousy, he demanded,

'Would you do this with any other man?'

'Are you mad?' she demanded fiercely. 'There could only ever be you.'

For her sake, he hoped that wasn't true.

A cry of triumph escaped Antonia's throat as Saif moved over her. This time he would take her. This time he would make her his. She had waited for this all her life, Antonia realised—this man, this moment. Whether Saif would admit it or not, he was part of her life now.

For a single night.

Could one night last a lifetime? It might have to, she accepted, seizing hold of his buttocks with fingers turned to steel. She drew her knees up and, with all the power of her sex, she urged him on.

Saif plundered her mouth while she sucked greedily on his tongue. He tasted ocean-fresh, pure, clean and strong, and with that all the spices of the east combined to seduce her senses. Every part of her was pressed against him and every part of her was keenly aware of him. That lovemaking came naturally to her was a revelation, and, feeling as safe as she did with Saif, made it perfect. She felt truly free for the first time in her life; free to be herself. There was only one jarring chord, which was the certainty that this level of harmony could only exist with one man.

He sank into hot, moist velvet. He was so much bigger than she was, he had intended to take it slowly, but she claimed him greedily, using her strong, young muscles to draw him in. He brushed her mouth and tasted her shock at this new sensation, and tasted her approval moments later. Withdrawing slowly, he plunged deeper still, while she sobbed her pleasure against his chest. 'More? You want more?' he prompted.

Her fingers closed around his buttocks. 'I want it all,' she assured him huskily.

Holding her wrists in a loose grip above her head, resting on the cushions, he made sure that was exactly what she got.

They made love all night and only drifted off to sleep in the quiet hours before dawn. She woke in time to see the waters of the Gulf glistening like a glass plate, with lilac fingers of light the only decoration. The waves were still, and seemed as content as she was, lying snug in Saif's arms to wait for the start of a new day.

But she wasn't content, because today everything must change, Antonia remembered. Today Saif might ask her name again and she must lie to him. She trusted him to take her back to the mainland, but when they arrived they would go their separate ways. Last night wasn't real, last night was a fantasy. They didn't know each other's names, jobs, lives, or even where they were from; they had no future, and there would be no togetherness ever again. The pain she felt at the thought of it was acute, the irony unbearable. If this was normal life, they wouldn't be facing the end, but the beginning; a beginning that might even lead to love. But as it was…

She could so easily fall in love with Saif, Antonia acknowledged, taking care not to wake him as she stirred, but loving each other wasn't an option for them. She still had a job to do—a job she was determined to finish, and to finish well. She couldn't settle for giving up now and going home. If anything, meeting Saif had only inspired her to do more, to achieve more.

'You're awake,' he said, shifting his powerful frame in lazy contentment.

'I'm sorry, I didn't mean to disturb you.' Or to do anything to hasten the day, Antonia thought wistfully.

'I want to be disturbed,' Saif assured her, drawing her close.

She shivered with desire at his touch and didn't have the heart to bring what must end soon to an abrupt finish now. 'You're dressed?' she said, tracing the lines of the top he must have tugged on some time during the night. He was wearing shorts too, she noticed.

'I had to go and check on the progress of the search,' he reminded her.

'Of course.' She relaxed. But even as they entered into this most normal of conversations she knew the spell was broken. The look in Saif's eyes had changed. He was already thinking about bringing the pirates to justice, which required a speedy return to the mainland.

He confirmed it, springing up and shrugging his massive shoulders. 'No time to waste,' he said, staring out to sea as if to assess the weather. 'Things look good.'

She had been expecting this, Antonia told herself firmly, but it didn't make the pain go away. It hurt to know the magic had vanished, only to be replaced by the cold chill of unease—something she must shake off when she had promised to help Saif in every way she could. 'I'll go below to freshen up and dress.'

She wondered if he even heard her as he began the process of preparing the yacht to sail.

Saif sailed with the total mastery with which he did everything else, and it would have been a pleasure watching him at the helm had Antonia not been dogged by the same dragging sense of dread. Of course things could never be the same again between them; she knew that. And of course she accepted the fact that everything must change when they reached the mainland. But the cloud hanging over her refused to budge. It was as if the same fate that had engineered their meeting now decreed that she must suffer for it.

She had been tested quite a few times on this trip and come through, she reasoned in an attempt to reassure herself. *But who knew if she could do it again?*

Antonia looked at Saif, who obviously didn't share her concern. If anything, he seemed to have gained new purpose. It was as if with every nautical mile they travelled he was slowly changing back into the man he must really be.

They shared the rhythm of the sea beneath their feet and little else now, Antonia reflected. He didn't need her help to sail the yacht, he'd told her, and so she was consigned to the role of passenger, a chance acquaintance who was being given a lift to port on a fabulous racing-yacht. 'Is that Sinnebar?' she said excitedly, catching sight of a coastline. She already knew it was. What she'd really wanted when she asked the question was for Saif to connect with her one last time.

'Yes,' he said briefly, but his focus was all on the coast. They had sailed past the lighthouse guarding the entrance

to the harbour before Saif spoke to her again. 'You'll have
to get changed,' he said. 'And clean yourself up.'

In a phrase, Saif had turned her back into a much
younger girl who needed his direction. 'You can use the
hose to get rid of the salt,' he went on. 'And you'll find
some robes under the bunk below. They'll be too big for
you,' he added as he swung the wheel hard to line the giant
yacht up with its berth, 'But you can't disembark in
Sinnebar dressed like that.'

Like what? In a few words he had made her feel
ashamed. What did he mean about the way she was
dressed? She was dressed like someone who had escaped
a pirate attack—the same way she had been dressed all the
time they had been together. Had Saif even looked at her?
Had he even realised what he'd said? He made her feel like
a piece of flotsam that had washed up on his deck and now
had to be swept away. She *had* hosed herself down with
the fresh water, and she *had* tied her hair back. She'd done
everything possible to make herself look respectable.

What Saif was actually saying, Antonia realised, was
that she must never refer to what had happened on their
desert island again. What they had shared had been great,
but as far as Saif was concerned it was over now, and she
was a potential embarrassment to him. 'I'll cover what
I'm wearing with a blanket,' she offered. 'No one will
expect me to be smartly dressed.' She was willing to show
her respect for tradition in Sinnebar, but had no intention
of making a bigger fool of herself than necessary by stumbling over some over-large robe when she disembarked.

Saif acknowledged this briefly. 'An ambulance will be
waiting at the dock to take you straight to the Al Maktabi

clinic for a check up,' he informed her, swooping by to complete some other task.

'Thank you,' she called to his disappearing back. 'I appreciate your concern,' she told the empty space.

It was a marvel to discover she could hold in tears for so long. But who knew what she could do? Antonia mused as she leaned over the prow while the yacht came in to dock. She had a feeling she was going to have to dig a lot deeper yet.

She was on her way down the companionway to get the blanket when Saif asked if she would do him a favour. 'Anything,' she called back, knowing this was no more than the truth.

'Take this down with you when you go, will you?' He'd lashed the wheel, and, peeling off his top, tossed it to her. She was determined to keep her gaze firmly averted from the body she loved—the body that had loved her so expertly.

'You'll find a cream robe hanging in what to you would be the front of the boat,' he told her.

'And you want me to bring it to you?' she asked. She caught the still-warm top he tossed to her, resisting the impulse to bring it to her face and drag in his scent.

'If you wouldn't mind?'

Then, like a spotlight on the star of a production, the sun caught him full on the chest and her mind went numb. She stared at Saif's tattoo. It occurred to her then that she hadn't seen him stripped to the waist in daylight—something that certainly put her moral code in question.

But right now her moral code wasn't uppermost in her mind. She had done her homework before setting out for Sinnebar, and knew what the tattoo over Saif's heart rep-

resented. The snarling lion with the sapphire tightly
grasped between its paws was the ruling sheikh's insignia.
Anyone could see the symbol online, where it was emblazoned on everything from the royal standard to the coin of
His Imperial Majesty's realm. It was said that Sheikh Ra'id
al Maktabi of Sinnebar—acknowledged as the most powerful ruler in the Gulf—had chosen the lion as his personal
symbol to reflect the power he wielded. It was also
rumoured in the wider world that the clarity of the cold,
blue sapphire reflected Ra'id al Maktabi's calculating mind
and his love-proof heart. So now it seemed that the man
she had dreamed of falling in love with, the man she had
had so brief an affair with, either had serious connections
with or was closely related to a royal family reputed to have
no finer feelings beyond the call of duty, which they took
very seriously indeed.

Or…

Antonia didn't even dare to contemplate this last possibility.

'Are you feeling ill?' Saif demanded when she groaned.

She stared at him, wondering why she hadn't seen it
before—the regal poise, the air of command, the confidence of kings. 'A little dizzy,' she confessed, turning her
back on him before she gave herself away. 'Maybe I'm suffering from delayed sea-sickness.' It was a lie, and a weak
one at that, but it was all she had.

'Well, take care as you go down the steps,' Saif advised.
'Sit down for a while. Put your head between your knees
and take some deep breaths.'

It would take more than a few deep breaths to blank out
what she'd seen.

But Saif couldn't be the ruling sheikh, Antonia decided. Where were his bodyguards, his attendants, his warships off the coast? It was time to stop panicking and start thinking clearly. With that tattoo, he must have some connection with the court, so that was good news. She might have a chance to ask him about her mother before she disembarked.

Nursing this little bud of hope, she went below. She couldn't pretend she wasn't excited by the chance to root around while Saif was busy up on deck. Who knew what she might find?

She found the cashmere blanket and not much else of interest. Saif's personal quarters were bare to the point of austerity. She found the robe exactly where he had said it would be, but, far from being some fabulous luxury garment that a ruling sheikh might wear, it was a simple cream linen *dishdash* of the type that could be purchased on any market stall.

That imagination of hers would get her into trouble one day, Antonia warned herself, collecting up a pair of traditional thonged sandals. There wasn't so much as a headdress, or a golden *agal* to hold that headdress in place, let alone a fancy robe. Saif was simply a patriot who chose to wear his leader's insignia over his heart. The fearsome ruling sheikh of Sinnebar, known to the world as the Sword of Vengeance, he was most definitely not.

CHAPTER SEVEN

ANTONIA was standing at Saif's side as he edged the giant yacht into its mooring at the marina in Sinnebar. She was covered from head to toe in the blanket. Her choice; her last defiant act. The ache in her chest at the thought of leaving him was so severe she felt physically sick. She hadn't expected parting from him to hurt like this, though neither of them had ever been under any illusion that their time together was anything more than a fantasy that would end the moment they docked. So she only had herself to blame for feeling this way, Antonia reflected as Saif called to the men on the shore to catch the ropes. Saif was her fantasy; she had never been his.

Grow up, Antonia told herself fiercely, biting back tears. Was this the girl who had set out from Rome with such determination? So, dealing with life outside the cocoon was sometimes tricky and often tough—get over it. She had that one day to remember, didn't she? And one day with Saif had turned out to be the best day of her life.

To avoid breaking down, she focused her mind on the stunning panorama beyond the harbour. Everything about Sinnebar gripped her. It was Saif's homeland, and a place where her mother had lived. So many impressions hit her at once: perhaps most significantly of all, the desert—stretching vast and silent beyond this billionaires' marina, as far as the eye could see.

The desert...

She felt a frisson of expectation just thinking about the desert. It had always been her dream to go beyond the silken veil and uncover the secrets there.

Well, she had the longed-for chance now, though it hardly seemed possible that she was staring up at jagged purple mountains, or the unfathomable desert. In the opposite direction were the gleaming white spires of an internationally renowned capital city. Immediately in front were low-lying white buildings. They lined the pristine dock, and all the paved areas were equally well maintained. Even the road was newly surfaced. There were colourful gardens and water displays, which she took to be a sure sign of wealth in the desert, and guessed that each entry point to Sinnebar would have similarly high standards so that the visitor's first impression could only be good.

She was a little surprised to see the number of security guards on duty, but then reasoned that it must be quite an event when one of the multi-million-dollar yachts came home to roost. If you had never seen a man like Saif climbing the yard arm to secure a sail, you would definitely want to add that to your scrapbook of memories. Saif had not yet put on his robe, and was balancing on what looked to Antonia like a narrow pole suspended at a dizzying height above the deck. She worried about him; she couldn't help herself. But he wasn't hers to worry about, she reminded herself, and some other woman would share his life.

She turned her face away so Saif couldn't see the distress in her eyes when he sprang down onto the deck. By the time he had taken the robe she was holding out for him and slipped it over his head, she was under control again. She wouldn't break down now, not now, not so close to the end of this journey. She turned her attention instead to the waiting ambulance, and noticed there was a low-slung limousine parked next to it. She guessed that was waiting for Saif.

Impressive.

So he was a wealthy man who drove around with blacked-out windows—so what? He could have been the lowliest member of the crew and she wouldn't have felt any different about him. Both vehicles were surrounded by security guards, but she'd be an important witness in the piracy trial, Antonia reasoned, so there would have to be precautions taken for her safety. She looked at Saif, who was greeting the paramedic. To her eyes Saif couldn't have looked more magnificent if he had been wearing the silken robes of her imagination. Even in plain linen he had the bearing of a king. It wasn't just that he was tall and imposing, or incredibly good-looking. He had such an easy manner—with everyone except her, she realised ruefully. She was apparently invisible now. In spite of everything she had so forcefully told herself, she yearned for a sign from Saif that said she meant something to him.

She would wait a long time for that, Antonia concluded as Saif brought the paramedic over to meet her. 'Take good care of the patient,' he said. 'She's had a rough time.'

As he spoke Saif didn't even glance at her, though the paramedic, a much older man, gave her a kindly smile, which she returned before bracing herself to disembark.

'*Kum shams ilha maghrib,*' Saif murmured as she passed within earshot.

'I'm sorry?' She didn't understand and turned to look at him for an explanation.

'Every sun has its sunset,' Saif translated, and for the briefest moment she thought she saw regret in his eyes.

That was his gift to her. Saif wanted her to know it had been a special time for him. It was the only gift she could ever want from him, just as leaving him without making a fuss would be her gift to him. 'You're right,' she said so that only Saif could hear. 'All good things must come to an end.'

And then, conscious that the paramedic was waiting for her, she left the yacht with her head held high.

As the limousine swept up to the steps of the palace he felt the return to reality more keenly than usual, but it altered nothing. The moment he stepped out of the limousine, he was changed. That was how it had to be. This was work. This was duty. This was his life.

The palace was set like a rose-pink moonstone on the golden shores of an aquamarine Gulf. It was an elegant marble paradise, where every luxury man could devise awaited him, and a fleet of servants was devoted to his every whim. He had never troubled to count the bedrooms, and doubted anyone ever had. Soon he would be making a gift of this towering edifice to his people, but until that time he called it home.

He strode inside, greeting people by name as they bowed to him, lifting them to their feet when they knelt in front of him. He loathed the deference some of his fellow sheikhs actively courted, and lived austerely considering his fabulous wealth. He valued all the treasures history had granted him, but he valued his people more.

He bathed and then clothed himself in the costume of power, adopting the shackles of responsibility with each new item. The heavy silk robe reminded him of the weight of duty, while the headdress spoke of the respect in which he held his country and its people. The golden *agal* holding that headdress in place was his badge of office, like the jewelled sash he wore at his waist. The sash carried his emblem, which he had personally designed as a representation of his pledge to Sinnebar. The rampant lion picked out in flashing jewels was a warning to anyone who threatened his land, and the cold, blue sapphire clutched in its claws was the heart he had given to his country and his people. On the day of his coronation, he had vowed that nothing would alter the pledge of that heart, or disturb the order he had returned to Sinnebar following his father's chaotic rule. That history had come back to haunt him in the form of a woman long dead, his despised stepmother Helena, something he intended to deal with without delay.

While he was away it appeared a letter had been found in Helena's room. Written before her death to an elderly maidservant, it contained a photograph of Helena holding a tiny baby girl in her arms. That was why they had called him back so urgently. Trusted advisors could be relied upon to keep this revelation under wraps, but not for long in a palace so heavily populated it was almost like a city in its own right.

The baby wasn't even his father's child, but the Italian Ruggiero's, and should have had no entitlement to land in Sinnebar. But when Helena had died the land had passed in equal part to her children. His father had paid her off, because Helena was the mother of his son. Razi ruled his own country and had returned the land to Sinnebar. Helena's daughter had not. It enraged him beyond belief to think that a woman long dead, a woman who had brought so much grief to his family while she was alive, could reach out even now from the grave to threaten his land.

He shouldn't be surprised to find his father had left him one last problem to overcome, Ra'id reflected grimly, checking his royal regalia before leaving the room. They had never seen eye to eye on matters of duty versus the heart.

He left the robing room with a purposeful stride, mentally preparing for the task ahead of him. The prospect of encountering anything connected to Helena was distasteful to him. It was an excursion into a world he had no wish to go to. Helena's heir should be clearing out her belongings, but the identity of the baby in the photograph had not yet been established. He would read through the documents and see what he could glean. At least it should prove a distraction, he conceded grimly, for a man tormented by the memory of a dancing girl invoking the moon, as he listened in vain for the sound of her voice.

He would never forget his desert-island castaway, Ra'id realised as he paused to admire the elegance of one of the inner courtyards. With its mellow fountains and counterpoint of singing birds, it was possible to hope that there were enough distractions here in Sinnebar, so that in time her voice would fade and her face would slip out of focus, until one day she would be just The Girl—a memory consigned to history along with all the rest. Closing his eyes, he inhaled deeply, breathing in the heavy perfumes of the

East, waiting for them to blank out the girl's fresh, clean scent. When that didn't happen, he frowned and turned away. The courtyard, with its fretwork screens and carved stone palisades, was made for the type of romance he had no time for. He didn't even know why he'd stopped here.

His robes rustled expensively as he strode away, the sound of them reminding him at all times of duty. When he reached his office he would read the letter again and study the land deeds. He would not tolerate part of Sinnebar being casually handed over to someone who cared nothing for the land of his birth and who didn't even live in Sinnebar. He would soon put an end to this outrageous claim and bury Helena's legacy of turmoil once and for all.

Before transferring Antonia to a luxury hotel, they had advised her to stay in a private clinic for several days, to check for concussion. She'd wanted to say she'd had a blow to the heart, not to the head, but the nurses and staff had been so friendly, and she had welcomed the chance to rest and regroup in such a clean and efficient place.

Her bills were covered, the staff had explained when she'd started to fret about expenses. She'd had no need to ask by whom, Antonia reflected, wandering out onto the balcony of the luxury hotel suite where she had just been transferred to. All of this had been paid for by Saif. It had to be Saif. Who else knew she was here?

Knowing Saif had paid for her care did nothing to ease Antonia's heartache. The fact that he hadn't tried to contact her once only rubbed salt in a wound she doubted would ever heal. How could it heal when there was no cure for her feelings for Saif?

The light of another day was fading, coating the city in a honeyed glow. The pink marble walls of the palace were tinted a deeper red as the sun drooped wearily towards the horizon. Leaning over the cool stone balustrade, Antonia pictured her mother catching sight of this same palace for the first time. Surely Helena must have seen the palace? It was impossible to miss the magnificent building on a visit to Sinnebar's capital, where the palace dominated the cityscape.

Knowing so little about her mother, Antonia could only guess that she was following in Helena's footsteps. She had to believe that whatever she found in Sinnebar would bring them closer in some small way. She wanted to understand her mother's early life. She knew that Helena had been very young when she had come to the Gulf, so it was easy to work out that she had probably been a student, back-packing her way across the world. Having discovered this beautiful desert kingdom, she hadn't found the will to leave. It would be easy to give your heart to a country where gilded cupolas and cream minarets stood proudly against a vivid electric-blue sky, Antonia mused. She thought the vista over the elegant city squares to the palace beyond was the most astonishing sight she had ever seen.

The second-most astonishing sight, Antonia amended, remembering the moment a sexy brigand had confronted her on board his yacht.

She must forget Saif, Antonia told herself firmly, staring at the palace again. She had work to do, and must devote herself to that. The hotel housekeeper had explained that the palace she could see was now called the Ra'id al Maktabi palace, after their new leader. The woman had excitedly gone on to confide that Ra'id al Maktabi's stated aim was to bring Sinnebar into the twenty-first century, which included equal rights for women for the first time in the country's history.

Antonia hadn't failed to notice how the woman's face had lit up when she spoke of the ruling sheikh, and had gathered that the hopes of the people were invested in their new leader. No wonder Saif had been offended when she had teased him about his sheikh. She understood now that Ra'id al Maktabi was looked upon as the saviour of his country.

Before he could deal with the Helena problem, he wanted to make sure that arrangements for the girl's safe passage home had been made. The sooner she went, the better. Reports on her progress were brought to him daily, which made it impossible to close that chapter until she was gone.

He rang his secretary to check that everything was in place, and, having been reassured that all the travel details were in order, he was reminded of an appointment that evening, a charity event he must attend. It was an event in the old style with no women present. He was in the process of putting an end to this segregation of the sexes, before any more good brains were wasted—a thought that immediately brought a flashback of a very determined young woman. What would Tuesday make of an event where she wouldn't be allowed past the door?

There was a smile on his lips as he shook his head at the thought of her reaction, but the event was for charity, and had been organised during his father's reign, so he would make time for it. Whatever his personal feelings, he could put up with one more evening of wall-to-wall men. When he returned from the event he would set about reclaiming the land that had been stolen from his people, and would be relentless in his pursuit of the missing heir.

She wasn't going to waste a second regretting things that couldn't be changed, Antonia decided as she came in from the balcony to her sumptuous hotel room. Everything was so beautiful in Sinnebar; how could she not be filled with a sense of optimism? And what else could life throw at her? She had to be over the worst now.

In fact, she was feeling quite positive, if only because this evening had provided her with an unexpected chance to put her plans for the charity into action. Her official appointment at the palace wasn't for three weeks yet, and she had intended to use that time to travel the country and learn more about the people. But fate had presented her with an unrepeatable opportunity to get a preview of the movers and shakers in Sinnebar. The moment the girl at the reception desk in the hotel had told her there was going to be a charity event that evening in the hotel ballroom, Antonia knew she must be there. She didn't have an invitation, because no one knew she was in the country yet, but there was nothing to stop her slipping into the crowded ballroom and mingling. At least she had to try. All the local officials were expected to attend, including the ruling sheikh.

The ruling sheikh!

The thought of seeing him both terrified and excited her. The Sword of Vengeance—who wouldn't be excited? And her heart rate soared to think that Saif might be there too. If he was a close supporter of the sheikh, surely there was a very good chance?

Society events were second nature to her, thanks to her

brother's high-powered life. She would blend in and get to know as many people as she could, taking the first steps towards making her dream of becoming an effective member of Rigo's charity team a reality. At last here was something she understood and couldn't make a mess of.

There was a shopping mall at the hotel where Antonia found everything she would need for the evening ahead. She chose a simple silk gown in apricot silk and teamed it with a pair of flesh-coloured high-heeled sandals, and a beaded clutch bag in the same soft shade. The girl in the hairdresser's suggested a fresh orchid to pin in her hair as a finishing touch.

Understated and discreet, Antonia thought as she took a twirl in front of the mirror in her room. The gown had a floating chiffon throw to cover her arms, and her back was covered too, so the dress was modest. It was a dream of a dress, she thought happily as she left the room, with nothing about it that could offend in this most conservative of desert kingdoms. No wonder she felt so optimistic about the evening ahead.

CHAPTER EIGHT

IT WAS an all-male gathering, which was definitely not what Antonia had bargained for. She was rocked back on her heels and hesitated outside the ornately carved double doors. She quickly gathered, from the glances she was attracting from the security guards, that she would not be welcome inside the ballroom. But they couldn't stop her peeping inside the room. It was an exclusive occasion, judging by the number of ribbons and orders worn by the robed men already seated at the beautifully dressed tables. Crystal glass and silver cutlery glittered in the muted candlelight, and there was a buzz of anticipation in the hall, but absolutely no chance to slip in unnoticed as she had hoped. She would stick out like a sore thumb as the only woman present.

This was definitely not a suitable forum in which to lobby support for her plan, Antonia concluded. She had no option but to wait another three weeks for her official appointment. But, as she drew back in disappointment from the door, her heart wouldn't allow her to leave. What if Saif was coming? What if he was already here? *What if she could see him one last time?*

She couldn't leave, so she came up with a risky plan. She would try to get in at the back of the ballroom, where she could see some steps leading up to a mezzanine area. She would be able to see everything from there.

Including the man who sat on the sapphire throne…

Antonia's gaze lingered. She'd seen images of Sheikh Ra'id's sapphire throne on the Internet, but nothing could have prepared her for the actual brilliance of the gold, or the lustre of the royal-blue sapphires with which it was so lavishly studded. Just thinking about the man who would occupy this legendary seat of power sent a shiver down her spine. You crossed the ruling Sheikh of Sinnebar at your peril, she had heard.

Dragging her gaze away from the blazing splendour of this formidable leader's throne, she crossed the lobby and slipped out of the building. Skirting the perimeter until she found a side entrance, she waited until the security guards were briefly distracted and then slipped inside through the staff entrance. Shoes in hand, she pelted up the back stairs, feeling certain her heart would explode with guilty fear.

Fortunately, the door to the mezzanine level was unlocked.

More tables had been set out for dinner on this upper level, for less important folk, she guessed. Taking quick stock of the situation, she decided if she hid behind a pillar no one would see her, while she could see everything that was happening below. This was her chance to weigh up the type of people she would be dealing with for the charity, and even the slimmest chance of seeing Saif made it worth the risk. The thought of seeing him and the fearsome Sword of Vengeance all in the same day made her heart thunder.

Taking a moment to calm down, she studied her surroundings carefully. She was at eye level with the royal standard, which was suspended behind the jewelled throne. That image made her heart leap when she remembered the last time she had seen it had been on Saif's naked chest. That was all the prompt she needed to begin scouring the rows of tables in search of him.

He wasn't there. She didn't really need to look to know, her heart would have told her if Saif had been close by. She was still trembling with emotion and disappointment when a noise like a wave breaking on the shore swept over the vast auditorium. As everyone rose to their feet, Antonia held her breath, realising the ruling sheikh was about to enter.

There was a peal of trumpets and then a procession began. A group of older men all dressed in elegant ivory robes walked proudly down the broad aisle between the tables. As all the other men bowed low to them, she realised that each of them must be a king in his own right, which was a reminder of the power their sheikh wielded.

As this group fanned out to take their places around their leader's throne, Antonia strained forward, still hoping for a glimpse of Saif. Once again, she was disappointed. He definitely wasn't amongst Ra'id al Maktabi's attendants— and probably wasn't even a member of the court, she thought, angry with herself for allowing her imagination to run away with her. There was certainly no one to compare with Saif here.

She was distracted and missed the moment when the ruling sheikh entered the room. She didn't see him, but she felt his presence. It was as if the room had suddenly been infused with greatness, and yet he had entered without a fanfare. He had no need of one, she realised when she saw the ruler of Sinnebar for the first time. She could only see him from the back, but even so, as Ra'id al Maktabi walked towards the platform with the easy loping stride of a panther, she thought him the most imposing figure she had ever seen.

At last here was a man to compare with Saif, Antonia decided. Dressed in robes of deepest blue, the ruling sheikh was easily the tallest man in the room, and far more powerfully built than any other man. She was transfixed by him, and couldn't wait to see his face, but just as he was about to turn the gold *agal* securing his headdress flashed in the light and she was momentarily blinded. It was then they seized her from behind.

This wasn't quite how she'd imagined spending the evening, Antonia reflected miserably, having made herself as comfortable as was possible in a dank, cold cell with very little light and no heating. She had asked for a blanket and they had brought her a thin, scratchy one, which was probably all she deserved. What her brother would make of this latest exploit, she had no idea. She had pleaded for the right to make a phone call to him, and had given the guard his number, but had no way of knowing if the guard would act on her behalf—no way of knowing if she would ever be released. Curling up into a ball, she covered herself as best she could and resigned herself to a long, dark night of fear and uncertainty.

She must have dropped off, Antonia realised when she was awoken by a crash of arms. Moments later her cell door was flung open and light streamed in. By this time she was huddled fearfully in the furthest corner of the wooden bench that passed for her bed.

'Stand up,' a guard shouted at her rudely.

She did so and stood trembling with her back pressed against the wall, expecting the worst. She was both surprised and relieved when the guard backed out of the cell, though that barely left enough room for the man who entered next.

She felt a sting of disappointment. What had she expected—the ruler of Sinnebar ducking his head to enter her cell? The ruling sheikh with his jewelled belt? Or perhaps Saif, her desert prince, the dark stranger of her dreams?

For the first time in her life, Antonia resented her over-active imagination. It was always tricking her into expecting the best.

The best?

The man facing her now in his smart suit couldn't have looked more disdainfully at her if he'd tried. 'I can confirm the identity of the prisoner,' he told the guard, ignoring Antonia completely.

'Please,' Antonia said as the man turned to go. 'Please don't leave me here.' She sounded so pathetic, but she was desperate. 'I have to get a message to my brother in Rome.'

The man paused and then turned to her. 'Nigel Clough, Foreign Office,' he said, making no attempt to shake her hand. 'I'm standing in for my colleague from Rome who is attending a charity function tonight. You're lucky that someone with influence has arranged for your immediate departure from the country.'

Antonia gasped. 'Do you mean I'm being deported?'

'I wouldn't quibble if I were you,' Nigel Clough warned her. 'Just take the chance to go while you have it.' The man's pale gaze flickered disparagingly around the cell. 'Unless, of course, you have some plan to stay?'

'No, none.' Tears stung her eyes. 'Will you call my brother just in case it all goes wrong and they keep me here?' She handed over a screwed-up note on which she had written Rigo's private telephone number with a pen she'd accidentally borrowed from an unwary guard. 'Thank you,' she called after the starchy civil servant. Now she just had to hope it wouldn't be long before she saw the outside world again so she could pick up her life.

But they left the cell door open, and with a rush of relief Antonia realised the guards were waiting for her to leave. She had no idea what lay ahead of her, but one thing was certain— she wasn't staying here. Drawing the flimsy blanket tightly round her, she followed the guards along the same dismal corridors down which they had first brought her, and almost cried with relief when she stepped onto the street. Of course there was no imposing sheikh, or sardonic Saif, waiting to greet her. She shaded her eyes against the glare of an unforgiving sun. This was a sorry end to a brave adventure.

She flinched as the prison gates slammed behind her. She had survived a pirate attack and an assault on her heart, but she doubted she could survive her own self-loathing if she returned to Rome without a single one of her goals having been fulfilled.

Well, that was just too bad, wasn't it? Antonia admonished herself, bumping around in the back of an old army Jeep on her way to the airport. She had to bite the bullet and get on with life like everyone else. She'd got into this mess, and now it was up to her to get out of it. She'd go back to Rome, face up to her brother and prove both to Rigo and to herself that she was worthy of her brother's trust and that she could do what she had set out to do. This time neither pirates, guards, nor even a man who had carved his name into her heart would stand in her way

It felt like she'd hardly had time to unpack her suitcase before she was standing in an austere cubicle in a private clinic in Rome, getting dressed after her examination. Of course, it had been a little longer than that, weeks in fact, Antonia reflected. She felt she was enclosed in a stark white eggshell—white walls, white floor; even the curtain shielding her from view was white. But in the past five minutes since the doctor had confirmed she was pregnant her life had blazed with vivid colour. Yes, it had been an incredible shock to discover she was pregnant, but when the doctor had confirmed it her horizons exploded with possibility. This was so far beyond the bounds of anything she believed she deserved; she could hardly take it in. Except to say that having a baby both terrified her and made this the happiest day of her life.

She couldn't tell Rigo, of course. He definitely wouldn't understand—and he would certainly never trust her again. But she must tell Saif. It might not be easy to track him down, but it wouldn't be impossible when he had commanded such a notable yacht.

A baby, Antonia mused, leaving the clinic in a bubble of happiness that grew and grew. She was going to have Saif's baby. What better gift could he have given her than a baby she would lay down her life for, a child she would protect and nurture as a lioness protects its cub?

Ra'id's fist thundered down on the top of his highly polished desk. Was this possible? Could the girl he had lightly dubbed Tuesday be the missing heir? Had he been duped? Had he harboured a thief hiding behind the guise of innocence? Had the thief of his people's land been lying in the arms of their king?

Springing up, he paced the room. He could not reconcile the feelings of loss and longing he felt for the girl he had known as Tuesday with his very different feelings for the person he believed posed the biggest threat to his people's happiness. The whole point of lifting a country out of chaos was to unite all the warring factions and keep them focused on one common purpose, which was the growth and prosperity of Sinnebar—something he was determined would be enjoyed by all, whatever their position in life. To think of one vast strip of land being teased away, leaving families stranded on either side of it, was something he would not tolerate.

CHAPTER NINE

MAYBE it was only a few months in real time, but it felt like ten years of growing up had passed since the last time she'd flown over this turquoise sea on her way to the Gulf. At least on this occasion she was prepared, Antonia reflected, and full of determination to finish what she'd started. There would be no hitching lifts on fishing boats, or desert-island idylls—there would be no distractions at all. This time she was here on business with a track record of success behind her.

After returning home in disgrace she had cancelled her initial meeting in Sinnebar to give herself time to regroup. The wounds from her ordeal with the pirates had gradually faded, but not so the wounds in her heart, and her brother Rigo had taken some convincing before agreeing to give her a second chance. It was then Antonia had discovered that a broken heart was the best engine for change. To forget Saif, she had thrown herself into her work, and in a short space of time had managed to double the number of children they were able to help. Having picked herself up, she had gone on to open branches of her brother's charity in Europe. Sinnebar was the next natural choice, and it was a place she couldn't wait to visit, though negotiations at the highest level had been necessary to arrange a visa for someone who had been deported from the country.

But this wasn't all about work. While she was here she would find Saif and tell him about their baby. What would happen next was a little hazy at the moment, but she was sure they could come to a civilised arrangement.

She would succeed in achieving all her goals this time, Antonia determined. She had a child to protect and set an example for now—a miracle she was still getting used to. And expecting a child had only intensified Antonia's longing to know her mother. She was more determined than ever to find out what she could about Helena's life in Sinnebar. Finding Saif was perhaps the most important goal of all.

She'd settle for that, Antonia realised, tightening her grip on the briefcase that held all the paperwork relating to the charity. If anything, it was Saif who had given her the courage to continue this adventure, and just knowing she was in the same country as the man was enough to make her heart fly. She had a good feeling about this as she disembarked the aircraft.

He had watched her progress over the past three months, knowing she would come back to Sinnebar. She had no other option if she wanted to extend the reach of her brother's charity. Antonia Ruggiero, daughter of Helena Ruggiero; Tuesday; Wild-child; Criminal; Cheat.

Lover…

She had bewitched him once and would never be allowed to do so again.

He thanked the immigration official on the other end of the phone for informing him that the individual under surveillance had landed, and replaced the receiver in its nest. He would see Signorina Antonia Ruggiero at the meeting in his government offices this afternoon. Antonia had no idea he would be there. He would surprise her at her appointment with his Minister of Charities.

Had it been a chance meeting on his yacht three months ago? How likely was that? He would trust no one with Helena's blood in their veins, and the coincidence was too much for him to swallow. Antonia had come to Sinnebar, like her mother before her, to weigh up the ground before greedily scooping up whatever she could. No wonder she hadn't been prepared to tell him her name. The charity she represented might be wholly above board—he'd had it checked out—but as far as he was concerned Helena's heir was a cheat out to rob his people of their land. The reckless escapade on a local fishing-boat was nothing more than vanity for the indulged wild-child of an Italian industrialist with more money than sense. Antonia Ruggiero had set out to deceive him. She was a criminal with a plan to steal his people's land—a woman who thought she could stroll back into the country and threaten him with her mother's bequest.

Let her try. He was ready for her.

Ra'id smiled grimly as he buckled on his belt with the royal insignia emblazoned on it.

'Signorina Antonia Ruggiero,' a quietly spoken man announced.

As the double doors shut silently behind her, Antonia was instantly aware of an atmosphere of ceremony and history. She could see the majestic council-chamber with its high, vaulted ceiling had been adapted to modern life with consoles and monitors positioned in the centre of a highly polished oval table, but nothing could take away from the craftsmanship around her. The gilt scrolling on the ornate plasterwork, like the exquisitely tiled floor and the artefacts decorating the room, was magnificent. Life-sized murals on the walls picked out scenes from Sinnebar's past, while giant gold vases at least twice her height stood like sentries at the doors. The floor-to-ceiling windows allowed honeyed light to flood in, and the air was scented and streaked with sunbeams. She felt it was a privilege to be here where time was measured in millennia rather than minutes.

Air-conditioning cooled her as she walked deeper into the room, and as she drew close the dozen or so men seated round the table stood and gave her the traditional greeting.

'Gentlemen,' she said, dipping her head politely before taking her seat. She had dressed for the occasion in a sober, beautifully tailored suit, in a subtle shade of dove grey that was both comfortable and modest, and she was wearing hardly any make-up. Her hair was neatly tied back, and though she had already given one presentation that morning her enthusiasm for the charity project had kept her fresh and alert.

She had left that last meeting with a positive feeling. Many of the men the sheikh had chosen to sit on his council were family men and they had quickly come to share her passion for the concept. This meeting was the final stage before Sheikh al Maktabi put his seal of approval on the scheme. She had been assured he would, as the ruler of Sinnebar always put the interests of his people first. She fully expected to start work on a centre for parents and children to enjoy in the next few weeks—providing the ruling sheikh would allow her to use some of his land for the project.

He had to—he must—Antonia determined. Ra'id al Maktabi famously cared about his people. How could he refuse such a simple request?

She was halfway through her summing up when the huge, arched golden doors at the far end of the room swung open. She felt a shiver of prescience and, following everyone else's lead, she stood up.

The thought of finally meeting the formidable Sword of Vengeance was both a thrilling and terrifying moment for Antonia, but as she turned to catch her first glimpse of him the light streamed into her eyes. It made no difference. She could still sense his animal power as he strode towards her.

Tall and lithe, the ruler of Sinnebar was bearing down on her like a jungle cat, deep blue robes rustling rhythmically as he walked. At his waist a jewelled symbol flashed.

Fear rippled down Antonia's spine. She had imagined the infamous Sword of Vengeance would be older. Sheikh Ra'id al Maktabi of Sinnebar's reputation was built on the solid rock of dedicated service to his country, but she could see now that this was a man in the prime of life—and that for some reason he disapproved of her.

'Signorina Ruggiero.'

'Saif…'

The breath shot from Antonia's lungs as His Imperial Majesty, Sheikh Ra'id al Maktabi, clasped her hand Western-style in greeting. She would have known that grip anywhere, and the name Saif had escaped her lips before she'd had chance to think.

But now…

Antonia began to shake as a debilitating fear swept over her.

'Water,' she heard a man's voice command and then someone was drawing out a chair for her and she sank back. That same someone had stopped her falling, and now he settled her into the chair, and she found herself staring down the long stretch of table into the face of a man who was both a stranger and her lover.

And the father of her unborn child.

The realisation that the father of her baby was none other than the Sword of Vengeance was a devastating emotional blow. Most things she could get around, but not this.

Any hope she'd had of finding Saif and living happily ever after had just been crushed. How could she tell this man—this formidable king—that she was carrying the heir to his throne? When would she tell him? Would he be willing to grant her a private audience—or would he find out somehow and steal her child?

He was darker than night and twice as dangerous, she thought as Ra'id al Maktabi stared coldly down the table at her. He would think her a gold-digger, or worse, if she told him about the baby, and would almost certainly demand that any child of his would be brought up in Sinnebar.

At his signal the hiss of the air-conditioning was instantly subdued to a hum. 'Don't let me throw you off your stride, Signorina Ruggiero,' Saif—the man she must now think of as His Imperial Majesty, Sheikh Ra'id al Maktabi of Sinnebar—insisted evenly. 'Please continue.'

He made a gracious gesture with his hand, but she wasn't fooled. This was a man everyone obeyed on the instant or suffered the consequences—which would be swift and terrible, Antonia suspected.

Sipping the water they had given her, she tried desperately to collect her thoughts. It helped to think about the child inside her, the child who depended on her, and then she widened these thoughts to encompass the many children who were helped by the charity she represented, and who depended on her getting this right. 'Gentlemen,' she began, determined to pick up the discussion without too great a pause. 'I do have some spare proposals with me.' She turned to one of the ever-present servants at her elbow. 'Would you be good enough to hand this copy to His Majesty?' she asked politely, passing over a neatly bound folder of printed notes.

'You make a persuasive case, Signorina Ruggiero,' Ra'id concluded as he brought the meeting to a close. 'I will consult with my council, but I am persuaded to allow you to open a branch of your charity in Sinnebar.'

'There is one other point I'd like to bring up.'

The surprise around the table showed itself in a collective gasp. No one interrupted the ruling Sheikh of Sinnebar, Antonia suspected, but in this instance she had no option as there was one item on which the ruler of Sinnebar's agreement was essential. 'The land...' She got no further. No one, especially not Antonia, could have predicted Ra'id's reaction. Wily gazes dropped before the power of their sheikh. Ra'id al Maktabi hadn't even moved, but all the men around the table had detected some subtle change in him, and it was a change that threatened all of them—especially her, Antonia suspected.

But when he spoke Ra'id's voice was perfectly calm. 'We have a number of matters to discuss, Signorina Ruggiero,' he agreed pleasantly.

Was she the only person in the room to hear the edge of menace in that voice? Antonia wondered. But wasn't this the opportunity she'd been hoping for? She could tell Ra'id about their child. It might come as a bombshell to him, but she had to believe he would be as happy as she was when he got used to the idea.

Ra'id's smallest emphasis on the word *we* had been enough to dismiss the council, who rose as one and, having bowed low to their sheikh, acknowledged her briefly before leaving the room.

CHAPTER TEN

SHE was alone with Ra'id. Even the servants had vanished. Now there was just echoing silence and the most powerful man in the Gulf—a man whose unwavering gaze was now fixed on her. This was no susceptible lover who would be thrilled to hear about a baby, but a hard man of the desert—a warrior who would stop at nothing to protect his people, a man without the luxury of a heart. She would have to be honest with him. She would explain first about the charity, and when the business part of the meeting was over she would tell him her most important news. She had to draw on her courage and remember the meeting earlier that day. The men who reported to the sheikh had all been broadly in agreement with her plan—subject, of course, to their sheikh's approval.

But had she made herself clear enough to Ra'id? Antonia wondered when he continued to stare at her as if she had unwittingly committed some terrible sin. Opening her hands in appeal, she pressed on. 'It goes without saying that the charity will stand all the expense incurred in building this facility, and we'll be happy to pay the going rate for the land.'

'The going rate?'

His reaction terrified her. Springing to his feet, Ra'id cast a long shadow over the table as he leaned his balled up fists upon it. It was almost a relief when he straightened up and turned his back on her to walk some paces away.

But what had she done? She could not remember feeling quite so threatened, and any thought she might have had of talking about their child had vanished. In fact, glancing at the door, she realised her primary concern now was to protect her child from this man she didn't feel as if she knew at all.

'Where do you think you're going?'

She shrank back as Ra'id spun on his heels to confront her when she started collecting up her things. 'I can see it's not convenient for you to see me right now.'

'When will there be a better time?' he said, cutting her off at the door.

'Ra'id, please...' Tears were threatening, and she hated herself for the weakness, knowing this was a man who would not care to see her cry.

'Ra'id, please,' he mimicked cruelly. 'What is it this time, Tuesday? Are you here for a pay-off—or would you like a little more action first?'

'Ra'id, don't,' she begged, turning her face from his stinging scorn. 'I can't talk to you when you're like this. Please, let me go.'

'Not until we've discussed this land that seems to mean so much to you.' His voice was harsh and cruel, and his touch was unrelenting as he steered her back to the table. 'Sit down,' he said, indicating the seat next to his. 'You've seen this, of course?'

As she shakily sank onto the chair, he pushed a sheaf of documents in front of her. 'No. What are they?'

'I have copies,' he said, when she didn't even know what he was talking about.

She glanced at the title on the topmost sheet. 'I don't understand—this is a deed of land granted by your father to my mother.'

'Well done,' he said derisively. 'One of your best performances to date. You almost have me fooled.'

Antonia shook her head in bewilderment. 'I'm trying to make sense of this. I'm sorry if I'm not as quick as you…'

'Take your time.' His voice was full of disdain.

'You knew my mother?' Antonia glanced up in confusion, and then her gaze returned to her mother's name as if just reading it could somehow protect her.

'It would be hard for me not to know my father's concubine.'

'What?' The room began to spin. She had heard Ra'id, and yet her mind refused to accept what he'd said to her. Pushing her chair back, she stumbled awkwardly away from the table. 'I don't understand what you're saying,' she admitted in a voice turned dry and faint.

'You don't?' Ra'id's hard face mirrored his disbelief. 'Let me stop your performance before you get started. And understand this, Antonia—I have no interest in learning how dear your mother was to you, or how much you meant to each other—let alone how passionately she wanted you to have this land in Sinnebar.'

'Land?' Antonia demanded with amazement. 'What land?'

'Oh, please,' Ra'id said, shaking his head. 'Can't you

do better than that? You will never rise from the ranks of the chorus to become a full-blown leading lady if you can't put on a better act.'

'This is no act,' she protested, feeling as if a vice were closing around her chest. 'I had no idea my mother even knew your father, let alone that she was his mistress.'

'That's a polite name for it.'

'Stop, Ra'id—please, stop it!' Holding out her hand as if to fend him off, she willed him to stop heaping insults on top of the confusion inside her. Then it occurred to her that as her heart had just been ripped in two he couldn't do any more harm.

She returned quietly to the table where she sat down and scrutinised the documents. She had inherited land in Sinnebar and a property from her mother. She couldn't have been more surprised. The news that Helena had been the late sheikh's mistress on top of this…

But Ra'id gave her no chance to recover. 'Do you still pretend you know nothing of this?'

'Nothing—I swear.' It was hard to take in the facts. Not only had her young mother been the late sheikh's mistress, but Helena had been paid off when the sheikh had tired of her with this gift of land. It was clear the late sheikh had thought nothing of this valuable gift of territory within Sinnebar, while Ra'id viewed it quite differently. Ra'id was the highly principled conservator of a kingdom and guardian of his people, and no greater sin could have been committed as far as he was concerned. She could understand his resentment. She had inherited a parcel of his people's land. It was a gift that had been passed from Helena to Antonia, who was not the daughter of the late sheikh but Antonio Ruggiero, the man who had rescued her mother from this life of…

She had no idea what her mother's life had been like, Antonia realised with a sharp pang of regret. Raising her gaze to meet Ra'id's hard, uncompromising stare, she knew she'd get no pity from him. But he still dazzled her, unreachable as he was. He was like a dark force framed in light, and one she must soften if her proposal for the charity was to succeed.

'I will use the land for the good of your people,' she said, feeling her strength and her courage return as a plan began to take shape in her mind.

'You can only do that with my permission.'

'But you will—' She had sprung up too quickly, and now she was paying the price. 'You must,' she said weakly, clutching the table for support.

'Are you ill?' Ra'id demanded, observing her keenly.

'No, I'm not ill,' she managed, instantly protective of her baby. Ra'id's child was a royal baby and could be stolen away from her by the stroke of his pen. She had to be cautious now.

'A drink of water, perhaps?' he suggested.

Antonia nodded, glad of the reprieve, and also relieved that even in his darkest rage Ra'id still had some flicker of humanity left in him. She sucked in a deep, steadying breath as he poured some water for her. Pregnancy might have weakened her, but what it couldn't do was lessen her resolve, and she would not fail for want of defending herself against Ra'id's unfair accusations.

'This doesn't change anything,' he said, handing her the glass of water. 'You have your mother's blood in you.'

'As you have your father's,' she flashed back. Ra'id might frighten her, but she was no doormat to be insulted by anyone. She wouldn't give up, her gaze plainly told him; she didn't know how to. This was her last chance to find out about her mother, to build a branch of the charity here and make it thrive. 'It would be a tragic mistake if you allowed your feelings for me to impact negatively on what we can achieve together with the charity.'

His expression remained unchanged. It was as hostile as ever. It wouldn't be so easy this time to build a bridge between them, Antonia realised, but she was as determined to push her proposals for the charity through as she was determined that her child would know its mother. Ra'id might be all ruthless, barbaric force, while she only had a dream to sustain her, but she had a store of stubbornness she hadn't even begun to draw on yet. 'I'll need planning permission.'

'To do what?' he demanded.

'Having read through this document, I see there's an old fort on the land I have inherited.' Ignoring his darkening expression, she went on. 'I shall restore that.'

'So you persist in this fantasy?' he interrupted.

'Obviously I would consult you first where any changes were concerned,' Antonia rushed on, determined he would hear her.

'You should know the land your mother left you lacks its own water supply.'

She made the mistake of staring into his eyes in confusion, only to see that the mockery she expected was mixed with slumbering passion in his gaze. 'You're enjoying this,' she said faintly, shocked to think that Ra'id could still want to bed his prey when he was so obviously relishing this opportunity to destroy her.

'The water course is on the wrong side of your border—and, unfortunately, you have no access to it.'

'Unless you permit it?' she guessed.

'And I won't permit it.' Ra'id's dark gaze glittered with triumph.

'So my land is...?'

'Worthless,' Ra'id confirmed.

'But not to me,' Antonia insisted, remembering her plans. 'The land is not worthless to me.'

'Arid desert? What will you do with it—offer camel rides?'

'That's cruel and unnecessary, Ra'id, especially with the prospect of you opening a branch of my brother's charity here in Sinnebar.'

'Only if I head up the ruling council of that charity.'

'Is there anything you don't rule?'

There was one thing—or rather one person—Ra'id reflected as Antonia pursued her argument. He had forgotten how persistent she could be. How irritating.

How desirable...

He watched her closely, noticing how her gaze softened when she spotted some ancient artefact, or when she stared dreamily into the middle distance as she formulated her plan, only for that gaze to harden and grow anxious when he'd mentioned the drawbacks to the old fort she had inherited. Would she fight for it? Remembering the girl who had swum through a storm to reach land, he had no doubt she would. Although she could only find the idea of visiting an ancient citadel where her mother had spent her last few months in Sinnebar incarcerated intimidating, rather as if the ancient building had the potential to become Antonia's prison too.

She had not yet broken free from her safe cocoon at home, though she badly wanted to, he concluded. So what was holding her back? Was it him? Was she frightened of him? Or was Antonia more frightened by the secret she was hiding from him?

As if sensing the way his thoughts were turning, she met his gaze, and that briefest of stares told him all he needed to know.

When Ra'id took a step closer Antonia's throat closed, and her gaze fixed on the jewelled belt on his robe. The rampant lion worked in gold thread clutching a very large sapphire in its deadly paws was exactly as she had pictured it, and she though it a perfect illustration of his power. But she had a small child sheltering inside her, and was responsible for other children who couldn't help themselves. She had to ignore her own fears and press on. 'If the old fort is habitable, I could live there myself and supervise the renovations.'

'Are you mad?' Ra'id thundered.

Mad? Yes, and very frightened, at the thought of taking a baby into the desert—a baby who hadn't even been born yet. But if she turned around and went home she felt sure she would never be allowed back into Sinnebar and everything she had set out to achieve would fail. 'According to those documents you showed me, I am entitled—'

'You are entitled to nothing without my permission,' Ra'id assured her in a deadly quiet voice.

He was very close to her, and his intoxicating scent was scrambling her brain. She had to forget everything they had ever been to each other. Ra'id must know she hadn't changed or weakened just because he was a king, and that she was as determined as she had ever been to carry all her plans through. 'So the rule of law means nothing in Sinnebar?' she challenged boldly.

She might not have spoken for all the good it did her. 'I will pay you for the land,' Ra'id told her coolly. 'Money is no object. Name your price.'

Her body shook with a tremor of revulsion. 'I don't have a price,' she said fiercely, searching for some semblance of the man she had known in Ra'id's eyes.

'I will *buy* the land from you,' he explained as if he thought her mind had failed her.

'It isn't for sale.'

This was truly a man she didn't know, Antonia thought as Ra'id's eyes narrowed. This fearsome ruler of Sinnebar bore not the slightest resemblance to the tender lover she had spent one glorious day and night with three months ago. This man was hard and brutal, and he didn't have a heart—or, if he did, it was as cold as the gleaming sapphire on his belt. Ra'id al Maktabi was a warrior forged from steel; a man she considered had nothing to offer the child she already loved so deeply and completely. But, with a mission to complete, she could allow no time for sentiment. 'Before I leave for the property I have inherited,' she said firmly, 'I would like to see my mother's room.'

The silence crackled with tension as they faced each other. Both of them were rigid with resolve. Ra'id was clearly astonished that anyone would challenge his authority, while Antonia was equally determined not to back down. It was an impasse from which there seemed no escape until, to her surprise, a faint smile tugged at his lips.

'I see no reason why you should not be taken to see Helena's room,' he said.

'By you?' Antonia demanded, feeling her confidence seep away.

'Who better to show you round? I am more than happy to take you to see your mother's room,' he said. 'And tomorrow morning I will take you into the desert to see your land.'

Even as Antonia's eyes widened and her lips parted with surprise, she wondered why she felt so sure that the granting of a wish had never carried greater danger. It wasn't just the thought of taking her unborn child into dangerous territory, she realised, but the very real threat radiating from Ra'id. Then she reasoned that the desert was not an environment to enter lightly, especially now she was pregnant, and who better to guide her than Ra'id?

But if she hoped to soften him…

Hope springs eternal, Antonia remembered, gazing up into Ra'id's cold eyes. But he held the key to turning her dream for the charity into reality. The old fort could only live again with Ra'id's water supply, and that was one dream she wasn't letting go of. And how better to find the chance to tell him the news about their baby than spending time with him?

No, she had no option. If she was to have a chance of success she must be as committed to her purpose as Ra'id was to his.

'Your mother's room?' he prompted.

'I'm ready,' she said.

CHAPTER ELEVEN

HE COULD feel Antonia's suppressed excitement as he led the way down gilded corridors to the east wing of the palace, where the shutters had remained drawn for years, and the rooms were neglected and cast in shade. He could feel her fear and apprehension too. He could feel everything Antonia was feeling in the same unspoken transfer of energy he'd felt between them on the desert island, when he had been Saif and Antonia had gone by the name he'd given her. But there had been a change in Antonia since then. She had matured. She might have trembled at her first sight of him, but the flame of purpose had returned to her gaze. This wasn't the adolescent who had ransacked his yacht to claim her piece of bread and cheese, but a woman who would not easily be dismissed. Perhaps the sight of her mother's room would change that, he mused as they reached the door.

Antonia could hardly believe she was really here, within touching distance of her mother's room. It was hard to catch her breath when Ra'id halted outside the golden door. The workmanship on the jewel-studded panelling was more fabulous than anything she could have imagined.

'Is it real gold?' she asked naively as she admired the intricate workmanship.

'Everything you see that looks like gold is gold,' Ra'id informed her with no emotion in his voice. 'Shall we go in?'

'Oh, yes please!' she exclaimed, hardly daring to blink in case she missed anything. Her sense of anticipation was indescribable, and she put all thoughts of Ra'id knowing something she didn't—something unpleasant, maybe—out of her mind.

'Could we turn on a light?' she asked, hesitating on the threshold.

'Certainly.' Reaching past her, Ra'id switched on a cobweb-strewn chandelier. Even now he made her tingle, Antonia felt, touching her cheek as she walked deeper into the room.

Whatever she had expected after seeing that golden door, it was not this shadowy interior, with sheets draped over the furniture and dust motes floating in stagnant air. But what affected her most was the atmosphere of abandonment, she realised, slowly turning full circle. It was as if the walls were soaked through with loneliness and sadness. Her first impression was that this was not the happy nest of a pretty girl, but a prison, a cage—a gilded cage for the discarded mistress of a ruler who had tired of her and moved on. But her mother hadn't moved on, Antonia thought sadly as she trailed her fingertips across the yellowing cover of a fashion magazine. She thought that the saddest artefact of all. 'It doesn't look as if this room has been touched since my mother left for Italy,' she said, rallying determinedly as she turned to speak to Ra'id.

She thought he seemed surprised she was holding it

together. She raised an eyebrow, as if to say that nothing
would shake her from her path—and that if anything this
clearer picture of the young woman who had been her
mother had only strengthened her resolve.

He watched her closely. Knowing Antonia's background, he had been half-expecting this indulged child of
a fabulously wealthy father to cross straight to her mother's
dressing table, where a tumble of priceless jewellery still
lay in a careless heap. The valuable gems were awaiting
collection and a detailed inventory by his team of asses-
sors, and would have attracted most people's interest. But
Antonia had stood in silence when she'd entered the room
as if she were battling some emotion greater than he could
grasp. It was an emotion that made her shudder and clamp
her jaw so hard a muscle jumped in her cheek.

The seconds ticked by while both of them remained
quite still, and then, instead of crossing to the dressing
table, she went to the wall of windows and started sliding
bolts back on the shutters. 'Can you help me?' she called
to him, as if this was just an ordinary task. 'No need; I've
done it,' she said, spinning round in triumph when he was
halfway across the room. She opened every window to its
fullest extent and light streamed in; with it came the warm,
scented air. 'That's better!' she exclaimed, turning back to
face the room.

She stood quite still for a moment and then proceeded
to examine everything in orderly sequence. Having apparently satisfied herself, she made for the large double bed
on its plinth in the centre, walking past the jewels flashing
fire on the dressing table and on across the room. She
ignored a silk gown glinting with rubies, that drooped

sadly from a padded hanger, until she reached the bed, where she stared down for a moment until inch by inch she sank into a heap on the floor, as if the bones were slowly melting in her legs.

He was a hard man, who had made many hard decisions since taking the throne, and had seen many things in his lifetime that should have affected him but had left his factual mind largely untroubled. Yet when he saw Antonia weeping by her mother's bedside he had to turn and leave the room.

He was showing respect, Ra'id reasoned, leaning back against the door. He drew breath to steady his emotions, but however hard a face he turned to Antonia he could not stand by and see her broken. Her defiance was so much easier to deal with, he reasoned, knowing deep down he had hoped she would exclaim with pleasure when she saw all the pretty things in her mother's room. But instead she had got to the heart of the matter.

The heart of the matter…

Yes; the heart of the matter was the searing sense of loneliness and rejection Helena must have felt before Antonio Ruggiero had arrived and rescued her. He could see that now, thanks to Antonia.

But he could not hark back to a happier time on the desert island, because that was stolen time, time he still regretted. His life, every moment of his existence, was devoted to a country and its people, and that was where his duty lay; on that there could be no compromise. Antonia was not simply a girl he was attracted to, she was a threat to his people's future happiness, with those documents granting her land in Sinnebar. He would not allow chaos to return to his country. He would bury the past, whatever it took.

Pulling away from the door, he opened it and stepped inside the room again. Whatever he had expected it was not this—Antonia seated at the dressing table, calmly reading letters.

'Why didn't you tell me about these letters, Ra'id?' she asked him in a voice that was calmer than he might have expected.

Had he anticipated hysteria—a broken woman, crushed beneath the weight of grief? Had he forgotten the virago who had confronted him on the yacht with a knife? This was no girl to be easily dismissed, but a strong and determined woman, even if that woman resided in a young girl's body.

'I had no idea my mother even had a maidservant in whom she confided,' she said, flourishing the bundle of letters she'd found. 'No letters were ever forwarded to Rome.'

'That might be because your mother wrote to her maidservant in English.'

'And the maidservant could only read Sinnebalese,' Antonia murmured, understanding. Then her face hardened. 'The maidservant might not have been able to read English, but she would have understood these.'

She was looking at photographs of herself as a baby in her mother's arms.

'I imagine so,' he agreed.

'You *imagine*?' Antonia bit out, springing to her feet. 'So why didn't I receive them?'

'They were overlooked, perhaps.' He made a dismissive gesture, but felt a surge of arousal as they confronted each other, both with passions raised. 'Are you finished here?' He held the door for her.

She shook her head slowly and her expression suggested she detested him. 'You have absolutely no heart, do you, Ra'id?'

He neither agreed nor disagreed with that assessment.

'I give up!' she flared. 'And don't think we're finished here.'

'You are finished here,' he told her coldly, pointing to the door.

She saw his shadow cross the courtyard from the window in her room and felt a pang of regret. Standing in her chaste, cotton pyjamas watching Ra'id stride purposefully towards some unknown destination, she realised he still had the power to take her breath away. If anything, the deep blue robes of office and the Arabian headdress, with its gleaming gold *agal* holding it in place, only added to Ra'id's menacing appeal. Though she had tried to hate him, that emotion was far too close to love. But how cold Ra'id had been when he'd looked at her, Antonia remembered; how dismissive.

And he was the father of her child...

As dusk thickened into glutinous night, she agonised over how to tell him. Was he visiting a lover now—perhaps some glamorous and frivolously dressed ladies in his harem? *The father of her baby.* The thought made her sick—sick and angry. Swallowing deep, she turned away.

Shutting the window to give the air-conditioning a chance to work, Antonia realised sleep was out of the question. How could she sleep with Ra'id in her head? But she had no rights over him; they were practically strangers, strangers who owed each other nothing, and who knew less about each other now than they ever had.

But she missed him, she realised, angrily biting back tears. And what would it bring her, this love of hers, other than distractions and more unhappiness? Antonia Ruggiero in love with the Sword of Vengeance? It sounded ridiculous even to her.

She padded barefoot across the room to her lonely bed. Some might think it generous of Ra'id to allow her to stay in such splendid accommodation, but she suspected it was his way of keeping her close so he would know what she was doing. He was orchestrating her every step, and what hurt the most was the knowledge that she was carrying his baby and couldn't tell him.

How much closer could they be than parents of a baby? Yet how much further apart? Antonia wondered, trailing her fingertips across crisp, white linen sheets on a bed she doubted she would spend even a moment on.

During the lonely vigil of the long night, Antonia considered what she had learned from looking through what remained of her mother's possessions. Helena had been very young, both in age and attitude, although she'd already had a son by the ruling sheikh when she'd moved to Rome to marry Antonia's father. Helena had never been allowed to see her son again. Poor Helena; a girl who had liked pop music and fashion, and who had traded on her looks, believing they were the key to happiness. She had discovered that in the end those looks were her downfall—for no one, especially not the ruling Sheikh of Sinnebar, had wanted beauty without substance when the novelty had worn off.

And, though Ra'id could never be called weak, he was his father's son, Antonia acknowledged, and that was the type of heartless individual she was dealing with. He couldn't even look at her without self-loathing, because she represented his one and only failing. Antonia was Ra'id's one breach of duty, and now she must be punished and driven away. Whatever was waiting for her at the fort, she suspected it was something Ra'id believed would end her quest once and for all and send her flying back to Rome in a panic. In one last act of cruelty, he was determined to be there to see her reaction for himself.

He drove his stallion hard. The horse was well-named Tonnerre, which meant thunder in French. When they galloped from yielding sand to a firmer path leading directly to the mountains, Tonnerre's hooves struck sparks off the moonlit track.

Then the horse smelled water and it took all Ra'id's riding skills to persuade the stallion to slow. When Ra'id mastered him, the stallion consented to walk, whinnying and snorting his disapproval. Ra'id loosened the reins, allowing Tonnerre to amble the last half-mile or so to cool him down.

When finally they reached the icy spring that emerged at the foot of the cliff, he sprang down, and, murmuring praise into one alert velvet ear, he removed Tonnerre's tack and allowed the horse to go free.

Free…

Something he would never be, Ra'id reflected as he leaned against cold, black granite watching his mount suck in water. He had chosen this path, though he would never be free from the ache in his heart. He thought of Antonia, asleep in bed, and had to wonder how one young girl could affect him so deeply. There was no future for them, and she was nothing but trouble. He had decided that the best course of action was to show her what awaited her in the desert, and then she would be pleased to go home, where he hoped she would fight some other cause.

Unwinding the black *howlis* from his face, he shrugged off his robe and dived into a pool turned frigid by snow-melt from the mountains. His last image before he sank deep was not that of a young girl sighing with passion in his arms but of an aircraft soaring into the flawless Arabian sky, as it carried Antonia and her foolish fantasies back to Rome.

By the time dawn peeped through the shutters, Antonia had drawn up a plan. She would use her own money to convert the citadel she had inherited without having to take anything from the charity's resources. She could only hope Ra'id might want to contribute his expertise and that of others around him to the project. Without their help, it could just be her best stab at an Arabian retreat, and she wanted it to be authentic down to the last detail. But before she could do any of that she must persuade Ra'id to give her the precious water supply.

She would have to appeal to his better nature and hope he had one, Antonia concluded, drying her hair after her shower. Startled by the sound of approaching hooves, she put down her brush and crossed to the window. Her apartment was on one of the highest floors of the palace, and she could see Ra'id returning to the stables. She knew it was him before she even focused on the man springing down from the ferocious-looking stallion. Even severe black robes only added to Ra'id's glittering majesty, but it was his barbaric vigour that had called to her before she saw him.

She shrank back. He stared directly at her. Could he feel

her too? It was as if he knew she was looking at him as surely as if she had called to him.

Pulling further back inside the room, she grabbed a steadying breath. She was right to think there was some invisible link between them, and wrong to believe it was fading when it had grown.

CHAPTER TWELVE

SO NEITHER of them had slept, Ra'id noted, carrying the image of Antonia's unusually pale face with him into his private quarters. There had been dark circles under her eyes and her face had been tense. Had she finally accepted there was no point in her staying on in Sinnebar? Would she return home without a fuss? And, if she did, how would that make him feel?

He showered fast before dressing in workmanlike robes, prior to striding at a brisk pace to the breakfast room where he had arranged to meet her. She was standing by the buffet table dressed in a safari suit, seeming uncertain while a manservant was doing his job well, trying to tempt her with morsels of food from the wide selection.

Everyone stood and bowed to him. Antonia looked troubled when she turned. 'Ra'id,' she said, causing a murmur of surprise by using his first name.

No one addressed him that way. In time he might have forgotten what his first name was, if it weren't for Antonia and his brother, he reflected wryly.

Desire for her swept over him as their gazes met and

held. But he had closed his heart to her, he reminded himself sternly, to protect her from a ruthless king.

'You had a good night, I trust?' he said, taking the plate out of her hands and choosing some delicacies for her himself.

'No. Did you?'

Would he ever get used to her bluntness? He saw hurt and disappointment mixed with the defiance in her eyes. She had expected him to come to her, he realised. However deep the rift between them, she thought they could get over it and pick up where they had left off. 'I rode out,' he said briskly. 'Is there anything else you want from here?' He scanned the buffet.

'No, thank you. Did you ride all night?' she asked innocently. 'Did you have things on your mind, Ra'id?' The look she gave him was fast and accusatory.

'No. Should I?'

She raised a faint smile. 'I guess not.'

Now her cheeks were flushed and her breath was coming faster, as if her heart couldn't keep pace with her emotions. He turned away, effectively dismissing her, but he carried with him her fresh, clean scent and innocent appearance. That and the appeal in her eyes had almost melted him, he realised, but thankfully he was ruled by his head and not his heart, so it was easy for him to walk away.

He had almost reached the door when he realised she was at his elbow. He glanced down. 'Yes?'

'I can't wait to see the citadel,' she said, as if this was a holiday for her and he was her tour guide.

He made a brief hum of acknowledgement, before sweeping on his way.

'What about your breakfast?' she demanded catching hold of his sleeve.

He looked down at her incredulously, ignoring the collective gasp.

She seemed unaware of it. 'Aren't you going to eat anything, Ra'id?'

His look hardened. 'I have more important things on my mind.'

'So you don't feel like eating either?' she said, actually tightening her fingers on his sleeve so the fabric was crushed.

'On the contrary—but I will eat in private.' He shook her off.

'Of course. I forgot,' she snapped. 'In your ivory tower.'

'Will you excuse me?' he murmured, ignoring the barb. Whether she would or not, he was going to the stables to make sure their horses were ready for them to leave at once.

She shouldn't have annoyed him. She ate breakfast, if only for the baby's sake, and returned to her room to get ready to leave. If Ra'id took her to see the citadel, which was by no means certain now, it would be no magnanimous concession on his part, but another opportunity to rub her nose in the fact that her dream of a fun-filled castle to be used to such good effect by the charity was a naive and frivolous plan. One which without Ra'id's water supply would fail utterly.

But she was going to call Ra'id's bluff. She refused to be put off by his threatening manner. She would go into the desert. Whatever it took she would find the water she needed somewhere, and then she would renovate the ancient building and make it live again.

The opportunity to tell Ra'id about their baby seemed

further away than ever, Antonia reflected anxiously, but she wouldn't get a chance to tell him unless she stayed close to him. She had to keep with her original plan to visit the citadel with Ra'id. How could she not when there was still this huge and pressing secret between them?

He watched Antonia stride across the stable yard in a blaze of purpose. She had put on a little weight, he noticed, and it suited her. She was glowing with health, in fact. Her hair in particular seemed to gleam more than it ever had, though she had made an attempt to tame the abundant locks in a severe chignon which did her no favours. The hairstyle was the one jarring note in her appearance—that and the look in her eyes.

So this was war, he thought with a mixture of anticipation and amusement. Excellent. Let battle commence.

'Are you ready to go?' she said, eyeing the quiet gelding he had chosen for her before raising an eyebrow when she viewed his stamping monster of a stallion.

He almost had to curb a smile at the sight of the girl he recognised even without a knife in her hand. This was Antonia white-lipped with determination, and even the kind gelding he had selected for her was hanging its head uncertainly, as if it sensed trouble approaching its back.

He soothed it with a gentle touch as she mounted up, and then said, 'Ready?'

Her gaze was like a lick of flame that wavered when he held it. Travelling into the desert with him wasn't so appealing, suddenly, he guessed. *On my own?* he imagined her thinking. *With you? Without anyone to take my part?*

'You have a hat, I hope?' he said. 'The sun is hot. You may have noticed?'

She crammed on the totally unsuitable headgear she had been holding crushed in her hand.

'That hat isn't suitable for the desert,' he pointed out.

'Well, it's what I'm wearing.' She gave the brim a defiant tug.

'You'll need this.'

She huffed contemptuously at the scarf he was holding out for her to wind about her face and head. 'Keep it!' she exclaimed, as if accepting anything from him was the first step on the road to damnation. 'I'm just fine as I am,' she assured him, wheeling her horse around.

One hour and a sandstorm later, she was begging him for the Arabian headgear.

'I suppose you think this is funny?' she demanded as he sipped cold, clean water from a ladle offered to him by the Bedouin who had set up temporary camp around a well of clean drinking-water.

'Not at all.' Having unwound the yards of fabric he wore to protect his head, neck and face, he was largely untroubled by grit and sand, while Antonia looked more like a sand sculpture, with her red-rimmed eyes the only sign that she was human. 'I have a solution for you.' He smiled.

'You do?' She glanced towards the stallion, where his saddlebags full of the supplies he considered necessary were hanging.

'Certainly,' he said, tipping the bucket of water over her head. 'That should clean you up a bit—and cool you down.'

Spluttering, she swore at him. 'Why, you—'

'Brute?' he supplied mildly, already on his way to retrieve the spare *howlis* he'd brought for her to wear.

By the time he had returned, the laughing women of the camp had helped Antonia to wash her hair, and were hustling her away between them, no doubt to find her something more suitable for the desert than her Hollywood gear. Bedouin were kind that way, he reflected; infinitely generous.

He waited with mounting impatience as the minutes ticked by, chatting with the men whilst keeping an eye on the women's tent where they had taken her. He wouldn't put it past Antonia to steal a camel and make a break for it—and this time when she left the country he wanted to be sure it was for good.

But as he held that thought Antonia just ducked her head to leave the tent, and now was coming towards him with her head held high and that seemingly irrepressible look of determination and challenge locked in her eyes. She was wearing a serviceable but undeniably sexy outfit. The Bedouin women knew a thing or two about such things. It comprised a robe and a headdress that both protected her and—regrettably, as far as he was concerned—made her seem only too well suited to the hostile environment. She didn't belong here, and in his opinion the sooner Antonia realised that, the better.

'Ready?' she said, taking her revenge cold as she sprang into the saddle of the gelding he was holding for her.

'Ready,' he confirmed, handing her the reins.

Far from buckling and demanding a helicopter out of what had to be both an alien and terrifying terrain for her, Antonia had adapted and was still intent on going forward.

So be it. He was equally determined that this would be Antonia's first and last taste of the desert adventure she so foolishly craved.

At least she was clean. The women had allowed her to use their private bath-house, which was basically a tent they had erected over the stream that bubbled up to the surface from some underground keep far below the surface. But never had a bathroom seemed more luxurious to her, or people more friendly and fun as they poured buckets of cold water over her.

It was the first time she had been able to relax in a long time, Antonia felt. The women had made that possible for her with their lighthearted banter and teasing looks through the tent flap, at Ra'id and then at her. She had tried to mime that he was way too important for her, and that anyway she wasn't interested, but they just laughed at her. And after an hour of constant teasing she found her hunger for Ra'id had only increased.

Black-hearted Ra'id, as she was determined to think of him, was already mounted when she stepped outside the tent. He was holding the reins of her horse with his gaze in-scrutable behind the folds of his dark and forbidding headgear. Thankfully, the women had arranged her own scarf so that, just like Ra'id, only her eyes were showing—which meant he couldn't see her blazing cheeks, or the way her lips had swollen with desire for him. Perfect. She angled her head to give him a glare. She wanted to be sure he could see her resolve, and that she would go on with this without allowing any personal considerations to get in her way.

The fact that she was terrified—of Ra'id, of the desert,

of the safety of their unborn child—was something she, like countless women before her, would simply have to take in her stride. There was a job to be done, and only un-flinching determination was going to get her through it.

Antonia's heart sank as their horses slowed to a trot outside the crumbling walls of the ancient citadel. This was not what she had expected at all. Instead of a fine fort sitting foursquare in the desert, the fortress she had inherited from her mother was a sad, run-down place with doors hanging off the hinges and windows boarded up. 'No wonder you wanted me to see it,' she said to Ra'id brightly, determined he wouldn't see her alarm. 'It's a blank canvas, isn't it?' she said, making the derelict wreck sound like the most de-sirable real-estate on the face of the earth.

'It's a blank something,' he agreed.

It was just a pity her horizons had been stretched somewhat since arriving in Sinnebar so that now they encompassed doors formed from solid gold, decorated with gem-studded handles. And windows—always made of crystal glass.

She smiled to herself at the irony of it all and was glad of something to cheer her up as she stared at the dried-out skeleton of a once-majestic home. Shielding her eyes against the glare of a sky bleached white by the sun, she tried to sum up her decrepit inheritance. 'A heap of stones' was a generous description. 'Is it safe to go inside?' she asked Ra'id, who had reined in beside her.

'I'll take a look.'

Before she could stop him he had urged his stallion into a brisk canter and was almost instantly swallowed up inside the walls.

Sitting alone on a fidgeting horse, breathing air that was heavy and still, was an unnerving experience. The heat was like a smothering cloth that choked off the last of her optimism, and the silence was overwhelming. There was no birdsong here, no leaves rustling, no sound at all.

Patting her horse, she rested her cheek against the firm, warm neck for comfort. She had never felt the need of a friend more. Had her mother felt like this? Antonia wondered, imagining Helena's feelings on being moved from one palace to the next by her disenchanted lover. This ancient fortress must have come as quite a shock after the opulent palace in the city. Her gaze swept the pitted stone, lingering on the mean little windows. How oppressive a building could seem, she reflected, remembering Ra'id explaining on the ride that the old fort had originally been built as a defensive outpost to guard the nearby water-supply—water that would now be held from her at Ra'id's whim.

She was beginning to hate it here, Antonia realised as the minutes ticked by. The ancient citadel was like nothing she had imagined, and had nothing to offer other than a home to desert rats and scorpions. It was ugly, and it stood in lonely isolation in the fire-pit of the world. She must have been mad to think she could restore it. Surely no human being could bear to live in a place that was so remote and hostile? It was sheer vanity on Antonia's part to think she could wave a magic wand and transform this tumbling ruin into a welcome retreat for hard-pressed parents and their children. That was definitely a fantasy too far.

And where was Ra'id? She was growing increasingly anxious about him. Old buildings could be dangerous, and he had been gone a long while…

Antonia's imagination started running riot. If Ra'id came to harm because of her, she would never forgive herself—and how would she help him here? The sooner they left the better, she concluded, regretting her earlier optimism.

She exclaimed with relief as he rode into view.

'It's safe to come in,' he said, reining in his prancing stallion. 'Antonia?' he pressed when she hesitated. 'Have you changed your mind? I thought you were on fire to see this?'

When she saw the glint in Ra'id's eyes and realised this was a test, and that he expected her to turn tail and run back to the city as fast as she could, she said, 'I am keen.' And picked up the reins.

CHAPTER THIRTEEN

ANTONIA dismounted and led the pony into the cobbled courtyard. It was impossible to know what to expect once she went beyond the outer the walls of the old fortress, and she didn't want to risk the horse stumbling. She felt sick and weak with disappointment—although pregnancy might have had something to do with it, Antonia conceded worriedly, unscrewing the stopper on her flask.

As she drained the cooling water she was conscious of Ra'id watching her. Had he guessed? Did he know that she was pregnant? She really couldn't find the energy to fight him now; all her earlier defiance had drained away. It was one thing taking on a major building-project in the desert when she only had herself to worry about, but the baby meant more to her than anything else, and she hadn't realised just how hostile and isolated an environment this was.

She was defeated before she even got started. She wanted to go home. The old fort was a dreadful place; no one could possibly live here. No wonder Helena had been miserable. It must have been nothing short of torment for a young girl to be shut away in the desert.

Lashing her horse's reins to a rail, Antonia sank down on a hard stone mounting-block and put her head in her hands.

'Are you all right?'

She lifted her head. Ra'id sounded genuinely concerned.

'This isn't too much for you, is it?' he said.

'No, I'm fine,' she said stubbornly. 'But, unlike you, I'm not used to the heat.'

'It's much cooler inside the walls.'

As he spoke, Ra'id was unwinding the folds of his head-gear, slowly revealing his brutally handsome face. How could she have forgotten how the sight of him affected her? Antonia wondered, holding on to her composure by the slimmest of threads. 'Yes, it is,' she agreed, as if her heart wasn't pumping furiously at the sight of Ra'id so close, so hot, so masculine. 'In fact,' she added, determinedly, 'If there was only water on tap, this castle would be ideal for my purposes.'

'Then it's a pity you don't have water on tap,' Ra'id observed smoothly, reminding her never to be off her guard where he was concerned. 'Shall we?' he invited, gesturing towards the entrance to the living quarters in the old keep.

She was determined this would not be an emotional re-run of her visit to her mother's forgotten room, though she was deeply conscious of walking in her mother's footsteps as Ra'id led the way up the stone staircase to the main building.

This had to be the strangest experience she'd ever had, Antonia concluded. She was bursting with emotion at the thought of finally visiting the place where her mother had been exiled; finding out about her mother's past was some-thing she had waited her whole life to see and understand. And here she was at last with the father of her child walking beside her. It should have been perfect. But this was the same man who wanted nothing more than to be rid of her. Where Ra'id was concerned she had a blind spot, Antonia admitted. She could never stop looking for a sign that he still felt something for her. *Keep looking*, she thought as they began the tour of dilapidated rooms.

How terrified Helena must have felt when she had arrived here a virtual prisoner, Antonia mused, discarded and exiled to the desert where she could cause no embarrassment to the ruling sheikh, parted from her child—could anything be more dreadful? And never knowing if she would ever see her little boy again. How must Helena have felt as she walked beneath this same cold, stone arch into an austere and forbidding citadel? A gift of land would hardly heal those wounds.

A glance at Ra'id made Antonia tremble inwardly. When Ra'id discovered she was pregnant, would he show her any more mercy than his father had shown her mother? The al Maktabis were warrior sheikhs, and Ra'id al Maktabi was the fiercest of them all. He thought the gift of this fortress and the land surrounding it had been a generous pay-off to her mother, but Antonia knew there were more important things than money and land. In her opinion there was nothing that could compensate for the crushing of a human spirit.

So what would she do if she were stranded here?

It was at that point, the same moment as they entered the dark and dismal building, that Antonia's empathy with her mother's situation began to waver, and she had to remind herself that Helena hadn't been as fortunate as Antonia, who had such strong support from a brother who adored her. It was easy to be strong when you had people behind you to give you confidence, Antonia reflected, knowing how lucky she was. And with that strength she would take a fresh look at the citadel, seeing the positive this time rather than the drawbacks. For instance, the small windows meant that the fortress would be cool by day, and she would make it even cooler by installing air-conditioning. The extensive terracing could be enjoyed in the cooler months, as well as at dawn and dusk, and if she took on the project she could even make it a practical memorial to her mother.

Would she take it on?

That all depended on Ra'id. Without his water, there was no project. She had to try the one thing that might touch him where she had failed. 'You've seen the photographs.'

Drawing to an abrupt halt in a shadowy rubbish-strewn hallway, Ra'id interrupted her. 'Photographs?'

'The photographs of the children our charity helps,' she said quietly. 'You saw the album during my presentation.'

'You can't seriously be thinking of bringing those children here?'

'Why not?'

'Do you want a list? And why would you even think of it when I have more palaces than I know what to do with going begging in the capital?'

'Because I want to do something, maybe? Because I don't want or need your handouts, Ra'id?' When his eyes narrowed with suspicion, her passion for the project overflowed. 'If you didn't expect me to make use of the fortress, why did you bring me here, Ra'id? Was it to teach me a lesson? Or to show me how inhospitable the place is so I will relinquish my claim on the land?' She found it impossible to keep the heat out of her voice.

'I thought you should see for yourself that your mother's legacy is nothing more than a meaningless sheet of paper—and if you weren't prepared to listen to me, then bringing you here was the only way I could make you see the truth.'

'The truth as *you* see it,' she returned hotly. 'You don't know me at all, Ra'id—though I can see how it would suit you to bring me here.'

'Suit me?'

'Yes.' She steadied herself by concentrating her thoughts on all those people who depended on her making a success of this visit. 'I think you pictured me taking a tearful look around before dejectedly mounting my pony and riding out of your life for good. Well, guess what, Ra'id? I'm not going anywhere. I'm going to stay right here.'

'And if you're deported a second time?'

Antonia firmed her jaw. 'If you do that, I'll shame you before the world.'

'You'd blackmail me?' Ra'id demanded incredulously.

'I'll do whatever it takes to see this project through.'

Now she knew she'd gone too far. She was alone with the Sword of Vengeance in the middle of the desert, where anyone could disappear without a trace...

'I suggest you consider very carefully what you say next,' Ra'id warned her in a voice that was all the more menacing for being low and calm.

Antonia held her ground, though she was trembling inside. Ra'id had to know she was no pushover, and that she would stand up to him, in this and in all the discussions to come—or else how could she speak up for her child?

There it was—the most important secret of all, glittering between them like the Grail. She could see Ra'id some time in the future, holding their baby, before handing the child back to her.

Was that wishful thinking?

The thought that it might be frightened her more than anything else. Surely they could come to a civilised arrangement where their baby was concerned? But was civilised even possible with Ra'id? This visit to the citadel where her mother had been incarcerated was bound to stir violent emotion in her, Antonia reasoned. But now she must control her feelings, concentrate on finding a way to touch Ra'id and convince him that her plan for the fortress would work if he would only agree to giving her the water she needed. If he agreed to do that, she could build the retreat for the charity, as well as a home and a purpose for herself and for her child.

'I understand why you think the worst of me.'

He looked at her with suspicion, wondering what this new, conciliatory tone heralded.

'But since the pirate attack,' she continued earnestly, 'my priorities have changed.'

His suspicions, already roused, grew. 'That's old news, Antonia. What's really on your mind?' He knew the answer to that question the moment Antonia's hands flashed across her stomach to protect it. *Antonia was pregnant?* 'Are you pregnant?' he asked her quietly.

'And what if I am?' she said defensively.

'Are you pregnant with my baby?'

'Do you really think there's any doubt?'

'How do I know?' Antonia's continued defiance in the

face of such momentous news drove him to explode. 'For all I know, you're like your mother in that respect too.'

If he'd thought the girl on his yacht a virago, this girl was a demon possessed. She launched herself at him. He captured her, holding her firmly in front of him. 'Think of the baby—if you can!' He was instantly aware of how it felt to hold Antonia, and was immediately remorseful for taking out his shock on the mother of his child. He let her go and stood back as she cried, 'There have been no other men, Ra'id—how could there be?'

This impassioned outburst revealed more than she wanted to say. 'Enough,' he told her softly. 'Do you want to upset yourself and the baby?'

'*Upset?*' Hugging herself, she turned away. 'Do you care about me now?' she demanded with disbelief.

If only she knew. He'd always known that one day he would face this dilemma: love or duty. But to him, with his father's history to draw on, there was no choice to be made. 'Of course I care about the child you carry. I have seen more grief than I care to think about brought down on a child thanks to the selfishness of its parents.'

'Don't tar me with that brush, Ra'id,' she warned him.

But as she confronted Ra'id Antonia knew that this was not one of her wild, romantic fantasies but a very dangerous situation. She had brought her unborn child into a desert kingdom where that child's father reigned supreme, and where its mother had no voice, no rights. She doubted Ra'id would let her go now he knew she was carrying his royal baby. What irony, Antonia thought as she stared up at the citadel's forbidding walls. She really was following in her mother's footsteps now. Would Ra'id make her a prisoner here like her mother before her? The loss of her freedom was a nightmare beyond imagining, and the very last thing she wanted for her child—but would Ra'id, a man driven so relentlessly by duty, respect that?

Ra'id would always do what was right, she concluded, but it didn't reassure her to know that he had accomplished many good things in Sinnebar without once involving his feelings. Plus, he had lashed out verbally at both their parents, whom Ra'id considered had failed his stringent test. With all his wealth and privilege, would Ra'id be so very different when it came to bringing up a child? For him, duty always came first. The only certainty, Antonia decided, was that she would never agree to be parted from her child, and neither duty nor self-interest would change that.

'You're going to live here?' The effects of pregnancy were more telling than he had realised, Ra'id concluded as Antonia stated her intention. 'Firstly, the place isn't habitable, and secondly, you would need my permission.'

'I can't do this without your help, Ra'id.'

'I'm well aware of that. But first I would have to agree to you remaining in the country.'

'Don't you want to keep your child in Sinnebar?' It was a passionate outburst in a last-ditch attempt to touch him. It was also the biggest risk she had ever taken in her life.

'I have a country to consider.' *And now a pregnant mistress*, Ra'id acknowledged tensely.

'And I would be superfluous to your plans?' Antonia suggested with biting accuracy. 'If you think for one moment you're going to part me from my child...'

He only had to picture Antonia staying in Sinnebar to know he still wanted her. And only had to think of his child to know he wouldn't let her go. But she represented everything he had pledged to avoid. The irony wasn't lost on him. Having shunned his late father's self-indulgent lifestyle, it now appeared that he was following his father's lead to the letter. Was he to lose everything he had fought for? Was the country he loved to be plunged back into chaos? Could he hide Antonia away as his father had hidden her mother? Just the thought of it disgusted him.

Would he pay her off when the child was born...?

Antonia might shun money now, but didn't they say everyone had their price? 'I won't part you from your child; I'll help you.'

'Thank you.' Her face softened and hope returned to her eyes.

'If only to ensure you do a proper job at the citadel.' His tone was brusque and businesslike as he struggled to remain immune to the Antonia effect.

'Oh, I will,' she assured him, her face transformed by happiness and wreathed in smiles. 'You have no idea how hard I'll work.'

'Not at the risk of your pregnancy,' he commanded.

'Of course not. I'll be sensible,' she promised him fervently.

'No more wild adventures.'

Only with you, flashed briefly across her eyes. 'None. I promise,' she said. And then she flung herself at him, hugging his unresponsive body, exclaiming, 'Thank you, thank you!'

There was such rapture on her face, and such vulnerability in her expression, while his mind was full of the fact that he was going to become a father—the very best of fathers—and he would be ruthless in achieving that end.

* * *

Thanks to the narrow windows it was surprisingly cool inside the many rooms, and far less threatening than Antonia had originally thought. In fact, now she was inside the citadel, it seemed to welcome her, though there would have to be some fairly major changes. During the renovations she would ask the architects to find a way to bring in more light and make the place seem more welcoming.

If only Ra'id could welcome her, Antonia thought wistfully as he accompanied her on the tour. But, of course, Ra'id was only doing this because she was expecting his baby. He probably wouldn't let her out of his sight now— but not for the reasons she had hoped. He might be walking at her side, but she was on her own—as her mother had been before her. Antonia was looking for a very different resolution. Her mother had wanted to escape, while Antonia was determined to stay. She wanted to bloom where she was planted and make a go of things here.

They had looked inside many rooms, but when Ra'id stopped outside a particular door she got the strangest feeling. 'This is my mother's room, isn't it?' she said, not really needing Ra'id to confirm that it was.

He said nothing as he opened the door onto what, at first sight, appeared to be yet another soulless, dusty room.

Antonia was determined to keep her emotions in check this time, but there wasn't a part of her that wasn't aware of Ra'id or a fragment of her heart that didn't yearn to have him close to her again. She missed the easy camaraderie they'd come to share on the island, when it had been just a girl called Tuesday and a man called Saif. But now there was a king and a girl who was nobody, except for the fact that she was expecting the king's child. She had value as the incubator of Ra'id's child, Antonia acknowledged, but equally she was a liability to him.

So she must plan for the future.

She stared around walls that seemed to beg her to linger so she could see the possibilities. 'I'd need some form of transport to get in and out of town,' she murmured out loud, thinking of all the shopping she would have to do to turn this place into a home.

He stared at her long and hard, and then he said briskly, 'A four-wheel drive should suffice. It isn't far to the city—and, of course, you'll have a full complement of staff. You can have a driver and a helicopter at your disposal, if you think that's necessary. I'm sure we can come to an accommodation that suits both of us equally.'

'An accommodation?' That sounded like a cold, soulless thing. And, as for suiting them both equally, she doubted Ra'id knew much about equality, and cared to learn about it even less. 'Will I be free to use the resources on my land?' She was thinking local wildlife, the flora and fauna, when Ra'id's expression darkened.

'Do you imagine you're going to find oil here?' he demanded.

'No, of course not, but I was hoping you might allow a number of specialists to advise me on the best way to showcase local wildlife and crafts.'

'I could make some enquiries when I return to the capital,' he conceded.

'When *you* return?' Antonia's courage dwindled to nothing, but then she firmed her resolve. Ra'id had never pretended they would be living anything other than separate lives; it was up to her to get used to it.

'I'll leave you to take a look around in private,' he said.

'No. Please stay.'

'As you wish. I'll open the shutters for you.'

As he did so the light streamed in, and she noticed something glinting so softly she almost missed it. Lying forgotten in the dust, a tiny necklace sparkled in the light. She scooped it up and slipped it into her pocket. It was a diamond-studded heart on a broken chain, and carried enough vibrations for her to know that it must have landed on the floor when someone had snatched it from their neck as they ran out of the room.

Her mother, maybe—tearing off the necklace before she'd left the citadel for good?

Ra'id remained silent in the background as she walked slowly round the room. It was impossible not to notice the many photographs, poignant reminders of a small boy with dark, curly hair and bronzed skin—a boy who looked a lot like Ra'id. 'So, this is my brother,' Antonia murmured, lifting up one of the frames to study the image more closely before carefully putting the frame back in its place.

'This room hasn't been touched since your mother left—in a hurry, I'm told.'

And who could blame her? Antonia thought, shivering as she remembered the tiny heart on its broken chain currently residing in her pocket. 'It seems unfair that anyone would accuse Helena of deserting her little boy.'

'What would you call it?' Ra'id demanded from his very different perspective. 'When she was heard crying out that Razi was the worst mistake she had ever made?'

'I would call this imprisonment,' Antonia said, gazing at the heavy door with its prominent lock and bolt. 'Maybe my mother was no longer attractive to your father once she'd had a baby—I don't know the reason. She was frightened and very young. But I do know Helena must have been distraught, losing her child, and she wouldn't have kept all these photographs around her if she hadn't loved her son.' Antonia's hand flew to her mouth as she stared around what to her seemed little better than a prison cell. 'I'm not surprised Helena seized the opportunity to escape.'

'And yet you want to live here?'

'I wouldn't be living here under duress.'

And she was a very different woman from her mother, Antonia realised, knowing all the fripperies of life she had previously thought so important to her had only left her hungry for real-life experience, like an unrelieved diet of canapés when what she longed for was steak and chips. 'And any time I want to leave, I'll just have to jump in the car...' The words froze on her lips as Ra'id stared at her, and somewhere deep inside her heart she felt a stab of panic.

CHAPTER FOURTEEN

HE LEFT her tidying her mother's room. He couldn't bring himself to stand over her, and any thought of gloating as Antonia viewed the sad trivia of a life given over to pleasure had vanished. Whether he cared to accept it or not, Antonia had made him see things differently. Helena had been a victim, and a very young victim at that, with no means of helping herself. He could see that now, and his father should have seen it years back, but it was too late to revisit the past and change the mistakes that had been made. Instead, he chose to do something about the present, which in this case meant getting down and dirty with the plumbing to see if it was possible to bring water here.

It would take major restoration work, he concluded, but it could be done. He found he was pleased about that as he closed the door on the ancient boiler-room and walked up the steps into the light. He was just brushing off his hands when he spotted Antonia heaving a sack out of the building. 'What do you think you're doing?' he said, racing across the courtyard to lift it out of her hands.

She squinted her eyes against the sun in order to stare

up at him. 'Collecting things for the thrift shop. You do have them in Sinnebar?'

'Yes, we do.' He gave himself a moment to rejig his air of command into something more accommodating for the mother of his child—a woman so determined to go ahead with her plan it wouldn't have surprised him to see Antonia with a spade, digging a trench to change the water course by herself, if she had to.

'You collect and I'll carry the bag for you,' he suggested, wishing he could remain immune to the fact that Antonia had obviously been crying. She'd put on a brave face for him while they had been in her mother's room, but the moment he had left it, she must have broken down. 'We'll stack them in here,' he said briskly, trying to harden his heart to her and failing miserably. 'I'll have everything collected and cleaned, and then distributed to the appropriate agencies.'

'So you do have a heart, Ra'id,' she said.

'I wouldn't go that far,' he said dryly, but he was relieved that Antonia was recovering. This visit couldn't have been easy for her, mentally strong as she was. So much for his determination not to get drawn in! He almost convinced himself that today was different, and that today he had no alternative other than to help her out; having agreed to help Antonia make the place habitable, he would delegate the work to the most appropriate team of experts the moment he returned to the capital, and at that time he would distance himself from her. 'Now, I think you should rest.' He was concerned for her, and worried that her enthusiasm for the project would make her forget that she needed to look after herself now.

'Rest? Rest where?' she said, gazing anxiously around the derelict ruin she had inherited.

Following her gaze, he felt her uncertainty, and her sense that the enormity of the task she had taken on might just be too much for her in her present condition.

Feeling nothing when she stared at him trustingly was a battle fought and quickly lost. 'I'm going to take you somewhere to rest up where you can bathe in fresh, clean water.'

'The water you'll be bringing here,' she said quickly, as if he might be allowed to forget.

'That's right,' he said, admitting to rueful admiration as he went to fetch her horse. 'The water you'll need if you're still interested in restoring this place?' He turned to look at her when he'd checked the girth.

'Still interested?' she demanded. 'You don't know me, Ra'id.'

But he was beginning to. This time she didn't pull away when he offered her a leg up onto her horse.

This just wasn't fair. Of all the things Ra'id had said or done, bringing her here was the cruelest—somewhere so beautiful, so tranquil, so instantly enthralling.

They rode the short distance in silence. She didn't know where Ra'id was taking her beyond his promise of rest and fresh water, but as they crested the dune and she saw his tented pavilion on the shore of the oasis she could have cried at the beauty of it—and with despair that this awe-inspiring wilderness she was quickly coming to love could never be hers to enjoy free of Ra'id's disapproval.

She felt gritty and grubby as she eased in the saddle to

survey the limpid and oh, so tempting waters of an oasis streaked with moonlight.

'What do you think?' Ra'id asked, reining in his prancing stallion beside her.

'I think it's the most beautiful place I've ever seen in my life,' she said honestly, starting the steep descent.

Leaning towards her, Ra'id steadied her horse. 'If you want to take a dip, I'll keep watch while you swim…to make sure you're safe.'

'You'd do that?'

'Of course,' he said, as if it were no big deal.

They had reached the flat ground, and Ra'id was waiting to help her down. 'I can manage, thank you,' she said, freeing her feet from the stirrups, but she was weary as she slid down from the saddle. She pulled herself round before facing him. The days of showing her soft underbelly to the world, and to Ra'id al Maktabi in particular, were well and truly over. 'Would you like me to light a campfire while you see to the horses?'

Ra'id unbuckled the saddlebags and threw them over his shoulder. 'If you're up to it.'

'I'm up to it.' She rested one hand on her horse's warm, steadfast neck for a moment, thankful for the survival course her brother had insisted she must take before involving herself in any more dangerous sports.

'Then let's set up camp.'

'Do we have food?'

He patted the saddlebags.

'You've thought of everything.'

Not quite. He had totally underestimated her, Ra'id concluded as Antonia walked ahead of him to the pavilion.

* * *

She wasn't quite out for the count, and had enough fizz left in her to agree when Ra'id offered to light the fire after she had helped him with the horses. 'You swim,' he said. 'Go on—you've earned it.'

She had nothing to prove, Antonia realised. She didn't have to stand on her pride, or work herself into the ground. They'd been a good team, and they could both cope with outdoor living, though Ra'id understood this terrain a lot better than she ever would, and he would know just where to look for tinder.

She couldn't see Ra'id when she reached the edge of the oasis, so she dropped her clothes and plunged naked into the water. The sudden chill on her overheated skin was like a healing balm, and as she powered into her first stroke she felt her cares float away. Everyone needed time out, Antonia reflected, rolling onto her back so she could stare up at the lantern moon. This precious time in the desert had been a welcome reminder that she could make a difference if she tried.

She would make a difference, Antonia determined, idly swishing her hands in the water to keep her afloat. Turning towards Ra'id's beautiful pavilion, she started swimming towards it. This was a scene that belonged in one of her fantasies, but if it had been she could have engineered a happy ending rather than this travesty: Ra'id and Antonia trapped in the middle of a drama of their own making, a drama that should have ended well before they made love…

But thank goodness it hadn't ended, Antonia reflected, caressing the still-flat planes of her stomach as she waded out of the water.

* * *

He watched Antonia until she was safely out of the water and dressed again, and then, without her seeing him, he returned to the campfire he had lit earlier. Should he show her what he had found in her mother's room? Was she ready for it, or had she suffered enough emotional upheaval for one day? Would it be better to throw it on the fire? While Antonia had been scooping something off the floor, he'd been too—something that had dropped off her mother's dressing table, another pathetic, hand-scribbled note.

'Ra'id!' Antonia exclaimed, drying her hair with a towel he'd laid out ready for her. 'You're cooking fish again.'

'In anticipation that you will fillet it for me again.'

'I might,' she said, her lips curving at the memory, though she hunkered down a good distance away from him. 'Of course I will!' she exclaimed now, as if some thought had suddenly occurred to her. 'If you promise I can have that water.'

'A filleted fish in exchange for my precious water-supply? Do you think I'm mad?' He might as well have added 'Do you never give up?' But he knew the answer to that already.

'Shake on it?' she said boldly.

He looked at the tiny hand stretched out to him, and just in time remembered how the desert affected him. It was another magical setting, where they could be anyone they wanted to be while they were here—the only difference now was they both knew there were consequences to embracing that freedom.

'You're smiling,' she said as he ate the morsels of fish she had prepared.

'Am I?' He frowned.

'What's wrong, Ra'id?'

He wasn't about to share his thoughts with her. He had concluded that the enemy to duty wasn't self-indulgence, but love. He wasn't sure he had the weapons to fight that enemy off. 'Why don't we have a swim?' he said, badly in need of a change of scene.

'It's too soon,' she cautioned him.

'Then we can stroll round the oasis, and when I judge the time is right I'll throw you in.'

She was off like a hare from the traps. 'Not if I see you first,' she called back to him, laughing.

They didn't make it to the water. The restrictions of the real world had been lifted again and nothing stood in their way. She was young, seductive and he wanted her.

She was fine until Ra'id brushed against her. He'd kicked sand over the fire and helped her clear everything away. She had identified the thick, nobbly palm-trunk behind which she intended to leave her clothes, and he was at the water's edge when something frightened her, a crawling thing...

A harmless lizard, Ra'id reassured her as it scuttled away.

'Okay, so I'll get used to them,' she said determinedly.

'If you intend staying in the desert, I'd definitely advise it.'

There was humour in Ra'id's voice and warmth in his eyes. She didn't imagine it. She had been hanging on for a sign that he would mellow so they could discuss the future together, and it turned out the desert had cast its spell over him again. In the capital he was the undisputed king, but the wilderness was a leveller that stripped everyone's position in life away. And Ra'id came out of that well...

Very well, Antonia reflected, feeling increasingly aroused as he continued to stare at her. There was so much strength in his dark gaze, so much wisdom and understanding of her needs.

'You're aroused,' he murmured.

'Am I?' she whispered, making it sound like a challenge.

'So aroused, if I touch you you'll come.'

She was too shocked to answer, by which time she was in his arms. He carried her into the pavilion and laid her down on the freshly laundered cushions. She was enveloped in the scent of sandalwood and sunlight as she sank into their scented folds. Moments later she was naked, and so was Ra'id; he had judged her level of arousal perfectly.

'You greedy girl,' he murmured as she abandoned herself to the onslaught of pleasure.

She was whimpering, open-mouthed in surprise that such levels of sensation were possible when he eased her legs over his shoulders. Being back with him was like a miracle, and so was the speed with which he could coax her into readiness again.

'Let me ride you!' she demanded, desperate to feel him deep inside her.

'You set the pace,' Ra'id agreed, settling back on the cushions.

She lowered herself cautiously. Ra'id was huge, and she had to take him in gradual stages. His touch was tantalisingly light on her hips as she sank slowly down. Then he was touching her, delicately, skilfully with one fingertip, and she was moving faster, with more confidence...wildly, and with abandon.

He turned her so fast she had no chance to protest—and why would she, when he was giving her exactly what she needed firm and fast?

Ra'id climaxed violently with her, and they clung to each other for minutes that turned into drowsy hours; two people, so close they were one.

'Do you ever tire?' she asked him a long time later.

'With you?' Ra'id gave her an amused glance. 'Never.'

This time he made love to her tenderly, as if he cherished her above all things. She wouldn't allow herself to believe that, of course. She knew it was some primal instinct at work that prompted a man to feel that way about the mother of his child. If she allowed herself to believe in his feelings for her, Ra'id really would possess the means to break her heart.

But he didn't make it easy for her. Brushing her hair back from her face, he moved slowly and deeply, kissing her eyelids, her lips and her neck, making love as if they had all the time in the world and he rejoiced in that as much as she did.

Dawn was busily brushing away the clouds of night when she woke in his arms. Would she ever become used to Ra'id's strength, or his beautiful body? Antonia wondered, snuggling close, determined to make the most of whatever time they had.

'So, you're awake,' he murmured.

'Just,' she admitted, loath to be the first one to break the spell.

'It can be like this always, Antonia. For you and me.'

'What do you mean?' She turned to look at him.

'We can be together,' Ra'id said, as if that were obvious.

'And the baby?'

'Of course the baby,' he exclaimed softly. 'We would be a family.'

She rested against him, thinking how wonderful that would be—how perfect. But life was never perfect. Ra'id was a king, and whatever plan he had brewing in his head she wanted to hear it before she agreed. 'Tell me more,' she said.

'Not now.' He smiled a slow, sexy smile. 'It will be a surprise.'

When had she learned to be such a pessimist? Antonia wondered, moving away. How much more did she want than this? Coming back to rest her head against Ra'id's naked chest, she inhaled his familiar scent, telling herself that nothing could be more perfect than this. She should be happy. She should be optimistic about the future.

So why wasn't she?

Because this was all an illusion, Antonia admitted; this wasn't right. Or, rather, she wasn't right for this. She wasn't her mother, and she wanted more than to be hidden away— the sheikh's plaything. She wanted a family. She wanted to work. She wanted to make a difference.

CHAPTER FIFTEEN

HE SENSED the change in Antonia and knew he would have to work hard to reassure her that his plan for her would work. His father had blanked out a son and had dumped his discarded mistress in the desert, but he would never do that. Freedom was as important to him as it was to Antonia, and was the bedrock of the constitution he had installed in Sinnebar. 'I'm going to take another swim,' he told her, 'While you can have your own private stream to yourself.' She smiled at him as he glanced towards the back of the tent where the luxurious bath-house was situated.

His life was nothing without Antonia's bright flame in it, Ra'id realised as he grabbed a towel and strode away. She consumed his every waking moment and invaded his dreams at night, filling him with hunger for her, as well as the absolute determination to keep her at his side.

She found what looked like a page from a diary underneath the robe Ra'id had worn the day before. She guessed he had found it in her mother's room at the fort and the sheet of paper must have fallen out of his pocket. Backing deeper into the pavilion, she began to read it.

She'd never tidy up again, Antonia determined, biting back tears. Like so many things at the fort, it must have been churned up, passed over and forgotten. She handled the single sheet of paper carefully, sniffing it, studying it, imagining her mother writing it, knowing it had been written in despair, and in hope that one day someone would read it.

I wanted everyone to know how I had to live in the last few years, so you would understand why I went to Rome.

It was a scrawled page that told of unbearable loneliness—of no one for Helena to talk to, or to share her fears with, and a child stolen away from her, a blow that no deed of land could ever soften.

Money, land and jewels, in however much abundance, had done nothing to ease a young girl's desolation, Antonia could see, and for a moment she felt numb. Then Antonia realised her main reaction to this page from her mother's diary was frustration, because it was too late for her to sort out her mother's life. She could only be glad her father had found Helena, and that they had been able to share a few months of happiness together before her mother's untimely death.

Realising she had scrunched the piece of paper in her hand, she carefully straightened it out again and put it with the other treasure she had found at the fort—the broken chain, with the tiny, diamond-studded heart. She would rather have these small things than all the riches in Ra'id's treasury, Antonia mused, because the broken heart and the note scrawled in the childish hand were in many ways her mother's true legacy. And if she didn't learn from them, she really would let her mother down, and the note would have been written for nothing.

Ra'id was with the horses when she came out of the tent with the intention of confronting him about her discovery. 'You've saddled up,' she said with surprise.

'I have something to do—for your benefit,' he assured her.

Ra'id was smiling, but she sensed that once again he was the autocratic ruler who had made some plan without consulting her. 'Don't I have any say in this?'

'You'll be quite safe here. Though you can't see them, there are security guards everywhere.'

'Oh, good…' That was supposed to make her feel reassured?

'Trust me—I'll be back within the hour.'

The gap between her belief they had grown closer and the true situation had just widened into a gulf, Antonia realised. She loved Ra'id and could never say no to him, but as she watched him ride away she thought that perhaps the time had come to do that.

No? Antonia had said *no* to his suggestions for her immediate future? They were in the pavilion, facing each other, and the atmosphere between them was as tense as it had ever been. He had offered her the sun, the earth and the moon, and Antonia had turned him down. 'I don't think you heard me,' he said as she stood with her back turned to him. 'I will have the fortress repaired and refurbished to your specifications. You will have your own palace in the capital, *and* I'll open a bank account for you with more money in it than you could ever spend. And you can spend that money on anything you want.'

'Subject to your approval?'

'Well, *obviously* I'll have a say in it!' he exclaimed impatiently.

'A *say* in it?' she echoed, spinning round. 'You'll choose. You'll pay. You'll install me in one of your fabulous palaces and visit me as and when you wish?'

There was no mention of their child, Antonia realised, hoping the terror didn't show in her eyes.

'I thought you wanted that?'

She did want to be with Ra'id, more than anything on earth, but not like this. If she agreed to his terms she was effectively giving over her life for Ra'id to control. He would hold the purse strings, the decision strings, and as he already held the strings to her heart that was one string too many. But how easy it would be to become dependent on him, a man so compelling and powerful; he exerted some hypnotic spell over her. It would be madness for her to fall under that spell, however much she wanted to. She must remain free to make her own decisions, even if sometimes she got it wrong. First off, she had to know his intentions regarding their baby so she could counter them if she had to. 'What about our child, Ra'id? Where will our baby live?'

For the first time since she'd known him, Ra'id's gaze flickered.

'No,' she repeated firmly, closing her fingers around her mother's note.

'You're being unreasonable, Antonia.'

'If it's unreasonable to defend my unborn child, then I am unreasonable,' she agreed.

'Defend the baby against me—its father?' he demanded incredulously.

'No, Ra'id, I'm defending our child against the past—a past that still seems to rule us both.'

'What are you saying, Antonia?'

'When were you going to show me this?' She produced the single sheet of handwritten despair that she had found by his robe-pocket and had the small satisfaction of seeing Ra'id reach inside his robe to check that it had gone.

'You took that from my pocket,' he accused her.

'No. It must have dropped out.'

Dragging off his *howlis*, he tossed it aside. 'I picked it up at the fort and intended waiting until you had recovered before showing it to you.'

'Recovered?' she said with only the smallest shake in her voice to betray her feelings. 'Let me assure you, I have recovered.'

'I was trying to protect you, Antonia.'

'I don't need that sort of protection, Ra'id. I need to face life, however ugly it is.' And it was ugly sometimes, Antonia thought, as an image of her mother as a very young girl, writing down her deepest thoughts and fears because she had no one to confide in, appeared to be.

'I have your best interests at heart.'

'And thought you could woo me with expensive trinkets and the promise of more money than I could spend? Do you really think you can buy me, Ra'id?'

'I'm doing everything I can think of to reassure you.'

'To reassure me that it will be cosy in my gilded cage?' Antonia's voice broke as she shook her head in despair. 'You really don't know me.' Would Ra'id never be Saif again? Would he never hear her again?

'I'm prepared to give you everything I thought you wanted,' he said.

In fairness, that was exactly the type of girl she'd been, Antonia reflected. How long had her journey been? And how short was Ra'id's? Very short, she concluded. Nothing about the all-powerful ruler of Sinnebar had changed. What was he thinking now? She could usually read him, but today that famous connection of theirs had interference on the line. Something big was brewing. Ra'id would never have left her side for a minute if it had not been to make some special plan.

'I want nothing but the best for you.'

'And the best is to be your prisoner, because I'm carrying the heir to the throne?' Ra'id's expression stopped her. She had come here with him willingly, and in doing had crossed into dangerous, uncharted territory—to take on a man who was accustomed to his every word being law. Ra'id frightened her, but her fierce maternal instinct turned out to be stronger. Brandishing her mother's note at him, she demanded, 'Have we learned nothing from this, Ra'id? Am I to be kept in a palace as my mother was—another bird in a gilded cage, awaiting the sheikh's pleasure, while you carry on as normal?' Shaking her head decisively, she exclaimed, 'I won't do it!'

'Think, Antonia.'

'Oh, believe me, I've thought about this. Why would I agree to your plan when my only purpose in life would be to perfect the art of becoming invisible? I'd spend every day waiting for you, never knowing if you would turn up.'

'You're growing hysterical. You will have the charity to occupy your time, and very soon your child.'

'A child to *occupy* me?' Antonia protested in outrage. 'Looking after my baby will be a privilege. Yes, I'm expecting motherhood to be demanding, but never a chore—never something to *fill in my time*. A child is far too precious for that, Ra'id—something I don't expect you to understand.'

'I understand more than you know.'

Something about the way he spoke sent a flash of guilt through her, and then she realised he was thinking about Razi, the half-brother Ra'id had brought up when his mother had been driven away and his father had cared for no one but himself. 'I'm sorry. I should never have said that. I'm just—'

'Frightened of taking a step into the unknown?' Ra'id suggested. 'Your life doesn't have to be a repeat of the past, Antonia.' He glanced at the sheet of paper she was still holding clenched in her hand. 'The path you decide to take from here is up to you, and not some letter written years ago.'

'You would allow me to choose that path?'

'Why are you so certain I want to crush you?'

'I don't know, Ra'id. Maybe it has something to do with the fact that you led me to understand our child would live with you?'

'I would never agree to a child of mine living apart from me.'

'So you would never agree to live apart from your child, but I must?' Her voice shook as he touched on her Achilles heel.

'You will have full access, naturally.'

'And for that I must be grateful?'

'For that you must obey.'

So there it was, Antonia thought, turning pale. After all

the niceties and tactics were out of the way. Ra'id was a desert king, a warrior; a man she was only coming to know. 'This is your country where I must live by your rules and forget that I was ever free?' When he didn't answer, she added passionately, 'I'm not my mother, Ra'id. I'm not Helena. I'm not looking to escape, or excuse, and I'm certainly not looking for a man to keep me. I'm going to stay here and work to make the best use I can of my inheritance.'

'But that's what I want too. I have a hunting lodge in mind where you can stay until the work here is completed.'

'A hunting lodge, hidden away? Is that so different?' She gestured around and then let her arms drop to her side. She wanted to stay and work as a team, as they had on the island, not because she wanted to profit from it in any way but because she loved him and wanted to be with him.

'I'll leave you to think about it.'

She might have matured and learned from her mother's mistakes, but Ra'id would never change, Antonia realised as he ducked his head to leave the pavilion. This was the man she had fallen in love with: a king; an autocratic ruler; a man who was master of all he surveyed.

But not her master, Antonia determined when Ra'id had been gone for some time and she'd had time to cool down. Mounting up, she pointed her kindly gelding in the direction of the fort. She would plough her own furrow, however long that took.

CHAPTER SIXTEEN

ANTONIA had looked stricken when he had left her in the pavilion, while he felt not a moment's guilt. He had tried the softly-softly approach, and much as he had expected it had got him nowhere. It was time to return to his default setting of intractable command. What he had planned for Antonia's future was not only for the best for all of them, it was the only way they could move forward. She could take it or fight back, but conflict between them would only mean an unnecessary delay in her settling-in process.

She had accused him of being incapable of feeling, and maybe once he would have agreed with her. But his life had changed on the day a young virago had accosted him with a knife. Since then he felt everything acutely. Taking care of Antonia was his primary concern, but the luxury of showing his feelings was the one privilege he did not enjoy.

So maybe he had to lighten up? Allow Antonia to take more risks?

The one thing he was determined on was that Antonia would never take another risk and would not be put in danger. She might be a formidable force in the making, but if she was going to fulfil her potential she had to stay on track—and that was a track only Antonia could find. She thought he meant to keep her captive, when he knew that only the hand of life could contain her. Staying in Sinnebar or going back to Rome was Antonia's choice, though he dearly wanted her to stay. But a royal child? On that there could be no compromise. His child would be brought up by him, under his roof and under his protection.

He was leaning against the trunk of a palm-tree, staring out at the desert, when he saw her mounting up. He couldn't say it surprised him. Nothing about Antonia surprised him. For the sake of the horse he was glad she was lightweight. The gelding was moving well at the moment, but he had bathed its foreleg earlier, having noticed the first signs of trouble. He doubted she would get far, but he'd ride Tonnerre bareback and keep an eye on her.

So much for her brave adventure. Her horse went lame and she ended up leading it back to the pavilion. She could see Ra'id's stallion tethered nearby, but not Ra'id himself. Maybe he had summoned some super-silent high-tech helicopter to whisk him back to the capital. So much for his protective instincts; she'd be better off alone.

She trudged back to the pavilion, having fed and watered her horse, knowing her options were shrinking. What kind of future awaited her if she didn't sort this out? Would she be a prisoner like her mother? It had already begun—the waiting. Ra'id had said he'd be nearby, but he hadn't even tried to stop her leaving, and now he'd gone.

Entering the silent pavilion, she tugged off her boots. Exhausted by everything that had happened that day, she just about managed to strip off her clothes before tumbling into a disillusioned ball on top of the silken cushions, where she quickly fell asleep.

She was dreaming of riding in front of a mysterious, dark stranger on a wild, black stallion across mile upon mile of desert when the sound of rustling skirts shocked her awake. Blinking against the light, she sat up, and it took her a moment to realise three women were bowing to her. 'Please,' she begged them groggily as she hastily dragged a sheet over her naked body. She whisked her hand around to mime that no one had to bow to her.

As the kohl-lined eyes smiled back at her, Antonia recognised the three Bedouin women she'd met a couple of days before. 'I know you!' she said, putting two and two together and realising that Ra'id must have left her to ask them to come and keep her company. 'My riding clothes.' She pointed to them, and the women nodded with enthusiasm, their ice-blue robes with the intricate silver cross-stitch decoration twinkling in the strengthening light as Antonia thanked them for lending her such sensible clothes.

Now she was a little embarrassed, and had to carefully manoeuvre herself off the bed. Wrapping the cover tightly around her, she did her best to make them welcome. 'Would you like a drink?' she offered, lifting the jug of juice that had miraculously appeared on a nearby pierced-brass table.

The women must have brought it while she was asleep, Antonia realised, along with the dishes of sweetmeats and fruit. 'You're very generous,' she said, bowing to them as best she could in her sheet ensemble.

The women giggled, as if she was the funniest thing they had ever seen and, shaking their heads, indicated that first she must follow them.

The bathing pool had been warmed by the fast-strengthening sun, and Antonia exclaimed with surprise and pleasure to see the women had scattered rose petals on the surface of the water. This was real luxury, she thought, quite excited at having her hair washed and then her scalp massaged with the most sweet-smelling products. The world should know about these, Antonia decided when the women explained to her with mimed actions that they had picked and prepared the herbs and flowers for the lotions themselves. Maybe that was something else she could do when she wasn't busy with the baby, the restoration work and the charity.

When they had patted her dry with soft towels, warm hands massaged her with more fragrant unguents. This should be part of her daily routine—not that she'd have time, Antonia thought with a rueful smile. And what was coming next? she wondered when the women slipped a plain, loose robe over her head.

Taking her by the hands, they ushered her excitedly into the pavilion, where they sat her down and dried and polished her hair before plaiting it loosely and decorating it with exotic flowers. More scent was applied, until Antonia decided she smelled like a garden, and then they put make-up on her and painted intricate designs on her hands and feet with henna.

This really was special attention, she thought, starting to wonder about it—but then they produced another robe for her approval, and she gasped. The women were pleased to see her delight at this first sight of a masterpiece of design in sky-blue silk chiffon. The delicate fabric floated as they showed it to her, and was decorated with tiny seed-pearls and sparkling silver coins that would jingle as she moved. Before she put it on, the women fastened anklets of jewelled bells above her feet, and more around her wrists, and then they slipped the whisper of highly deco-rated silk-chiffon over her head. She was just revelling in those silken folds when, with some ceremony, they prepared to veil her.

She felt a real frisson of excitement now, realising this must be the culmination of the ceremony. They had even brought a full-length mirror into the pavilion, and placed it in front of her so she could see the finished effect.

She looked amazing—amazingly different, Antonia realised, seeing sultry eyes she hardly recognised flashing back at her. But the question uppermost in her mind was why? Why now? Why were the women doing this for her? What was this all about? And how could she ask her newfound friends what was going on, when no one spoke the same language? She couldn't be so rude as to stop the women when they were having such fun attending to her—and, truthfully, so was she—but she couldn't deny a nagging sense of doubt that suggested she was being prepared to take on the role of His Imperial Majesty's concubine.

She would bring everything to a halt if that were the case, Antonia determined, but for now... The women carried a twinkling veil reverently over outstretched arms. To try it on, just once, was irresistible. The veil sparkled bewitchingly, exceeding any fantasy image she could ever have come up with—and were those tiny jewels sewn onto the floating panels? Blue-white diamonds? The veil was clearly precious and significant to the women, judging by the way they handled it.

And they weren't finished with her yet, Antonia realised when they had draped it over her head and shoulders. Now they were going to secure it with the most fabulous rope of turquoise-and-coral beads. The turquoise toned beautifully with the robe, while the coral could have been chosen to point up the warm-blush tint in her cheeks.

What on earth had she done to deserve this?

That was her first thought, and it was swiftly followed by *who is this?* as an older woman entered the tent.

The older woman shocked Antonia into silence by explaining that Signorina Antonia Ruggerio had been adopted as a daughter of her tribe. 'And my name is Mariam,' she said. 'I will be your advocate, should you require me in the discussions to come.'

What discussions? Antonia wondered. And she could speak for herself, though she nodded and smiled politely. It must be something to do with the charity, she reasoned. This was a culture she knew little about, and if she wanted to forge ahead with her work it would be wise to have an interpreter— at least until she was fluent in the language herself. But a daughter of the tribe? That was a good thing, wasn't it?

Mariam pretty much confirmed these thoughts, explaining that once the most powerful tribe in Sinnebar had accepted Antonia as a daughter she would have no trouble persuading the rest of the country to support her.

Well, anything that would help to spread the reach of the charity was a good thing, Antonia supposed. Learning that Ra'id was the head of this most powerful tribe came as no surprise—but if he was also the head of the ruling council, who was going to refuse him? 'How does that work?' Antonia murmured, thinking out loud.

With a faint smile and a low bow, the woman called Mariam walked gracefully out of the pavilion.

Ruling council, my foot! Antonia thought, starting to pace. Once again, everything had been decided by Ra'id. She could see the point of the fabulous costume now. This wasn't a treat, it was a set-up, a shrewd move by Ra'id to involve her in some ceremony far away from the prying eyes of the world in an exotic setting he believed would seduce her. The ceremony probably wasn't even legal. She would be no more secure than her mother—no more visible, certainly. So much for her fantasy of the silken veil! She would be a prisoner in a silken veil, Ra'id's love-slave, until he tired of her.

She whirled around when he strode into the tent. 'Ra'id!' Mariam had entered behind him, and she was followed by the girls who had helped to prepare Antonia for their sheikh.

Ra'id stood in the centre of the pavilion, an ominous force dressed all in black, still with the *howlis* wrapped round his face. 'From now on,' he informed her, 'this is how it will be. These women will wait on you and I will not see you alone again until we are married.'

'Married?' The word choked off any air supply she might have had in her lungs.

'That is what you wanted, isn't it?' And before she could protest—*Yes! No! Not like this!*—he went on, 'Now you are an accepted daughter of the tribe, I must observe the formalities laid down.'

'Centuries ago?' Antonia challenged him, almost beside herself with shock.

'Oh no,' Ra'id replied evenly. 'Somewhat longer than that, I should think.'

'You are joking?' Then, realising the women standing behind Ra'id were still waiting for her instruction, Antonia remembered her manners and invited them to sit down.

Once everyone was seated, she went up to Ra'id; staring into his eyes, which was all she could see of his fierce face behind the headdress, she hissed, 'Did you think to ask me first? Did I miss something before you disappeared yesterday?'

The expression in Ra'id's eyes remained as shrewd and as dangerous as ever. 'I thought you liked surprises,' he said mildly.

'Some surprises,' Antonia agreed. But surprises came in many forms. The chance to dress up in pretty clothes was nice, but when it came to matters of the heart—things that really mattered—like a marriage between two people...

She'd done with surprises, Antonia realised. It would be helpful if an alarm rang on the day you grew up, she reflected—helpful to everyone, especially Ra'id. She could no longer be seduced by a visit behind the silken veil, or by fabulous jewels and clothes that looked as if they had been sequestered from the set of a Hollywood movie. Or by some hasty marriage ceremony that probably had no legal standing outside this tent. Before she'd come to Sinnebar? Yes; she had been impressionable then, before she had met and fallen in love with a man called Saif. But now there was just one man and one woman, or there should have been. And you could forget the trimmings; she didn't need them. She would never settle for anything less than a real marriage based on love. She certainly didn't intend to be bulldozed into the most important decision of her life just because this was expedient for Ra'id.

'What do you think you're doing?' he demanded as she started tugging off the rope of jewels holding her veil in place.

Ra'id had underestimated her for the last time, Antonia determined. 'If you don't know…' she said, and then, conscious that they weren't alone, she added more discreetly, 'Do you mind if we walk outside? Only I'm feeling a little faint in here.'

'Of course.'

Ra'id was immediately concerned about her.

About her *pregnancy*, and the welfare of his child, Antonia amended as the ruler of Sinnebar escorted her out of the tent.

He was at her side in a moment. Pregnancy must have weakened her, he realized. There was some shade inside the pavilion, but no air-conditioning, plus he and the other women were used to the heat.

Having removed her veil and carefully placed the rope of precious jewels on top of it, she took a moment to reassure the women and thank them by miming with expressive hands. They looked at him for reassurance too, and with a brief dip of his chin as he strode past them he confirmed Antonia's wishes. This was not the child-woman he had first encountered on his yacht, but a woman of purpose who made her own decisions.

She made for a group of palm trees where he had sheltered the previous evening and there she stopped. 'What's wrong?' he said, joining her in the shade.

'This—all this,' she said with a sweep of her hands over the jewelled gown. 'More toys for me to play with, Ra'id? I grew up with this—I thought you knew that. I have fourteen wardrobes crammed full of clothes back in Rome. My brother gives me everything that money can buy; at one time I thought that beautiful clothes and wonderful jewellery, eating at the best places in Rome, was all it took to make me happy. I took it for granted, because that was my life. But it's not enough, Ra'id. I've seen more now, and I want more.'

'More?' He hated the disillusionment spilling from Antonia's lips, though he wondered if he had ever seen her looking lovelier than she did now with the morning breeze tossing her hair about and a vision of the future in her eyes.

'I don't mean more stuff,' she said, perhaps sounding younger than she had intended. 'I mean more time to be us—to be real—to do real things.'

'If you mean time to work for the good of the charity?' he said.

'Yes!' she exclaimed. 'If you'll let me work for Sinnebar, I'll put my whole heart into it. I don't need this pomp and ceremony, Ra'id. And, as for becoming a daughter of the tribe, it's very kind of you—but it's too late for me to become anyone's daughter. I'm not a child any longer, Ra'id. Can't you see that?'

His proposal for the tribe to adopt her had been his way of smoothing Antonia's path so that they could be married. He had come to this conclusion without consulting her, he realised now. He hadn't even told her how empty his life would be without her. In fact, life without Antonia was unthinkable. But had he told her that? Slowly unwinding his *howlis*, he stood staring out at the desert over which he ruled. He had made much of that desert into a garden for his people to enjoy and to nurture and harvest crops on. Was there as much hope for him?

Then she placed her hand on his arm and stared up at him, pleading. 'Don't drive me away.'

'That's the very last thing I'm trying to do.'

'Then you must know I would never settle for anything less than a marriage based on love?'

Ra'id held her gaze. He looked more magnificent than she had ever seen him. There wasn't a single item of his clothing, or even his expression, his hair or his eyes, that wasn't unrelieved black, but she loved him without fear or favour. What did his outer coating matter? When she had seen him in regal robes of royal blue trimmed with golden thread and yellow sapphire, had she loved him more? Saif, in his worn, frayed shorts and faded top was the man she had fallen in love with, and they were one and the same. Except, Ra'id al Maktabi was a man turned hard by duty. But Ra'id's fearful title didn't frighten her. She wouldn't allow anything to stand in the way of the people they could be. 'You were wrong about me liking surprises,' she told him softly. Still with her hand resting on Ra'id's arm, she explained, 'There are some surprises I do not like at all.'

Her heart faltered when he looked down at her and then she saw Saif in his eyes. 'I think I get that,' he said.

'Can we talk?' she whispered, hardly daring to believe what was happening.

'We can talk,' Ra'id confirmed, and, finding her hand with his, he linked their fingers together and, turning, they slowly walked together back to the tent.

He dismissed the servants so he and Antonia could be together.

'It will cost you nothing,' she told him earnestly, fixing her gaze on his. 'No jewels, no land grants, nothing except you and me together, forging a future.'

He heard the question in her voice, and it was a question he couldn't wait to answer. Drawing her to him, he kissed her gently on the brow. 'Your wish is my command,' he murmured.

He had dreams too, and his dream had grown to encompass the two of them standing together—but not too close for, in the words of the poet, even the pillars of the temple stood apart.

CHAPTER SEVENTEEN

THE VALUE of a hug could not be overestimated, Antonia realised as Ra'id held her close. Sometimes she needed a hug more than anything, and it turned out that Ra'id was really good at that too. They were talking now and he was listening, really listening; she was back with the man she loved, the man she had known as Saif. She had changed into a casual robe and was reclining on the cushions with Ra'id, staring out across the ocean of sand through the silken curtain that covered the entrance to his pavilion. 'I could never live as my mother lived.'

'You won't have to. And, before you accuse me of fiendish plots and insurmountable character-flaws, let me reassure you that I do understand love. I also understand that love takes many forms and that sometimes fate doesn't allow enough time for love to be proven.'

'You're not defending your father, I hope?'

'He gave your mother land. People show their love in different ways, Antonia, and though I think my father loved himself best of all I also think he finally discovered a conscience.'

'But he abandoned his son, Razi, for reasons of self-interest.'

'I can't argue with you on that point, but neither can I continue to believe that your mother didn't care for you.'

'What?' Antonia turned to him in surprise.

'She must have done.'

'Or wanted to cause the maximum upheaval in Sinnebar as some sort of revenge.'

'Isn't it time to give her the benefit of the doubt?'

'I never thought I'd hear you defending her.' This was the pivotal moment, Antonia felt, when Ra'id would make sense of her past as she was beginning to understand his.

'Helena must have known her life in Sinnebar would end some day.'

'And in such a terrible way—locked up, incarcerated, forgotten. No wonder she bolted into the arms of my father.'

Ra'id nodded 'Your mother escaped, as she saw it. And went on to make your father very happy, I believe. And when your mother wrote her will she wanted to be sure her children had something significant to remember her by.'

'Her land in Sinnebar? But in leaving it to her children she must have known how much trouble that would cause.'

'In Sinnebar when a parent dies their property is divided equally between their surviving children, so Helena had no choice in the matter. And, maybe, the country meant more to Helena than we know. She had that friendship with her maidservant, remember? Maybe Helena was just starting to grow up when my father decided he was tired of her.'

'I can't believe you're taking her side,' Antonia said, feeling as if a great weight had been lifted from her shoulders.

'Why should you find it so hard to believe? You're Helena's daughter. I have to believe there was some good in her—unexplored possibilities.'

They remained quiet for a while, and then she said softly, 'Thank you, Ra'id. I understand now why you wanted to be with me when I read that page from my mother's diary.' But she was thanking Ra'id for more than that, Antonia realised; she was thanking him for his ability to see through the muddle of the past to a place from where they could both move forward.

'Don't forget this when you put that page away safely, will you?'

Antonia gasped when she saw the necklace Ra'id was holding out to her. 'Where did you find that?'

'It dropped into my hand,' he said, tongue in cheek.

She blushed. 'I hope you don't think...'

'That you stole it?' With a wry smile, he shook his head and then handed her the slender chain with the diamond-studded heart dangling from it. 'This has always belonged to you, along with the rest of your mother's possessions. I can only apologise that, like anything else that was left behind, it wasn't found earlier and sent to you in Rome.'

'I'm rather glad it wasn't,' Antonia admitted, knowing this was a much better way to receive it. 'And you've mended it!' she exclaimed.

Reaching behind her neck as Ra'id fastened the clasp for her, she rested her hand on his. 'Do you think your father gave this to my mother?'

'Who knows? And does it matter?' he said. 'All that matters is that you have it now. I believe your mother would have wanted that.'

'You really are turning into a romantic.'

'Let's not get carried away,' Ra'id cautioned. 'A few romantic minutes a day are the most I can manage.'

'So, not long enough—' She had been about to say 'for a wedding', and only just managed to stop herself in time.

But Ra'id would not be distracted. 'Not long enough for what?' he said. 'What were you about to say to me, Antonia?'

'Nothing,' she said, but her blazing cheeks gave her away. 'Do I expect too much?'

Antonia's face was as serious as he had ever seen it; this was the closest they had ever been, and she needed him to be absolutely honest with her. 'You've certainly tested me to the limits of my endurance.'

'I don't know what you mean.'

'Yes, you do,' he said, his lips tugging in a smile. 'Why don't you test me again?' he suggested. And this time she knew exactly what he meant.

It was much later when he caused her to cry out again, and this time with surprise. 'Sorry,' he mocked gently, removing the velvet box from her hand before she had a chance to open it. 'I forgot you don't like surprises.'

'Just a minute,' she admonished him, sitting bolt-upright, naked and beautiful. 'Like you said about love, surprises come in many forms—and some of them aren't so bad.'

'Well, if you're sure?' he said, pressing his lips down in a pretence of doubt as he opened the catch on the velvet box to reveal the magnificent royal-blue sapphire surrounded by blue-white diamonds he had picked out in the hope that Antonia would wear it on her wedding finger.

'Are you suggesting a partnership?' she said, narrowing her eyes.

'I was rather thinking a marriage. Isn't that the same thing?'

'No, it isn't the same thing at all,' she assured him with all the defiance in her voice that he loved.

'A marriage and a partnership, then?' he amended.

'If I can have both…' She appeared to think about it.

'If I can have you standing beside me, you can have anything,' Ra'id said.

'In that case…'

'I love you,' he said simply as she threw herself into his arms. 'I love you and I want to marry you, Antonia. Unfortunately that means you will have to be a queen, and for that I apologise. I know you, above all people, understand what is involved in loving a country and its people as I do.'

'And I love its king,' she assured him. 'But, most of all, I love you…Saif, Ra'id, Sword of Vengeance—whoever you are.' And then she laughed and warned him, 'You'd better not use that sword on anyone else, or you're in serious trouble.'

'Grow up,' he said, tumbling her onto the cushions.

'In that respect? Never,' she promised him defiantly.

Then he kissed her with all the passion with which only Ra'id was capable, and in a way that convinced Antonia she'd found not her lover, or even her husband, but her soul mate; there could be no other. Ra'id had kissed the last of her fears away until she was triumphant and strong. There was only one thing missing, Antonia realised as Ra'id pulled away.

But then he did that too.

'Antonia Ruggiero,' he whispered, kneeling in front of her with his head bowed. 'Would you do me the honour of becoming my wife?'

'Yes…Oh, yes!' she exclaimed.

'Will you be my queen, the mother of my children, and will you work at my side for the good of Sinnebar?' Ra'id demanded, lifting his proud, formidably handsome face to stare her in the eyes. 'Because I love you—and will always love you.'

'I will,' she said fearlessly. 'I will.'

Moving to embrace her, Ra'id cupped her face in his hands. 'If you look with your heart, you will find as I did that the most important things in life aren't land or possessions, they're invisible.'

'As long as *I'm* not invisible.'

'You, Antonia?' Ra'id's expression changed from irony to sincerity. 'You could never be ignored—you'd make sure of that. But please be serious for a moment. I'm saying I love you, and I'll take a lifetime to prove it to you if I have to. And, as for the land, it will always be yours—'

'Or I could give it to the people of Sinnebar,' she interrupted him, which felt right to her.

A faint smile tugged at Ra'id's firm mouth. 'Now do you see why I love you?' he said, and, taking the fabulous sapphire ring out of its velvet nest, he placed it on Antonia's wedding finger.

SHE couldn't have everything her own way.

Which wasn't such a bad thing, Antonia conceded, staring at her wedding dress twinkling in the faint, pink light before dawn. Ra'id had insisted that their people required their queen to look like a queen, and that Antonia could have her wedding dress adapted at some later stage and wear it again if she felt bad about the extravagance.

It was a dream of a dress, Antonia reflected, holding back the folds of the lavish bridal-pavilion where she had spent the night. She had tumbled out of bed in time to see Ra'id leave the encampment. He had galloped away on his fierce black stallion, with his younger brother Razi at his side, their very masculine silhouettes framed against a brightening sky as they rode across the brow of the dune. They were two unimaginably powerful men like heroes of old, leaning low over the necks of their straining horses as they raced away, no doubt to enjoy an early-morning swim in some lush, green oasis.

The wedding gown the tribeswomen had created for their queen was an exquisite column of a dress in heavy ivory silk, embroidered for this occasion in gold thread by specialist craftswomen who lived deep in the interior of Sinnebar. It managed to be both demure and sexy, with long sleeves to preserve Antonia's modesty, but body-skimming to hint at what lay beneath. She hoped Ra'id would take the hint, as they hadn't made love since their last night in the desert. Far from dulling her sexual urges, pregnancy had only made her hungrier for him, a fact she was sure he knew, but which he cruelly refused to take action on. The thought that this would be their wedding night made desire cry deep inside her, and it was a voice she was determined he would hear.

The sexual tension between them had become unbearable, Antonia realised as she walked deeper into the luxurious womb-like interior of her tent. The bridal pavilion was decorated in many shades of crimson, fuchsia and rose-pink silk, and was a delicately scented sanctuary where she was supposed to be resting before the rigours of their week-long marriage ceremony. But wanting Ra'id made rest impossible. It felt as if they were starting over from the moment they had met. Her body yearned for him so shamelessly, only now it was worse, because now she knew what she was missing.

The wedding ceremony was to be at dawn and already a tented city had grown up on the ivory-sugar sand. Lights glinted as far as the eye could see, as Ra'id's subjects had gathered from every corner of the kingdom to see him wed the girl who had laboured night and day at their side to prepare the renovated fort for the first of the children it would house. Antonia had wanted to name the centre after her mother, but the people had ruled that they would name it after her. Ra'id had compromised when he'd opened the

Queen Antonia Children's Centre, adding a small plaque signed by Antonia in memory of Helena Ruggiero that said quite simply: *She looked into the future and believed.*

That plaque was the best gift Ra'id could ever have given her, Antonia reflected, gazing at the casket of fabulous jewels he had given her the previous evening. She smiled, remembering him commanding her not to take them off during their wedding ceremony, as she had removed her jewels once before. 'Our people must see you,' Ra'id had insisted, when she protested at the size and quantity of the sparking diamonds.

'They'll hardly miss me wearing these,' she had replied, touching the glittering stones he had fastened around her neck. 'They must be worth a king's ransom.'

'No—a sheikh's,' he had told her dryly. 'You may consider me your hostage for life.'

She would, Antonia thought, hugging herself in anticipation.

She turned at the sound of footsteps. The women had come for her, she noticed, her excitement mounting as they slipped silently into the pavilion. She still couldn't believe they had come to dress their queen.

They bathed her, prepared her, scented her and polished her, until her skin glowed and her body yearned for the touch of Ra'id—her lover, her soul mate, her king. They laced the diamonds in her hair and arranged her filmy, ivory-coloured veil beneath them—the veil that Ra'id would remove in their wedding tent prior to...

The sound of the *nafir*, the horn with a single true note, was a fortunate disruption to Antonia's progressively sensual thoughts. There were people to greet, and a ceremony to undergo with grace and dignity, before the longed-for moment when she could be alone with Ra'id.

And when that moment came she trembled like a virgin. Or, at least, that was how she felt as Ra'id removed her veil with a teasing lack of speed. She felt like a virgin waiting to be kissed by her lover for the very first time. But when Ra'id kissed her brow, and then the swell of her belly where their baby lay safe and loved, she knew this was going to be better and far deeper than anything she had experienced before.

'Our child,' he murmured, sharing her sense of wonder.

'Our family,' she answered, quivering with enough expectation to found a dynasty as Ra'id's lips brushed her mouth. That kiss was all the more arousing for his lack of haste or pressure, she realised, shivering with frustration beneath Ra'id's tantalisingly light touch.

'We have all the time in the world,' he murmured, teasing her as he always did.

'Don't make me wait that long,' Antonia protested, while Ra'id laughed. And, falling back on the bed, he drew her on top of him. 'Tiger woman.'

'Meets rampant lion?' she suggested, tracing the lines of the tattoo on Ra'id's chest.

'An interesting coupling,' he agreed.

'Let's find out, shall we?' Antonia suggested, slipping out of her fabulous robe.

THE SHEIKH'S
RELUCTANT BRIDE

TERESA SOUTHWICK

To Susan Mallery, Maureen Child
and Chris Rimmer—the best plot group ever

CHAPTER ONE

"FEAR is my friend."

As the plane touched down on Bha'Khar's runway, Jessica Leigh Sterling prayed she spoke the truth. Except the statement was fundamentally flawed. Fearful flyers usually freaked out on takeoff, not so much on touchdown. But nothing about this flight was usual and she'd learned there were lots of ways to be afraid.

This wasn't like when she was a girl and her mother had gotten so sick that Jess had been sent to the state home. This was scary like the hopeless romantic who finds out it might be possible to get what she's wanted her whole life only to find out her dream really is hopeless.

She was afraid it was going to be like that old joke: everyone who has a family, step forward. Not so fast, Jessica. There are people who share your DNA, but they don't want to know you so forget about them helping out if you need a kidney or bone marrow transplant.

Oh God, to be this close to meeting someone who'd known her mother, someone who might care about Jessica because of that connection. Might. But, maybe not. And she was still a little weirded out because the family she'd come to meet lived in a country halfway around the world from California. But the potential benefits trumped fear and, although important, matching kidneys and compatible bone marrow were not an issue, thank goodness. It was the simple things she wanted to know—like where her brown hair and hazel eyes had come from.

And, just this once, couldn't life come down on the side of the hopeless romantic? That's what she was here to find out.

As the plane slowly turned toward a group of buildings, it hit her that this was really Bha'Khar, her mother's country—the country Jess had never known about while Mary Sterling was alive. The mounds of paperwork necessary to make this visit happen had made her eyes cross and—good lord—the king of Bha'Khar had sent an aide to cut through the red tape. Why had her mother kept secret her connection to royalty? Jessica never would have known if an attorney from the Department of Children and Families hadn't contacted her about the letter from her mother that he'd found in her old file.

The King had sent a plane, too. When it stopped,

the captain turned off the Fasten Seat Belt sign and she released hers, then stood, stretching cramped muscles. She'd been told that someone would be here to meet her, but her nerves didn't seem to care. Then the curtains parted in the forward cabin and a tall man in a close-fitting and elegantly tailored navy-blue suit walked toward her. He looked familiar, but no way could she have ever met him.

He looked about thirty and moved with confidence, predatory grace and an air of controlled power. His thick black hair was long enough to scrape the crisp white collar of his dress shirt. The barest suggestion of arrogance mixed with the sensual curve of his mouth and his straight nose flared a little at the nostrils, hinting at a depth of passion that could rock a girl's world. Only a vertical scar on his lip and a crescent-shaped one on his sharp cheekbone marred his male perfection. And mar was the wrong word. If anything, the imperfections enhanced his masculinity.

He stopped in front of her and smiled. "Jessica?"

That smile could start the average woman's world rocking, but she wasn't the average woman. His deep voice and attractive accent made her name sound like a caress.

"I'm Jessica."

"Welcome to Bha'Khar." He took her hand and bent over it.

Along with the plane ride, this was a first. Kids

from the state home didn't grow up and rub shoulders with the sort of men who kissed women's hands. It made her feel awkward and ill at ease. Like that first night after being taken from her mother's hospital room to share a room with other girls who had no one. All the hopeless, empty, scary feelings came back in a rush.

Then his soft lips grazed her knuckles and the touch unleashed other feelings that had nothing to do with anxiety and everything to do with awareness.

"Th-thank you," she said.

Dark brown eyes assessed her. "Please forgive my boldness, but I am compelled to say that I did not expect that you would be so lovely."

English might be his second language, but certainly he was fluent in flattery. Could flirtation be far behind?

"Thank you," she said again.

It was the polite response to the man who'd probably been sent to take her to her relatives. But every single instinct she possessed elevated from alert-level-orange to run-don't-walk-away red. Suspicion was the by-product of a childhood spent watching alcohol destroy her mother's body as surely as the string of two-timing men through her life had destroyed her spirit. Jessica had learned to spot a player by the time she was ten years old and this guy was definitely a player.

But that wasn't her problem. He was probably another of the king's aides and she was nothing more than his job. After he connected her with family, his work would be done.

"I trust your journey was pleasant?" He continued to hold her hand and for some reason she continued to let him.

Pleasant? She glanced at the plush, customized interior of the royal jet. "There was some turbulence." Her heart had raced then, too. "But mostly the flight was smooth. Although I have nothing to compare it to. This was my first time."

A gleam stole into those dark eyes. "So... You are no longer a virgin—" Two beats later he added, "Flier."

That, too. She'd never slept with a man, either. Many had been willing to be her first, but she'd been unwilling to participate. She didn't believe there was a faithful guy out there, let alone one who could sweep her off her feet. An unfortunate characteristic of the hopeless romantic was the yearning to be swept away, which put her idealistic and rational selves in constant conflict. She wanted a completely romantic meltdown that would prohibit logical thought and just let her *feel*. So far she'd come up empty on all counts.

Although the way her stomach had dropped when he'd kissed her hand made her feel like she was still in the air and the plane hit a downdraft. Imagine if he kissed her for real—on the mouth. Darned if her lips didn't tingle at the thought. This so wasn't the time to abandon logical thinking. What had he just asked? Her journey. Right.

Time to cleanse the virgin remark from the air and turn the conversation to the mundane. Make that nonpersonal because there was nothing ordinary about this guy or the royal jet. "This plane is amazing. It's like a flying living room."

"There is a bedroom as well," he said, suggestion in his tone adding to the gleam in his eyes.

So much for nonpersonal communication. "I noticed."

"You found the bed comfortable?"

More comfortable than the way he made her feel. It was like every nerve ending in her body had received a double dose of adrenaline.

"I found everything perfect."

"Excellent. There is a car waiting. I will escort you to the palace."

"The palace?" She knew her eyes grew wide, and tried to stop, but couldn't, what with her heart pounding so hard.

"Is there somewhere else you wish to go?"

Yes, she wanted to say. And no. "Going to the palace" didn't fit into her frame of reference even after reading her mother's letter. She remembered the handwriting, as familiar as if it were the day's grocery list instead of the last thing her mother had written ten years ago. The words still made her heart hurt. *I know I did everything else wrong, but it wasn't wrong the way I loved you.* Since then, Jess had read the message over and over but still couldn't grasp that she was distantly related to Bha'Khar's royal family.

"I'm sure the palace is fine, but—" Fine? It so wasn't fine. She wasn't a palace kind of person. She was burgers and fries, sweatpants and sneakers.

"But?"

"I was sort of hoping I'd be meeting my family."

"And you will," he promised. "Arrangements are being made. In the meantime, permit me to make you comfortable."

Comfortable? What did that mean? And how could she be comfortable with strangers, however distantly related, who were royalty?

As he started to turn away, she put her hand on his arm and felt the material of his suit jacket. "Wait."

Concern that seemed to be genuine slid into his eyes. "Is there a problem?"

The problem was the material just felt like material to her. It was probably expensive material, but she had no frame of reference for that any more than she did for a palace. Most little girls grew up playing pretend princess, but the fantasy was usually limited to the great gowns and a tiara or two. Not living under the same roof as the king and queen. This was a fear she'd never felt before.

"Maybe it would be better if I stayed at a hotel."

He looked puzzled. "The king and queen would be disappointed."

How did she explain this? "There's a saying in my country—it's better to look stupid than open your mouth and prove it. This is kind of like that."

"I like this saying. But you do not look stupid so I am unclear on your point."

"They're certain to be disappointed in me, but staying at the palace—I'm bound to do something that will let them down for sure," she explained.

He shook his head. "You need only be yourself."

"That's what I'm afraid of."

"There is no cause for fear."

"Yeah, there kind of is. This is a perfect example." She held out a hand indicating the plush plane interior. "I grew up in a run-down, one-bedroom apartment on Stoner Street in Los Angeles. That was until the state of California took over. I wouldn't know a shrimp fork from a forklift."

"You are exaggerating."

"Yes. But you get my point."

"If it becomes necessary for you to know these things, just stay very close to me and follow my lead. I promise to protect you."

She studied the oh-so-sincere expression on his handsome face. "That sounds very much like 'trust me.'"

"Exactly."

"In my country when someone says that it's usually a good idea not to."

"You are most cynical," he commented.

"I have good reasons."

"I look forward to hearing them," he said, probably just being polite.

He smiled, showing off straight white teeth, then he covered her hand with his own, a gesture meant to comfort but brought back the spiraling-plane-sensation.

"The king and queen are looking forward to meeting you, the daughter of their dear friends' daughter, for whom they've been searching so many years."

"They've been searching?" she asked, her gaze jumping to his.

In the letter, her mother had confessed that she'd become pregnant by a married diplomat and ran away because shame prevented her from going to her family. Jess had feared the same family would shun her and to find out they'd been looking gave her hope a double dose of adrenaline.

She smiled up at him. "Thank you—" Had he introduced himself? Was she so caught up in her nerves, skepticism and his charming flirtation that she'd forgotten? "I'm sorry, I don't know your name."

"My apologies. I have been remiss." He bent slightly at the waist. "I am Kardahl, son of King Amahl Hourani of Bha'Khar."

That name sounded familiar. Probably because he was part of the royal family. "So are we related?"

He shook his head. "Your lineage can be traced

back to royalty, but the bloodlines split off over a hundred years ago."

There was no reason to feel relieved about that and yet she was, right up until she realized why the name sounded so familiar. And why she'd thought she'd seen him before. Because she had seen him in print. He was better looking in person. "You're the playboy prince." Did she say that out loud? Oh God, the look on his face told her she did.

His eyes narrowed. "You have been reading the tabloids."

"I don't buy them," she said. It was a minor distinction, but a distinction just the same. "But it's hard not to see them in the grocery store, the beauty salon, the doctor's waiting room."

"You might want to choose a physician who does not patronize disreputable publications," he said.

"I don't have a choice." This was proof that they could be living on different planets. He had no clue about her reality. "My kids go to doctors contracted with the state and we don't get a vote on the publications in the waiting room."

"You have children?" he asked, a flicker of surprise in those dark eyes.

"I've never given birth if that's what you're asking. I'm a social worker and kids in the state's care are my responsibility."

"I see."

"I doubt it. Probably you never had to worry

about medical attention, or your next meal or a roof over your head since you grew up in a palace not a group home." She made a mental note that irritation cancels out fear.

"You would be correct."

Lucky him. "What should I call you? Your Highness? Your Worship?"

"He who rules the universe is my preferred title."

She blinked. "I'm sorry. Were you being funny?"

"Apparently not."

But he smiled, a charming smile that made her want to grab hold of the nearest chair. Another mental note: this playboy had a sense of humor and it packed more punch than his charm. She didn't know whether to be grateful that her player radar was alive, well and functioning with one hundred percent accuracy or unsettled to have proof that she'd inherited from her mother the playboy-magnet gene. The thing was—she wanted to be swept away, but by someone who sincerely wanted *her* and men who were players didn't do sincere.

She'd just confirmed that he was everything she didn't want in a man. Not that he would hit on her. According to those questionable publications, his taste in women ran to models, actresses and world-famous beauties. She was not, not and *so* not.

"My friends and family call me Kardahl," he was saying.

She nodded. "Kardahl it is. I'll just get my bag—"

"It will be taken care of." He rested his hand at the small of her back.

She swore the heat of his fingers seeped through the material of her suit jacket and made her want to melt. Probably that was because he smelled really good. She'd read somewhere that sense of smell was a powerful weapon in the arsenal of seduction. Still, there was the whole willingness thing and he'd just kissed the hand of maybe the only woman on the planet who was immune to his tabloid-worthy charisma.

Kardahl did not miss the chill that slid into Jessica's large hazel eyes when he had introduced himself. Or the way she quite deliberately moved away from his touch now. Given their relationship, her reservations were puzzling.

He held out his hand, indicating that she precede him. "Let us go."

He settled her in the back of the limousine and supervised the removal of her luggage. There were only two pieces, a meager amount of belongings all things considered. It was his experience that women always brought more than necessary and she was moving her entire life. Strange, indeed.

Kardahl slid into the back of the car beside her and met her gaze. The scandal precipitating her arrival was entirely his doing. He'd lost the only woman he would ever love and when he had grown weary of being told life goes on, he had thrown himself into the business of living—with many women. And he was guilty of the abundant yet judicious use of flattery. But he had told *this* woman the truth about being quite lovely. Her sun-streaked brown hair fell past her shoulders, with shorter strands framing a delicate face and cheekbones that revealed her noble heritage. She had also inherited lips that were full, well-formed, and quite frankly, the most kissable mouth he had ever seen.

"Tell me about yourself," he said.

"I'm disappointed."

"You have only to tell me who has done this and I will see that a high price is paid for the transgression."

"Look in the mirror," she said dryly. "Surely you can do better than 'tell me about yourself.' I've heard some of the world's best pickup lines. For instance— 'here I am, what are your other two wishes.' Or, 'do you have a Band-Aid? I scraped my knees when I fell for you.' Or, my personal favorite—'Do you believe in love at first sight? Or should I go out and come in again?'"

"You do not believe that I sincerely wish to know you?"

She slid him an assessing glance. "How's that uber-sincere line working for you?"

The puzzle of Jessica Sterling deepened. Revelation of his identity had altered the obvious female interest he had first recognized when her pulse raced and her hand trembled in his. Gone was the friendly, open woman he had first met. Now he found her prickly. Skeptical. And if he was not mistaken, suspicious. This was a reaction he had never before encountered from a woman. It was remarkably refreshing.

He smiled. "The line works quite well, actually. When I politely and sincerely inquire to know more about a woman, she invariably rewards me with information about herself. Intimate information."

"Okay. I'll play along."

"Play? This is a game?"

"What else?" she asked. "This is you."

He nodded. "Then if you choose to treat it as a game, I will play along, too."

"I figured you would," she said.

"So, if you please, tell me about yourself."

She blew out a long breath. "I was born in Los Angeles, California. My mother died when I was twelve. I grew up in the child welfare system. Went to college and received a degree in social work." She shrugged. "Those are the highlights of my life."

Kardahl did not believe that was so and only now recalled that his father had intended to have Jessica's background investigated. Undoubtedly it had been done, but Kardahl's indifference to the situation had prevented him from reading the report. He regretted that now.

As the car sped smoothly toward the palace, he

looked at her. "I suspect there is more you are not saying."

A frown marred the smooth skin of her forehead, then she turned to look out the window. There was tension in the line of her jaw, the length of her slender neck, the set of her shoulders. Her hands rested in her lap, fingers intertwined, but there was nothing restful about her as she rubbed one thumb over the other.

"There's a lot I'm not saying, but it's not important." Finally she met his gaze. "Tell me about you."

She did not wish to talk about herself, which made him all the more curious. But there was time to learn what he wanted to know. "I am the second in line of succession to the throne of Bha'Khar—"

"The spare heir?"

"Some would say."

"So you're like the equivalent of the vice president in my country."

"I suppose that is true."

"You're so busy keeping women happy all over the world. When do you have time to get ready?"

"For what?"

"To rule the country. If you're called on."

He did have a reputation—some of it deserved, some embellished. But no one knew why he took pains to cultivate it. "I will do my duty should the need arise, but I pray it will not because my brother, Malik, will one day be king."

"Of course. Tell me more."

"What do you wish to know?"

"I wish to know how someone like you who was born with so many advantages and opportunities to do really good things can turn into a self-absorbed pleasure seeker who's only interested in his next romantic conquest."

Her tone was friendly, conversational. And because he liberally used flattery, he recognized it in women. He was accustomed to it. He definitely did not see it now. "You have quite a low opinion of me."

"It's hard not to, what with all the stories printed about you and women who are equally self-absorbed and pleasure seeking."

His emotions had shut down two years ago after burying his beloved Antonia and he almost didn't recognize the prick of anger now. "Do you believe everything you read in those publications?"

"At the very least there has to be a grain of truth or they would be subject to accusations of slander followed by expensive lawsuits. And how many times have denials been issued only to find out the story was true? So, yes, I do believe a lot of what I read." She met his gaze directly. "Although I have to say you look nothing like your pictures."

"The paparazzi are not interested in taking favorable photographs. Their goal is to take infamous ones." And they did not care who they hurt in the pursuit of that goal, he thought bitterly.

"And you certainly give them ample opportunity."

"If you have such a low opinion of me, it begs the question. Why did you agree to come here?"

"You know why. The king's representative promised to make it possible for me to meet my family." She met his gaze. "After that, I'm going back home to my job with the department of social services—important, relevant work. Something you probably wouldn't understand."

"You would be wrong." He was the minister of Finance and Defense. "I am quite social."

She smiled. "No doubt about that, but the services you provide are questionable."

She was making assumptions without knowing him and it was beginning to grate. It was as if she were trying to elicit emotion from him, even if that emotion was negative. If that was her objective, she was destined for more disappointment. The passion he had once felt was big and blazing, an entity with a life of its own and an excitement that had consumed him. When he lost that, he lost everything. He was empty inside. He had learned to go on by embracing that feeling of nothing and Jessica could not do or say anything to make him care.

This was about duty—in his case duty had been helped along by the unfortunate photographs of him with a certain still-married and much divorced actress. With negotiations in progress for Bha'Khar to join other nations in the Global Commerce Union, a scandal in the royal family would not be tolerated. As the public relations minister had pointed out— the only thing the media loved more than a salacious story was a salacious *love* story that included a wedding.

But that was not the real reason her presence in Bha'Khar had been expedited. The woman Kardahl had loved was dead, along with their unborn child and a part of him had died with them. Now one woman was the same as the next. It had ceased to matter to him that the king had chosen his bride when Kardahl was just a boy. His heart had turned to stone.

But his confusion was increasing. What was this about her going back to a job? It would explain her scarcity of luggage, but created more questions.

Kardahl frowned. "One who takes vows so cavalierly should not be so swift to point accusing fingers."

"Vows?" Her smile disappeared. "What are you talking about? What vows?"

"The vows we took by proxy."

Her eyes widened. "I don't understand."

Neither did he. But this he knew for certain. "You are my bride."

CHAPTER TWO

THREE hours ago Jessica had been afraid the family she'd only just found might reject her because she was the result of her mother's out-of-wedlock pregnancy. Now she had bigger things to worry about, like marriage to a man who didn't know the meaning of the words vow, dedication and loyalty.

In his palace suite, she paced back and forth in front of the French doors that opened to a balcony overlooking the Arabian Sea while she waited for him to return and tell her it was all a big mistake. They'd have a laugh, then she could get on with the reason she'd come here.

At least she had a great view for her pacing and his suite wasn't bad, either. Not bad was a gross understatement. It was big. And while she was tempted to explore, she didn't want to lose her way and get caught snooping. What she could see right here was pretty awesome. Celery-green sofas done in a suedelike fabric faced each other in front of a white brick fireplace. Pictures, each with their own lighting, hung on the walls throughout the spacious living and dining rooms. She didn't know a darn thing about art but would bet each one cost more money than she made in a month because they were filled with difficult to identify body parts. And they were difficult to identify because they weren't where they were supposed to be. Kind of like the mess she now found herself in.

How could she be married and not know it? What about the white dress, flowers, rings and vows— preferably of the verbal kind. Her low-heeled pumps clicked on the mosaic tiles in the suite's foyer as she checked the door to make certain it wasn't locked, then peeked outside to see if anyone was standing guard there. No and no, she thought, closing the door.

That didn't mean she wasn't a victim in some bizarre sex slave ring. She'd seen stories. Granted it was far-fetched. When the royal family had taken her under their wing, she'd never suspected another agenda, but what did she know? She thought proxy marriages had gone out with horse-drawn buggies and hoop skirts.

While she was trying to decide whether or not her luggage would slow her down too much when she made a run for it, the door opened and Kardahl joined her in the living room.

"I have news," he said.

She tried to read his expression and when she couldn't, made a hopeful guess. "We're not married."

"On the contrary." He held out a piece of paper. "Is this your signature?"

She took it from him and stared at the familiar scrawl beneath the foreign words. "It looks like mine, but—"

"Were you coerced?" he interrupted.

"No. But I remember a stack of paperwork taller than me and—"

"Not such a very great stack of paperwork then," he interrupted, looking her over from head to toe.

She was going to ignore that. "Not being fluent in the Bha'Kharian language, I couldn't read this. The man who was supposed to be helping me said it was nothing important. That I was simply giving my permission to open records that would unite me with my family."

Kardahl nodded as he took the paper she handed back and set it on the glass-topped coffee table. "In his overzealous desire to serve the king, he may have stretched the truth."

"He lied?"

"Not exactly. Your signature gives your permission to access records, but it also bears witness to your agreement to the marriage by proxy."

"That's absurd. This is 2007. No one gets married by proxy."

"I assure you it is quite real and legal."

As yet, she wasn't outraged to the point where she missed the irony of being this man's bride. Nine out of ten women would be alternately doing the dance of joy and counting their lucky stars. But Kardahl got reluctant woman number ten. But irony worked both ways. She was apparently *legally* married to her worst nightmare. That kicked her outrage into over-drive.

She put her hands on her hips. "How do you know I'm not already married?"

"Do you not think someone would have checked that?"

"I never thought I'd be in a proxy-marriage situation. How did this happen?" she asked, pacing again. "Why did I draw the short straw?" At his blank look she translated, "Why me?"

"Your mother's lineage can be traced back to royalty and there is a long friendship between our families. Many years ago it was decided that her offspring would become the bride of the king's second son—"

"What if she'd had a boy?" Jess demanded.

"But she didn't," he pointed out, far too calmly as his gaze lingered on her breasts. "So when your attorney made inquiries and you were located, plans for the union proceeded."

This was wrong in so many ways, she didn't know where to start. Actually that wasn't entirely accurate. "Did you sign one of those papers, too?"

"Yes."

"Voluntarily?"

"Yes," he answered far too patiently.

The playboy prince signed a marriage agreement without a gun to his head? "Why?"

"It is my destiny. The spare heir is required to marry and produce children."

Since when was he the poster boy for following the rules? "What if I'd never been found?" When he opened his mouth, she held up a finger to stop him. "Don't you dare say 'but you were.'"

The corners of his mouth curved up. "It is not necessary since you have said it for me."

"Then I'll rephrase— What prevented you from getting married before this? If I'd never turned up, would you never have married?"

"A suitable bride would have been selected." He shrugged. "When the time was right."

"So the time was right now? Because I was located?"

"That—and other things." He looked like a naughty little boy caught red-handed.

The expression was cute, she thought, before her outraged self scratched the observation and replaced it. He was no boy. The girly parts of her recognized and responded to his masculinity against her will and better judgment.

"What did you do?" she managed to ask.

"Why do you assume that I am at fault without really knowing me?"

She folded her arms over her chest and looked up. "How can you ask that with a straight face. This is you we're talking about. The whole world knows about your romantic escapades. Of course you did something. What was it this time? I'm sure a woman is involved," she guessed.

"She left her husband, although the separation is not yet legal."

"That would make her a *married* woman. I guess the king wasn't too happy with you."

"Not me so much as it is the pictures of myself and the lady taken with the telephoto lens." He shrugged, but his eyes narrowed. "My father and his advisers made it clear that this was an opportune time to—what is the expression—kill two birds with one stone."

"Squash the scandal and do your duty?"

"Exactly," he agreed.

So the king had one nerve left and Kardahl had gotten on it—and dragged her along with him. She put her hands on her hips. "There's just one problem. I don't want to be married."

"May I ask why?"

"So many reasons, so little time," she said. "And if I did decide to walk down the aisle—and I mean walk down the aisle, not sign a piece of paper and presto you're hitched—you're the last man on the face of the earth I would choose."

Instead of irritation, amusement sparkled in his eyes. "Is that so?"

"Your behavior proves you're not capable of commitment." She waited for his expression to change and when it didn't, she said, "Feel free to deny it and set the record straight. The basis for that opinion comes directly from the tabloids."

"There is no need to deny it. You are correct."

"Then why didn't you refuse to go through with this proxy thing?"

The amusement finally disappeared, replaced by a dark look that made his eyes hard as granite. "It is the price of royal birth. This marriage is about duty."

"That's the thing. There is no marriage because I didn't knowingly give my consent." She never would have given it, especially if she'd known who she was marrying. "In case there's any question, I am not happy about this."

"That is understandable. You have been ill used."

He was agreeing with her again. Why did he keep doing that?

"Come again?"

"You should have been apprised of all the facts of the situation. The aide responsible for this will be severely disciplined."

"That's a start. How severely?" she asked cautiously.

"How severely would you like?"

Good question. How did you chastise someone responsible for marrying you to the kind of man you'd avoided like the stomach flu?

She looked at him. "If the punishment were to fit the crime, he should be forced into a marriage with the last person on the planet he would choose."

"He is already married."

Laughter slid into Kardahl's eyes indicating he got her drift and didn't care that she'd slighted him. Why should he when the world was his playground and all the women in it his adoring toys.

"I see. And does he also have children?" she asked.

"Three."

Ouch. She didn't want to be responsible for the man losing his job when he had a wife and kids depending on him. "Maybe a severe talking to would be enough. Along with a warning not to play with people's lives."

"I will arrange it," he said. He bowed slightly and smiled.

"Don't do that."

"It is a gesture of respect," he explained.

"Not the bow. Don't smile at me."

He tilted his head as he studied her. "You would rather I frown?"

Yes, she thought. For many reasons. Not the least of which was the way his smile made breathing a challenge and threatened her equilibrium. "How can you smile when we still have a big problem? How are you going to get me out of this marriage?"

"It is possible to obtain an annulment," he said.

"Okay," she said nodding. "I'm almost smiling. What do I have to do?"

"You must not consummate the marriage."

This must be hopeless romantic hell. She was discussing sex as if it were a business deal. So much for being swept away. "Okay then, start the paperwork. I promise not to seduce you and I'm quite sure you can't seduce me."

"Are you so very certain?" There was a gleam in his eyes. The glitter of competition, a challenge issued.

"Oh, please. I'm looking for a man who can put his heart and soul into a relationship. You're not that man and we both know it."

"Do we?" He looked at her for a long moment, then shrugged. "If you wish it, I will begin the process of dissolution."

"I wish it very much." Clearly he was being so agreeable because he didn't want to be married. Then a thought struck her. "Is this going to get you in more trouble?"

"Do not worry about me. I will explain to the king and queen."

"There won't be more scandal?" she asked.

"My public relations staff will issue appropriate statements. But—"

"What?"

"If I could prevail upon you to play the part of my wife—only in public," he added, "until any hint of scandal has faded away. You would have my gratitude. And although my family has caused you some distress, they would be forever in your debt as well.

And in the meantime, I will give you every possible assistance in meeting your family."

Family. It's why she'd come halfway around the world. Because she'd had no one after her mother died, she'd always longed to have the problems with relatives that others moaned about. She would cherish interference, being judged and unwanted advice if she gained unconditional love.

"It's a deal," she agreed. "As long as no one expects me to produce children."

His only response was a smile and a look that reminded her of a large hunting cat selecting his prey.

As the limousine drove past the colorful booths of the open marketplace and continued toward the heart of Bha'Khar's capital city, Jessica stared out the window shaking her head.

"Something is not to your liking?" Kardahl asked.

"Everything is fine."

And that was an understatement. True to his promise, he had shown her to her own room and she'd spent the night—alone—in the most beautiful bedroom she'd ever seen with a closet as big as her whole apartment in L.A. The bed was so high, she'd half expected her nose to bleed. The bathroom vanity was marble and all the fixtures were gold. After a pleasant breakfast, Kardahl had told her his staff was contacting her family and while they were waiting for a response he offered to take her on a tour of the city. It was very sweet, but probably part of his scandal-suppressing charade. And she was okay with that.

What saddened her in a soul-deep way was that this lovely, graceful city with its white and pink stucco buildings and red-tile roofs had been her mother's birthplace and Jessica had never known. It was part of who she was and made her feel as if pieces of her heart were missing.

"Tell me what troubles you," he said, his voice deep and gentle.

The gentleness got her. That and the fact that he'd read her so right and wouldn't let her brush him off. "I can't believe that my mother never talked about her country and her family."

"It must have been a bitterly unhappy time for her."

"Why do you say that?" she asked.

He shrugged. "It is a reasonable assumption. One tries to forget unhappy times. Talking of them would simply keep the pain fresh. In addition, the burden would be heavy enough without weighing down a child."

So he thought her mother was protecting her. He looked sincere and it made sense, although she hadn't expected such a depth of understanding from a man with his reputation for superficiality.

She smiled at him. "Whether or not you're right, I find that very comforting." When his cell phone rang, she looked out the window at the Arabian Sea.

The sparkling blue expanse disappeared as they drove down a narrow street with fashionable shops on both sides.

He folded shut his phone and said, "That was my secretary."

He looked at her. "I waited until your arrival to confirm a visit to your family."

"When can I meet them?" she asked eagerly. "I don't know much about them."

"You have two aunts—"

"My mother had two sisters?" Duh. He'd just told her as much. What she'd meant was, she'd always wanted a sister, or a brother. She'd desperately wished for someone so she wouldn't be alone. Her mother had sisters and she'd walked away from that, never looking back. Why?

"One of your aunts," he continued, "is married to the ruler of Bha'Khar's desert people. The other is a doctor who lives in a city to the north of the capital. I have arranged for you to meet them both."

"That would be wonderful." She was almost afraid to ask. "And my grandparents?"

"They are on an extended diplomatic assignment at the request of the foreign service minister. They've been informed of your arrival and will return as soon as possible."

"I see." She sighed.

He frowned. "What is it?"

"I'm disappointed that I have to wait," she

admitted. "I'd hoped to spend as much time as possible getting to know them before I have to return to my job."

"Can you not extend your leave of absence?"

"I suppose I'll have to, but I hate to do that to the kids."

"They are not being cared for while you are gone?"

"It's not that simple. Getting kids to trust when they've lost everyone isn't easy." She knew from personal experience. In fact, she still never let herself believe in anyone with her whole heart. "It's a leave of absence for me, but to them it's one more rejection. One more person who abandoned them."

"They must learn not to put their trust in a single person," he said. "It is a lesson that will serve them well. Would they not be better off without you?"

She shook her head. "Everybody needs somebody sometime. If they don't engage emotionally, they become isolated and antisocial."

"Is not detachment more uncomplicated?"

She stared at him. "This from a man who attaches himself to anything in a skirt—" She pressed her lips together and sighed. "Never mind."

"Do not misunderstand. I have great admiration for your devotion and the conviction that you can make a difference." His tone said it was a waste of time.

"The world would be in sadder shape than it already is if no one tried."

"I wish you luck in your efforts."

This attitude was what she'd expected based on what she'd read about him. And if not for his insight moments ago she never would have questioned it. But she wondered how he could be so understanding and so jaded at the same time.

She was about to ask when she glanced out the window and realized they'd stopped. "Is the tour over?"

His smile was mysterious. "Yes. And now I have a surprise." When the driver opened the door, Kardahl slid out, then held a hand out for her. She took it and he closed his fingers around hers, drawing her to her feet on the sidewalk in front of a dress shop. Then he slipped her hand into the bend of his arm and said, "Come with me."

Inside, the perimeter of the store was lined with women's clothes—dresses, suits, full-length gowns. If one couldn't have a fairy godmother with a magic wand, shopping was the next best thing. But there was nothing magic about her budget and she was pretty sure it wouldn't withstand the prices in this place.

"Why are we here?" she asked.

Before he could answer, a saleswoman appeared, smiling broadly when she recognized Kardahl. "Your Highness, I was delighted when you called. Please give the queen my regards. As you can see, I have canceled all other appointments and closed to the public as you requested. So this is your wife?"

"Jessica," he said.

"She is quite lovely. My congratulations on your marriage."

"Thank you," he said, glancing down at her. "My wife is in need of some clothes. And there is a reception tomorrow night."

"There is—" Jess stopped, not wanting to blow his cover. But it would be helpful if he didn't spring stuff like that on her in public.

The next thing she knew, the woman had whipped out her tape measure and after taking measurements said, "She is a perfect size two. I have some lovely things that will be most flattering to Her Highness."

Jess wasn't anyone's "Highness," but she didn't quite know how to phrase it even if she could persuade someone to listen. Not to mention outing their marriage for the sham it was. The woman bustled around the room plucking a sage-green suit, black silk slacks and several coordinating blouses before disappearing, presumably to a fitting room. When she returned, Kardahl pointed to a slender, black evening gown. "I wish to see her in this."

The saleswoman smiled. "It is fortunate that the gown is her size. And Your Highness has excellent taste."

As well he should, Jess thought. His Highness was a notorious flirt and playboy who no doubt had intimate experience sizing up women as he removed their clothes. The thought made her shiver and that was a problem. Jess's mind was saying no, no, no, while her body grew more curious. And her heart was telling her she'd have to be six feet under to not salivate at the chance to at least try on these clothes. But how could she tell the woman she was wasting her time?

When she disappeared with the evening gown, Jess turned to Kardahl. "Listen up. This isn't necessary. I don't need anything. We both know the annulment is coming. And—"

"And until then, the world will be watching my wife. There is the matter of the reception tomorrow evening." He smiled. "I saw your eyes light up as you looked at everything. It would please me to do this and the least I can do for the inconvenience imposed on you. At least try the things on. The woman would be disappointed if you do not."

"So you're playing the disappointment card again." She sighed. "Is that a royal order?"

"Would you like it to be?"

She sighed. "Yes. It has to be wrong to defy a royal order."

"Indeed," he said.

She heard the smile in his voice as she turned away and left to find the saleswoman. Around the corner was a fitting room with the clothes she recognized hanging on various hooks. Jessica figured she was probably a spineless slug, but what the heck? She was stuck and might as well enjoy the experience.

Everything fit as if made for her and her female

heart was full to bursting at the prospect of wearing such exquisite styles, such delicate, shiny fabrics that rustled when she moved. The saleswoman, Jasmine, bustled in and out, removing items as she brought in more. The black dress Kardahl had picked out was the last thing she tried on.

Jessica looked at herself in the full-length mirror and her eyes went wide. The neck was high and the sleeves long but the soft satin clung to every curve and revealed as much as it concealed. She turned and gasped at the flesh-baring back.

"It is perfect for you." The woman ran her hands over the hips and waist. "His Royal Highness requested only to see you in this."

"He did?"

The woman nodded. "He said to tell you it is a royal order."

The downside of orders were the ones you didn't want to obey. But her choices were to either suck it up, or cause a scene. As she left the dressing room, Jess held the skirt of the gown up to keep from tripping on the long hem. When she walked into the room where Kardahl waited, she held her breath. He stood and took her hand, helping her onto the dais in front of a bank of mirrors before stepping behind her.

Jess could see him in the mirror, the smoldering look in his eyes as his gaze took in every inch of her. Her feet had been on solid ground for twenty-four hours, but her stomach dropped as if she were taking off in the royal jet. The only explanation was emotional drought, she thought. She wasn't used to men looking at her the way he was and it was like setting fire to the dry brush of her romantic heart.

"I don't think this suits me," she said breathlessly.

"It suits me," he said, his voice as deep and appealing as sin. "We will take it with us," he informed the saleswoman.

Jess said nothing because she wouldn't embarrass the royal family in public. But elegant and costly clothes wouldn't change anything. She might have been chosen for a prince, but she wasn't raised as a princess. All she wanted to do was get to know her family, then go back to her life.

By the time she was dressed in her off-the-rack slacks and shirt, the dress was in a protective bag and Kardahl had arranged for the rest of the clothes to be delivered to the palace. When they stepped out of the store, the crowd gathered outside suddenly surged forward, flashbulbs exploding from every direction.

"Who's the lady, Your Highness?" asked one reporter.

"Is she married, Your Highness?"

Someone shoved a microphone in Jessica's face. "How did you and Prince Kardahl meet?"

Without comment, Kardahl pulled her to him, using his body to shield her from the cameras. Then he thrust her into the waiting limousine.

As she struggled to control her hammering heart, Jess looked at Kardahl. The expression of fury on his face was completely and utterly shocking. Something told her this reaction wasn't about unauthorized pictures or unflattering photo angles. This was a deeply emotional response.

She wondered where the easygoing, charming flirt had gone when she didn't want to wonder about him at all.

CHAPTER THREE

How ironic to have a skirmish with the paparazzi only hours before this meeting with the king and queen. Kardahl had once hoped the woman he would be presenting to his parents as his wife would be another, but thanks to his father, that was never to be. Still, the time had come for introductions.

Now he sat beside Jessica on the sofa in his parents' living room. Faline and Amahl Hourani, made the side by side overstuffed chairs look like thrones as they studied their "daughter-in-law." They had once scrutinized the woman of his choice and found her wanting, but tonight they looked pleased. At least someone was, he thought.

His father's dark hair was flecked with gray on the sides, giving him what most thought a distinguished look. Kardahl had no feeling one way or the other. He only knew the king was a rigid and uncompromising man, difficult to please and stubborn. Kardahl would never forgive him for refusing to waive tradition so that he could marry the woman he wanted.

Unlike her husband, his dark-eyed mother would not permit a gray hair to invade her lustrous, shoulder-length hair. For a small woman, she possessed a strength of will and sense of humor that kept her husband both intrigued and in line. At one time, Kardahl had hoped to emulate their relationship. Those hopes had died with his beloved.

"Are you sure you will not join us in a brandy, Jessica?" his mother asked.

"Thank you, no. Coffee is fine." Jessica set her china cup on the saucer resting on the side table.

She was casually dressed in black slacks and a co-ordinating silky black and white blouse. Her hair was pulled back into a loose bun at her nape, with numerous sun-kissed strands escaping the confinement to caress her graceful neck. The scent of her skin filled his head with the fragrance of sunshine and flowers as her shoulder brushed his own. She seemed unaffected by the nearness, but he was not so fortunate.

"I understand you had your first experience with reporters today, my dear," the king was saying.

"Yes, Your Highness."

The king turned a displeased look on him. "How did this happen, Kardahl?"

He had wondered also and made inquiries of his security staff. "It seems there is a site on the Internet where the sighting of a high-profile individual can be posted practically as it is occurring."

Jessica stared at him. "You mean anyone monitoring that site who happened to be in the area could walk up and shake your hand?"

"Yes," he said grimly. "My guess is that the news media monitors the site."

"But that's practically stalking."

"In a free society," the king said, "it is the price we pay. Also part of the cost is minding one's behavior. As Kardahl knows all too well."

Jessica glanced up at him with what looked like sympathy in her eyes, then back to his father. "I can't help feeling responsible. They found him because he surprised me with a detour to the dress shop—"

"You took her to Jasmine's as I suggested?" his mother interrupted.

"I did," he confirmed, sliding his arm along the top of the sofa, then resting his fingers close to Jessica's shoulder.

Until that first meeting on the plane, Kardahl had been annoyed at the turn of events, but had subsequently learned that Jessica was even less pleased than he about the situation. She was an unwilling participant and unprepared for this life. And the look on her face when the paparazzi had besieged him had made him want to protect her. As he had been unable to protect Antonia.

"Those people are predators who feed off others," he commented.

The queen sighed as she shook her head. "The press can be difficult."

"I just wasn't prepared for them," Jessica said. "Up until today the most excitement I ever had shopping was when the clerk forgot to remove one of those security devices and I set off the alarm when I tried to leave the store."

The king smiled indulgently. "My dear, if you would change your mind and stay with Kardahl here in Bha'Khar, you would be given instruction in dealing with the media."

"Probably not by Kardahl," Jessica said, glancing up at him with humor sparkling like jewels in her eyes. "Unless he used himself as a cautionary tale."

His father laughed. "No. I think my son would not be the best instructor." Then he turned serious as he met her gaze, "I urge you to change your mind about the annulment."

"You're very kind—"

"I hear a 'but,'" the king interrupted. "Your grandparents are dear friends. They would be greatly pleased by a real marriage to join our families."

"You're very kind," Jessica said again. "*But,* I'm not royal family material. In spite of the betrothal, circumstances intervened and I wasn't raised to be the wife of a prince."

Kardahl saw her fingers clasp and tighten until the

knuckles turned white as she rubbed one thumb over the other. When he glanced at her face, the tension in her delicate jaw and shadows in her eyes did not escape his notice.

"You would have a staff to help and the queen and I would—"

"Enough." Apparently Kardahl had to protect her from his father as well as the press. He rose. "Jessica has expressed her feelings and I will not permit you to pressure her."

"Kardahl." The queen frowned. "That is no way to speak to your father."

"For the time being she is my wife and in this instance, it is precisely the way. I have promised her a tour of the palace. We are leaving now."

Surprise flickered in Jessica's expression when she looked up. Before she could expose his lie, he held out his hand. "Are you ready?"

"Yes." She put her fingers in his palm and stood up, then smiled at his parents. "Thank you for dinner."

"You are most welcome," his mother said. "We look forward to seeing you at the reception tomorrow evening."

"And you as well, my son." There was anger in the king's order.

"I will be there."

For Jessica. Kardahl led her to the elevator that would take them to the first floor. He was impervious to his father's moods now. Once he had cared, but that ended when the king chose tradition over happiness. If Kardahl had been allowed to marry the woman he wanted, she might still… But that was something he would never know. His fingers clenched into a fist as the rage-fueled powerlessness blazed through him. He had learned it was preferable to the pain.

Jessica looked up at him. "Are you all right?"

"I am fine."

She pointed. "That vein throbbing in your forehead says you're lying."

Instinctively he touched his temple and smiled reluctantly. "Let me rephrase. I will be fine."

"Thanks for coming to my rescue in there, but you didn't need to. Your father didn't upset me. I know he was just trying to help."

"He was attempting to impose his will on you. Tradition is more important to him than anything."

She folded her arms over her chest and stared straight ahead. "I understand that my opinion is flawed because I never had traditions or relatives telling me what to do. But I don't think you appreciate how lucky you are to have a family who cares about you."

When the elevator doors opened, he waited for her to precede him, then pressed the button. "You are correct."

"I'm glad you see that they love you."

He smiled. "Your opinion is flawed."

"Right." She smiled. "Everyone has flaws. We learn to overlook the worst in the people we love. But I got the feeling that there's something going on between you and your father."

Not any longer. "You are mistaken."

She studied him. "No. You were really angry with him and it was more than the fact that he was trying to change my mind about the annulment."

"We disagree about many things."

"I gathered. But it was also clear to me that your parents love you." She held up her hand when he started to say something. "When you've longed for it like I have, you learn to see it in others. So don't even tell me my opinion is flawed."

"I would not dream of it." On the ground floor, they stepped from the elevator onto the marble tile and Kardahl held out his hand. "This way."

At the end of the short hall, he pulled wide a door that opened into the garden and surrounded them with the scent of flowers and warm sultry air. Inside the walls surrounding the extensive palace grounds, strategically placed lights underscored the proud palms, fragrant jasmine and lush greenery.

Eyes wide, Jessica looked around and breathed deeply. "Kardahl, it's beautiful."

"I thought you would like it here. It is where I come when I wish to—"

"Let your testosterone levels return to normal before you put your fist through a wall?"

"Just so," he said, his mouth twitching as a grin threatened.

Kardahl found himself intrigued by his reluctant bride.

It was said that misfortune built integrity and by that measure, he had much character to spare as did she. Although that was just a guess based on what little she had said about her life. She had edited out almost everything, claiming it was unimportant. He had heard the words, but the pain in her eyes and tension in her voice had said she was lying.

"It's perfect," she said, clearly awed. "I wish I could stay here forever."

He watched her wordlessly take in the garden's natural beauty and thought her own natural beauty a pleasing addition to this serene place. She was like a flower in the desert—strong, resilient and unexpectedly lovely.

"You may come here whenever you wish." He took her hand and placed it in the bend of his elbow, leading her down the path that curved through the flourishing plants.

"But I won't be here that long," she reminded him.

"All the more reason to take advantage while you are able."

"Do you appreciate this? Or do you take it for granted? Like your family?"

"Perhaps," he said with a shrug. He did not take

offense at the question because he had finally read the investigator's report on her life and knew for a fact she had left out much, including that the cause of her mother's death was alcohol abuse. "I cannot change my father any more than you could change what happened to your mother."

She pulled away from him and folded her arms protectively over her chest. For many moments she was silent but finally she met his gaze. "What do you know about my mother?"

"Everything."

"How?"

"When you were located, my father had your background researched."

"And our 'marriage' moved forward even though my mother never married anyone, including my father." Her tone was rife with bitter irony. "But she never stopped looking for 'Mr. Right,' even though every time she thought she'd found him, he let her down."

"Yes." The report had been quite thorough.

"And each time she lost a little more of herself."

"That must have been very difficult."

She looked at him and a fierce protectiveness flashed in her eyes cutting through the pain. "When she was really there, she was my best friend. She listened and we talked. And I miss her still."

"I understand."

"No, you don't. How could you? Your family is

alive and well and all living here in this big, beautiful palace with the gorgeous grounds. And you don't appreciate them." She stopped suddenly at the end of the path and pointed. "What's this?"

He glanced at the salmon-colored stucco walls with their stained-glass windows and graceful red-tile roof. The structure had been closed up since before he was born. "This is the harem."

"Really?" Curiosity shimmered in her eyes, replacing the sadness and successfully distracting her. "So this is where the royal men stash their women?"

"Actually, no. There is a dungeon beneath the palace and secret passages—"

"You're joking," she said.

"Yes." He tried the door to the building and found it locked. "The harem has been abandoned for many years. I believe my grandmother delivered an ultimatum to the king who bowed to her wishes."

"Wow. That sounds like a romantic story."

"I do not know." But if it would keep her eyes shining, he would find out the details.

"I wonder—" She peeked through the window.

He moved beside her, leaning a shoulder against the wall. "What do you wonder?"

"What it would be like to live in a harem." She bent from side to side and stood on tiptoe, trying to see through the stained glass. "Waiting for the call to get in the game. When you're chosen."

"It was more than sex," he explained, noting the

blush that pinkened her cheeks. "Years ago it was a necessity to produce many children in order to ensure the line of succession. The infant mortality rate was very high. Now medical advances make it less important."

"And the women of the world are your harem." She met his gaze, daring a contradiction.

He had sought comfort and forgetfulness in the arms of many and achieved it with none. In this, too, her opinion was flawed, but there was no point in correcting her misconception. Her favorable opinion of his character mattered little to him because it would change nothing.

She met his gaze and smiled. "So, when my background was researched, was there anything about me being harem-worthy?"

Kardahl's gaze was drawn to her mouth and his pulse quickened along with his heart. What would those lush lips feel like? Taste like? "There is only one way to answer your question."

"How?"

He straightened, then cupped her cheek in his palm as he brushed his thumb back and forth over her mouth. "Like this," he said, lowering his head.

The lips that could coax a man into sin without uttering a word tasted even more exceptional than they looked. Softness he had expected, but the innocence he sampled ignited his blood like a torch to kerosene. He cradled her face in both hands and tunneled his fingers into her hair, drinking from her mouth yet unable to quench his passion.

He caught her breathy purr of desire on his lips and felt her hand settle on his chest, over his heart. The touch pitched him into a stormy sea of need, tossing in the turbulence of her temptation. This he had not felt for… Lifting his head, he stared at her bewitching, kiss-swollen mouth. Her breathing was uneven, her eyes glazed with an erotic expression he did not believe she knew was there.

"It is time to—" He swallowed and willed indifference into his tone. Dropping his hands as if she had suddenly burned him, he said, "I will take you back inside."

"G-good idea."

Kardahl was careful not to touch her as they walked back. For two years he had lived with the ghosts of what would never be. Since meeting Jessica, the ghosts had receded for a time, which was unexpected. And unfortunate.

He was comfortable with the pain he carried and did not wish for more. He would not add to his burden by caring again and this bewildering attraction made him grateful that his wife wished to pursue an annulment. He had allowed himself to want women, but this woman could be dangerous to the indifference he had so carefully cultivated.

Knowing she would meet the press, Jessica had thought she was prepared for the reception. She'd been wrong. The black designer gown didn't help. The diamond tiara in the upswept hairdo crafted by the queen's personal hairdresser didn't help. And the professionally applied makeup didn't help. The only thing that kept her from full and humiliating retreat was Kardahl's presence beside her.

He looked pretty spectacular in his black tux and snow-white shirt. But she hadn't had time to fully appreciate that either before this command performance when the announcement of her marriage to His Royal Highness Kardahl Hourani had been made. After a silence that hadn't lasted nearly long enough, the press started firing questions. Kardahl had fielded them easily.

"How did you meet?" someone shouted.

"Are female hearts breaking around the world?"

"Are you really settling down?"

That question brought back memories of the harem where the royal men had gone in years past to satisfy needs. Needs she understood a little better after Kardahl's kiss—a kiss that had come dangerously close to sweeping her away. The feel of his muscular body against hers had ignited a yearning she hadn't known was there.

"Where are you from, Princess?"

The called out question jarred her back to the far less pleasant present.

"How do you feel about landing the playboy prince?"

"You make him sound like a fish," she said. The bright lights made her squint and she resisted the urge to raise a hand and shield her eyes from the constant flashes of light. It was blinding; it was disorienting. It was weird not to be able to see who you were answering.

"What do you do?"

"Will you keep working?"

"When are you going to have a baby?"

"Are you already pregnant?"

The personal questions shouted out so indifferently, so publicly, felt like a personal violation. The last one made her gasp as if she'd been slapped.

Kardahl put his arm around her waist and drew her to his side. "Enough. This interview is over."

The next thing she knew, he was escorting her from the room. After he'd guided her through several doors and shut each one after them, the noise finally receded. He took her hand and led her through a set of French doors and outside onto a balcony with a view of the city lights in the distance. Blessed quiet embraced her along with the pleasantly warm night air.

She breathed in deeply. "I take it back."

"What?"

"When I said you wouldn't be the right person to advise me about dealing with the media. I was wrong. That escape was well done."

He bowed slightly. "I am pleased that you approve."

This knight-in-shining-armor impersonation

didn't fit her formed opinion of him. Was it flawed along with her family sensibilities? Her only legacy from her mother was caution toward men. And this man's exploits chronicled in publications around the world had proven that he wouldn't know commitment if it walked up and shook his hand. So was she wrong about that, too? Or was he a heroic rogue? Was that an oxymoron? Or was she simply a moron for giving this situation more thought than it warranted.

She stood on the tiled balcony in a puddle of moonlight. The last time she'd been outside with him alone, he'd kissed her. The memory made her mouth tingle and she needed to say something to take the edge off her tension.

"You're good at handling the press."

"I have had much practice. As a member of the royal family, I was born into the life of public servant. It is my duty to serve the people of Bha'Khar."

"Female people?" she couldn't help asking. Apparently the tension still had an edge. The words popped out before she could stop them. She didn't mean to be abrupt, opinionated and abrasive. She wasn't normally like this. But he, and more to the point his kiss, had brought out the worst in her. Maybe it was her defense mechanism.

With the French doors behind him, he was backlit and his facial expression concealed in shadow. But the statement had barely left her mouth when his body went rigid with tension.

"I am the minister of Finance and Defense." The words were clipped and precise.

"I'm surprised you have the time, what with pursuing women all over the world." There was the legacy of caution rearing its ugly head again.

"Is it so hard for you to believe that I can put my responsibilities before personal pleasure?"

"In a word? Yes."

"Little fool." His tone made her shiver even though the evening was far from cold. "I am not an unfeeling man."

"Then the scandalous photos are misleading? And everything I've read about you is wrong?"

"You should not believe everything you read in anything but an approved interview."

"So, in spite of what they print, you are open to love?"

He slid his hands into the pockets of his tuxedo pants, marring the perfect line of the matching black jacket. When he turned to the side, light from inside revealed the muscle tensing in his jaw. She thought he wasn't going to answer.

"No," he said. "I am not open to love."

She was surprised he would admit it. "Have you ever been in love?"

She hoped her voice was calm because the rest of her was anything but. His answer shouldn't matter to her but she found every one of her senses finely tuned as she waited for his response.

"Yes," he finally bit out. "I have loved. And she is dead."

CHAPTER FOUR

IF THERE had been anything in the press about this, Jessica had missed it, but that wasn't surprising. Between college and part-time jobs, the world went by and she'd missed everything until after graduation. But everything she'd said to him and the raw pain on Kardahl's face now made her feel lower than a slug. Whatever life-form that was, she was worse. Her only defense was that nothing like this had crossed her mind. Death didn't touch the fabulously wealthy and famous.

She realized that was stupid and knew she tended to romanticize. Everyone got sick; fatal diseases didn't discriminate between old and young, rich and poor.

She needed to say something, but all she could think of was, "What happened?"

His jaw was rigid and edgy anger rolled off him in waves. "It was two years ago," he started, his voice even and low and all the more dangerous for its softness. "An accident."

Not an illness? "How?"

"We were chased relentlessly by reporters who wanted a picture, a story, a word that could be made into a story." He walked to the low balcony wall and looked out into the distance where the lights of the city on the coast twinkled brightly. "Antonia was upset that we were followed, as we had taken great pains to be alone. She absolutely insisted the driver attempt to outrun the horde of photographers although both of us tried to calm her. The roads were wet. The car flipped. She died instantly. Unfortunately I did not."

Now it was the lack of anger in his voice that frightened her. She moved beside him and settled her hand on his arm. When he met her gaze, light caught the scars on his lip and cheek. She reached up and started to touch them, but he ducked away.

"Is that how you got those?" she asked.

"What does it matter?"

That would be yes. Oh God. An apology would be in order, but she didn't even know where to start. "Kardahl, I didn't know. If I had, I'd never have brought up such a painful subject. I'm very sorry. Please accept my deepest condolences on the loss of your wife—"

"Not my wife," he bit out, the anger spontaneous and underlining each word.

"But if you loved her—I don't—"

"The king held tightly to tradition and I was betrothed to another."

He'd been betrothed to her, Jessica realized.

She'd stood between him and the woman he'd desperately wanted and couldn't have—now he would never have his Antonia. She felt responsible, which was stupid since she'd known nothing about him, Bha'Khar or the tradition that was responsible for her being duped into this marriage. But the resentment and lingering pain in his eyes told her he wouldn't want to hear any of that.

"I think now I understand the animosity between you and your father. Under the circumstances, why did you agree to go through with the proxy marriage?"

The hard expression in his eyes made her flinch when he turned his gaze on her. "Because it ceased to matter."

As in he disregarded all women equally because he'd cared too much about one. Jessica was shocked and ashamed in equal parts. She'd misjudged him horribly and insulted him to his face even though he'd been unfailingly polite to her. This rage and resentment were emotions he'd kept well hidden.

From her own experience she knew that the bitterest of tears shed over a grave were for words left unsaid or things left undone. What was it that Kardahl had not been able to say or do?

"I have arranged for you to have riding lessons," Kardahl said the morning after the reception.

During breakfast, he was still trying to understand why he had told Jessica of Antonia. Perhaps because Jessica had provoked him. Or he'd grown weary of her low opinion. Either way, she'd caused him to feel something and he did not like it. All the more reason to facilitate the meetings with her family and send her back to America.

He had instructed Jessica to put on jeans, then escorted her from the palace to the extensive equestrian area where he would personally instruct her. They were standing just outside the stable and the mount he'd chosen for her was saddled and waiting by the fence beside them. "Have you any experience with horses?"

"Why do I need to learn to ride?"

"I was under the impression that you wished to meet your family."

She tucked a strand of hair behind her ear. "Call me dense, but I don't see what one has to do with the other."

"You will need to learn basic riding skills if you are to meet your aunt."

"I can hardly wait," she said eagerly. Her joyous expression turned to puzzlement. "But why do I need to learn to ride?"

"The desert wanderers have settled into their summer encampment in the hills. Horseback is the favored mode of transportation."

She took a step back and looked up at him. "Why can't we take the helicopter? You've got one, right?

Your brother was telling me about the royal yacht and I've already seen the plane. Surely there's a chopper in the family."

"There is. But the terrain is too mountainous." He folded his arms over his chest and struggled not to smile. She had a way about her that reduced the monumental to mundane. "So—I must know what you know about horses."

"I've seen them in the movies and on TV. Does that count?" When the animal beside them shook its head and snorted, she laughed and said, "Busted."

But the look of wariness on her face answered his question more completely than her impudent reply. Kardahl watched the sunlight pick out the gold in Jessica's hair.

He decided she was much like that precious metal—gold—there was a richness to her spirit that was only uncovered when one searched deeper.

As she continued to study the horse, she caught her top lip between her teeth. He was unwillingly reminded of the unfamiliar kind of need her kiss had unleashed inside him. It was a weakness he could not repeat. She thought him shallow and unfeeling, but he would prove that he was trustworthy and would not break his promise. Another kiss would sorely test that resolve.

"Only hands-on experience counts," he said and winced.

"Okay. If that's the only way, then point me in the direction of whoever's going to show me what to do."

"I am going to teach you."

"You?"

He could have assigned one of the eminently qualified grooms, but he'd been unwilling to do so. As to his motivation? It was a decision for which he had no answer.

"Yes. I am an expert rider—" When she opened her mouth to say something, he touched his finger to her lips to silence her, and hated himself for wishing to use his mouth instead. "Do not say you have read of my exploits."

"I wasn't going to." The pink on her cheeks made it appear that she was blushing. A decidedly innocent and refreshing reaction. "I was going to say that you've been very generous with your time since I arrived and I'm feeling guilty about that." She looked down at the red dirt where they stood then backed up.

Traces of guilt lingered in her eyes, but he was certain that had more to do with what he'd revealed to her on the balcony last night. That was less important than why he'd revealed the tragedy. Perhaps her uneasiness at the barrage of media curiosity had unleashed his instinct to protect her along with some deeply buried feelings of grief.

He nudged her chin up with his knuckle as he wished to really see into her eyes. "I do not believe it is my time that is the source of your guilt."

"What other reason could there be?" The question was a diversion but couldn't hide the truth.

"Perhaps you feel that you have misjudged me?"

Her gaze skittered away again. "I'll admit that I was wrong in believing you incapable of sincere feeling. But the fact is your name is linked to many women."

So, she still thought him a womanizer. That was good. He had nothing to give any woman and her poor opinion would keep her at arm's length.

"There have been many women," he said. "But now I am married to only one," he reminded her.

"Temporarily."

"Agreed. But for the duration, you will have my undivided attention."

"That's what I was afraid of," she muttered.

"I beg your pardon?"

"I'll show you what I'm made of," she amended.

He smiled. "In return, I will make certain you are prepared for the journey and I will accompany you myself to see that no harm comes to you."

"Again— Don't you have more important things to do?"

"I have made arrangements. Besides, I promised to help you meet with your family. Despite what you have read about me, I am a man of my word."

"Okay." Then she looked at the horse and caught her top lip between her teeth again. "So… Where do we start?"

"As with any relationship, you must begin by making friends."

Her look was wry. "There are so many things I could say, but it would be too easy. I'm holding back."

"A wise decision." He took her hand and placed it on the animal's neck. "Stroke her and let her become accustomed to your touch and your scent."

As Jessica obeyed his command, he observed her small white hand move hypnotically up and down the chestnut nose and neck of the animal. The scent of this woman invaded *his* senses and he was suddenly and acutely aroused.

"If you are ready," he said, wondering if she heard the rasp in his voice, "It is time to mount."

She let out a breath. "Okay."

Fortunately she did not look at him. "Put your left foot in the stirrup, your hand on the saddle. Then push yourself up and swing your right leg over the horse's rump."

Her movements were slow, awkward, and his fingers itched to reach out and help. But he did not— for two reasons. She needed to learn. And the white cotton shirt and worn jeans that hugged her body intrigued him. He did not trust himself to touch her.

When she was securely sitting atop the animal, she smiled down at him. "Mission accomplished."

"Hardly." He laughed as he handed her the reins. "Mission begun."

He explained how to control the horse by right and left movements with the reins. Then he guided the animal into the corral and with a gentle pat on the rump, it started to walk in a circle. As with all beginners, her backside slapped the leather of the saddle as she bounced up and down.

"Grip with your inner thighs to go with the animal's gait."

Her face wore a look of fierce concentration and he knew she was trying to comply. But Kardahl pictured twisted sheets and her legs around him and the vision produced an intense state of sexual frustration. Forcing away the images, he said, "Don't bounce."

"It's not my fault. The horse is bouncing and I'm just going along for the ride. No pun intended," she said breathlessly.

She continued to bobble like a rag doll and he knew the best and fastest way to get his point across was hands on instruction. Against his better judgment, he swung up behind her and put his hands on her thighs. "Press with your inner thighs. Use your legs or your backside will be most unhappy."

"That makes two of us," she snapped. "I'm trying to use my legs."

And he was trying not to picture them around his waist.

He forced himself to focus on the task at hand. Pressing against her, he used his body to help her get the feel of controlling the animal. For the next hour, he tortured himself, feeling her close. Touching her. Smelling the floral scent of her hair. With every ounce of his will, he attempted to douse the fire she started inside him, but was less than successful. That was unfortunate, because he'd given his word that he would not seduce her.

But it had been easy to give his word before he'd begun to want her.

Anger welled up inside him, like it had last night on the balcony. But now he understood why. He'd forced himself to feel nothing for the last two years, and Jessica was changing that.

Kardahl had promised not to touch her and he would keep his word even though her kiss had told him it was possible to have her despite her denial. He would keep his word because he had no wish to hurt her. He would keep his word because fate had taken from him what he cherished most. At night when he closed his eyes, he remembered the sounds—the screech of brakes, the crash and grinding of metal. Antonia's terrified scream—the last sound he ever heard from her.

He had not been able to stop the reeling and rolling vehicle. In the dark he had not been able to find her. He had been able to do nothing to change the fact that he had lost the woman he loved and the child she carried that he had only just begun to love. He never wanted to feel so out of control again and since then had learned to control the only thing he could—his feelings. He ruled them with an iron will because the only way he could be sure he would never go through such agony again was to never again let himself feel.

CHAPTER FIVE

As HER horse skittered and danced on the mountain trail, Jessica wasn't so much worried about pain in her backside as she was about keeping her backside in the saddle. Riding beside her, Kardahl reined in then reached over and patted her horse's neck as he spoke soothingly. He had worked with her every day for a week and finally pronounced her skills limited, but adequate for the trip.

"You must relax," he said to her. When she opened her mouth to deny it, he simply cocked his head and stared.

"All right. It's my own fault. When you said we'd be there soon, I got excited."

"Your mount senses this and reacted."

"Even though I'm excited in a good way?"

His serious expression turned wry. "She is smart, but incapable of discerning the fine distinctions of your mood. She knows only that you are not relaxed and this makes her afraid."

"She's not the only one."

"I told you that I would let no harm come to you."

His look was ultrasincere, identical to the one he'd worn when he'd first made that promise and insisted he accompany her on this trip. She'd tried to talk him out of it without revealing the real reason she was reluctant for him to come along. She didn't want to spend time with him.

Since he'd told her about losing his love, she could feel her attitude slipping and she was counting on it to defend her against his three-pronged assault: charm, humor and looks. She needed time to reassert her neutrality, but he hadn't given it to her. Because, she realized glancing around the isolation of the mountains, she figured he was using the time, too, time to let the news of his marriage settle in with the press.

She glanced at him beside her, and her heart gave a little lurch. Although she wanted to blame it on the horse, it was all about the dashing figure he cut in the saddle. Sitting tall and proud, he looked every inch a prince of the desert. High polished boots covered his muscular calves. She'd have thought snug riding breeches would make a man look like a sissy, but not this man. And the loose cotton shirt with wide sleeves that caught the wind was buttoned to a vee that revealed just a hint of dark chest hair, making her want to see more. So much for shoring up her attitude.

"I'm not afraid of falling off my horse," she explained. "At least that's not the only thing."

"What else troubles you?"

Scanning the grass and trees of the hills, she wondered at a country with such diversity of terrain. This was so different from the sand and rocks in the desert below. With a security detail discreetly in attendance, they'd driven from the palace as far as possible, then climbed on horses for the part not accessible to even the sturdiest vehicle—or the family helicopter. Now she could see why. The path was narrow and wouldn't accommodate anything wider than the hips of her trusty mood-sensing mount. And of course Kardahl's.

The thing was, in thirty minutes she might get a family, something she'd wanted for as long as she could remember and thought she would never have. Or, they might shun her because she was the result of her mother's affair with a married man. They'd agreed to meet and that boded well, but she knew nothing about her family. Maybe her mother had good reason for running away and never contacting them again. Jess had always wondered and wanted family, but now that there was a chance, if it didn't work out she knew the fall would be bad. A bruised backside was nothing compared to the bruising her soul would take.

"What if they don't like me?" she blurted out. She sounded like a kid and knew her insecurity was showing. And she wished anyone but Kardahl had seen it, but he was the only one here.

He put his hand over hers. "If they don't like you, then they are stupid and the loss is theirs."

The words pushed the lump of emotion from her chest into her throat and she swallowed once. "I'm sorry. Were you being funny?"

"No."

"Just checking." Her voice cracked and she wished he wouldn't be nice. Although, with the exception of that kiss, he'd been unfailingly nice. And she couldn't blame him for her own wicked streak that made her want him to be less polite and give her another chance to kiss him.

She looked away from the sensual curve of his mouth, at the sun descending toward the top of a distant peak. She didn't want him to see that her tension went deeper than humor could hide. She'd already let him see too much and blamed it on the fact that he'd shown her deep feelings of which she hadn't thought him capable. It just made everything more complicated and would have been so much easier if he'd stayed back at the palace like any self-respecting playboy prince.

They rode in silence for a while and when she felt her nerves pull tight again, she decided it was in her best interest to let him take her mind off things so her horse wouldn't spook.

"Tell me about the desert people," she asked.

He glanced over, then back at the path. "They are wanderers."

"Why? If anyone knows the value in putting down roots, it's me."

"Tradition is their roots. Two hundred years ago a son of the king challenged the rightful heir to the throne." He looked at her. "That is when the bloodlines split."

"So there's a rebellious streak in my family tree."

His only answer was a smile that turned her insides to liquid smoke. "The rebel and his followers were turned away and took refuge in the far reaches of the desert, far from the capital. Since then, they have protected Bha'Khar's borders from invading enemies. Now they maintain the customs of their ancestors and live off the land. They raise cattle, sheep and some of the finest horses in the world. To escape the heat and find grazing land for the stock, they take to the mountains as the summer months approach."

"When I was a little girl, my mother told me stories at bedtime, about the mountains and skilled riders. But I thought it was something she made up."

As Jessica watched the sun disappear behind the mountain, she felt a connection. Maybe she'd inherited a little of that skill and it's what made horseback riding come easily to her. The downside of inherited traits were the less positive ones—like attraction to what you knew was bad for you. Like Kardahl, she thought, glancing over as the wind blew his black hair and highlighted the noble brow and strong jaw. He might be capable of deep feeling once. But now he went from woman to woman on a regular basis, just like every man in her mother's life.

But as they reached the top of the mountain and a village came into view, she was awfully grateful for his presence. His brief history of her people had taken her mind off her anxiety. His steady voice and presence had kept her calm when fear washed over her, the same fear she'd felt when her plane landed in Bha'Khar. She looked at him and realized it wasn't the same fear at all because she'd been alone in that plane and she wasn't now.

As they rode into camp, women and children lined the dirt road, smiling shyly. Kardahl reined in his horse when they reached the center of the village. Jess could see now that the buildings were wooden frames, and semipermanent, but the walls were canvas that could be rolled up for easy transport.

By the time her horse stopped, Kardahl had dismounted. When she prepared to slide down, he reached up and lifted her to the ground. The feel of his strong hands as he let her body graze his own sent tingles of awareness arrowing through her and she realized she was feeling a fear like she'd never felt before.

She'd grown up believing she was alone and had come halfway around the world to meet someone who shared her DNA. It was about to happen. Not only had he facilitated this moment, Kardahl hadn't left her alone. And it was wonderful.

Impulsively she threw her arms around his neck in a hug. "Thank you for bringing me."

"Had I known such a sweet reward awaited, I would have increased the pace," he said, pulling her tight against him.

The seductive humor in his voice brought a flush to her cheeks as she stepped out of his sheltering embrace. This was just part of their deal and so far he'd been her sheikh-in-shining-armor. But it wasn't something she could count on; it was a temporary truce. When she was alone again, and there was no doubt in her mind she would be, unlike her mother she wouldn't be devastated—for two important reasons.

Jessica wasn't expecting romance. And she would be the one to walk away.

She turned and saw a woman with dark hair and eyes coming toward them. "Jessica?"

"Yes."

"I am Aminah. Your mother Maram was my older sister. It is my pleasure to meet you." She smiled her mother's smile.

Jess's eyes filled with tears. "I don't have the words to tell you what it means to me to meet you—" Her voice cracked and she pressed a hand over her mouth as emotion swamped her.

Arms enveloped her again, this time maternal. It was her mother's sister holding her and patting her

back and hair as she whispered words that were
nothing—and everything.

"Do not weep, little one. This is a joyous occasion."

"I know." Jess pulled back a little then hugged her
aunt again. After all, she had twenty-three years of
hugs to make up for. Beside her, the horses snorted
and pawed their hooves across the dirt. She glanced
at Kardahl. "This is His Royal Highness Kardahl
Hourani. My husband," she added. She met his gaze.
"This is my aunt Aminah."

Her insides lit up like a Christmas tree at being
able to introduce a family member, other than her
mother, for the first time in her life.

Aminah nodded. "Your Highness, welcome."

"Thank you."

"We received word of your impending arrival and
my husband regrets that he could not be here to greet
you. He is overseeing the birth of a prized foal. It is
unexpected and he sends his apologies to you and the
niece he is most anxious to meet."

She had an uncle, too, Jess thought. Along with
her inner-Christmas tree, she felt like the kid who'd
just opened the gift she'd asked Santa for.

"Please come inside. Rest after your journey."

Her aunt turned away and Jess noticed that the
dress she wore was a colorful fabric made of inter-
woven blue and gold strands. Inside the house
propane-fueled lanterns illuminated the interior. In
the corner, a wooden frame piled with pillows and

blankets served as the bed. There were more pillows grouped around a table in the living area and a small wooden table and chairs sat off to the side.

"Please sit," her aunt instructed.

When they did, she poured water into glasses and set out bread and cheese.

Jessica was too excited to eat. "Now that I'm here, I don't know what to say," she admitted.

"Nor I. Although there is much to catch up on."

"Kardahl said that you—my family—searched after my mother left."

She nodded sadly. "That is true. Maram—"

"To me she was Mary," Jess explained. "I'm not sure where the name Sterling came from."

Her aunt looked puzzled. "It was not your father's surname."

"You know him?" Jess asked.

"I know who he was. And that he betrayed my sister's trust." Her aunt sat and took Jess's hands into her own. "Do not feel shame, my niece. There is none for you. Sadly my sister— I wish, as do my parents that she had come to us. But pride prevented it and we cannot change the past." She smiled at Kardahl. "Tradition has found a way and your betrothed returned. It pleases my family."

"Mine as well," he said.

Jessica couldn't tell what he was thinking, but his tone was polite, although when his gaze collided with hers the gleam there told her he was thinking of their nonconsummation pact. Then she was distracted when her aunt asked questions about her mother and growing up in America. Jess decided to keep the painful details of her mother's illness to herself, but her aunt was distressed about the fact that she'd grown up in a state home.

Her eyes filled with tears. "Had we but known, you would have been brought to your family. That I was not there for you is a regret that I will carry all the days of my life."

"You had no way of knowing," Jess said. But it was as if the good intentions started closing up the hole in her heart. "It's all right."

"It is not. I know how swiftly the years pass and what I have missed. My own children have grown so quickly—"

"I have cousins?"

Her aunt nodded. "Three. All girls."

"I want to meet them."

Her aunt smiled, but it was a little sad. "They are at school in the city. Because we are herders, our life is not permanent and their father and I insist on their receiving a level of education they could not otherwise have if they traveled with us. I miss them terribly."

"What about the school-age children we saw when we rode in?"

"I teach them. But we have not many resources to offer when they become teenagers."

"So you're separated for months?"

"Unfortunately, yes." Her aunt sighed, then shook off her sadness. "But you must be weary from your journey. I will show you and your husband to the place I have prepared for your stay."

Jessica had a bad feeling that it wouldn't be as big as Kardahl's palace suite. In fact it was probably a single room like this. And that would reduce the wide-open spaces to not-so-wide, not-so-open and space? Not so much. She'd appreciated having him there, but hadn't thought through the fact that he would be *there* 24/7.

Jessica looked around the little house, tent, cabin—she didn't know what to call it—where her aunt had left them alone for the night.

"It's a little isolated from the rest of the village," she said.

"We are on our honeymoon," he reminded her. "Your aunt is most considerate."

"I suppose it's not a good idea to clue her in that there won't be any horizontal hokeypokey because of the annulment."

"No," he agreed. "Even as isolated as we are, that kind of information has a way of being given to the press before it is expedient to do so. For such news to get out too soon would be counterproductive to what we are trying to accomplish."

"That's what I thought." She kept her back to him, hoping the dim lantern light hid the flush creeping up her neck into her cheeks. Glancing around at the place that was the mirror image of her aunt's she said, "This is nice."

"Indeed."

Her nerves jumped and twisted at the pleased note in Kardahl's voice. "It's not what you're used to, though," she commented.

"Rumor has it that I am accustomed to many bedrooms."

Jess glanced over her shoulder and couldn't be sure, what with the subdued light, but it looked like he had a gleam in his eyes to go with his pleased tone. What was that about? An expression came to mind—no good deed goes unpunished. The thing was, accompanying her here had been his good deed, so why was she being punished?

She could have spoken up and told her aunt that they weren't really a couple, but several things stopped her. Number one: she wouldn't embarrass Kardahl or his family. Whatever the state of his morals, he'd only been kind and considerate to her. Stalwart was another adjective that came to mind, but there was no point in carrying it too far. Number two: her aunt seemed so pleased that destiny had taken a hand in their betrothal. Jess had just met her. She didn't want to be a self-fulfilling prophecy, as in the family was going to reject her, therefore she should hand them, on a silver platter, a good reason to hate her.

So she was stuck. And when she found herself stuck, her attitude took on some sass.

She walked over to the wooden-frame bed and met his gaze. "How does this compare to all those other bedrooms?"

His direct look said I'll-see-your-sass-and-raise-you. His eyes smoldered as he deliberately let his gaze wander over her. "It has quite a unique charm."

The look, the words made her shiver and attitude abandoned her. She walked over to the table and bent to smell the wildflowers in a metal pitcher. "It is charming. And my aunt clearly went to some trouble."

"The flowers are indeed a nice touch."

The seductive deepening of his voice on the last word made her shiver again and the surge of awareness warmed through her, then settled like a glowing coal low in her belly. If he could do that to her body with a single word, imagine what he could if he actually *touched* her.

"We need some ground rules," she said quickly.

"Oh?"

"When bathing or dressing or at such time any clothing is removed or—"

"When you wish privacy," he said, far too calmly.

"Yes. When privacy is required, the other person goes outside."

"Agreed."

"As far as the bed—" She looked at it again. It

was roughly the size of a standard double mattress. "You take it."

He frowned. "Where will you sleep?"

"I'll make a place on the floor."

"I cannot allow that. I will sleep on the floor."

"And I can't let you do that."

He rested his hands on narrow hips and somehow the stance highlighted his wide chest and the unmistakable power in his shoulders. Response to his overwhelming masculinity shimmered through her and it wasn't helpful to this discussion.

"How do you intend to stop me?" he asked

What he meant was that he was bigger, stronger and could make her if he chose.

"Be reasonable, Kardahl."

"Very well. We will share the bed."

"That's not reasonable. That's—"

"What?" he asked, his chin lifting as a challenge slid into his eyes.

She'd been about to say it was crazy. But he would ask her why and she would have to admit it was because she was afraid. And it was a kind of fear she'd never felt before. It was fear of going where she'd never gone before with a man.

She'd always believed she wanted to be swept away. Now she knew she had to put qualifiers on that wish. And she would. Right after he stopped looking at her as if he knew what she looked like naked.

"I was going to say that's a lovely gesture, but you'll be more comfortable if you sleep alone."

"Do not worry about me. I am accustomed to sleeping with a woman beside me."

The flash of his white teeth made her want to blink and she felt like the mouse to his predatory cat. He was toying with her and doing a fine job. Anything he could do she could do better? That would mean a bald-faced lie—telling him that she was accustomed to sleeping with a man beside her. If she continued to protest, the situation would become much ado about nothing meaning it was definitely something. And she didn't want him to know it was something.

She looked at the bed, then forced herself to meet his gaze. "All right. We'll share the bed."

"Excellent."

CHAPTER SIX

"ARE you comfortable?" Kardahl asked.

That all depended on how one defined comfort. She'd never shared a bed with a man before and here she was, flat on her back beside the world's most notorious playboy.

Jess stared up into the darkness and contemplated her answer. She was huddled between Kardahl's back and the canvas wall. He'd turned away and no part of his body touched hers—as agreed. But she could *feel* him. The sound of his even breathing, the wonderful deep voice, the radiating warmth of his skin combined then curled inside her and added up to temptation.

"I'm completely comfortable," she lied.

"And you had adequate privacy when I left you alone?"

Since she was sleeping in her clothes, the mocking note in his voice wasn't lost on her. "Yes."

"The mountains of Bha'Khar turn cold at night."

"I noticed."

"You are warm?"

Oh, yeah. Especially after seeing him strip off his shirt before joining her in the bed. Unlike her, he hadn't required privacy. "I'm perfect," she said.

"I would be agreeable to sharing the warmth of my body should you require it," he offered.

His deep voice oozed phony innocence, yet it still tweaked the knot of temptation inside her. "I don't think that will be necessary."

Underneath the cover, his body gave off heat like a coal-stoked furnace. And that was before factoring in her own fired-up hormones.

"If that changes in the night, you have my permission to move close."

They were three inches apart, not on opposite sides of the room. And if he expected her to make a reciprocal offer, he was doomed to disappointment. "How self-sacrificing of you."

"Indeed."

It had been a long time since Jess had even had a roommate. And before that, when she was in the home, she'd shared a room, but the temporary situation didn't contribute to an atmosphere of trust or sharing feelings in the dark. She'd always felt isolated and alone. Although she didn't feel that way now, it wasn't an entirely happy sensation. Was this feeling of having someone the reason her mother had gone from man to man? Or was it more than that?

"If my body can bring you comfort, it would be my honor to do so."

"You're a prince of a guy."

His laugh was warm and rich, like coffee and chocolate. And his kiss. She'd never slept with a man, but she had been kissed. Although never the way Kardahl had kissed her. And she wanted that feeling again. So much.

The depth of her longing convinced her she couldn't let it happen again.

"Good night, Kardahl."

"Sweet dreams, Jessica."

Kardahl had flattered and flirted his way into many beds and always he had slept deeply and felt rested the next morning. That was not the case after spending the night beside his wife.

It had taken every fragment of his self-control to keep from touching her when she brushed against him or sighed sweetly in her dreams. He had not been fortunate enough to dream since that required actually falling asleep.

After waking beside her, they had gone their separate ways. Jessica had spent the day with her aunt, seeing the village and teaching the children. Kardahl had watched the men and marveled at their way with the horses in training. As he walked toward the tent where he'd been told the school was located, he found himself anxious to see his wife.

He saw her on the dirt path playing ball with a group of children. The sun was bright and a pleasant breeze drifted through the trees. Jessica was wearing a short-sleeved white cotton shirt and jeans. Sun-streaked brown hair danced around her cheeks and her eyes were bright as she laughed. Surely his reaction was the result of too little sleep, but the tight, heavy sensation in the lower part of his body was sudden and intense. He wanted her.

She waved when she saw him and the children grew quiet, their dark eyes wide and shy as they warily watched him come nearer. When he stopped in front of them, the boys and girls scattered.

Jessica's look was teasing. "Way to clear a room, Your Highness."

"That was not my fault."

"They're a little shy," she admitted. "And how was your day, dear?"

He lifted an eyebrow. "I bought a horse."

She looked surprised. "You don't waste any time. Is it for you?"

"No. My brother, Malik, asked me to pick out a suitable animal for his betrothed."

"I hope his bride-to-be can translate the fine print before she signs on the dotted line."

"He is the Crown Prince. There will be no mistakes."

"Famous last words," she teased.

"And how was your day, my sweet?"

Now *she* raised an eyebrow, but did not comment on his use of the endearment. "I spent the day with my aunt in her classroom."

"You are frowning. Did something happen?"

She shook her head. As they strolled along the path, she picked a leaf from a bush and rolled it between her fingers. "But education here is an uphill battle. No pun intended. There aren't enough books for all the children and the situation is fairly primitive. There's no access to computers or any other technology that would supplement education."

"To do that would take money," he agreed.

"In a prosperous country like this, it's inexcusable that they don't have more." The look she leveled at him was taut with accusation. "And that *is* your fault."

"How so?"

"My aunt said that several years ago her people petitioned for the necessary funds to improve education. As the minister of Finance, the appeal went to you and died on your desk."

"I see."

"Do you?" she asked.

Two years ago he had been lost in his own pain and could not clearly recall that time. He had gone through the motions, but his heart had disconnected.

When he did not answer, she said, "These are your people, too. I know their lifestyle makes it a greater challenge, but there must be a way to get technology to them. It's an oil-rich country, but the children are the most precious natural resource. Someone needs to champion them."

He felt the weight of her reproving stare. "Your passion on this particular issue would make you an exceptional champion. It is unfortunate that you are not staying."

He found that was the truth. She was worthy of respect and her spirit and sense of humor were most engaging. She intrigued and delighted him, which meant he had not disconnected from her as completely as he would have liked.

"I wish my visit could be longer," she admitted.

"Then you are not so very sorry you signed on the dotted line in error?"

Her mouth curved up. "I'm still sorry about that, but not that I'm here. I can't tell you how wonderful it is to meet family."

"Your aunt seems like a fine woman."

"She is." Jessica tore the leaf in her fingers to shreds. "I was just afraid that—"

He stepped in front of her on the path and stopped. "What frightened you?" When she looked down, he slid a finger beneath her chin and nudged, forcing her to meet his gaze. "Tell me."

"I—I didn't know whether or not there was strength of will for me to inherit. I was afraid I was destined to be like my mother."

"In what way?" He had made certain to read the

investigative report his father had requisitioned, but did not know to what she referred.

Jessica's eyes turned dark and troubled. "She never married. There was one man after another in her life and each time she believed he was the one who would be her 'happy ending.' Every time it didn't work out, she drank more—more wine, whiskey, vodka—whatever alcohol she could get her hands on—to help her forget. And that made it easier for men to use her. It was a vicious cycle that cut short her life."

Hearing her speak of it made him sad for the child Jessica had been, a little girl alone. "An alcoholic."

She nodded. "They say the tendency is inherited, so I always wondered. She was the only outline I had and that's hard to ignore even though all the books say it's about choices."

If it were all about choices, the woman he loved and the child he would never know would be here now. There was always pain when he thought about them, but he found it a little less now. Maybe because he found himself involved in someone else's pain and the fear of not knowing whether any of her people possessed the strength of character to fight the demons and had passed on that strength to her.

"I did not know your mother, but I know with a great deal of certainty that she was a fine woman."

"How can you be sure?"

He cupped her face in his palms. "If it was not true, she could not have produced a child who grew into such a beautiful, strong woman."

She smiled, a small smile, but it chased a few of the shadows from her eyes. "Thank you for that."

He dropped his hands and stepped back, because he wanted very much to kiss her. "So you do not regret coming here?"

She shook her head. "I could never regret the opportunity to learn about the traditions I always thought were just make-believe, just a part of the bedtime stories my mother told me."

"Traditions are not always a good thing."

"You say that because you haven't known a life without them."

"That is true. But if not for tradition, we would not be married."

"I see what you mean." She slid her hands in her pockets. "That is a problem."

More even than she knew. He had hoped this sojourn in the mountains would decrease his awareness of his wife, but had found it to be just the opposite. He was having a more difficult time resisting the urge to make her his.

"Actually I'm glad you found me," she said.

"Is that so?"

"Yes. We're invited to a welcoming celebration. The whole village will be there and festivities will be commencing at sundown."

He glanced at the sun just disappearing behind a peak. "Now?"

"I guess so," she said, her gaze following his. "Aunt Aminah says that there will be food and dancing and that we should be prepared to be worn-out."

From her mouth to God's ear, Kardahl thought. If he did not find a way to resist her presence beside him in bed, he would be going to the seventh level of hell. His indifference was fading. He knew this because it was more than lust coursing through him. Jessica would agree that if anyone knew the difference, it would be him. And this was distressing because lust was all he wanted to feel for her. It was far less complicated.

Jessica stood beside Kardahl and looked down at her feet, trying to memorize the steps to the traditional Bha'Kharian folk dance. The villagers played the music on guitars, a violin and harmonica, instruments that traveled well and produced a lively tune. In the open area centered among the tents, a big fire was burning. Men, women and children, including toddlers barely walking, sang and danced.

When Jess tried to follow Kardahl's lead in a crossover step and stumbled, she laughed ruefully at herself and shook her head. "I think I have two left feet. This pathetic attempt to dance proves that I should have left them in America."

"As with all physical activities," he said, "it merely takes practice."

All physical activity? What did that mean? Was she reading a significance into those words that he didn't intend? Given his reputation, it was a logical assumption.

"I've had lots of practice waltzing, but this is more like line dancing and I've never been able to get the hang of that."

"Then we will waltz," he said.

The next thing Jess knew, she was in his arms, following his lead in a slow dance. She felt his hand on her back, holding her close but not close enough. The fingers of his other hand curled possessively around hers, but not possessive enough. As their bodies moved and brushed together in time to a tune only they could hear, the dance was intimate—yet not intimate enough.

In his eyes she could see the bonfire flames flickering and snapping and wondered if he saw the same in hers. And whether it was in actuality burning logs or a fire inside them. They had arrived in the mountains twenty-four hours ago and this was the first time her breathing had been affected by the altitude. She prayed that, combined with the exercise of dancing, was the reason drawing air into her lungs became a challenge.

She prayed it had nothing to do with the solid, masculine contours of his body pressed to the feminine parts of hers. She hoped it wasn't the spicy scent of his skin invading her senses, dividing her rational and sensuous selves as he scaled her resolve on the way to conquering it. If he had an ulterior motive, she didn't want to know. If he was up to something, she wouldn't be his willing fool.

She moved out of the circle of his arm, executed a deft twirl, then put her own contemporary moves— as in hip action and footwork—to the music. Everyone clapped, including Kardahl, as he smiled broadly.

"You most definitely do not have two left feet," he assured her, a gleam that had nothing to do with the fire lighting his eyes. "That leaves only practice."

"Right," she said wryly. "About that—"

"Jessica." Her aunt Aminah joined them. "Your Highness," she said, with a slight bow. "I have arranged a surprise for you in your tent."

Jess frowned. "I don't understand."

"It is time for you to retire."

Since she knew her aunt wasn't talking about an end to her productive working years, this had to be about going to bed. "But the party is still going strong. And I'm not tired," she protested.

In the glow from the fire, Aminah's teeth flashed in a wide smile. "That is good. You and your husband are newly married and one needs only to see you in each other's arms to know that you wish to be alone."

"No. We're enjoying spending time with everyone," Jess insisted.

Aminah held up a hand. "Do not feel that you are hurting our feelings. We will not think you rude. It is understandable that you are anxious to spend time only with each other."

"No—"

"It bodes well for the duration of the union," her aunt added.

Jessica looked at Kardahl, willing him to jump in any time and help her out, but he just smiled and she wanted kick him. He was a prince, for crying out loud. All he had to do was issue a proclamation that they were staying at the party and everything would be fine. But he just stood there, giving her no choice.

"Thank you," Jess said.

Kardahl held out his arm. "Come, my sweet."

She put her hand in the bend of his elbow and said through gritted teeth, "You're incorrigible."

He laughed. "How you flatter me."

"It wasn't a compliment," she whispered.

When they were in their tent, Jess planned to tell him what he could do with "his sweet" until she spotted a tub of steaming water in the corner. Beside it was a stool with two towels and there were lighted candles scattered throughout the room.

"This must be the surprise," she said.

He glanced down at her. "From the expression on your face, I would say it is most welcome. If you looked at me in such a way, the matter of consummating our union would not be in question."

Oxygen went missing from her lungs again and she couldn't blame the sensation on the fire stealing it. Clearly her aunt intended for them to use this "surprise" together, but no way would she take off her clothes in front of Kardahl, let alone get into that tiny tub with him naked, too.

"Per our agreement, you have to wait outside." They were far enough from the festivities that there was no way he could be seen by the others. "This comes under the heading 'Private.'"

"As you wish."

When he was this close and there were candles and a steaming tub of water, she couldn't think clearly enough to decide what she wished.

"I'll be quick," she promised.

When his eyes caught fire, there was no question that he wasn't talking about a bath. "That is the difference between us. I would *not* be quick."

But he left her alone and she wasted no time undressing and stepping into the tub, immersing herself up to her shoulders in the warm water. It felt heavenly, almost as good as being in Kardahl's arms. That was a dangerous thought considering his reputation and the fact that to keep their union temporary and uncomplicated she had to stay out of his arms. Before journeying to the mountains with him she would have thought herself too smart to fall under his spell. If not too smart, then too cautious. Jess had vowed not to be like her mother and let men take advantage of her inherited romantic streak. Now here she was, struggling against her own nature.

"Is everything all right?"

Kardahl's voice, just on the other side of the canvas from where she sat naked in a tub, startled her and she jumped. Just a thin material separated them, but since she couldn't see him, she figured he couldn't see her.

"I'm fine," she answered. "How are you?"

"As I cannot bask in the warmth of your presence... Cold," he admitted.

There was that fluent flattery again. Two could play games. She splashed loudly. "The water is perfect. Not too cold. Not too warm. Just right."

"I am pleased."

"Wasn't it nice of my aunt to do this?" she asked.

He laughed, but there was more tension than humor in the sound. "I do not believe this is precisely what she had in mind."

"No? I suppose I could have set her straight. But I didn't figure it was time for that yet."

"Your discretion is appreciated."

"Always happy to oblige."

"Not always," he muttered. "Any time you would care to show off attributes of a more *physical* nature, I would be more than willing to participate."

He *was* incorrigible, but she couldn't help laughing. "If I decide to do that, I promise you'll be the first— To know," she added.

But literally the first. With every ounce of her willpower she had to fight the temptation. If she gave in, there would be no going back, and she wanted a clear exit strategy from this marriage.

"I do not wish to rush you, but the air does get cold in the mountains after dark."

The water was starting to cool off, too. A shame since she was thoroughly enjoying herself and being in control of his discomfort. But he'd been a good sport and a gentleman, which she would never have expected when she'd first met him. She washed quickly, then reached for a towel and let out a screech.

"Oh God—"

"What is wrong?"

The biggest, hairiest spider she'd ever seen in her life was parked on one of the towels. She stood, jumped out of the water, then carefully watched that the creature didn't pounce in her direction as she grabbed the other one and wrapped it around her. She'd barely covered herself when Kardahl rushed in.

"Jessica, what—"

"Bug," she said, waving her finger at it. "Do something."

The insufferable man just smiled indulgently. "It is a harmless spider."

"You are so wrong," she said. "Anything that ugly has to be pretty darn harmful."

"It is more afraid of you than you are of it."

"I sincerely doubt that."

He moved closer and captured it in his bare hands.

"Eww. I can't look." She closed her eyes and heard his footsteps, then the flap of canvas that served as a door. Moments later, she smelled the spicy scent of Kardahl and knew he was right in front of her, close enough for her to reach out and touch him. This time all that stood between them was a flimsy towel.

"It is gone. You are safe," he said.

When she opened her eyes, the smoldering look in his told her she was anything *but* safe.

CHAPTER SEVEN

THIS was another in a long line of firsts. Jessica had never been this close to being naked in front of a man, which didn't even register on the safe scale. No part of Kardahl's body touched hers, yet the look in his eyes made her feel as if he touched her everywhere. His breath stirred the loose hair around her face and his gaze lowered to the spot where she fisted her hand in the towel that barely covered her breasts. His eyes grew darker and his nostrils flared slightly, signaling his leashed passion. Her first impression of him had been right. He was rocking her world, big time.

Things tilted more when he bent his head and oh-so-gently kissed her. The butterfly-soft touch was like an electric jolt to her heart and more effective than a finger in an electrical outlet.

A small step forward brought his body in contact with hers, although her fist and the towel kept him at bay. But he continued kissing her, peppering her lips with soft touches that were like a kaleidoscope of passion, brief glimpses of something unbelievably mind-blowing just out of reach.

There was no way to hide her ragged breathing and she didn't try. She should put a stop to this, but she couldn't manage that, either. She'd thought so much about that kiss in the garden, wanting another, and now her wish was coming true. If there was a God in heaven, this heaven would go on forever. But forever wasn't to be, she thought, when he pulled away. This time when she opened her eyes, she saw that his breathing was uneven, too.

He ran unsteady fingers through his hair. "I do not expect you to believe me, but I did not plan to kiss you."

He was right. She wasn't sure she believed him. But the fact that he stopped kissing her when he had her right where he wanted her would give playboys everywhere a bad name.

"Why did you?" she whispered.

His eyes darkened even more if possible. "I could not help myself."

Very original. "Why did you stop?" That was the burning question.

"My conscience compelled me to. Unless—"

"What?" She gripped the towel tighter.

"It is a woman's prerogative to change her mind."

"About?"

"The consummation of our union." He let out a

long breath. "If you are willing, I would be most agreeable to making this a marriage in the physical sense."

Physical meant kissing and she wanted to do more of that. When he kissed her, the world disappeared. It was him, her and a want that took on a life of its own. But he was talking about more than kissing. Before she could tell him she was agreeable, he stepped back. A chill came over her and without the heat of his body, cold reality set in. If she agreed to consummate the marriage, there would be no going back. She felt like that scared girl whose mother was dying, leaving her no choice but to go with the social worker. She didn't ever again want to be without alternatives.

She shook her head. "I haven't changed my mind. I still want the annulment."

"As you wish." The coolness of his voice made her shiver. He grabbed the other towel beside the tub. "You are still wet. Forgive me. I will leave you to your privacy and bathe in the mountain stream."

The next thing she knew he was gone, she was still wet and colder if possible. Quickly she dried off and dressed in sweats and a T-shirt, then slid into bed. A long time later, she heard footsteps before Kardahl lifted the tent flap and came back inside.

His dark hair was still damp and her fingers tingled with the need to run them through the wavy strands. But that wasn't the biggest challenge to her willpower. His chest was bare, revealing a dusting of dark hair across the broad expanse that tapered over his flat abdomen, disappearing into the waist-band of his cotton pants. She closed her eyes and every muscle in her body tensed as she prepared for her second night sharing a bed with a man.

The lantern went out and she was plunged into darkness, just before he slipped into bed beside her. His arm brushed hers and his cool skin was a contrast to her warm flesh. He smelled like fresh mountain air and powerful male.

"I know you are not asleep," he said, humor in his tone.

"How could you tell?"

"Tension rolls from you like waves on the shore."

She didn't know what to say to that. He'd nailed her. So to speak. "How was your bath?"

"Not as warm as yours."

"Sorry."

"Not as sorry as I."

She thought about that and he was right. The realization made her laugh. And the more she tried to stop, the more she couldn't.

"You think that is funny?" he asked, but there was laughter in the tone, followed by the deep rumble of it beside her.

"No, it's not funny." She hesitated a moment before saying, "I'm lying. It's very funny. But I can't believe what a good sport you are about all of this."

"I live to serve," he grumbled. "Playboys are not all bad."

"You'll get no argument from me." And she would never have known without spending time with him, time that had brought her a childhood dream come true. "I can't help thinking about how different my life would have been if I'd met my aunt and uncle sooner."

He put one hand beneath his head. "If they had known of your whereabouts, there is no question that you would have had a home with them in Bha'Khar."

She had to agree. Her reception with the people here in the mountains had been warm and friendly. She couldn't imagine a childhood, an actual carefree growing up without insecurity and fear. It might have been enough to erase the emotional baggage she still carried from her mother's heartbreak, weakness and decline. But she would never know.

"Yeah," she said sadly.

"What troubles you?" he asked sharply.

"I'm not troubled. Not exactly."

He was quiet for several moments, then his deep voice warm as chocolate, cut through the darkness. "Life is not a destination, but a journey. Each of us has a destiny at birth and there are many paths to finding it."

"So you believe in destiny?"

"I believe that fate will find a way. If it were not so, your mother's letter would have remained buried in a lawyer's file forever."

"But it didn't."

"No. The discovery restarted a series of events that were set in motion a long time ago."

"Our marriage."

"Just so. You are living out your destiny—for the time being. And it was your family who set that in motion."

"Yes. And I can hardly wait to meet the rest of them."

"Patience, little one."

Easy for him to say. He'd never had to wonder about his family. Clearly there were issues, but the bad you knew was better than no information at all. She was anxious to meet her other aunt and grandparents. If not, she'd take her annulment and run. Because every second spent with Kardahl made her more restless and edgy.

He was the first man she'd let close enough to sweep her off her feet, but her hesitation had stopped him.

In her wildest dreams, she'd never expected to be married to an international playboy. When she'd learned about the legal tangle, she'd assumed her contempt for his type would be enough to protect her and never anticipated that she could be wildly attracted to someone like him. And it just kept getting stronger. The longer she knew him, the more he tempted her. She'd come frighteningly close to throwing caution and good judgment to the wind.

After watching men use her mother, she'd never thought this could happen to her, but she'd underestimated Kardahl's magnetism. She'd pathetically misjudged her own passion. And the worst of all: she'd gotten used to having him around.

She rolled on her side and turned her back to him. She wouldn't misjudge the situation again. There was a lot to like about her husband, but he had already loved and come right out and told her he wouldn't do it again. At the rate he went through women, he'd proven that he meant what he'd said.

Early the next morning, Kardahl had ordered the horses to be ready for their journey back to the capital. The villagers were gathered for the farewells and he watched Jessica hug several people, including her uncle. She saved her aunt Aminah for last and when she pulled away both women had tears in their eyes. Jessica hesitated a moment, then threw herself into the other woman's arms and hugged her one more time, just a little longer.

"I wish I didn't have to go," she said, taking a step back.

Aminah cupped her niece's face between her palms, then kissed each cheek in turn. "Fate has brought you back to us. We will see each other again soon. In the meantime, know that when you go, my heart goes with you."

"And mine stays with you," Jessica answered.

Her aunt smiled, then met his gaze. "You are a prince of the royal blood and my niece's husband. My parents chose you to care for the granddaughter they loved even before she was born. I entreat you to take this responsibility most seriously and hold it in the highest regard."

When he glanced at Jessica, he did not miss the guilty expression on her face. Now was not the time to make known their temporary arrangement. He nodded solemnly. "Consider it done."

Aminah smiled sadly. "Knowing she will be safe makes it easier for me to let her go. Thank you, Your Highness."

He held the stirrup and steadied Jessica's horse as she mounted, then handed her the reins. After he swung into his own saddle, they turned toward the path down the mountain.

Jessica glanced over her shoulder. "Goodbye—"

Kardahl heard the catch in her voice and glanced over. She was looking back, waving, smiling though her lips trembled and the sheen of tears glistened in her eyes. Her reluctance to leave tugged at him, but he did not share it. His relief that their time in the mountains was over could not be measured. One more night tortured by Jessica's nearness while he was shackled by his vow not to touch her would be more test than his self-control could endure.

There was an innocence about her that he found far too appealing, but he was troubled by the sense that it kept her passion prisoner. He had felt it in her kiss and did not wish to risk another opportunity to find out he was correct. That would break his vow and in the grand scheme of things it would change nothing. He would not care again. He could not.

His spirit grew less burdened the farther down the mountain they traveled. The sky above was blue and cloudless. Hawks, with their wings spread wide to catch downdrafts of air, floated above them. His horse and hers were well-behaved and surefooted. Life was good.

Until he glanced at Jessica's face. One look told him there was more on her mind than a bittersweet farewell to the family she'd just found.

"You are uncharacteristically quiet," he began.

"Is that your way of saying I have a big mouth?"

"Absolutely not." As he watched the corners of her mouth turn up in a smile, the knot of need he had not left on the mountain tightened within him. "Let me rephrase the question. What is on your mind?"

"Is it that obvious?"

"Yes. I believe it is more than the sadness of saying goodbye."

"You're right."

And that surprised him. He was not in the habit of deciphering a woman's mood. Since losing his beloved, he'd immersed himself in the complicated task of bringing Bha'Khar into the world order as a financial force to be reckoned with. Between his work and a series of forgettable women who brought relief to his body but none to his spirit, he'd managed to put aside his pain for long periods of time.

But he was beginning to realize that Jessica was not the latest in a string of unremarkable women. She was a woman whose moods he was coming to recognize without effort. Something was troubling her now and he wished to know the source of her agitation.

She sighed. "Aunt Aminah misses her daughters and I feel as if I'm abandoning her, too."

"Her children will be home soon."

"For a visit," Jessica said. "Children shouldn't have to leave their parents at such a young age to receive an education."

"It has been that way for many years," he explained.

"So if it ain't broke, don't fix it? That doesn't make it right. It's not broken, but it could be better. Traditions are good, but sometimes they need shaking up."

"The people who dwell in the desert have chosen this way of life."

"Oh? Like I chose a mother who wanted so desperately to be loved that the bottom of a liquor bottle was the only safe place when she couldn't find it? Or the way you chose to be born into a family who picks out your bride?"

It was a circumstance he had once railed against, then it ceased to matter at all. But learning about

Jessica was making everything change, a fact that was becoming disturbing.

He rested his palm on his thigh, then met her gaze as their horses meandered down the trail. "What is your point?"

"I don't know." She sighed and looked away, shaking her head. "I guess I'm trying to reconcile two such extreme ways of life. You grew up surrounded by luxury. The desert people don't have a permanent roof over their heads."

"Your words sound like an accusation. But it would be idiotic to try to defend myself against the material benefits I enjoy. Regardless of how it looks to the outside world, my life is far from perfect."

Her gaze slid to his. "It must have been difficult losing someone you loved."

"Just so."

"And it would be glib and callous of me to say snap out of it. But fate put you in a situation of enviable advantages and with that comes great responsibility."

"Duty," he agreed.

"As in serving the people of Bha'Khar. *All* the people. Including the ones who alternate homes in the desert and the mountains. You admit you had advantages and one assumes those included an education?"

"Indeed."

"Possibly tutors who came to you?"

He could see where this was going and could only be grateful she had chosen a career in social work instead of the legal profession. She had backed him into a corner and made him feel the need to explain. "I excelled in studies and was at the top of my class in college, up to and including a master's degree in business."

As she studied him, her body swayed from side to side while her horse picked its way carefully over the stones in the path. Her hazel eyes were fervent with what she believed in her heart.

"And what have you done with that exemplary education?" she challenged.

"I am working to ensure Bha'Khar's financial power in the global community."

"What about the community closer to home?"

"Your people," he confirmed.

"My people," she agreed. "I never thought I'd be able to say that. I didn't think I had 'people.' Now that I know about them, I can't turn my back. And I don't see how you can, either."

"I am not."

She sighed. "I know technology has made the world smaller. In the big picture, it's important for the country of Bha'Khar to be a political player. But people make up the country and their needs are vital. People like Aunt Aminah who doesn't get to see her children as much as she'd like because she knows it's important for them to get an education and they have to do that within the existing educational system."

"Education is the key to everything," he agreed.

"But you said yourself that learning could be brought to the high school level without the kids leaving home. All it takes is money and someone who cares."

That was the problem. In the general sense, he was concerned about his people. But the passion had been ripped from his life and he did not wish to resurrect it. "You care. If you wished to discontinue your pursuit of the annulment, you could stay and sponsor the cause."

"I can't stay." She glanced at him and her eyes were troubled. "But you're the money guy. You're in a position to get things done in a hurry." She stared at him and something she saw in his face made her frown. "If you want to."

"It is not as simple as you make it sound."

"It never is."

The trail narrowed and forced them to ride single file. In truth, he was relieved. She was uncompromising, single-minded in championing a cause. Her passion shamed him. She had been orphaned at an early age, yet still truly believed the world could be a better place. He had grown up knowing the price of his advantaged lifestyle was a responsibility to his people. Then fate took the light from his life and he became jaded, disconnected.

Jessica would be an asset to the man persistent enough to chip away at the defenses she had built up. She deserved someone worthy of her and he was not that man.

She put her heart into life and there was no life left in his heart.

CHAPTER EIGHT

JESSICA cradled a cup of coffee in her hands as she leaned against the low wall on the balcony outside her palace bedroom. The silk nightgown and robe were soft against her skin and the most luxurious sleepwear she'd ever worn—and very different from her clothing in the mountains. Staring out at the crystal clear blue water on the coast, she realized that the contrast between the Bha'Kharian lifestyles and terrain was as wide as the sea she was looking at. Fear had receded after meeting her aunt. One hurdle behind her, two to go.

She hoped it was only two. This morning she was troubled. One would have thought she'd have slept better all alone in her comfortable palace bed, but one would have been wrong. She and Kardahl had spent the last two days practically joined at the hip. He'd seen more of her—inside and out—than any man ever had. She'd spent two nights in his bed with the seductive masculine scent of his skin curling inside her. Surely the fact that she missed him was rooted in habit and nothing deeper.

Her feelings had been far less complicated when she'd thought him too shallow to care for anyone but himself. Finding out he'd cared too much was a shock that had gone straight to her heart.

A noise behind her made the hair at her nape prickle and her pulse jump. The familiar zap to the heart told her who was there but she turned to confirm.

"Kardahl," she said. His name came out just above a whisper and the worst part was she couldn't seem to help it.

"Good morning."

He smiled and it affected her like a sweeping martial arts movement that knocked her legs out from under her. Or maybe not just the smile, but the total package. He was wearing jeans, boots and a long-sleeved white cotton shirt with the sleeves rolled to just below the elbow. She'd seen him in suits, a tux and riding attire, but this was the first time she'd seen him dressed this way. It was just as good as all the other looks—maybe not quite as outstanding as shirtless, but darn close. What annoyed her most was that he appeared exceptionally well rested.

His gaze took in her appearance, from the top of her tousled hair to the tips of her red-painted toes—and everything in between. This balcony was shielded from the public and she hadn't thought about putting on clothes before walking outside. When a gleam slid into Kardahl's eyes, liquid warmth trickled through her and settled low in her belly.

This awareness had to be about spending so much time together. The joined-at-the-hip thing had to stop.

"You slept well?" he asked.

"Fine," she lied. "Never better."

"I am glad."

"You?"

"I missed you beside me."

He was lying. He had to be. "It was only two nights."

"But they were memorable nights," he said, flashing his white teeth.

For what didn't happen? Or what almost happened? "I guess you're not used to being in bed with a woman and actually sleeping."

"Just so."

"It was memorable for me, too," she said. Because he was the first time she'd actually been tempted to give herself to a man. "I've been thinking, Kardahl—"

"A dangerous prospect."

"Are you being funny?"

"Yes."

"Just checking." She couldn't help smiling. "You must have better things to do than tagalong with me on this family quest. Aunt Aminah told me her sister is a doctor in the northern city of Akaba. If you could just put a driver at my disposal—"

"That is what I have come to tell you."

"That you're handing me off to a staffer?"

He shook his head. "Your other aunt has responded to the palace inquiries and has sent word that she is eager to meet her niece."

"She is?" Even after her aunt Aminah's warm and loving welcome, Jess needed reassurance.

"She has been told to expect you later today."

"How far is Akaba from here?"

"It is a good distance."

Jess frowned. "Too far to get there today?"

"Not by air."

"I don't want to put anyone to any trouble," she said. "If it's an inconvenience, I'll call her and maybe we can reschedule—"

"It is no inconvenience. The aircraft will be readied."

"I saw that plane. It's pretty big—"

"There is a smaller one—an executive jet," he said, shrugging.

"I guess you can't have too many planes," she said wryly. "Think of all the educational technology that money could provide."

"You are relentless."

"Thank you."

He met her gaze. "We can be in Akaba—"

"We?" She sipped cold coffee as her mind raced. She needed to do this on her own. Not that she didn't appreciate his support. That was the problem. She appreciated it far too much. It was time to cut herself off before the point of no return, which she sensed was dangerously close. "Surely you have better things to do."

One dark eyebrow rose in surprise. "No cynical remark about women?" he asked.

"I guess I deserve that."

After judging him by the standard of tabloid stories, she'd jumped to conclusions. Now she understood why he was never seen with a woman twice. In a weird kind of way, it was sweet that he was protecting them from being hurt. Her mother had been the classic romantic who'd believed she would be the one who could make that elusive alpha male fall in love with her. At least Kardahl didn't lead anyone on.

"I'm sorry, Kardahl." Jess met his gaze. "I don't think I've ever apologized for misjudging you."

"I accept your apology." He looked at the Rolex watch on his wrist. "The plane is being prepared. If you can be ready in an hour, I will fly you to Akaba—"

"You?"

"Yes." His gaze narrowed. "You have apologized once already. Take care with your words."

She winced. He was right. She'd been about to say something snarky, like when had he had time to learn. The thing was, the question was still relevant. He was busy overseeing the quickly expanding economy of Bha'Khar.

"I was just wondering," she said, struggling for diplomacy, "what with all your responsibilities as the minister of Finance, when did you have time to learn, let alone practice?"

"When I was ignoring the needs of my people," he explained.

"Are you being funny again?"

His reply was a shrug. "There has been adequate opportunity to hone my skill on this aircraft. If you believe anything, believe this— I would never put your life at risk."

"It never occurred to me that you would. The thing is, I don't want to keep you from more important matters."

"Right now you are what matters most."

No one had ever put her first. Not ever. So how did she tell him she didn't want to be his priority at all let alone on top? That she needed physical distance to get her balance back.

"Look, Kardahl, it's not that I don't appreciate everything you've done for me, but—"

"Are you attempting to get rid of me?" He folded his arms over the chest she'd seen naked. "Do I make you nervous?"

Yes, she wanted to say, but a thousand horses couldn't drag the information out of her. "Of course not. It's just that you're a man with a public duty and I'm on a personal mission. I just don't want to bother you."

"Correct me if I am wrong, but the sooner you fulfill this personal mission, the sooner you can return to the children in your care. Is this not so?"

Most people would have said it was no bother whether or not it was the truth. He hadn't and the hopeless romantic in her went to the place where she wanted to know if she *did* bother him, the same way he bothered her.

"Yes. I do want to get back to work," she admitted. If they were on opposite sides of the world he couldn't bother her.

"Then I am at your service. I will fly you to Akaba. And I promise that I will let no harm come to you."

There was a point where you just had to give in gracefully and this was it. "Okay."

After that she only needed to see her grandparents before returning home. The thought should have brought comfort, but not so much. And it wasn't life and limb she was worried about. It was her heart. One by one his flaws were disappearing. He was dashing. He was kind. On top of that, he could fly a corporate jet.

Was there anything he couldn't do?

Yeah. He couldn't care for her and the more time she spent with him, the more it mattered.

Kardahl shut down the jet's engines, as always, grateful that the trip had been without incident. And yet, somehow it had felt eventful. He could only attribute that to Jessica. Had he been alone, he would not have been tempted by her voice, her scent and her shapely curves.

He could have made arrangements for someone else to accompany her, as she'd suggested, but he could not. She was his wife—for the moment. But duty only explained part of his motivation. Until the annulment severed their ties, she would be a paparazzi target. He wished only to protect her. But there were ways to do that without becoming personally involved and he was at a loss to explain why he had ignored them.

After unbuckling their seat belts, he left the cockpit and pressed the red knob that released the air from the door seal. Then he pushed down on a lever that freed the stairs for gravity to lower them. After descending, he escorted Jessica to the waiting limousine and handed her inside, sliding in after her. Instantly she folded her hands in her lap and rubbed one thumb over the other.

Kardahl put his hand over hers to still the movement. "Do not be nervous."

She jumped, as if she'd been lost in her own thoughts. But her familiar defensive spirit was evident in her gaze. "That's easy for you to say."

"Actually it is." He smiled at her surprised look. "And before you ask, I was being funny. At least I was making an attempt."

"You could jog in a circle and squawk like a chicken—"

"On the contrary, I could *not* do that."

"Now that's funny," she said, laughing.

He was pleased to see her smile, even though it increased the ever-present temptation to touch his lips to hers. His growing attraction for her continued to be a puzzle. She was not the most beautiful woman he had ever seen. She did not go out of her way to flatter him. And she did not want to share his bed. He could only credit his obsession with her as a challenge to unlock the passion she kept hidden. What stopped him was the risk that he would reveal the heart he had locked away.

"Your aunt will be most pleased to know you. Why do you doubt it?"

"If you'd grown up without anyone, you wouldn't take it for granted, either."

"Perhaps."

And there was probably a great deal of truth in what she said. Since nothing he could say would reassure her, he didn't try. He simply took her hand in his and laced her fingers with his own until they reached Akaba Medical Center where her aunt was the chief of staff. As the car pulled smoothly to a stop in front, he saw the crowd gathered. Word of their visit preceded them and the security detail he had sent ahead had called in uniformed law enforcement officers for backup.

Kardahl looked at her. "I am not pleased to add to your burden, but doubtlessly you have already noticed that reporters are gathered."

"Yeah."

"I feared this might happen. The announcement of our marriage was made, followed by our disappearance for several days. That tends to whet the press's appetite for more."

"I can see why they would be curious." She blew out a long breath. "Let's get this over with."

As they got out of the car, Kardahl felt the crowd move forward as a single entity. He put his arm around Jessica as bodyguards and police surrounded them while they mounted the steps leading to the automatic double doors at the entrance. The click of camera shutters was like the angry buzz of insects as reporters shouted out questions, none of which could be heard.

He would have hustled her into the building, but she turned unexpectedly to face the press.

"I'll answer a couple of questions," she said.

"Are you going to have a baby?"

"Not today."

"Are you pregnant, Your Highness?" someone else shouted, putting a finer point on the inquiry to pin her down.

She laughed and glanced up at him with the absurdity of the question shining in her eyes. "No."

"There's a rumor that you and the prince are having trouble conceiving."

"Not true," she said.

Only because they had not yet tried. And it was not for lack of desire, he thought.

"Are you here because of fertility issues?" someone else asked.

"Why would you think that?" she shot back.

"You've come all this way to Akaba to keep it quiet."

"Also not true. And before you ask, Kardahl and I are not ill. We're here at the Medical Center to visit my aunt, Dr. Janan Fahrani."

"Are you trying to have a baby right away?"

"We haven't talked about it." Jessica smiled enigmatically. "Now, if you'll excuse us, I'm anxious to see my aunt."

She turned away and ignored the relentless media who continued to toss out questions until the automatic doors closed and the quiet, cool marble floors and walls of the hospital lobby embraced them.

Kardahl stopped and looked down at her. "Why did you do that? We could have simply ignored them."

She shrugged. "A split second decision. Gut instinct, I guess. It occurred to me that it's human nature to want what you can't have. If we continue to dodge their questions, everything becomes so much bigger. If you stand and face it, get it over with, it takes away the power. I'm not running away."

Like Antonia, he thought. Her anger at being the prey of the media had incited the tragic series of events that cost her life. It had all spun out of control so quickly. If only he could go back…

Just then, a dark-haired woman in her late forties approached. The embroidery on the breast of her white lab coat read, Janan Fahrani, M.D.

She glanced at both of them but her eager gaze rested on Jessica as she smiled. "I cannot tell you how very pleased I am to meet my sister's child."

"And I'm happier than I can tell you to meet my mother's sister. You look so much like her—" Jessica's voice cracked and she pressed a hand over her mouth.

The other woman opened her arms and Jessica moved into them as the two embraced.

"I met Aunt Aminah," she said, pulling back after a long moment.

"How is my sister and her family?"

"Fine. She misses her daughters," she answered glancing up at him. "I'm sorry. This is His Royal Highness Kardahl Hourani—"

"Your husband. I have seen the news reports of your marriage."

He held out his hand. "It is a pleasure, Doctor."

"The pleasure is mine, Your Highness." She slid her fingers into his. "I apologize that I could not meet you in the capital. My work is demanding. I regret that you had to come all this way."

Jessica smiled. "It was no problem. Kardahl has a plane and he knows how to use it."

Her aunt laughed. "Still, it was good of you to bring her to me."

"It *was* good of him." Jessica smiled and when she met his gaze, there was warm affection in her eyes.

He liked it when she looked at him that way and could too easily grow accustomed to seeing that winsome expression on her face. "Would you still think me good if I told you I was showing off for my bride?"

"I doubt it was just that," the doctor said. She looked at her niece. "I have spoken with my parents and they wanted me to tell you that they are most anxious to meet you and will be home soon. Their schedule of meetings with foreign dignitaries could not be called off, not even for something so important as meeting their granddaughter."

Jessica swallowed hard. "I've been told they searched all these years for my mother. She changed her name, which is probably why the search was unsuccessful."

Janan sighed. "I wish it could have been different, but we cannot alter what has been. We can only be grateful for what is now. And I am most grateful that you have come."

"Since we are here," he said, "would you be so kind as to show us around the facility?"

Her black eyes glowed with pride. "It would be my pleasure."

For the next hour Jessica's aunt took them through Radiology, Cardiology, Surgery, Respiratory and Outpatient Services. She showed them the building where various research studies were being conducted, with revenue spent on promising cancer drugs and diabetes treatments.

As they were walking down the hall, Janan announced, "I have saved the best for last."

She pressed a square metal pad on the wall and the double doors opened automatically. On the left was a large window. Behind it was an open room with rows and rows of newborns and nurses attending to the ones in most need of attention, a fact revealed by their red-faced crying.

"This is the newborn nursery," the doctor explained.

Jessica moved close to the glass and smiled as she stared beyond it. "They're so sweet."

"Our most precious natural resource," her aunt agreed.

"I said that to Kardahl once," Jessica said. "They're just too precious for words. Don't you think so, Kardahl?"

He moved beside her and saw the infants, some squirming and flailing tiny fists. Others sleeping the sleep of the innocent. He barely heard Jessica's words as pain punched through him, and it was like none he had ever known. He had never let himself picture his son or daughter as a living, breathing child. Now he knew why. He had not wanted to think about the fragile life lost, the dreams and deeds that were never to be.

Until this moment he had been successful in

burying this part of his grief but now it sat like a stone on his chest. He could not breathe.

Without a word, he turned and walked away.

CHAPTER NINE

"KARDAHL! Wait."

"I wish to be alone."

"What is it? What's wrong?" Too stunned to move at first, Jessica stared at his broad back for several moments before running after him. When she caught up at the elevator, a brief view of his dark expression put fear in her heart as the doors whispered shut.

"I don't know what's wrong with him," she said to her aunt who had followed. There must be something wrong because just a glimpse of the stark misery on his face convinced her there was something terribly not right.

She pushed the down button. "I have to go after him."

"I have seen that look before," her aunt said.

"What do you mean?" she asked, turning. "You've seen Kardahl before?"

"Not him specifically. The expression. Pain. Loss.

As a doctor, I use my skill and knowledge and everything I have for my patients. But sometimes there is nothing that can be done. And I have to relay this information to the family that their loved one is beyond help." She met Jess's gaze. "He had the look of one who has heard, but has not yet let go."

Jess jabbed the elevator button, as if that would make it come faster. "I have to go after him," she said again. "He shouldn't be alone."

"It is what he wants."

Jess turned on her. "That's what he said, but it's not what he really wants. He lost someone he loved very much. So did I. When my mother died, I was all alone in the world.

Her aunt looked stricken. "Jessica, we did not know—"

"I'm not blaming you. I'm just saying I know how alone feels. Then I came to Bha'Khar and Kardahl has been here for me."

"Of course. He is your husband. You care for him. That is obvious."

Obvious that she cared? Jess hoped that wasn't true. Although she knew it was hard not to care for a man who had been there for her practically from the moment she'd arrived in his country—her country. His support had given her confidence and smoothed the way for meeting her family. Whether he knew it or not, he needed someone now and she wouldn't abandon him.

"He is my husband, Aunt Janan. And I must go to him."

Her aunt nodded. "Go. We will see each other again soon."

Jess hugged her tightly for several moments, then released her and stepped into the elevator.

Jessica paced the penthouse suite at the Ritz-Carlton Akaba. Kardahl had given instructions for her to be brought here but he was missing and she was getting frantic for him to return. If she'd had any idea where to look, she would have, but she knew nothing about the city or where he would go.

Hours of this waiting was driving her crazy with worry. In her work she saw kids like herself who'd lost everything. She'd seen desperation and loneliness mixed with gut-wrenching grief. And she'd recognized it again in the soul-deep sorrow in Kardahl's eyes. Where did a desperate man go? What would he do to outrun whatever demons chased him?

She walked out on the balcony that overlooked the cosmopolitan high-rises that made up the skyline of this bustling city. Far below there was traffic noise. She heard the occasional horn honking and the screech of brakes. The sun had gone down and still there had been no word from Kardahl. Apprehension knotted inside her and squeezed out hunger and every other need but the one to know he was safe.

How could she do anything until she knew where he was, how he was and what was wrong?

Instinct told her this was about something more than losing the love of his life. He'd told her about that and she'd been almost certain that afterward the shadows had lifted from him.

Back inside the suite she paced into the marble-tiled foyer with the circular table and vase filled with red roses. She stood on tiptoe to peek through the security peephole, hoping he would be there, disappointed when there was no sign.

She wandered back through the living room, glancing at the elegant floral love seats, rich dark wood tables and the graceful dining room set with the matching breakfront. In the bedroom, a plasma screen TV was mounted on the wall across from a king-size four-poster bed. As a kid, she'd always longed for pretty clothes and plush surroundings as if lack of it was all that was wrong with her life. Now she had things but everything was wrong. Nothing could erase the worry gnawing away at her. And she realized the finest material things in the world wouldn't have made a difference while she waited all those long nights for her mother.

It wouldn't have eased the anxiety of wondering whether or not her mother would come home at all, or in what condition. It wouldn't have helped when her mother was drunk or when the man she'd thought would love her had let her down again and Jess held her while she cried. It wouldn't...

She heard the door open and close and relief broke through the worry gripping her. Hurrying into the living area, she saw Kardahl lower himself to the love seat. Lines of weariness carved grooves on either side of his nose and mouth. He scrubbed both hands over his face as he let out a deep, sad sigh.

She didn't know why the sight of those innocent babies had triggered this reaction in him, but every instinct she had urged her to comfort him, touch him, let him know he wasn't alone.

She sat down beside him and put her hand on his arm. "Kardahl, what is it?"

He shrugged her off. "I do not wish to speak of it."

"Tough." She touched him again and her determination got his attention.

"Leave me."

"No." She put her arms around his shoulders and rested her head against his cheek. Her hair caught on the stubble as she nuzzled him. "You don't have to talk. You just need to know I'm here for you. I'm not going anywhere."

He turned his head, meeting her gaze with surprise in his own.

"Jessica—" Her name, a whisper on his lips, was a plea for something she didn't understand.

She touched her mouth to his and felt his conflict, his reluctance to take the comfort she offered, but she wouldn't be discouraged. She deepened the kiss and his shoulders tensed, his breathing grew faster, and the groan that sounded in his throat came from somewhere deep down inside him.

He gathered her onto his lap and wrapped his arms around her, burying his face in her neck. He held her for what seemed an eternity before cupping her cheek in his palm and capturing her mouth with his own. Need crested through her on a wave of heat that scorched rational thought and turned it to ashes.

She couldn't kiss him hard enough, deep enough, or get enough air into her lungs. She pressed her breasts to his chest, straining to get closer.

The next thing she knew, Kardahl stood with her in his strong arms and walked into the bedroom. Settling a knee on the mattress, he placed her in the center of the bed with exquisite gentleness.

"I want you." His voice was warm and soft and seductive as black velvet.

He stretched out beside her and undid the buttons on her blouse. Looking his fill at her virginal-white cotton bra, he leaned close and peppered kisses over her neck. Then he parted the sides of her shirt and pressed his mouth between her breasts, tracing her cleavage with his tongue. It was like a jolt of electricity that zapped her from head to toe and made her fingertips tingle.

And she knew. This was what she'd been waiting for—to be swept away by desire, to feel such passion that nothing else on earth mattered but being with this man.

"I want you," she answered, meeting his gaze before wrapping her arms tightly around him.

Rational thought slipped away as her senses took over and reveled in touching and being touched.

If one could be damned to hell twice, Kardahl knew it would still not be sufficient punishment for what he had done. Not only had he broken his promise not to touch his wife, but he had taken her virginity. How was it possible that she had never been with a man? She was so beautiful yet she had come to him pure as the driven snow and he had callously stolen her innocence.

Mesmerized by the rust-colored evidence on the twisted sheets, he damned himself in four languages. He truly was the bastard prince—every bit the rogue and scoundrel the tabloids portrayed him to be. A better man would not have savored the feel of her bare flesh pressed to his as he had held her in his arms through a night that had been far too short. A better man wouldn't want her again, but Jessica had told him more than once that he was not a better man.

He whirled at the sound of the bathroom door opening. Steam from her shower followed Jessica into the room. The perfect body he had memorized every inch of the night before was swallowed by a thick, white terry-cloth robe. Her still-wet hair hung straight around her small face, a face naturally beautiful and free of cosmetics.

When she noticed him watching, she smiled and the look was like an arrow to his heart—an arrow comprised of passionate intensity with a sharp tip of guilt. She was spirited and generous as well as smart and beautiful. Had he but known she had never been with a man he would have…

"Why did you not tell me you were a virgin?" he demanded, putting emphasis on the past tense.

Her hands, in the act of drying her hair, instantly stilled. When she met his gaze, her smile wavered, then disappeared. "Some men would think it was a good thing. You make it sound like a disorder. I promise it's not contagious."

"That is not— You twist my words." He ran his fingers through his hair, struggling with what to say. He had never faced such a situation. "Why did you not say something before it was too late?"

He remembered wanting her more than his next breath, needing to be inside her. He had never felt such passion, and he knew it had been fueled by her simple and unsullied desire, an innocence he now understood. But there had been a moment after entering her, the briefest of seconds after her gasp of discomfort that he had thought was passion. Awareness of her virginal barrier had penetrated his desire-fogged brain, but he failed to grasp the significance in time.

"Too late?" she repeated. "That implies regret. I suppose a good deal more experience on my part would be required to achieve your accustomed standards."

"That is not what I meant—"

"I have to tell you as standards go, it was all a bit disappointing for me. I'm having a little trouble understanding what all the fuss is about."

How did he tell her what she had given him was a most precious gift? She was right. Most men, unless they were complete idiots, would be giddy with joy and probably feeling a healthy dose of pride at being her first. But it was so much more complicated than that.

Kardahl saw the hurt in her eyes and knew he was handling this badly, almost as badly as he had handled her last night. But that was not completely his fault.

"With pertinent information, there are things a man can do to make the first time easier for a woman, more satisfying. If you had told me—"

"So you're saying we have to work on our communication." She dropped her arm and let the towel dangle from her fingers. Her full lips pressed together into a straight line. "Right back at you."

"I beg your pardon?"

"You have some explaining to do, too."

"I do not understand."

"Yesterday— Why did you walk out of the hospital without a word?"

"I do not wish to speak of it."

She tapped her full lips with a finger. "See, that's the thing about communication. It works both ways."

"Your meaning?"

"I didn't wish to speak of the fact that I'd never slept with a man, and yet somehow we just talked about it."

"We did not. You never told me why I was so honored to be the first."

"An honor?" She turned away and settled the wet hand towel on the bathroom doorknob. "Just now, you didn't act honored. However, you're changing the subject. Why did you walk out of the hospital when we saw the babies?"

He closed his eyes as a vision of new life flashed into his mind. Then he felt Jessica's hand on his arm.

"What about the babies?"

"No—"

"You need to talk about it, Kardahl."

"Why?" he demanded. "What is the point of re-membering what you can do nothing about?"

"You can't change it," she agreed. "But if you don't deal with heartbreak, the pain becomes like a festering wound. You need to let out the poison. Talk. Air out everything. Eventually healing happens."

"A wound this deep will not heal."

"You won't know unless you try," she pleaded.

He turned away and went to the window, watching the sun's rays peek over the top of a jagged mountain. "Antonia was pregnant."

Several moments of stunned silence followed before she said, "She was carrying your baby?"

"Yes."

"Did your family know?" she asked.

He shook his head. "I was going to tell them. Then— There was no need."

"Oh God. You didn't just lose the love of your life. You lost your child, too."

"She was just starting the second trimester." He recalled putting his hand on her belly, feeling the subtle changes in her body brought about by the life their love had created. "The child was real to me. That night, the night of the accident, we were discussing our marriage."

"The prospect of going against tradition?"

"I did not care about that." He turned, his chest knotting at the sympathy in her eyes. "And after losing them, I only wished to never care again."

He was seen with women all the time, but never let anyone into his heart. Until Jessica, he had been successful in that endeavor, but she was making him feel again. That did not mean the behavior was to be encouraged and he would not. Caring was a pathway to pain.

"Kardahl, I don't know what to say. I'm so terribly sorry."

"It is in the past."

"Right. If you believe that, then you're lying to yourself. The look on your face when you saw the babies—" She pressed a hand to her chest. "It broke my heart. And when you left so suddenly— I was worried about you."

"I did not mean to distress you."

"That's not what I meant. I was concerned about you—"

When she touched him, he pulled away because he so badly wanted to pull her into his arms. Last night he had found comfort with her as he had no one else. She was making him want to forget his promise and let the tenderness he felt bloom. The sooner she completed her family obligations, the sooner she could go back to America, which would be best for both of them.

Unfortunately consummating their marriage would make the process of ending it more difficult. He did not wish to think about the personal cost and the longer he knew her, the more certain he was that there *would* be a personal cost.

"There is a concern, but it is not so much about me. It is about us. And what we are going to do now. We have consummated our marriage."

"I noticed." Her cheeks flushed pink.

"Then you realize that there is now a problem with the annulment."

Her eyes widened. "Oh. I forgot all about that."

Until this moment, he had as well but could not help being pleased that he was not alone in the overwhelming passion, that he had driven everything but making love from her mind. It had consumed him, a force of nature, like trying to walk through a cyclone.

"What are we going to do?" she asked. She walked outside, to the low wall and leaned her elbows on it, staring out at the rising sun as it made the shadows in the valley disappear. "I guess we'll have to get a divorce, then."

"The legalities will be a bit more complicated."

"If you're talking about alimony or anything like that, let me assure you I don't want or expect anything. I'll be grateful forever that you were here for me in one of the most emotional and difficult times of my life. That's priceless. So I don't see why it has to be complicated if it's what we both want. Neither of us will contest it—"

"What if there is a child?"

She went completely still, then turned to look at him. "No way."

"It was my fault. I did not once think about doing anything to prevent conception."

"It was just once," she whispered.

"That is enough." Even as the words left his mouth, something inside was telling him that once would not be enough with Jessica.

"Of course. I knew that. It's just—" She shook her head, then rubbed shaking fingers over her forehead. "I can't believe it. I'm the perfect example of the idiot woman who doesn't believe she could get pregnant the first time."

"So—"

"So," she echoed.

"If there is a child—"

"No." She straightened away from the wall and met his gaze, her own filled with fear, shock and disbelief. And something else unrecognizable. "There is no child. Fate would not be so cruel."

CHAPTER TEN

A WEEK LATER, as the limousine drove through the city to the outskirts where her grandparents lived, Jessica pressed a hand to her flat abdomen and prayed that she'd spoken the truth to Kardahl and right now she was feeling nerves. It was too soon to know if a baby was on the way.

That didn't mean she was opposed to the idea of children someday. Just that she'd tried so hard not to make the same mistakes her mother had. As far as Jess could tell, the only one she hadn't made was being married the first and only time she'd had sex.

Before she had a baby, she wanted to be in love with the father. Hopeless romantics wanted to be in love period. But while she'd waited these few days for her grandparents' return, Kardahl had been conspicuously absent and that was probably a good thing. She hadn't been completely truthful when she'd told him sex was a little disappointing.

After the first minor discomfort receded, she'd

seen the potential. And the fuss? She'd thought a lot about his comment that there were things a man could do to make it more satisfying for a woman. Her skin tingled and her breasts tightened at the thought of how lovely those things might be. And that was why his absence had been a relief. She didn't trust herself not to fall into his bed again.

She'd also had lots of time to analyze her situation. Jess had grown up without a father's influence on her life, without a father's unconditional love to shelter her. She didn't know anything else and had come to terms with that.

However, it was one thing not to know a father's affection and never miss it, but quite another to grow up wondering why your father can't love you at all. She knew that Kardahl could never love her and she could deal with it. She was a grown up. But she couldn't stand watching him not love her child.

The most frustrating part was that she couldn't even blame him. Not after the tragedy of losing the woman he loved and his unborn child along with her. It was so much easier when she thought him a shallow cad. Now she felt just the opposite and had come to respect him very much. As the big car drove through the security gates and the palatial white stucco house with red-tiled roof came into view, Jess missed his solid, comforting presence.

All her life she'd wanted a grandmother and grandfather who would spoil her rotten and she was about to get her wish. At least to meet them. The spoiling rotten part wasn't as important now as it had been when she was ten. She was nervous, but not nearly as much as when she'd met her aunts. Kardahl's presence had gotten her through and the void left by his absence today was so big it scared her. How could his impact on her life have grown so large in such a short time?

When Antonia was alive he'd been ready to throw tradition out the window. He'd only involved himself in their arranged marriage because love didn't matter to him anymore. But he mattered to her so much more than she'd ever thought possible.

The car moved smoothly up the driveway and stopped in front of the house. An archway with tall, square columns shaded the double doors with their intricate stained-glass design. She'd barely stepped out when one of the doors opened and an older couple came out. Jess's heart pounded as she walked up the stairs.

The woman was a combination of Aminah, Janan and her own mother, Maram. But Jess felt the pieces of her soul come together when she recognized her own brown hair and hazel eyes—eyes shimmering with unshed tears.

"Grandmother—"

As with her two aunts, the older woman word-lessly opened her arms and Jess moved into her embrace. A sensation of peace settled over her and when she was released, her grandfather pulled her to him for a hug.

"I am Esam," he said, holding her at arm's length to study her. "And this is Leena. Welcome, dear child."

"Thank you." She smiled at each of them. "All my life I've dreamed of a meeting like this."

"Our prayers have been answered," the older man said simply.

Her grandmother nodded and slipped an arm around her waist. "Come inside."

The spacious interior was cool and serene. The foyer was covered in stone tiles that stopped at twin curved staircases leading to the upper floor. In the living room, she was settled on a plush white corner group across from a wall of French doors that opened onto a patio and a view of the jagged mountain peaks in the distance. Her grandmother brought a tray with a pitcher, glasses and a plate of sugar cookies and set it on the mahogany coffee table. How cool was this, she thought.

"Tell us about yourself." The older woman handed her a tumbler of ice cold lemonade.

"I don't know where to start."

"Start at the beginning," her grandfather suggested, taking a seat beside her.

She was surrounded by love and felt it with every fiber of her being. Taking a deep breath, she said, "I was born December 2 in a county hospital in Los Angeles."

She told them a version of the truth that edited out the bad parts. But when she related being taken to the state home and growing up with other kids who didn't have family, her grandmother took her hand and nestled it between her own warm wrinkled ones.

"If only we had known—" Her grandmother sighed, shaking her head.

"Tell me about my mother, before I was born," she said.

"Maram was a headstrong girl," Leena began. "Too beautiful for her own good. Stubborn. Sweet."

"She was our best and brightest," Esam added.

Jess looked at each of them. "But Aunt Janan is a doctor. Aunt Aminah is married to the leader of the desert people. My mother—"

"Ran away." Her grandfather's eyes were sad, a sorrow that went very deep. "She was our youngest, our shining jewel. So beautiful."

"Yes. We still miss her terribly." Her grandmother met her gaze, studying her. "You look very much like her."

Jessica wondered if the resemblance ended with looks and she hoped she wasn't destined to repeat her mother's mistakes.

"Tell us about our Maram. After she left. What happened to her?" Leena asked.

Jess didn't want to tell them the whole ugly truth. Not yet. "She was a good mother. Every night when she tucked me in bed, she told me stories of a faraway kingdom called Bha'Khar and handsome princes and beautiful princesses. I thought she'd just made it up." She smiled at the older couple. "But she got sick, and kept getting worse. Social Services took me away because she wasn't strong enough to care for me. I loved her very much and still miss her."

Esam's mouth trembled, and he pressed his lips tightly together. When he was under control once more, he said, "Let us speak no more about the painful past. Tell us of your impressions of Bha'Khar."

"What your grandfather means is that we would like to know about Prince Kardahl, your husband."

"Yeah, about that—"

"We were in Washington, D.C. when we saw news coverage of the palace reception when the announcement of your marriage was made public," her grandfather explained. "You make a handsome couple. I think you looked happy."

Was that hope she heard in his voice? "I understand you and the king are responsible for the betrothal between Kardahl and myself."

"Yes. The king is a dear friend. We felt it was advantageous to join our families through marriage."

"So you and the king were playing Cupid?" she teased.

He sighed. "It did not work out precisely as we planned. Children have a way of—"

"Doing their own thing?" she suggested.

"Just so."

"But fate has a way of stepping in and righting things," Leena said. "You found your way back to Bha'Khar and the family who loves you. Prince Kardahl is your husband and finally settled down, to the relief of his parents *and*, I suspect, the minister of Public Relations. He simply needed a good reason to stop his high jinks and tomfoolery. He will be a good and devoted husband. All is as it should be."

Not so much, Jess thought. She didn't want to spoil this perfect first meeting by telling them that she and Kardahl had agreed to stay married to take the heat off his "high jinks" while she met her family. After that, she was going back to America, although the means of dissolving said marriage was now a big question mark since they had consummated the union. Looking at the older couple, she decided that was too much information for the brand-new relationship they were beginning. She was simply going to enjoy them.

And she did. Jess spent all afternoon listening to stories of her mother's childhood. She learned about her aunts and cousins and toured her grandparents lovely home and soaked up the attention they lavished on her. But there was a state dinner at the palace and she was still playing the part of devoted bride, albeit reluctantly.

She stood. "I'm afraid it's time for me to go."

"So soon?" Leena looked genuinely disappointed. "But you'll be back, yes?"

"Yes." But Jess knew it would be to say goodbye, and the thought made her chest tight.

With her between them, they walked her to the door. She looked from one to the other. "This day has been a wish come true and every bit as wonderful as I dreamed it would be."

Leena's eyes filled. "For us as well, little one. And the first of many visits."

"You must come back soon," her grandfather agreed. "Your grandmother—Leena—her name means tender. In translation, Esam means safeguard. For all these many years we have been deprived of the opportunity to live up to our names with our granddaughter. We have much time to make up with you. If there is anything you need, you have only to ask and we will make it happen."

With a lump the size of Bha'Khar in her throat, Jessica didn't trust herself to speak. She just hugged them both as hard as she could and found it was more gratifying than any words could be.

As the car pulled away, she looked back and waved. She was no longer alone in the world. She had family. And they had offered to do anything for her. But even the world's most doting grandparents couldn't make it so that she wasn't falling in love with Kardahl.

"Kardahl, we need to talk."

He was just pouring himself a brandy from the

decanter on the bar tucked into the corner of the living room and thought how perfect Jessica's timing was, because he would no doubt need the drink. Those words coming from a woman never induced peace of mind in a man.

"Do we?"

He took a sip of the liquor, then savored the warmth as it slid down his throat. Lifting a hand, he pulled at his black tie, loosening it to let the ends dangle before twisting open the top button of his dress shirt. The state dinner for the Chinese minister of Finance had been long. Only Jessica had been a bright spot in an otherwise tedious evening.

Even now—especially now—the sight of her had need pulsing through him. He knew the jewel-toned green gown covering her from her long graceful neck to her slender ankles was deceptively chaste. The back dipped provocatively low, flirting with the curves of her delightful derriere. He remembered every inch of her soft flesh from that night they had been together.

Kardahl had unburdened his soul and still did not know whether it had been a mistake. But he knew two things—the loss did not weigh so heavily on his heart. And that night had been abundant with intensity, emotion and the satisfaction of learning he had been correct and innocence masked the depths of his wife's passion.

It was later that guilt had settled over him, shame

for his broken vows. But guilt and shame were not enough to keep him from wanting her again. Once had not been enough and doubts hovered at the edge of his mind that he could ever get enough of her. So he had kept his distance but that had done nothing to temper the temptation to touch her and most definitely had not taken the sting out of his need.

She stood in the center of the room, hands clasped, one thumb brushing over the other. A single lamp was lit and he was jealous of the shadows that caressed her lovely face. They were alone and the need to feel her bare skin beneath his hands consumed him. The last thing he wanted to do was talk.

"What is it you wish to say?" he managed to ask.

"I saw my grandparents today."

The inner joy lighting her eyes made him smile. "I can see from your expression that it went well."

She nodded. "They're wonderful. Everything I hoped they would be and more."

He risked moving close enough to crook a knuckle beneath her chin and nudge it up. "Now you look most serious. What troubles you?"

"How much time do you have?" she asked with her characteristic impudence.

"As much as you require."

"Now that I've met them my mother's behavior is even more confusing. I can't imagine why she would run away and never come back."

"I cannot answer that," he said, daring to brush a

finger over her cheek. "No one can. And you probably will never know what was in her mind."

She sighed. "I guess I knew that. It's just they were so warm and welcoming. The house is amazing. And I felt that they would have been there for her whatever she had done, whatever she needed."

"It is not necessary for you to know what was going through your mother's mind. Now that you know your family, the relationship you forge with them from this moment on will be what you make of it."

"I know." She caught the corner of her lip between her teeth. "That's really what I wanted to talk to you about."

"I do not understand."

"I won't have an opportunity to make much of a relationship with them. My goal was to meet them and I've done that. Now I have to find a way to tell them goodbye. It's time for me to go back to America."

The words seized his chest and squeezed the air from his lungs. Before he could stop the feeling, everything inside him cried out against what she had just said. He had known from the beginning that this was the course of things, but... What?

That was before he had come to know her? Before he had come to like her? A time when he had not expected to grow accustomed to her face across from his at the breakfast table. Or when he had saved her from a harmless spider. Or made love to her and yearned for more.

"You cannot go," he blurted out.

"Oh?" Her chin lifted. "I thought we had an agreement."

"It was altered when you came to my bed. By mutual consent," he added

"So what you're saying is that I can't go because I might be carrying a baby?" She turned away from him and started pacing. The sight of her bare back did little to restore rational thought. He had the absurd desire to pull her against him and kiss her until she could not think straight, either.

"A *royal* baby."

She stopped in front of him and looked up, her eyes clouded. "I'm not pregnant."

"You are certain of this?"

"Almost," she said, her gaze sliding away.

"That is unacceptable."

"Right back at you. It's unacceptable to me to give a child to a man who's incapable of loving it."

"That is what you meant when you said that God would not be so cruel."

"Exactly." She blew out a long breath. "You told me that you will never care again. That's not the ideal environment for a child. I should know. My mother loved me, but she loved the bottle more. If and when I have a child, I want it to have uncondi- tional love from both parents and you aren't capable of that. I understand. You went through an unimaginable loss and at first you get points for just breathing in and out when your life stopped. But time has passed and life never started again for you."

Was she right? Was his heart poisoned against a child they might have made? He did not know what to think. He just knew he could not let her go. Not like this. Not yet.

"Jessica—"

"You can't change my mind. There isn't anything you can say—"

"The baby—if there is one—would be in the line of succession to the throne of Bha'Khar. There is a duty to train the child in the ways of royalty should the responsibility of leadership fall to him."

She sighed. "Darn it. That's a low blow."

The miserable expression on her face again made him want to take her in his arms, yet he was the one who had put it there. "I cannot change the circumstances of my own birth and being a prince of the royal blood."

"Yeah, I get that." She folded her arms over her chest. "Okay. You win this round. I'll stay in the country until we know whether or not I'm pregnant."

That was good. The relief pouring through him elevated his mood instantly. "Excellent."

"But I'm moving in with my grandparents. If the press gets wind of it, just tell them I'm taking some quiet time to get to know them. Or come up with a better story. The last thing I want is to cause you or your family trouble."

That was not good. He much preferred that she reside in the palace, near him, but little clue why her close proximity made a difference. Surely it was all about rehabilitating his image, polishing the perceptions of the world in order to facilitate Bha'Khar's acceptance into the ranks of a global economy. But if that were the case, his chest would not feel so tight.

He did not wish her to go. But if she was not pregnant, he did not know how to make her stay.

CHAPTER ELEVEN

IF KARDAHL had said he cared about her, she would have happily stayed in the palace while they waited to see if she were pregnant, Jessica thought. He didn't even have to tell her he loved her, although she realized that's what she wanted to hear.

She just didn't get him. He'd told her she couldn't go and his eyes blazed in a way that had made her heart pound with something pathetically close to hope and a healthy dose of desire. Then he used the excuse that she might be pregnant as his reason for the order. He made no fuss when she'd said she was going to stay with her grandparents, yet a few hours later, after successfully dodging the press, here he was escorting her there in the limo.

When the big car pulled smoothly into the drive way and stopped in front of the house, Kardahl looked at her, but his blank expression gave nothing away. "Have you discussed this with your grandparents? After all, they are responsible for our betrothal. Would they approve of you leaving your husband and taking shelter with them?"

"My grandfather is my protector. He said so. My grandmother— They said if I needed anything, I should ask." She squeezed the hands clasped in her lap until her knuckles turned white. "And, yes, I called to make sure it was all right if I stayed here."

Anger darkened his eyes to twin black coals. "So," he said, "the fruit does not fall far from the tree."

"What does that mean?"

"Perhaps you are like your mother after all. You are running away."

Without responding, Jessica got out of the car, then climbed the front steps to knock on the door. That turned out not to be necessary as her grandmother opened it instantly, as if she'd been waiting. While the driver carried her luggage into the house, she glanced over her shoulder and saw Kardahl.

Her heart stuttered at the sight of his lean elegant body standing by the open car door. Remembering the exquisite feel of that naked body cradling her own, she shivered with yearning. She had never met anyone like him—kind, supportive, too handsome for his own good. As if all that wasn't enough, he had a pretty decent sense of humor. Quite simply, he was the most wonderful man she'd ever met.

She had her reasons for voluntarily walking away and in no way could it be construed as running.

In a familiar gesture, he ran his fingers through

his thick, dark hair and her heart caught again. How well she'd grown to know him. It surprised her just how much she'd come to rely on him. But a double tragedy had killed his will to reciprocate tender feelings and anything less than a committed relationship was intolerable to her. Now here she was walking into the arms of the family she'd finally found. She'd made the break from him because her heart was breaking. The man she loved could not love her back.

She waved to him, a small gesture and saw him respond before letting her grandmother lead her into the house.

"Now then," the older woman said, "I have requested tea be served in the living room and we can talk."

"Where is my grandfather?"

"He is giving his report on our trip to the Foreign Service minister and will not be home for some time. We will not be disturbed."

Jessica sank into the soft sofa cushions. "Thank you for letting me come here."

"Thank you for turning to us. It is what families are for. But I am curious about why you felt it necessary to leave the prince. Is there a problem?"

Only if she was pregnant. "Kardahl and I have some things to work out and I felt I could do that better if I had some distance."

"I see."

Was she running? Like her mother.

Jess folded her hands in her lap and crossed one thumb over the other. "Why did she run? My mother, I mean. Why didn't she turn to you and my grandfather for help?"

"I do not know for sure."

"You knew her. She was your jewel, your best and brightest. You must have an idea why she didn't feel she could come to you when she found out she was in trouble."

"Pride. Shame." Her grandmother stared sadly out the French doors.

"According to the letter she left me, my father was a diplomatic attaché," Jess confirmed.

The older woman nodded. "Maram met him right here in this house, at an embassy party that your grandfather and I hosted. He was married and far from home. She was young and quite lovely. They flirted and she began to make excuses to see him at the Foreign Ministry office. He made a pretext of coming here to see your grandfather. We knew what was happening and sternly warned her away from him. Esam and I argued with her many times, but our disapproval only seemed to make her want to be with him more."

"So she refused to stop seeing him?"

Leena nodded. "We were beside ourselves with frustration and worry. She was stubborn and so very young."

"And then she got pregnant." Jessica watched the bewilderment turn to pain on her grand-mother's face.

"We did not know that at first. She simply dis-appeared. Then we began to hope it was a child making her too ashamed to come to us and nothing far more sinister."

"Did you go to my father?"

"Of course."

"Cad."

"Yes. Although he had no knowledge of her whereabouts he confirmed that she had come to him and revealed her condition. He told us about his last conversation with Maram and that he'd made it clear he was an ambitious man. He would not leave his wife and risk a scandal."

"Big cad."

"Indeed." Her grandmother's eyes were hard.

Jess smiled at the hostility she exuded, a mother lioness protecting her brood. And Jess was part of the brood. How wonderful it felt to be part of something. She was beyond glad to have someone in her corner. "Did my father stay here in the diplomatic service?"

"He took our daughter from us, we took his pro-fession from him. I'm not proud of it, but…" She shrugged.

"I see." Jess met her gaze. "Considering that, I'm a little surprised you embraced me so warmly. I'm the child of the man who disgraced your daughter."

"She was not without blame." Her grandmother put a comforting hand over hers. "But we never stopped loving her. You are the child of our child and we love you."

Behind the sofa, a low wall separated this room from the dining area and sitting on top were framed photographs. Jess reached over and picked up one of her mother as a young girl.

"Was my mother a hopeless romantic?"

Leena frowned as she thought about the question. "If you mean was she possessed of a soft and romantic heart, I believe the answer is yes. She cared with every part of herself—mind, soul, body. She loved well, but not wisely."

"Do you think I'm like her?"

"I cannot say, as we are just getting to know each other. Clearly you are troubled about something." She smiled, a small upturning of her mouth. "I would have to be very dimwitted not to know that whatever has made your eyes so sad has something to do with His Highness, the prince."

"No wonder my mother couldn't fool you," Jess answered, trying to make light of it.

"I am old, not deaf, dumb and blind."

"You're not old."

"And you are trying to flatter me. I like that in a granddaughter. And I believe it to be sincere, although it is rooted in the fact that you do not wish to discuss what is really bothering you and are attempting to distract me." Her eyes brooked no evasion. "Tell me what is wrong."

"Because I wouldn't stay at the palace Kardahl said that I was running away—like my mother."

"Running from what? Your mother left us because she was embarrassed and feared that she had disgraced her family."

"It's still sad."

"Yes. Although, from the perspective of many years passed, in a way I find her flight oddly comforting. She knew we were hurt and she did not want to see the pain she had caused. What she failed to take into consideration is that hurt heals."

Not in Kardahl's case. He'd made it clear that he would never get over the love he'd lost and the child she'd carried. She put her hand over her abdomen and prayed that they hadn't made a baby.

"You and Kardahl were betrothed and against the odds have found each other and from what I can see, there is a romantic spark."

On her part, not so much his. "I think you're seeing static electricity."

"Joke if it makes you feel better, my dear. But simply because a child shares characteristics of the parent, they are not necessarily predestined to repeat the same mistakes."

"I hope you're right."

"Of course I'm right. Your mother's heart was

stolen by a man who was not free. She fell hope-lessly in love, but it was doomed from the start."

And those words did not make Jessica feel better. Because of Kardahl's past, her love for him had been doomed from the start—just like her mother's. And she wondered which was worse—a series of men who used and abandoned you while you searched for love. Or never trying again because you'd found the one man who'd once loved so well the pain of his loss would keep him from giving his heart ever again.

Her grandmother frowned. "But when you speak of running, are you talking about going back to America?"

"I have a job there," Jess admitted. "Working with children who need me."

"I am certain they do. But consider this—would you be giving to others for all the right reasons?"

"I'm not sure what you mean."

"Just this—I will not pry into your feelings for Prince Kardahl. And you will always have a home here with your grandfather and myself. We understand if you decide that your work is the right reason to go back to your home. But before you make that decision, remember what your mother did not—you can leave Bha'Khar, but you will take all your troubles with you."

There was a reason they called it emotional baggage. Jess had come here with very little of it, but if she left now, ten trunks wouldn't be enough to carry all her problems.

When she couldn't hold back the tears a moment longer, her grandmother gathered her into her arms and held her tight. She'd come here looking for family and found it. She hadn't been looking for love, but she'd found that, too.

At least she had someone to hold her while she cried. It was definitely the best and worst of times.

From the moment his secretary told him Jessica called to set up a meeting, Kardahl had been unable to concentrate. It would have been better if the young man had interrupted his conference call. Had he spoken with his wife, far more would have been accomplished this morning. Now he could not get her out of his mind. Truthfully that was not new. It was a condition he had become accustomed to ever since his first sight of her on the royal jet.

The condition had escalated to a state of acute distress in the past several weeks, after he had left Jessica with her grandmother. His suite seemed too big, too empty without her there. But how could that be? It was not as if her petite presence took up so very much space. He leaned back in his office chair and stared at a computer screen that no longer interested him. Nothing held his attention unless it included thoughts of his wife.

In truth, the size of her form, lovely and curva-

ceous though it might be, was not the issue. It was
the size of her character, personality, heart and spirit
that made him miss her with every part of his being.

So lost was he in his thoughts, the buzz of the
intercom startled him. "Your Highness?"

He pushed the button to answer. "Yes?"

"Your wife has arrived."

Kardahl's heart lurched and a feeling of height-
ened anticipation surged through him. It took all of
his considerable self-control to keep his voice level.
"Send her in."

It seemed a lifetime before the office door opened
and she stood there. In evening gown or jeans, she
had never looked more beautiful to him than she did
now wearing a floral print skirt, cream-colored
blouse and loosely crocheted sweater. Her sun-
kissed brown hair was pulled into a casual knot at her
nape with loose strands caressing her neck and
cheeks. The blood pounded through his veins and
roared in his ears as the need to take her in his arms
became almost more than his considerable self-
control could withstand.

He stood but did not come around to meet her. He
kept his glass-topped desk between them. "Hello."

"Hi. This is nice," she said, looking around the
spacious office with the thick Berber carpet and
leather furniture. "I never saw where you work."

One corner of his mouth lifted. "You did not believe
I worked so it would have been an exercise in futility."

"I was wrong." She pointed a finger at him. "And that's the last time I'm going to say it."

"Very well." He held out a hand, indicating the two chairs in front of his desk. "Please sit down."

"Thank you." Her tone was very formal now.

He preferred the seductive whisper in her voice when he had held her in his arms and made love to her. He favored the teasing tone just now when she had admitted her erroneous first impression of his character. He desired almost anything to the aloof and distancing manner she had assumed just a moment ago.

"I regret that my secretary did not put you through when you called earlier," he said. "I was involved. Had I but known you were trying to reach me, I would have interrupted the proceedings. It was a budget conference—" He stopped. Since when did he babble about trivialities? "To what do I owe the pleasure of your first visit to my office?"

"This is something I thought I should tell you in person."

The look on her face was difficult to read and he wondered when she had learned to mask her emotions so well. She had agreed to stay in Bha'Khar until she learned whether or not she carried his child. Since he had not seen or spoken to her in several weeks, it was an educated guess that her visit to the lion's den was in regard to her physical condition.

"Are you pregnant?" he asked bluntly.

She sighed. "No."

"No?"

She shook her head and he read the truth in her eyes. His spirits plummeted and until that moment he had not realized he had carried inside him a high level of anticipation that her answer would be different.

"I see," was all he said.

She looked surprised. "I thought you'd be more relieved."

As did he. But it was not so. He became conscious of the fact that he did indeed want a child with Jessica and the awareness stunned him.

Before he could formulate a response to that, she spoke again. "That's one hurdle out of the way."

"Of what?" he asked.

"Dissolution of our union. Since there can't be an annulment, we need to go ahead with the divorce."

As the words penetrated, again he was stunned. It was thickheaded of him to believe she would have changed her mind, but he realized the hope had been there all along.

"Have you spoken with your grandparents regarding your wishes?"

She nodded. "They're disappointed. They'd hoped I would stay in Bha'Khar, but ultimately they want me to be happy."

"Are you so very certain you cannot be happy here in the palace?"

"With you," she clarified.

"Yes." He did not wish to look deeply into his feelings, but one thing was quite clear. He did not want her to go. "I respect and care for you."

She clasped her hands in her lap and rubbed one thumb over the other. The gesture had become so familiar. She was nervous and he was glad.

"I've come to respect you, too, Kardahl. And that's saying a lot considering my opinion when I arrived."

"I am glad. Life here could be very rewarding. You could champion the causes of the desert people and there are children in Bha'Khar who would benefit greatly from your interest and support."

She shook her head. "It's not enough."

"Those two causes are quite a challenge," he argued. "You would—"

"That's not what I meant. It's not enough for me personally. I'm a hopeless romantic. Like my mother. All my life I've dreamed of being swept off my feet by the man of my dreams." She laughed self-consciously. "I know that sounds foolish, but it's the truth. And I won't settle for less."

Kardahl didn't know what to say. In the beginning, it had all seemed so simple. They would help each other. But that was before he had come to know her. And want her. And love…

No. Not that.

But he could not say the words that would keep her here. He was loath to think it let alone give weight and importance by voicing it. That would tempt fate and he just wished to go on as they were. His greatest pain had been precipitated by this condition and he would not let himself ever experience such a thing again.

"I won't agree to a divorce," he ground out.

Her gaze jumped to his and something flashed in her eyes. "Then you leave me no choice but to hire an attorney, one whose specialty is international law."

"Is that a threat?"

"No. But the thing is, we both know I have a good case for dissolving this marriage. I signed the proxy under false pretenses."

"Have you been so unhappy in Bha'Khar?" he demanded.

She hesitated for a split second. "That's not the point," she finally said. "You've made it clear that you can't love me. You'll never know how deeply I wish it could be different. And how sorry I am for you. And angry. To withhold your love is disrespectful to the memory of the woman you lost and the child who will never live except in your heart."

The truth of her words pierced his heart and he winced at the pain. "Jessica, I—"

She stood. "The thing is, Kardahl, your heart is dead. That means your child will never live at all. And I won't be tied by a binding legal agreement to a man who can't love me. That's no life at all."

CHAPTER TWELVE

KARDAHL stared at the divorce papers on his desk. It had only been a week since she had sat in the chair across from him and said that she would not be legally bound to a man who could not love her. He had made known his positive feelings. Why was that not enough for her? They got on so well together, why did she need more?

The intercom on his desk buzzed and he answered. "Yes?"

"The Crown Prince is here to see you, Your Highness."

"Send him in." Kardahl smiled. He knew what this was about and relished the opportunity to do battle with his brother.

Malik entered his office and sat down in front of the desk. He did not look happy. "Father sent me to speak with you. You are asking for a lot of money, Kardahl."

"Yes. But it will be well spent on programs that have been too long neglected."

His brother's gaze narrowed. "This is the first time you have expressed such a viewpoint."

With Jessica, it was the first time he had met such an extraordinary woman who had a way of cutting to the heart of a matter. He had been operating under the belief that he was handling his responsibilities as a member of the royal family. She had made him see that he was isolated and out of touch with the needs of the people. He was detached from life in general and simply going through the motions of his work without an emotional connection. That was not enough in order to be an effective public official whose primary interest should be the welfare of the citizens of Bha'Khar.

Kardahl linked his fingers and rested his hands on the divorce decree on his desk. "It has been brought to my attention that the government is not doing all it could and should to invest in the future of Bha'Khar."

A gleam stole into Malik's eyes. "Lately your attention has been concentrated on your wife. Would I be wrong to think that she is the one who has altered your views?"

"It does not matter. The point is that the allocation is necessary."

"I agree, but you are the minister of Finance. It is up to you to convince father to change his mind." Malik leaned his elbows on his knees and his look was sympathetic. "You know better than anyone that he holds in high esteem the traditions of the land of our birth."

"Sometimes traditions need shaking up." But with the power of passion for his cause, he would be persuasive. "I am prepared to change his mind."

"Are you prepared to forgive him also?"

Kardahl knew what his brother was asking. All this time he had held his father responsible for the tragedy that took the woman he had loved. The truth was, it was an accident and Kardahl had felt the need to hold someone accountable. Perhaps in time the king would have been convinced to alter the tradition and allow him to marry the mother of his child. They would never know. He would always have tender feelings for them, but the paralyzing pain no longer held him in a state somewhere between life and death. In truth, tradition had brought him Jessica. It was he, Kardahl, who had erred badly and he did not know how to make things right.

"Yes." He sighed. "I am no longer angry at father."

Malik nodded. "I suspect Jessica is responsible for this as well?"

"In a circuitous way."

"That heartens me," his brother said, smiling broadly. "My own betrothed will be here from America in a number of weeks."

"Tread cautiously with your optimism. You know the circumstances of our marriage?"

"That father's overzealous aide obtained her signature on the proxy in a deceptive manner? Yes. I heard."

Kardahl held up the legal document. "And you know that she is determined to obtain a divorce."

"I do. And you do not wish it?"

"No."

"That is a problem. You seem confident of persuading father of the wisdom of your budget allocations. Yet you cannot convince your wife of the wisdom of remaining married to you?" The gleam in Malik's eyes was clear evidence that he was enjoying this far too much.

"The two matters are completely unrelated." As, at the moment, he wished he and his brother were.

"I will be certain not to make the same mistakes when my own bride arrives. Although, I am assured that the bride chosen for me is well-trained in the matters of discipline, royal protocol and tradition. And, unlike your wife, she is obedient."

"You are in for a rude awakening, my brother," Kardahl assured him. "Obedience does not guarantee a successful marriage."

"It does not hurt."

Hurt. Kardahl sighed. Both he and Jessica were wounded souls. She was a young and vulnerable witness to her mother's downward fall into alcoholism while searching for love. He had found it once, only to have it ripped away, making him determined not to care or hurt again. What a pair they were.

He refused to debate the virtues of an obedient bride. Soon enough his brother would deal with the issue on his own. But Kardahl did wish to unburden himself as the knot of pain inside him would not go away. Maybe Jessica was right and talking would help.

"Jessica has longed for a romantic relationship and will not settle for less than her expectation." He met his brother's gaze. "And I have stubbornly resisted loving again."

"To no avail," his brother commented.

As much as he disliked feeding his brother's ego, he could not deny the truth of the statement. "You would be correct."

"Then you must talk her out of the divorce," Malik said seriously.

"How do you suggest I do that?"

"Convince her of your deep and tender feelings."

"I have shown her in every possible way that I care. So, again I say, how do I go about that?" Kardahl demanded.

"You have a certain reputation with the ladies—"

"Do not go there." This was not the time to inform his brother that reminding Jessica of his reputation would be counterproductive to his goal of changing her mind.

"Let me finish. I'm simply suggesting that you should do what you do best. Court her. As I intend to do with my betrothed when she arrives."

"Flowers? Moonlight? Promises?" Cold showers in a mountain stream, he thought with a shudder. Lying beside her without touching when all he wanted was to pull her into his arms and kiss her until neither of them could think straight.

"Exactly," his brother agreed.

"She is not susceptible to traditional courting methods."

"If they were accompanied by a sincere declaration of your feelings that might alter her perception," Malik pointed out. He leaned back in the chair and steepled his fingers as he studied Kardahl. "If you love her and I feel certain that is the case, you must tell her so."

"I cannot."

"Rubbish."

Kardahl stood and started pacing his office. "It would test the boundaries of fate. The last time I said those words to a woman I lost her."

"It seems to me that you will lose again if you do not say it." Malik stood and stepped into his path, making him stop, meeting his gaze to get his point across. "This time the loss would be unforgivable because it is within your power to control."

Kardahl felt the air leave his lungs as surely as if his brother had made a fist and punched him in the stomach. All this time he had been trying to control his feelings because that was the only thing he had power over. Except with Jessica, he had no power to resist her. She forced him to feel again and he was in love with her.

He hoped he had not realized the truth of his feelings too late.

* * *

Excitement raced through Jessica as she walked into the palace ballroom filled with men and women wearing tuxedos and gowns. She'd dressed with great care in a floor-length strapless black satin dress and her grandparents thought she looked beautiful. They were here somewhere, hanging out with their friends the king and queen of Bha'Khar, soon to be her ex-in-laws. The ball was held annually to celebrate national pride and when Kardahl had called and invited her to one last palace function, she hadn't been able to refuse him. His charm had nothing to do with her decision to attend. Being in love with him had everything to do with it.

Foolishly she'd once thought that if he told her he cared it would be enough. The last time she'd seen him he'd said the words, but it wasn't all right. She didn't want just all right, she wanted fireworks and moonbeams.

She stood just inside the door as the royal family took their places on a dais at the front of the ballroom. The king made a speech and said the world was changing and Bha'khar needed energy and youth to guide it into the world order. He planned to step aside soon to let Prince Malik assume the throne with the counsel of his brother Prince Kardahl.

Even the sound of his name made Jessica's heart beat faster. She was going to miss him terribly. And not only him. She would miss the country, the people, her family. The downside of knowing them was having to say goodbye. As she watched, Kardahl stepped to the microphone. He was a sight for sore eyes and an even sorer heart. As if he had a special radar, his gaze met hers across the crowded room and he smiled the smile that made her stomach drop and her knees weak.

"Good evening. My parents, my brother and I thank you all for coming tonight." He glanced at his father and the two exchanged a smile. Then Kardahl looked into the crowd, finally meeting her gaze. "Someone whose opinion I respect very much recently pointed out to me that I have been neglecting our most precious natural resource. That ends tonight. The king has approved my proposal to appropriate a great deal of money for educational endeavors for the children of Bha'Khar. I will personally oversee the dispersal of these funds. But talk is cheap. It is action that shows the sincerity of a man's heart. If I do not fulfill this promise, I expect the citizens of the country to hold me accountable as I shall hold myself accountable." After a burst of sudden and enthusiastic applause tapered off, he said, "We are here tonight to celebrate. Our country has long and distinguished traditions. Talking is one of them, but I have done enough for tonight. On behalf of the king and queen and the Crown Prince I wish you all to enjoy yourselves."

Stunned didn't begin to describe what Jessica was feeling. Kardahl had been talking about her. He respected her. He'd told her so, when he'd said he cared. Tonight he'd said so publicly. And he was right. Actions spoke louder than words. Everything he'd done said he cared and she'd thrown that away.

She looked up and saw that he was coming toward her, making his way through the crowd. Her first thought was to run and that was exactly why she stood her ground and smiled when he finally stood in front of her.

"Hello," she said.

"You came."

"I did. And I see that you've been busy making up with your father and finding money for the kids."

He grinned. "The king and I have indeed come to a new and pleasant understanding. After much discussion he saw the wisdom of investing in the youth of Bha'Khar."

"I'm so glad, Kardahl," she said.

His smile disappeared and a fierce intensity darkened his eyes. "I must speak with you alone."

"All right." How could she say no? She wanted nothing more than to be alone with him—even if it was for the last time. Especially because of that.

He took her arm and they slipped out the door and into the hall. Just outside, a group of reporters waited, like circling sharks who smelled blood in the water and were waiting to pounce. He put his arm around her and they continued to walk as questions peppered them.

"There's a rumor that your marriage is falling apart. Would you care to comment?"

"Your Highness, we heard your speech. Did your wife talk you into appropriating the money for the kids?"

"She's a social worker in the United States, right? Can you confirm that she grew up in a state run home?

"Is it also true that her mother died of alcoholism?"

Kardahl turned on them, his lean jaw tight with fury. "My wife has the greatest heart of any woman I have ever known. I will confirm what is public record and that is that she has known some adversity. Without that, she would not be as beautiful on the inside as she is on the outside."

A microphone was thrust at him. "Would you care to comment on the state of your marriage?"

When he answered, his voice was hard as steel. "My wife made me think about many things. And she is responsible for the fact that I have put aside my selfish ways. She made me want to be a better man. But hear me, and hear me well—I need you, all of the media to spread my message for the children. But I will tolerate no further intrusion into my private life. Do I make myself clear?"

Jess was as speechless as the reporters. Before any of them could answer, he took her hand in a firm grasp and escorted her down the hall and to the elevators. He pushed the button for the ground floor. The next thing she knew, they were in the palace garden. This was where Kardahl had kissed her for the first time. The lighting and lush plants had made it magical then, and the memories made it even more magical now. Sadness swamped her at the thought of leaving everything she'd ever wanted. She'd been too angry and defensive to recognize it, to fight for it.

He held out his arm, indicating the wrought-iron bench. "Will you sit with me?"

"Yes."

One word was all she could manage since her throat was thick with emotion. So much for going away quietly. The press had dug into her past and it would be out there for all the world to see. But once again, Kardahl had been there for her, defending her. And the things he'd said… More importantly, the things he was going to do. Suddenly the feelings grew so big she couldn't hold them back. A single tear slipped from the corner of her eye. Then another. And another.

"Jessica—" He cupped her cheek in his hand and brushed the moisture away with his thumb. "The reporters will not bother you again. I will not allow it."

She shook her head. "That's not why I'm crying."

"Tell me who is responsible for your unhappiness and I will see that they are severely punished."

"You are responsible."

"I?" If she'd slapped him, he couldn't have looked more surprised.

She nodded. "You're going to use your power for good. For the children."

"I was under the impression that is what you wished."

"I do. And it makes me very happy."

Confusion creased his forehead. "I do not understand. If you are happy, then why do you cry?"

"I'm sad, too. You would have been an amazing father."

She had nothing left to lose by telling him that. Since the day she'd told him she wasn't carrying his child, she'd had a lot of time to think about things. How her mother must have felt—pregnant, alone, scared. And in love with a man she could never have. But knowing love once made her want the feeling again and she had looked, but was doomed to the disappointment of never finding it. Loving Kardahl, wanting to be with him and only him, made Jessica understand. The power of love, the unbelievably wonderful feeling was why her mother had kept searching to find it again.

Something inside Jess melted away and she suspected it was bitterness she hadn't even known she carried. She hadn't realized she needed to forgive her mother, but she felt the burden of resentment lift from her heart.

Kardahl took her hand in both of his. "I am pleased that you think I would be a good father. But I find myself in need of a woman who would be a good mother."

Her gaze jumped to his as hope swelled inside

her. What if just once life came down on the side of the hopeless romantic? But what if she was wrong?

"It's too late, Kardahl. The divorce is proceeding. Maybe it would be better just to let it go on. Maybe we'd be better off apart—"

"No." His eyes were fierce and stubborn determination pressed his mouth into a thin line. "I cannot speak for you, but I know for certain that I would *not* be better off."

"But we—"

"I love you," he said simply.

"What?" She couldn't believe her ears weren't substituting words that her heart desperately wanted to hear.

"You can go through with severing our union, but that will not end it. I will continue to pursue you and as you have pointed out on numerous occasions, I have had much practice in successfully pursuing women."

"There is a saying—never judge a book by its cover. I am guilty of that. I didn't know you or understand what you'd been through. I didn't realize that you were capable of deep and lasting feelings. And now—"

"Now, my darling, I am in love with you. I have courted and won many who were unimportant, but I love only you. That makes you beyond important, it makes you priceless."

She struggled against all her perceptions honed by sadness and loss. "It's difficult for me to believe—"

He touched a finger to her lips to silence her.

"Believe it. You are the one who breathed life into my soul once again. You are the one who brought me out of the shadows. Your fingers touched my unresponsive heart and pulled it free of the dark place where I have hidden it to keep it safe. And now that I have begun to feel again, I can no longer be satisfied with this empty life I have known."

"Oh, Kardahl—"

He took her face in his hands and there was a desperation in his touch, in his gaze. "If you do not return my feelings now, at least give me another chance. I will do everything within my power to change your mind—"

"I do love you."

He went completely still, then slowly a smile relaxed the tension in his mouth. "That pleases me." Lowering his head, he touched his lips to hers in the most exquisite kiss. When he pulled away, he said, "I am humbled and honored. And very grateful."

Then he went down on one knee as he slid his hand into his pocket and pulled out a ring. "Your courage and spirit in facing life are an inspiration and I wish to be your equal, to embrace life with you by my side. This ring has been in my family for generations and it is fitting that one who knows the fragility and value of family be the one to wear it." He met her gaze with an earnest sincerity that took her breath away. "Will you do me the honor of being my wife?"

"It's the most beautiful ring I've ever seen." She

was dazzled by the sapphire surrounded by diamonds as he slipped it on her finger. Then she smiled
into his eyes. "I'm already your wife."

"I wish to have a ceremony, an exchange of
vows—face-to-face this time. Vows spoken with the
love we have found through the tradition of betrothal by our beloved families, the love we will share
for the rest of our lives. Will you do that?"

"I will."

He stood and pulled her to her feet and into his
arms. "Oh, my heart, you have made me the happiest
man in the world."

She rested her cheek on his chest and heard the
solid steady beat of the heart she'd brought back to
life. A happiness she'd never known before
expanded inside her. "You're a good man, so different from what I thought at first. Now I know you
simply lost your way for a while."

"And you have shown me the path to contentment."

"Right back at you. Nothing would make me
happier than to be your wife and have children with
you. Together we can make the world a better place."

He nodded. "It is my solemn promise to my reluctant bride."

She wasn't reluctant any longer. She was a
hopeless romantic who'd found the love of her life
halfway around the world and validated what she'd
always believed.

Love will find a way.

ACCIDENTALLY THE SHEIKH'S WIFE

BARBARA McMAHON

Barbara McMahon was born and raised in the US South, but settled in California after spending a year flying around the world for an international airline. After settling down to raise a family and work for a computer firm, she began writing when her children started school. Now, feeling fortunate in being able to realise the long-held dream of quitting her day job and writing full-time, she and her husband have moved to the Sierra Nevada of California, where she finds her desire to write is stronger than ever. With the beauty of the mountains visible from her windows, and the pace of life slower than that of the hectic San Francisco Bay Area, where they previously resided, she finds more time than ever to think up stories and characters and share them with others through writing. Barbara loves to hear from readers. You can reach her at PO Box 977, Pioneer, CA 95666-0977, USA. Readers can also contact Barbara at her website, www.barbaramcmahon.com.

To Carol, Barbara, Kate, Diana, Lynn and Candice.
Thanks a bunch.
Lunch is always great fun.

CHAPTER ONE

BETHANNE SANDERS lined up the aircraft with the designated runway and began the final descent. The new jet handled like a dream—all the way from Texas to the coast of the Persian Gulf. It was the first time she'd flown halfway around the world and she wished she could continue on until she circled the globe. When she left Quishari, it would be by commercial flight back through Europe.

Maybe she'd get another dream assignment like this one in the not-too-distant future. For now, she continued to scan the landscape as far as she could see as the plane began descending. Excitement built. The Persian Gulf was magnificently blue, from deep, dark navy to shades of azure and turquoise. The strip of sandy beach now visible was almost blinding beneath the sun. She had read so much about Quishari and heard so much from her father, she almost felt like she recognized the landmarks as she came in for the landing. Her heart raced at the thought of actually being here. It was like a dream come true.

Had this assignment not materialized, she still would have come—but it might have taken longer as the cost was exorbitant and savings accumulated slowly.

But fate had stepped in—almost like the answer to a

prayer. She was delivering a brand-new Starcraft jet to Sheikh Rashid al Harum—and bringing in a priceless cargo. His soon-to-be fiancée.

Except for the shakedown trips around Texas, the only hours on this jet were the ones taken to fly it here. If the sheikh liked it and accepted delivery, he'd be the proud owner of the latest and greatest of the Starcraft line.

She hoped the sheikh's fiancée enjoyed the detailing of the luxury appointments and had enjoyed the flight. Bethanne had taken extra care to make the journey as smooth as possible. She found it vastly romantic that they were planning to marry—and neither had yet met the other.

A bit odd in the twenty-first century. Still, to have been chosen to be the bride of one of the fabulously wealthy sheikhs of Quishari had to be thrilling. Pictures had been exchanged, the parents had made the arrangements. How did a thirty-four-year-old man feel about having his bride hand-picked? Not too different from some of the online dating services—match likes and dislikes, find someone compatible, and there they were.

Would they kiss when meeting? Seal the deal, so to speak? Or would the woman be too shy to be bold enough for physical affection at the instant of meeting?

She had daydreamed on the long portions of the flight when autopilot had taken care of flying that she was being met by someone who would sweep her off her feet, make her feel cherished and special.

Or, alternatively, she'd also imagined her father striding along the tarmac, gathering her into his arms for one of his big bear hugs.

Blinking, Bethanne brought her attention back to the task of landing this multimillion-dollar jet.

The snowy-white exterior had already been detailed with

stripes using the colors of Quishari—blue and gold and green.
The interior resembled a high-end hotel lobby. The lush
Persian carpet in golds and reds supported cushy sofas and
armchairs, all with the requisite seat belts. The small dining
area was elegant with rich walnut furnishings. The galley was
fully stocked, and included a stove, oven and microwave in
addition to the lavish below-counter refrigerator, wider than
long, capable of carrying any supplies necessary for the
sheikh's pleasure. Even the sole restroom was spacious.

Bethanne had shown Haile al Benqura all the features of
the cabin before going to the cockpit for her preflight routine.
The chaperone accompanying the young woman had not
spoken English, but Haile had. She'd taken in everything with
a solemn demeanor. Wasn't she the slightest bit excited?
Apparently when the sheikh had mentioned something to the
president of Starcraft, her boss had immediately offered to fly
Haile from her home in Morocco to Quishari as a favor to the
prospective buyer of their top-of-the-line private jet.

Bethanne glanced at her copilot, Jess Bradshaw. It was his
first long-distance delivery as well and they had taken turns
flying the aircraft to minimize delivery time.

"Want to bring it in?" she asked.

"No. We want this to go perfectly. I'm not as good at it as you."

She shrugged and then brought the plane down with a kiss
against the asphalt.

"Nice job," Jess said.

"Thanks. This is a sweetheart of a plane. The sheikh is one
lucky man."

She followed directions from the tower and taxied to an
area away from the main terminal. The immaculate hangar
was already swarming with ground crew; everyone had eyes
on the jet as she pulled it into the designated slot. She and Jess
ran through the checklist as they shut down. She wanted to

10 ACCIDENTALLY THE SHEIKH'S WIFE

dash out and breathe the Quishari air. But duty first. She had scheduled several days here to see if she could find her dad. And to see the towns and desert that made Quishari famous.

"I'm glad we get to sleep on the way home," Jess mumbled, waiting for her to get up first. He followed her from the cockpit to the outside door of the jet. With minimum effort, Bethanne opened it, watching as stairs unfolded. She glanced back and saw the chaperone. Where was Haile? In the restroom? Probably primping to look her best when seeing the sheikh for the first time. Bethanne hoped she hadn't been there when they landed. Jess had announced their approach and told the passengers to fasten seat belts.

The chaperone looked worried, her eyes darting around the cabin, refusing to meet Bethanne's gaze. Had she been afraid of flying? Bethanne couldn't image anyone not loving it. She'd wanted to be a pilot since she turned five and first been taken up in the cockpit of a small plane. Of course, wanting to follow in her father's footsteps had also played a big part.

Two men waited at the foot of the stairs. When the steps unfolded and locked in place, the taller began to ascend. Bethanne watched him approach. He was maybe six-three or four. Which Bethanne found refreshing. Her own five-ten height usually had her eye to eye with men. His dark hair shone in the sunlight, his skin was tanned to teak. The closer he came, the more she could see—from dark eyes that watched her steadily, to a strong jaw that suggested arrogance and power, to the wide shoulders encased in a pristine white shirt and dark charcoal suit.

Her heart began to beat heavily. She was fascinated by the man. Awareness flooded through her, as did a sudden need to brush her hair—she hoped it was still neat in its French plait. Studying him as he drew closer every step, she noticed the hint of wave in his hair. She wondered what he'd look like if he ran his fingers through his hair. Or if she did.

She swallowed and tried to look away. Fantasies like that would get her nowhere. This had to be Sheikh Rashid al Harum. Almost-fiancé to the woman in the back of the plane. Oh, lucky Haile al Benqura. She had undoubtedly fallen in love with the man from the pictures exchanged. Now she would be greeted and swept off her feet with one of the most gorgeous men Bethanne had ever seen.

"I am Rashid al Harum. Welcome to Quishari," he said in English as he stepped into the aircraft.

"Thank you." She cleared her throat. That husky tone wasn't like her. This man was rattling her senses. "I'm Bethanne Sanders. My copilot, Jess Bradshaw." She saw the surprise in his eyes. Despite all the headway women had made in aviation, it was still considered primarily a male profession. She was growing used to seeing that expression—especially in locales away from the U.S.

Rashid al Harum inclined his head slightly and then looked beyond them into the cabin.

The older woman rose and began to speak in a rapid strained tone.

Bethanne still didn't see Haile. Was she ill? As the chaperone continued, she glanced at the sheikh, wishing she understood the language. His face grew harder by the second. In a moment he turned and glared at Bethanne. "What do you know of Haile's disappearance?" he asked in English.

Bethanne looked back into the cabin. "Disappearance? Isn't she in the restroom?" she asked, suddenly worried something was wrong. What had the chaperone said? Where was Haile al Benqura?

"Apparently she never left Morocco," the sheikh said in a tight voice.

"What? That's impossible. I showed her around the plane myself. She was on board when we were ready to leave." She turned to Jess. "You saw her, right? When you boarded?"

Jess shook his head slightly. "I don't remember seeing her when I closed the door. A maintenance man ran down the stairs just as I was rounding the back to board. No one else got off the plane."

"There shouldn't have been a maintenance man aboard— there's nothing wrong with the plane," Bethanne said. What was going on? Where was Haile? "What did she say?" Bethanne gestured to the chaperone, still standing in front of the sofa.

The sheikh glared at her for a moment, then in a soft, controlled voice that did not soothe at all, said, "I suggest that you and I speak alone."

She stared at him, suddenly worried things had gone terribly wrong. He seemed to tower above her, anger evident.

"I'll check on things on the ground," Jess said with obvious relief. He eased by the two of them and hurried down the stairs. Once he was out of earshot, the sheikh turned to the older woman and spoke briefly.

She dropped her gaze and nodded. Gathering her few things, she walked to the back and sat on the edge of the sofa, gazing out one of the small windows.

"According to her, Haile took off before the plane departed Morocco, running to meet a lover."

"What? How is that possible? I thought she was coming here to meet you—your fiancée, or almost," Bethanne blurted out before thinking. How could the woman choose someone else over this man? was Bethanne's first thought.

"So she is, was, to be. Her family and mine have been in negotiations for months over an oil deal that would prove advantageous to both countries. Included in that was the merger of our two families through marriage. Now my entire family—

not to mention others in this country—expects the arrival of a woman who is to be my wife—and she is not on board."

Bethanne swallowed hard at the anger in his eyes. Surreptitiously wiping her palms against the fabric of her uniform, she raised her chin and said, "I'm not responsible for her leaving the plane. I thought she was on board. She was when I last saw her."

"You're the captain of the aircraft. What goes on is your responsibility. I hold you accountable. How could you let her leave?" His dark eyes pinned her in place. His entire demeanor shimmered with anger—controlled, which made it seem even stronger.

"How was I suppose to know she didn't want to come here? I thought everything was arranged." She would not tell him how romantic she found the scenario. Maybe she hadn't thought it through if the woman had fled rather than come to Quishari. "Though if I had known the circumstances, maybe I would have questioned whether anyone wanted to be *negotiated* into a marriage. I thought it was an old-fashioned mail-order-bride situation. But if the bride wasn't willing, I'm glad I did not have a part in bringing her here." She looked at the older woman. "She's the one you should hold responsible. Bringing them from Morocco to Quishari was a favor to you by our company."

"But the favor was not fulfilled. She is not here."

"I can see that. What do you want me to do about it now?" Bethanne said.

"The marriage would be an arrangement that benefits both countries," he said with a dismissing gesture. "That is not any concern of yours. The decision has been made. What is of your concern, is the fact Haile went missing on your watch."

Bethanne met his gaze bravely. It was not her fault the woman had deplaned. Why hadn't the chaperone stopped her? Or told someone before they took off from Morocco? What else could she say?

This was certainly not the happy arrival at Quishari she'd anticipated.

"The immediate need, now, is for damage control," he said after a moment. The sheikh looked back at the woman sitting so still in the back of the jet. For a moment Bethanne imagined she could see the wheels spinning in his head. How could she have known Haile wasn't as interested in the marriage as she had thought? She would never have suspected a young woman like Haile would disguise herself and slip away between the time Bethanne went into the cockpit and Jess joined her. It couldn't have been more than five minutes. Obviously it had not been a spur-of-the-moment decision. It had taken planning and daring. Bethanne's romantic mind imagined Haile deplaning surreptitiously and finding her lover and both fleeing, whilst her father and his minions followed on horseback. She blinked. Her overactive imagination could get her in trouble.

"I'm sorry I can't help you," she said, hoping to ease the tension that was as thick as butter. Her primary goal was to deliver the plane, which she'd done. Now all the sheikh had to do was accept the delivery, sign the paperwork and Bethanne could begin her vacation in Quishari while Jess would be flying back to Texas on the next available flight.

"Ah, but you can help. In fact, I insist." He turned back to her. The serious expression in his eyes held her in thrall. What did he mean?

"How can I help? Fly back to Morocco and find her? I wouldn't begin to know where to look."

"Despite my family's efforts to keep the entire matter solely within the family, rumors have been flying around the country. I've ignored them, but I know they speculate a special visitor will arrive soon. My coming to meet this plane would have fueled speculation even more. So, you're it."

"I'm what it?" she asked, wondering what would happen if there was no special visitor. Some gossip, more speculation about when his fiancée would arrive.

"The woman I came to meet. It's as if it was meant to be. What are the odds of having a female pilot bringing the plane— and one who is young and pretty enough to pass muster?"

"Muster for what?" Bethanne wondered if she'd fallen down the rabbit hole. Nothing was making sense.

"To pass as my special guest, of course."

She stared at him. "Are you crazy? I mean…" Ever conscious of the fact he was an important client of her company she didn't want to insult, she stopped. But he couldn't be serious. Thinking she could pass as a fiancée for a sheikh? He had to have half the money of the country. She'd learned that much about the al Harum family from her father. They controlled vast oil deposits and dealt in the world market for oil. They played a major role in the government of Quishari and had for generations.

Bethanne's head was spinning. He wanted to pretend she was his fiancée?

He spoke to the chaperone who came reluctantly to stand beside him. For several moments, he spoke in rapid Arabic. The woman glanced at Bethanne and frowned. The sheikh continued to speak and resignation settled on the woman's face. Finally she answered, bowing slightly.

Bethanne hadn't understood a word. But her mind had quickly considered and discarded one idea after another. The one fact that shone above all was she would be dealing with Rashid al Harum for days. Awareness spiked. She wished she had checked her makeup and hair before opening the door. Did he even see her in the uniform? Feeling decidedly feminine to his masculinity, she let herself consider the out-landish suggestion.

Special guest to a sheikh. They'd spend a lot of romantic moments together. Would he kiss her? Her knees almost melted at the thought.

"It is settled. Haile's chaperone will serve as yours for the time being. Her name is Fatima. She doesn't speak English but we'll get around that somehow."

"Wait a minute. I'm not—"

He raised his hand. "You are in my country now, Ms. Sanders. And my rules apply. Certain influential people are watching to see the young woman that I am interested in. It is fortunate that my family kept a tight lid on the negotiations. No one knows who I have selected. It would not be a good thing at this point to disappoint them. You are my choice since *you* lost my other one."

"That's totally ridiculous. How can you say that? Maybe you need a few minutes to come up with an alternative plan."

"This suits me. Time is short. Please put on a happy face and accompany me down the stairs," he ordered.

"Wait a minute. I haven't agreed to anything."

"Would you prefer to fly this plane back to the United States immediately? Canceling the sale?" he asked. "And perhaps putting in jeopardy the relationship Quishari holds with Morocco?"

His implacable expression confirmed he was completely serious. She tried to comprehend if he really thought she could divert an international incident. She opened her mouth to refute it when a thought occurred to her.

She had another agenda in Quishari. She had hoped during her vacation to find her father. It wasn't exactly the kind of stay she'd envisioned, but maybe agreeing to his pretense for a short time would work to her advantage as well. Certainly the special guest of the sheikh would be afforded more access to information than a mere visitor. She had contacts to find, places to visit. Wouldn't it be easier with the help of Sheikh Rashid al Harum?

She closed her mouth while she tried to see how this odd request—no, demand—could work to her benefit. "What exactly are we talking about?" she asked, suddenly seeing the situation advantageous to her own quest.

"A short visit. We'll tell people you've come to meet me and my family. If they think you and I are making a match, that's their problem. After a few weeks, you leave. By then, I'll have the contract finalized and who cares what the rumormongers say. In the meantime, you would be my honored guest."

"I don't see how that would work at all. We don't even know each other." She had never been in love. Had dreamed about finding that special man, one who had likes and interests similar to her own. Never in a million years could she envision herself having anything in common with a sheikh. But there was that pull of attraction that surprised her. She couldn't fall for a stranger. Not right away. It had to be jet lag or something.

Still, he fascinated her. And she was pragmatic enough to realize she could get a lot of help in searching for her father.

The way he put things, it wasn't quite as if they were supposed to be lovers. They were to be still in the getting-to-know-you stage. The thought of getting to know him better tantalized. And people who were almost engaged did kiss.

Why did that compel her? she wondered as she looked at his lips, imagining them pressed against her own.

"Have you considered all the ramifications? What will you say when asked how we met? Why we are attracted to each other? My background is not that important that a sheikh would view it as any kind of advantage."

"Perhaps we could say we fell in love," he suggested sardonically.

She frowned. His tone suggested he didn't believe in love. The dismissing glance he gave proved the thought never crossed his mind. And it wasn't as if she'd fallen in love with him. A strong interest in an intriguing man—that's all she felt. Once she got to know him better, she'd undoubtedly find him a bit annoying.

"It's important even in an arranged marriage for the partners to at least be cordial to each other," she replied with false sweetness, wondering if she could spend much time in his company without coming completely unglued.

"Do you not think I can be cordial?" he asked in a silky tone, leaning closer. He brushed his fingers against her cheek as he pushed back a strand of hair. His dark eyes were so close she could see tiny golden flecks in them. The affinity she felt was drugging. She wanted to close the scant inches separating them and touch his face, feel his mouth on hers.

She drew a breath to get control of her senses. But the scent of his aftershave set her senses to dancing. She opened her mouth to offer a hearty no, then closed it.

Think.

It would help her look for her father. Using her unexpected position to gain access where mere visitors might not have was a bonus she never expected. Don't hastily reject this, she warned herself.

"Perhaps," she conceded.

"And you?" he asked. The intensity of his gaze had her mesmerized. She could no more look away than she could fly without a plane.

"I can be cordial. But not lovey-dovey," she said. There was a limit she dare not cross lest she be lost. One kiss would never be enough. She'd become demanding and forget why she'd come to Quishari if the tempting allure was given free rein.

Amusement flared in his eyes. "Agreed, no lovey-dovey. You must call me Rashid and I will call you Bethanne. In public you will appear to be devoted to me."

"And in private?" she asked, already wondering if she'd lost her mind to even consider such a bizarre plan. Still, if it gave her the answers she craved, who was she to say no?

"I'd settle for devotion, but can understand if you feel more reserved," he said. Laughter lurked in his eyes.

The amusement confused her. Was he serious or not?

"I will have Fatima accompany you to a villa I own by the sea. It was where Haile was to stay. You'll have privacy there. Of course, I expect you to attend the celebratory functions that have been planned. And to convince my mother we have a chance of making this work."

"Your mother? You want to pretend to your mother? I think you're crazy."

Bethanne was not close to her own mother but lying to her would never be an option. Were the sheikh and his mother on no better terms?

The amusement vanished. "I want nothing to ruin the deal I still have pending with Haile's father. There are factions here who oppose the proposed arrangement. The finance minister, for one. He would consider Haile's actions an insult to our country. He'd love nothing better than to drive a wedge into the negotiations. As it stands, perhaps it is even better that things turned out this way. Al Benqura will feel guilty at the actions of his daughter so be more willing to concede some points still to be agreed upon. Help me and I will do something in return for you."

Mixed feelings washed through her. She could never pull off being a woman of interest to a dynamic man like Rashid al Harum. She'd be spotted for a fraud the first time she ventured out. Yet the thought of being escorted around by him had her stomach flipping over in giddy anticipation. She'd never have this kind of chance again.

She had only seconds to make a decision.

Jess stepped to the door. "Everything okay?" he asked.

Rashid did not look away from Bethanne. Her gaze met his, seeking assurance that if she complied with this wild scheme, it would end up all right for all.

"Everything is fine," she said at last, hoping she wasn't making a monumental mistake.

There was an almost imperceptible change in the sheikh's manner. Had he doubted her? Well, he should. If not for her goal of finding her father, she would have categorically denied his request. Or maybe thought about it a bit longer. She had trouble looking away.

The sheikh spun around. "There is no need for you to remain. We can get you on a plane within the hour to return to the United States." The sheikh summoned the other man still standing at the foot of the stairs. In only seconds, Sheikh Rashid al Harum had given him orders.

One less person who would know about the charade, Bethanne thought. She was still a bit bemused with the entire matter. This man knew what he wanted and went for it without hesitation.

"Bethanne?" Jess said, looking between her and the sheikh as if suspecting something was amiss.

"I'll be fine. Just a few details to work out. If you can get on a plane within the hour, you better take advantage of the flight."

"In the meantime, I will examine the interior and cockpit," Rashid said.

Jess came closer to Bethanne when Rashid went to inspect the rear of the plane. "Is everything really okay? What happened to the fiancée?" he whispered.

"Um, change of plans."

Jess still appeared doubtful, but he nodded and turned to retrieve his bag from where he'd stashed it. With one more look down the cabin, he turned and left with the sheikh's man.

The sheikh peered out of one of the side windows and watched as Jess entered the car that had been waiting and was soon heading for the main section of the busy airport.

He nodded as if in satisfaction and headed for the front of the plane.

"I assume you have your own bags," he said.

She nodded and pointed out the small travel case she used.

"You travel light."

"It carries enough clothes for me. Two more uniforms like the one I'm wearing. And some off-duty outfits. I have reservations at a hotel in the heart of the city," she said.

"You were planning to stay in Quishari for a while?"

"Yes. I've heard about it for years. Have pictures and books and pamphlets about the beaches, the history and the stark desert dwellings. I'm quite looking forward to learning more firsthand. I think I'm already in love with the country."

"Where did you learn this?" he asked.

"From my father, Hank Pendarvis."

For a moment she wondered at the change in attitude of the sheikh. His face tightened as it had when he learned of Haile's defection.

"Your name is Sanders," he said.

"My stepfather's name. My mother remarried when I was young and he adopted me. We do not get along. My father has been missing for three years."

"He is a thief. He stole one of our planes."

She blinked. "That's a lie!" Her father was not a thief.

"So you are the daughter of a thief." Rashid shook his head.

"No, I'm not. That's not true. My father would never steal

anything—especially from your family. He wrote how he loved working for Bashiri Oil and for Sheikh Rabid al Harum."

"My father. Who died when he learned of Hank's theft."

Bethanne felt sick. Was it possible? No, not her father. She hadn't seen much of him over the years, but she had scads of letters. And he'd phoned her once a week for most of her life. Whenever he was in the States, he came to visit. They flew over Texas, had picnics in meadows and spent time at the beach together. She loved those visits when her father would tell her of the ideal life he enjoyed flying for the senior al Harum.

She raised her chin. "You are wrong."

Rashid uttered a word in Arabic she did not understand. But the intent was clear. He did not like this situation at all. Did he want to change the role she was to play?

He leaned forward, anger radiating from him. "My family has been hurt by yours already. Do not betray me in this charade or it will be the worst for you. I am stuck—temporarily—but do not think I shall forget for an instant."

"If you want my help, you need to make good your offer to do something for me in return."

"And that is?" he asked, his demeanor suddenly suspicious.

"Help me find my father."

He stared at her for a long moment, then stepped to the door. He gestured to someone on the ground and the man entered a moment later. He lifted Bethanne's carry-on bag and went back.

"Agreed. But if we find him, the law will take care of him."

"Not if he didn't steal a plane," she countered. She wasn't sure if she was relieved or stressed at the thought of being the sheikh's girlfriend. But if it helped her to find her father, she would make the best of it.

"So we begin," the sheikh said and stepped to the top step.

Bethanne followed, Fatima behind her. There were now several men in suits at the bottom of the stairs and they came to attention as the sheikh appeared. Bethanne felt caught in a dream. She glided down the stairs and before she knew it, she was in the back of a stretch limousine that seemed to take up a city block. It was a luxurious machine, gleaming white beneath the hot sun, with fancy gold Arabic script on the doors. When she stepped inside, Bethanne was delighted with the cold air that greeted her. Fatima rode in front beside the driver. Rashid slid onto the wide backseat with her. A few words and the driver had the glass wall slide up, separating them from the front of the vehicle.

She glanced at the sheikh as they drove away. He flipped on a cell phone and was speaking rapidly, the Arabic words beyond her. He didn't look like he was taking all the air in the car, but she felt breathless. Gazing out the window, she tried to quell her riotous emotions. She could reach out and touch him—had she the right? Clenching her hands into fists, she refused to give way to the clamoring attention his presence demanded. He thought her father was a thief. How dare he! She had best remember this was only a game of pretense while he went after that oil deal. For her part, he agreed to help her find her father. It would be worth it in the end as long as she kept her head.

Fruitless daydreams of a relationship between them would contribute nothing. She had to keep focused and ignore the awareness that seemed to grow the longer she was around him.

Hank Pendarvis had disappeared three years ago. She feared he was dead. Her mother, long ago divorced and re-married, had tried to obtain information from the oil company for which he flew—the one owned by the sheikh—but her inquiries had produced no results. Bethanne had tried letters to people her father had mentioned over the years, but only one had gone through and that person had not known anything beyond Hank had flown away one day and never returned.

Bethanne missed the larger-than-life man, her secret hero from childhood. He'd been the one to spark her interest in flying, her passion for exploring new places, meeting new people. He would not have ignored her this long if he were alive.

Sad as it was to think of him as dead, she wanted closure. To know what happened to him. And if he were dead, where he lay. She tried to convince herself he was dead or would have contacted her. But the faint hope he was just caught up in something could not be quenched. Until she knew, she hoped he was still alive somewhere.

"We are here," Rashid said.

Bethanne blinked and turned her head to peer out his window as the car slowed and turned into the wide driveway that led to a beautiful white villa. A stunning expanse of green grass blanketed the area in front of the structure. It looked like an Italian home or French Riviera villa. Nothing like what she expected in an Arabic country.

"Wow," she murmured softly. The home was amazing. Two stories tall with a wraparound veranda on both levels, its white walls gleamed in the sunshine. The red terra cotta roof sloped down, providing cover to the upper veranda which in turn shaded the lower level. Tall French doors opened from every room.

The driveway curved around in front, flanked by banks of blue and gold flowers. The chauffeur slowed to a stop in front of wide double doors, with wooden panels carved in ornate designs. The heavy wrought-iron handles added substance. The right door opened even before the car stopped. A tall man wearing traditional robes stepped outside and hastened down the shallow steps to open the passenger door.

The sheikh stepped out and returned the man's greetings.

"Mohammad, this is Ms. Sanders. She has come to stay for a while as my special guest," he said in English.

Less than five minutes later Bethanne stood alone in the large bedroom that had been assigned to her. It held a huge canopy bed in the center, complete with steps to the high mattress. The chandelier in the center of the ceiling sparkled in the light streaming in through the open French doors. Gauzy curtains gently swayed in the light breeze.

Two sets of French doors gave access to the wide upper veranda. She stepped outside and immediately inhaled the tang of the sea mixed with the fragrance of hundreds of flowers blossoming beneath her. She crossed to the railing and gazed at the profusion of colors and shapes in the garden below. A wide path led from the garden toward the sea, a glimpse of which she could see from where she stood. Walking along the veranda toward the Gulf, she was enchanted to find a better vantage point at the corner with a clear view to a sugar-white beach and the lovely blue water.

The maid who had shown her to her room had thankfully spoken English. She told Bethanne her name was Minnah while she unpacked the few articles of clothing in the small bag and asked if Bethanne had more luggage coming.

At a loss, she merely shook her head and continued staring at the garden.

She'd have to suggest to the sheikh that a woman coming to visit would bring more than a handful of uniforms and an assortment of casual clothes. This stupid plan of his would never work. What did he hope to achieve? Save the embarrassment of people learning his intended bride had run away rather than go through with a marriage? Get the business deal completed without anyone knowing how insulting Haile al Benqura's actions had been?

She had no idea of how long he expected this charade to last. So any investigations for her father needed to be done swiftly in case her visit was cut radically short. The sheikh had canceled her reservations at the hotel. She wondered if she should make new ones, just in case.

After she'd changed and freshened up, Bethanne headed back down the way she'd come. The villa wasn't as large as she first thought. Probably only eight bedroom suites. She almost laughed at the thought. Her tiny apartment in Galveston would squeeze into her assigned bedroom here.

She didn't see a soul as she went back to the front door and let herself out. The limo was gone. The lawn stretched out to a tall flowering hedge of oleander, sheltering the house from any view from the street.

Following the lower veranda to the path she'd seen, Bethanne walked through the garden and out to the beach. There were several chairs and tables on the white sand near the edge of the garden. She could sit and relax after her walk.

In the distance she saw a large container ship slowly moving through the Gulf. Happily Bethanne walked to the water's edge, kicked off her shoes and started walking north. Her mind was already formulating where she could begin with her inquiries. When she returned to the villa, she'd summons the maid to begin with her. Had her father ever visited the house? Maybe the staff would remember him. She wanted answers and didn't plan to leave Quishari until she had them. Neither the difficulty of the task nor language barrier would stop her!

"What's got you upset?" Khalid asked from his position lounging on one of the chairs in Rashid's office at Bashiri Oil. The corner office had a splendid view of Alkaahdar and the Gulf. On the highest floor of the building, it rose above most other buildings in the capital city and gave an unimpeded view.

Rashid paced to the tall window and glared at the cityscape, annoyed afresh that his brother had picked up on his irritation. It was not new. Twins had an uncanny intuition concerning each other. Rashid could recognize his brother's moods in a second. Of course Khalid could recognize his.

He knew he had to contact Haile's father. The longer he delayed, the more awkward it would become. Did the man know yet his daughter had run off? Had he known about the other man all along and still expected Haile to consider marriage to him?

He turned from the window and met his brother's eyes. Khalid had the knack of instant relaxation. And then instant action when called for. He was slouched on one of the visitor chairs. Rashid noted his brother was wearing a suit again, instead of the more traditional robes. A concession to being in the city. First chance he had, Rashid knew his brother would head for the interior or the derricks along the coast to the south. Khalid was not one for society or social niceties.

For a second he debated trying the charade on his twin. But it would not take long for Khalid to figure things out. Besides, they had never lied to each other.

"It appears the glowing bride-to-be is glowing for someone else."

"Huh?" Khalid sat up at that. "What do you mean?"

"She never arrived."

"I heard she did and that she's blonde and tall and you whisked her away to keep her from the prying eyes of everyone."

"The rumor mill is even faster than I knew. That's the idea. Haile never arrived. I want to finalize the deal with al Benqura before letting the world know I've been stood up. You know what the minister would say if he found out. This deal's too important to me to let some flighty woman screw it up." Briefly Rashid outlined the situation.

"What does al Benqura say to his daughter's no-show?" Khalid asked.

"I'm not sure he knows."

"And the blonde you escorted from the plane?"

"I hope a substitute until the deal is done."

"Where did you conjure her up?"

"Turns out she's the pilot delivering my new plane—that was supposed to bring Haile. She thought Haile was on board and was as surprised as I was to discover she was not."

"Ah, yes, the new jet you're buying. The pilot is a woman? That's odd."

"Or providence in this situation."

"And she agreed to this charade? What am I saying, of course she did. How much for her silence?"

Rashid shrugged. "So far no monetary demands. But a twist I never expected. She's Hank Pendarvis's daughter."

"What?" Khalid sat up at that. "You're kidding. I didn't even know he had a family."

"And she's looking for her father."

Khalid sat up in his chair. "He took that jet some years ago."

"And disappeared. Apparently starting life anew, he cut all ties with his past. She wants to know what happened. As do we all."

Khalid shrugged. "Don't get in too deep," he warned. "I wouldn't trust her, if I were you." He shifted slightly and tilted his head in a manner that reminded Rashid of his own mannerisms when confronted by questionable behavior. "Are you sure she won't give away the scheme at the first chance? European tabloids would love such a story. And she has nothing to lose and lots of money to gain."

"So far she seems more interested in searching for her father than acquiring anything. But I will keep in mind her relationship to Hank."

Rashid glanced back out the window, but he knew he wasn't fooling his twin. That Bethanne would refuse to cooperate was a true risk. One he was willing to take to insure the finalization of the deal he had been working on for months.

He needed the support of the ministry to finalize the deal of such magnitude. Otherwise he wouldn't care two figs about the minister's position.

He was not going to tell his brother how he had grown to regret agreeing to an engagement that had been so strongly encouraged between his mother and al Benqura. Haile had the perfect background to be his wife. And after his aborted attempt to marry the woman of his choice when he was twenty-two, Haile seemed more than suitable.

He also was not going to mention the flash of desire that had surprised him when he met Bethanne. She was so different from the women he knew. If asked for a type, he would have said he preferred petite and dark, with brown eyes and a lush figure. Bethanne didn't meet a single criterion. She was tall, blonde, blue eyes and almost as slender as a boy.

But that didn't stop his interest. Which hadn't waned even when learning she was Hank's daughter. There could be nothing between them. Not once the relationship was made known. In the meantime, he hoped they could carry on until the oil deal was signed.

"I hope you know what you're doing," Khalid said. "I'm off to the south for a few days. I want to check out the pipeline from the number four oil rig. There's a leak somewhere and so far no one's found it. If it catches fire, there'll be hell to pay." Khalid rose. "Maybe I should take the new jet and vet it for you."

"It's my new toy. Get one of your own."

Khalid's sarcastic snort of laughter conveyed his amusement. "Don't need one. I use the company's," he said, referring to the fleet of small aircraft the oil company owned.

"You don't have to have hands-on surveillance of the rigs," Rashid said. "And if there is a fire, let someone else deal with it."

"Hey, that's my job."

He and Khalid had this conversation a dozen times a month. He glanced at his brother, his gaze focused briefly on the disfiguring swath of scar tissue running from his right cheek down his neck to disappear beneath his shirt collar. The oil fire that had caused the damage had eventually been extinguished—by Khalid himself. The devastation hadn't stopped him from turning his back on office work and continuing in the oil fields. His elite company of oil firefighters was in high demand whenever an oil fire broke out.

Both of them had inherited wealth when their father had died. Both had a strong sense of obligation to the family oil business. Rashid preferred to hire competent help for routine tasks. He loved dealing in the world markets. But his twin had always found the drilling sites fascinating. Not to mention finding the conflagrations that could ruin a site a challenge to extinguish. Khalid drove their mother crazy with concern.

The phone rang.

"Did she arrive?" His mother's voice sounded in his ear.

Khalid gave a mock bow and left his brother to the phone call.

"My guest arrived and is staying at Grandmother's villa," Rashid said. Another front to deal with. His mother had been instrumental in the arrangement of the alliance with Haile. She herself had had an arranged marriage and she wanted her sons to follow the old ways.

"I can't wait to meet her. I know you were hesitant about this arrangement, but it'll work out for the best for all. Plan to bring her to dinner tonight."

"Ah, I believe you misunderstood me, Mother," he said. The charade started now. "Haile had other plans. My guest is Bethanne Sanders. Someone I know from Starcraft." When concocting a magnificent lie, it was best to stick as close to the truth as possible.

"What do you mean?" He heard the bewilderment in her tone.

"I will be happy to bring Bethanne to meet you tomorrow. For tonight, we wish to be together. She's had a long flight and is tired."

"But Haile? What of her?"

"I'll explain when we meet," he said.

"Rashid, don't be impetuous."

He almost laughed. It had been years since he'd been impetuous. His brief aborted love for Marguerite when he'd been younger had ended that streak. Now he kept careful control of his emotions and actions. "Rest assured, Mother, I do not plan to repeat the past."

When the call ended, he reached for the folder on the new jet. He needed to know more about the woman he had ensconced at the villa and quickly. His assistant had approved the requests for visas for both pilots. He took the photograph of Bethanne and stepped closer to the window, his curiosity raised. Blond hair, blue eyes, tall for a woman. A standard passport photo, yet the playfulness lurking in the depths of her blue eyes contrasted with the severe hairstyle, pulled back probably into a ponytail. He'd seen the anger flash in her eyes on the plane. And the shrewd bargaining to help find her father. Was Khalid right, she would be looking for some way to gain money or prestige from the charade?

She didn't look very old. Yet he knew she had to be experienced. Starcraft was an established firm that didn't take chances with the multimillion-dollar aircrafts it built.

How novel to have a woman pilot. Had that fact made the rumor mill yet? He put the photo back, wondering what the financial minister was making of the situation. Rashid had to make sure he did not learn the true circumstances until the deal was consummated. Or even then, if he could help it.

For a moment he remembered their meeting on the plane. She had caught his attention instantly. She was far different from anyone he knew. Wasn't it his luck she was off-limits because of her father. He would love to explore the attraction he felt when he first saw her standing proudly at the top of the stairs. But as the daughter of a thief, he could not let himself enjoy their relationship. He needed to be on guard for any nefarious activity on her part. The apple never fell far from the tree. Was she also not to be trusted?

Hank had worked for his father for many years when he stole the latest jet in their fleet. What had caused his actions? They'd probably never know unless they found him. But he'd watch his daughter. Their family would not be caught unawares a second time.

He was in a tight spot—balancing the minister on one hand, his mother's interest on another, and needing to keep his guest visible enough to satisfy curiosity, and secluded enough to insure she could not threaten the situation.

In addition, he was now committed to delving into the old business of the theft of their plane. Three years ago, when his father died, Rashid had stepped into his place at the oil company. Khalid had worked on locating Hank and the plane—with no tangible results. They'd accepted the loss and moved on. Would they have any more success now?

CHAPTER TWO

BETHANNE wondered how much of the beach she was walking on belonged to the sheikh. She had not seen any sign of other people as she walked, and she estimated she'd gone almost a mile. The water was warm on her feet. The sand swished around her toes as the spent waves swirled around them. She wished she'd worn a hat or something; the sun was burning hot on her head. She was reluctant to return, however. The walk was soothing and just touching the ground where her father might have once stood gave her a connected feeling that had been missing a long time. She could imagine she'd run into him and they'd both express surprise and immediately begin talking and catching up. Then she'd realize he'd been extremely busy and had not died alone and unlamented somewhere unknown, but had simply let time slip by. He had never done so before, but Bethanne clung to hope.

Finally she turned to retrace her steps. Glad she'd left her shoes above the tide line as an indicator of where to return, she studied the lush vegetation that bordered the beach. The villa was almost invisible from the shore. When she caught a glimpse of it, she also saw someone sitting in one of the chairs near the path.

Her heart rate increased as she walked closer. Even before she could recognize him, she knew it was Sheikh Rashid al Harum. Rashid. She said the name softly. He rose as she approached, watching her. Conscious of her windblown hair, sandy feet, khaki pants rolled up to her knees, she knew she must appear a sight. Why couldn't she have brought a dress that would look feminine and sexy? No, she had to be practical. What would he think?

"Did you enjoy your walk?" he asked.

She nodded, leaning over to roll down her pants and dust the sand off first one foot and then the other. Slipping on her shoes, she wished she had worn sandals. Glancing at her watch, she saw she'd been gone longer than she realized. It was approaching the dinner hour.

"It's quite lovely," she said, standing again. "I'd like to go swimming while I'm here."

"My brother and I enjoyed the beach when we were children. The villa used to belong to my grandmother. It's been a long time since I've gone swimming here."

End of conversation. She cast around for something else to say. But the topic she wanted to discuss was, of course, the charade he'd insisted upon. So—

"I don't think this is going to work," she said.

"Because?"

"I've had time to think about it. No one's going to believe you have fallen for some jet jockey from America. First of all, where would we have met? Then, let's face it, I'm no femme fatale."

His gaze skimmed over her. Bethanne felt her blood heat. She wished she could read minds. What did he think when he looked at her? When he again met her eyes, he smiled.

Bethanne's heart flipped over. The way his eyes crinkled with that smile had her fascinated. It changed his entire demeanor. He was the best-looking man she'd ever met. He had to know the effect he had on women. On her.

Flustered, she tried to appear unaffected, but suspected the color rising in her cheeks gave her away.

"You look like you could be most intriguing, with the right clothing."

"And that's another thing. I would not have come to visit bringing only uniforms and casual clothes! I expected to be searching for my father, not going anywhere where I needed to look like I could attract a sheikh."

He laughed. "Even in your casual clothes, people would know why you would attract a sheikh. But clothing is easily remedied. In fact, I took the liberty of having some dresses sent to your room. Please accept as a token of my appreciation for your help."

"Help? You practically kidnapped me." What had he meant by *people would know why you would attract a sheikh?* Did he like the way she looked?

"Hardly that. You agreed to help in exchange for my resuming the search for your father. I don't think we'll turn up anything at this late date, but I will make some inquiries."

Bethanne considered the terms. She was not going to stop believing in her father just on the sheikh's say-so. She knew her father would never betray anyone. Still, any help would be appreciated. "Okay, it's your party. If you think we can fool people, good luck."

"You underestimate yourself. No one will ever doubt that I could be interested."

"Nicely said. Maybe there is a ghost of a chance," she said. Her heart rate increased with his compliment. And the look in his eyes. Definite interest.

"Dinner will be served at seven. Perhaps you would join me on the veranda then?" he asked.

"Thank you, I should be delighted." She nodded regally and swept by, wishing she wore a lovely dress and didn't have sand chafing her feet.

Bethanne gazed at the closet full of clothes five minutes later. Rashid's last words echoed in her mind. No one could doubt he could be interested if she wore some of these dresses. How had he arranged to have so many different ones delivered in the few hours since he deposited her at the villa?

Duh, money can accomplish anything, she thought as she fingered the light silks and linens. She pulled out a blue dress that matched her eyes.

Pampering herself with a luxurious bath and then paying careful attention to her hair and makeup, Bethanne felt a bit like she'd imagine Cinderella felt dressing for the ball.

Fatima had knocked on the door as she was slipping on the dress. She smiled and nodded, saying something in Arabic that Bethanne didn't understand. But the universal signs of approval were obvious. What had the sheikh told this woman about their charade?

The blue of the dress did indeed enhance the color of her eyes. During her walk the sun had tinted her skin with a light tan and the constant hint of excitement at the thought of dining with a sheikh had her on tenterhooks and brought additional color to her cheeks.

Descending the stairs shortly before seven, she wished Rashid were at the bottom to see her descend. The designer dress hugged her figure and made her feel as sexy as a French movie star. She hoped it would replace the image he had of her windblown and disheveled from her walk.

Reaching the ground floor, she headed toward the sound of male voices. She entered a formal sitting room a moment later, just as the butler left. She took a deep breath, dismayed to find her stomach full of butterflies and her palms growing damp. Why this sudden attack of nerves? He was the same. Nothing had changed. But she felt as if the stakes had been rachetted up a notch. She had to find her father to prove his innocence. It became important that the sheikh not think she came from a dishonored family.

As if sensing her arrival, the sheikh turned.

"Thank you for the dress. It's more than expected and quite lovely," Bethanne said quickly, her words almost too fast to understand. Her heart rate tripled and she gripped her poise and tried to act as if she were comfortable greeting Arabian sheikhs every day.

"It is of no consequence. I hope your stay in Quishari will be enjoyable. If you need anything while here at the villa, do ask."

"I look forward to seeing Quishari while I'm here. Since I assume I'll have some free time while you're at work, perhaps you could recommend a guide who speaks English? If I can hire a car, I can explore on my own. I've heard so much about the country for years. I can't believe I'm here." Or at least under these circumstances. Her father had loved Quishari. She knew she would as well.

"I shall put one of my drivers and cars at your disposal. Do allow me to show you the major sights of my country. I am anxious to try out the plane. If you would fly it for me, we can put it through its paces tomorrow."

"I'd love to. I am at your service," she said, feeling almost giddy with the thought she might actually fly where her father had flown. And find time to talk to maintenance men who might know what happened to him. She was a bit surprised the al Harum family had not done more to pursue the issue. Had they merely dismissed it as casual theft and written off a plane? she wondered.

Perhaps in the greater scheme of things, it didn't cost much from their perspective. But she would have thought Rashid the type to go after someone who had done him wrong and make sure justice triumphed.

"Then I will see that you have every opportunity to explore. I'm quite proud of our heritage and history. Some of the architecture in the old section of town is renowned."

"I look forward to seeing it all." In truth, she never expected Rashid to spend a moment with her if not in a public forum in an attempt to discourage gossip.

"Did the dresses fit?"

She loved hearing that deep, melodious voice with its trace of British accent. Why were Americans such suckers for accents? Her Southern drawl sounded out of place in the posh cosmopolitan sitting room with elaborate brocade sofas and antiques dating back centuries.

"The ones I tried on fit perfectly. I loved this one the best."

"It was the color of your eyes," he said.

She caught her breath. Had he noticed enough to request this special color? She searched his eyes for a hint of the truth, but though he looked at her for a long moment, his expression gave nothing away. He'd be terrific at high-stakes poker.

"I thought from your visa photo that you seemed young to be an experienced pilot. Now it appears you're far too feminine to fly planes."

"I've had plenty of training." She didn't know whether to be flattered at the subtle compliment or defensive for her abilities. Did he think women weren't as capable as men to pilot aircrafts?

"You graduated from the U.S. Air Force Academy, took flight training and flew a number of fixed wing crafts and helicopters while serving," Rashid said. "I read your background sent from Starcraft."

"You needn't worry I can't handle your new jet."

He laughed, amusement dancing in his eyes. "I never

doubted it. You brought it safely from the United States. Come, dinner will be ready by now." He offered his arm to Bethanne. She took it, feeling awkward. She was more at ease in the casual restaurants she normally patronized than dining with an Arabian sheikh. But her experiences taught her how to meet every challenge—even this one.

Dinner proved to be less disconcerting than she'd expected. Once seated, the conversation centered around the new jet, its performance and the enhancements Rashid had ordered. After they ate, Rashid insisted they share hot tea on the veranda overlooking the garden. By the time it grew dark, Bethanne was glad to retreat to her bedroom. It had been a long day. One that had not ended as expected.

He bid her good-night at the foot of the stairs and even as she climbed them, he left the villa. The sound of his car faded as she shut her bedroom door.

Bethanne twirled around the large room in sheer joy. She felt as if she were a part of a fairy tale. Handsome sheikh, beautiful setting, lovely clothes and nothing to do but fly a plane at his whim. Could life be any better?

Falling asleep to the soft soughing of the sea relaxed Bethanne like nothing else. Before dropping off, she vowed she'd begin her search for her father tomorrow. But for tonight, she wanted to think about the dashing sheikh who chose her for his special guest—if only temporarily.

Minnah awakened Bethanne the next morning when she entered the bedroom carrying a tray of fragrant hot chocolate and a basket of fresh pastries and croissants. Breakfast in bed was not a luxury Bethanne enjoyed often and she plumped up her pillows and took the heavy silver tray on her lap with delight. There was an English newspaper folded neatly on one side.

"Thank you," she said as the woman went to the French doors to open them wide to the fresh morning breeze.

"I will bring you bathing suits after your breakfast. His Excellency suggested you'd like a swim before starting your day." The maid's English was practically flawless. "Later a driver will pick you up to take you to the airport. His Excellency is anxious to fly in the new plane."

"Sounds like a plan," Bethanne said, already savoring the rich dark chocolate taste of the hot beverage. The feeling of being a princess living in the height of luxury continued. But she dare not waste a moment.

"Before you leave," she said to Minnah, "did you know Hank Pendarvis? He was also a pilot for the sheikh. Or at least the oil company."

The maid tilted her head slightly as she tried to remember. Finally she shook her head slightly. "I do not know him."

That would have been too easy, Bethanne thought. She thanked her and resumed eating breakfast.

Selecting a one-piece blue swimsuit from her new wardrobe a short time later, she donned the accompanying cover-up and headed for the beach. A short swim would be perfect. It was warm enough to enjoy the water without the blazing heat that would rise later in the day. Fatima accompanied her. She had been informed of Bethanne's plans by the maid. For the time being, Minnah would act as the go-between. Bethanne wondered how she'd learned English. When they reached the beach, Fatima sat on one of the chairs near the edge, apparently content to watch from a distance.

Feeling pampered and spoiled, Bethanne relished each sensation as her day started so differently from normal. Shedding the cover-up near the chairs, she ran to the water, plunging in. It was warm and buoyant. Giving in to the pleasure the sea brought, she swam and floated and thoroughly enjoyed herself. She had a goal to reach and a job to do. But for a few moments, she felt carefree and happy.

At the airport an hour later, Bethanne's attitude changed from bemused delight to efficient commander. She talked to the ground crew through a translator the sheikh had provided, reviewing items on the checklist. She listened to how they had refueled the aircraft. She did a visual inspection of the jet. She wasn't sure when the sheikh would want to take the maiden flight, but she was ready when he was. Now she had nothing to do but await his arrival.

She beckoned the translator over. "Can you ask among the crew if any of them knew Hank Pendarvis? He was a pilot and probably flew from this airport," she said.

He nodded and walked back to the group of men.

Two spoke to his question and both looked over at Bethanne. Breaking away from the rest, the two men and the translator walked to her.

"These men knew him. He was a pilot for His Excellency's father, Sheikh Rabid al Harum."

"Is he dead?" she asked bluntly, studying the two men who had known her father.

One man looked away when the question was posed in Arabic. The other looked sad and shook his head at Bethanne, speaking rapidly.

"It is unfortunate, but it appears he has vanished. Was he a friend of yours?"

Bethanne didn't want to reveal her connection to all and sundry. "An acquaintance. I heard he had a job in Quishari and hoped to look him up while I am here."

There was lengthy conversation between the three men, with a couple of glances thrown her way as the one man grew quite passionate.

Finally the translator turned to her. "The man was a pilot. One day he took a plane without permission. He never returned. It is surmised he either flew to another country or the plane crashed. No one has heard from him in almost three years. And the plane has not flown over Quishari skies since then."

She wanted to protest that her father was not a thief, but these men confirmed what Rashid had said. But it couldn't be. Her father was nothing like that. He was loyal to the al Harum family. Loved his job. He would not risk it to steal a plane, no matter what the provocation.

"Did they search for a crashed plane?" she asked, holding on to her composure with effort. Had no one been concerned when he disappeared? Had they so quickly condemned him as a thief that no one searched in case there had been an accident? Her heart ached. Her father had to be dead. He would have contacted her long before now if he could have. She refused to believe he stole the plane.

Another bout of conversation and then one of the men shrugged and turned to walk back to the group. The other continued talking and then watched Bethanne when the translator told her a search was impossible when no one knew where he'd gone. The desert was vast, uninhabited for the most part. Without knowing the direction he'd taken, it was fruitless to search.

"And no one knew why he took the flight?" she asked. How far could she push without giving away her avid interest?

"He was pilot to the old sheikh who died shortly after the man disappeared. His son had no knowledge of the reason he took the plane. There is no more," he ended sadly.

"Thank you." She forced a smile at the man who had conveyed the information. Refusing to let her dismay show, she walked back to the plane.

She wished she had some time alone to assimilate the cold facts. What would have compelled her father to take a plane if not authorized? He hadn't owned a plane, just flew for whoever hired him. Where could he have been going? Why was there no debris if he'd crashed? Someone flying over an accident site must have seen it. Maybe he'd flown off the normal route. Maybe he had not filed a flight plan and no one knew where to look. Yet, how could he have flown without filing a plan? She'd had to fill out enough paper to fill a box when requesting routes into Quishari. Even this morning when saying she wanted to take the jet up, she'd had to fill out a half-dozen forms.

She entered the plane and wandered through the sumptuous cabin. The interior had been designed to the specifications requested by Rashid al Harum. She sat on the sofa, encased in comfort. The microsuede fabric was sensuous to the touch, feeling like velvet. The thick Persian rug on the floor felt sumptuous beneath her feet. She'd like to take off her shoes and scrunch her toes in the luxury. It was like a fine drawing room. The only time she flew, when not piloting an aircraft, she was crammed into the cheapest seats possible returning to base. What would it be like to fly high above the earth in such elegant furnishings? Nothing like the flights she knew.

For a moment she imagined herself sitting next to the sheikh as they cruised high above the Arabian desert. He'd offer her a beverage. They'd sit close together, heads bent toward each other, enjoying each other's company.

Rashid Al Harum entered, ducking his head slightly to clear the lintel. He looked surprised to see her.

Bethanne jumped to her feet instantly, her face growing warm with embarrassment. Bad enough to be daydreaming, but to be caught sitting as if she had nothing to do was problematic.

"I'm sorry. I just took a moment to test the sofa," she said in a rush. She had no business imagining herself as a guest aboard this lovely plane. She was here to work!

"And is it as comfortable as it looks?" he asked, taking her presence in the cabin of the plane instead of the cockpit with equanimity.

"Fabulous. The seat belts are discreet. I feel like I'm in a small living room somewhere. I hope it meets your expectations." She stepped toward the front of the plane, hoping to squeeze by, but his presence filled the narrow space.

"If you're ready to depart, I'll begin the preflight checklist," she said, overwhelmed a bit by his proximity. It wasn't only his sheer masculinity, which made her feel quite feminine, it was the way he carried himself—with all the confidence in the world. And his good looks would give anyone a run for his money. Tall, dark and handsome was such a cliché—and now Bethanne knew exactly why. He looked like the dream of every young woman anywhere with his fabulous features, dark hair and chiseled lips that she'd like to touch hers just once.

Get a grip, girl, she admonished herself. They would never have met in other circumstances. And the only thing he wanted to touch was the fancy furnishing of his new jet. Or the signed copy of the contract for the deal he was working on.

To further her efforts to return to reality instead of indulging in fantasy, she reminded herself the man thought her father a thief. But instead of putting a damper on things, it strengthened her resolve to find her father to clear his name. For his sake, and for hers. She wanted Rashid to think well of her no matter what.

He stepped aside and Bethanne squeezed by, careful to make sure she didn't touch however much tempted. Breathless with the encounter, she hurried to the pilot's seat and sank down, grateful for the few moments' solitude. She ran through the preflight checklist in the cockpit, hoping she could concentrate on flying and not have her mind winging its way back to the cabin and the sexiest man she'd ever encountered.

"Ready when you are," Rashid said, slipping into the second seat a few minutes later.

"You want to fly up here?" she squeaked.

"Why wouldn't I? Wouldn't a man want to spend time with his special friend?"

She glanced out the window at the scurry of activity in preparation for departure. The ground crew could easily see into the cockpit. Of course he wanted to bolster the conception they were involved.

"Okay. Ever flown up front before?"

"From time to time."

In only minutes they were shooting into the sky, the power of the rear engines thrusting them effortlessly into the air. Bethanne had no trouble focusing on the controls. The best part of everything was soaring above the earth. She had calculated the route south along the coast and had it approved by ground control. Flying for one of the top businessmen in the country gave her special privileges not normally afforded.

Slowly Bethanne leveled out and then gradually climbed to their cruising altitude. She prided herself on her smooth flights. The smaller planes were more susceptible to variations in air currents. Today was all about showing off how smoothly the jet rode.

Once they reached cruising level, Rashid nodded. "Good ride."

For a few moments, she'd forgotten he was there. Now, suddenly the space seemed to shrink. The scent of aftershave lotion the sheikh used tickled her nose and made her heart beat faster. She kept her eyes ahead, but could still envision every inch of his face as if he had put a photograph in front of her.

"Do you fly?" she asked.

"No. I leave that to the experts. But I sit up here with my pilot sometimes. I like the panoramic views which I don't get from only one side of the airplane. And I like the feeling of freedom. Must be one reason you enjoy it."

"The primary reason, I guess. It's fabulous." She wished her pulse would slow.

"Unusual profession for a woman, at least in Quishari."

"Not that many women pilots in the U.S., but we're growing in numbers."

"Did you always want to fly?"

She nodded. "From when I was a little girl. It was always magical to me. Soaring high above the earth. My dad—" She stopped abruptly. "Sorry, I'm rambling on."

"If I didn't want to learn more, I wouldn't have asked the question. Your father got you interested?"

She nodded stiffly, still feeling raw with what she'd learned this morning. She wanted to defend him to the sheikh. But she had only a daughter's loyalty to offer. She needed more facts.

"I, too, am following in my father's footsteps. He and my uncles built the oil company to the stature it is today before they died. The loss of them has been a tragedy for my family. My father built an empire through hard work and integrity. My brother and I and one remaining uncle are hoping to build it to even new levels."

"Lofty plans. From what I know, Bashiri Oil is already a leader."

"I hope to be remembered as my father is—someone with vision and the ability to achieve results."

Rashid was charming, Bethanne thought to herself. It was probably second nature to him, which would go a long way in achieving his ends.

"So how is our charade going? No accusations of impossibility?" she asked.

"No one would dare question my word," he said.

"Good."

"My mother expects us for dinner tonight. I accepted on behalf of both of us."

"She'll spot the incongruity."

"I fully expect her to question you about everything. It's up to you to make sure you allay any suspicions. One thing to keep in mind, if she discovers who your father was, she will never believe the relationship."

She resented his suggesting she would be less than worthy of being considered as a wife for the sheikh because of her father.

"I have done nothing wrong. And I don't believe my father has, either."

"Nevertheless, don't volunteer that information."

The sooner she found out the truth, the better, Bethanne fumed.

"Down there, circle around," he said.

Spotting a chain of oil rigs off the shore, she angled down slightly. "Are those the rigs you wanted to see?" One in the distance seemed to shimmer in the heat, gold flames reaching high. "Is that one on fire?" she asked in disbelief as they flew closer.

"Damn. I was hoping it wasn't. If Khalid is in the midst of it, I'll skin him alive."

She blinked at the vehemence of his tone. Who was Khalid? Did Rashid suspect the man had started the fire?

She contacted air traffic control to alert them to her altered plan, then began a wide sweep to the right around the chain of derricks. The last one in the line billowed flames, easily seen from their height. How frightening it would be if they were closer.

"How do you put out oil fires?" she asked, keeping a distance from where the heated air would be rising. Even at this distance they rocked slightly from the thermals.

"Best left to the experts. Which Khalid is. Not that it's any guarantee of his safety."

"And Khalid is?" she asked quietly, taking in his tenseness as he stared at the scene below.

"My brother."

"Oh."

Bethanne made the wide circle twice, then Rashid told her to return to the airport. "I need a phone."

"Don't forget this aircraft is equipped with the latest in satellite technology," she said, feeling a bit like an ad on television.

"I had, thank you." He rose and headed for the back of the plane.

"Whoosh," Bethanne said, feeling the atmosphere around her grow lighter with him gone. She hoped Khalid wasn't in the thick of things or he was sure to get the full brunt of his brother's anger.

How odd that his brother fought fires. They had more than enough money to hire the best. Why put his life on the line?

She wished she knew more about Rashid and his family. Her father had held the family in high esteem. He had enjoyed working for them, although he hadn't told her much about them. She couldn't deny she was attracted to the man, but it would be wiser to ignore that attraction. Where did she think it could lead? The pretense would end once Rashid finalized his important deal.

A short while later, she lined up the jet on the glide path the tower indicated. The landing was as smooth as silk. She taxied to the hangar and cut the engines.

"Now what?" she wondered aloud as she began the end of her light checklist.

"You return to the villa, I to work," Rashid said from the door. "Nice flight, thank you."

Bethanne felt a rush of pleasure at his words. Not every

multigazillionaire even noticed the people who worked for him, much less offered any praise for a job well done.

"Nice aircraft," she responded. "Were you able to use the phone feature?"

"It worked perfectly. The ride was comfortable. The appointments are just as I wanted. I'm sure I'll have years of use from it."

Bethanne pictured him lounging in the cabin for flights around the Middle East or as far as Europe. This model was the best plane Starcraft produced and she was pleased the buyer seemed satisfied.

"Was your brother at the fire?"

"Yes, and says he has it under control."

"Scary job."

"Dangerous, too. I have instructed one of my drivers, Teaz Suloti, to drive you wherever you wish while visiting. Teaz speaks English. Of course, you have complete use of the villa. The library has a number of books in English."

"Thank you."

"I'll pick you up at six-thirty tonight. We'll dine with my mother at her place at seven."

"Right. Shouldn't I know more about you if we're pretending to be involved?"

"Like?"

"Oh, come on. People who know each other and are attracted to each other want to know more about the other person. The early stages are questions and reminiscences and all. Did I misunderstand or do you want people to think we are on the brink of an engagement?"

"You are correct. I had forgotten."

"Forgotten what?"

"How people who are involved act."

She frowned. "I'm not sure I follow."

"Nothing you need be concerned with. I'll come earlier than planned and brief you on important parts."

"So I should have a dossier on myself prepared as well?" she asked.

"Not necessary. We have information on your visa request. I can wing the rest."

Bethanne settled back into the luxury seats of the limousine a few moments later, wishing she could have continued to spend time with the sheikh—if only to listen to his deep voice with its pleasing accent. She also had a bunch of questions. She knew so little about the man. She couldn't face his mother and not give away the show. She hoped he knew what he was doing.

When they reached the villa, she'd ask about her father to everyone she came into contact with on the sheikh's staff. Someone must have befriended him. He had a sparkling wit and genuine interest in people and places. Had they all condemned him without a fair hearing?

When they reached the villa, the driver opened the door and stood by, waiting for her to get out.

Once on the pavement, Bethanne stopped and looked at Teaz. "Did you know Hank Pendarvis?" she asked.

For a few seconds he made no move or response. Then he nodded abruptly—once.

"Do you know what happened to him?"

"He was the pilot for the old sheikh. He flew away one day and never returned." His English was heavy with Arabic accent, but Bethanne had no trouble understanding him.

"Do you know where he was going?"

The same stare, then a quick shake of his head.

"Thank you," she said. She started for the front door when a thought occurred. Turning, she saw Teaz still staring at her. "Do you know where he lived?"

"In the Romula section of old town."

She waited, hoping for more, but he said nothing. She had the address. Might as well go and see if she could find someone there who knew him.

"Maybe you could drive me there tomorrow if the sheikh doesn't need me." She'd love to see the old city. Match photos with the historic buildings. See a square with coffee cafés and stalls of goods for sale. Skirting Alkaahdar from the airport to the villa showed only the modern high-rises of shining steel and glass. She knew the older section would have been built in the more traditional Moorish architecture that she'd so loved in southern Spain.

"I am at your service," he said with a slight bow.

Entering the quiet villa, Bethanne paused at the bottom of the steps, then on a sudden whim turned and headed toward the sitting room she'd been in last night. A quick glance showed it empty. Moving down the wide hall, she peered into the dining room they'd used. The last room in the hall was the library the sheikh had mentioned. Books lined three walls. The French doors stood open, keeping the room fresh and cool. Stepping inside, she saw a large desk to one side. From the computer on top and the scattered papers, she knew it had been recently used. Who by? From their conversation, she'd surmised Rashid lived elsewhere. This was a second home.

She stepped in and crossed to the desk. She wouldn't open drawers and nothing was visible that would tell her anything about her father. It had been three years. Time enough to put away anything of interest.

"Where did you go, Dad? And why?" she muttered softly.

She sat in the desk chair, picturing Rashid sitting behind the desk, working on major deals for oil exports. What did he do for leisure? How come he was not married at his age? Most men she knew had married in their twenties. Rashid had to be close to mid-thirties.

Though she herself was still unwed.

She swiveled back and forth in the chair. Spotting the computer, she sat up and turned it on. Maybe she could search out what she could find about Rashid al Harum. She would not go to dinner unprepared.

Rashid leaned back as the car pulled away from the office. He was on his way to pick Bethanne up for the command dinner. He had thought about her questions, wondering what she felt important to know if preparing for a confrontation with a future mother-in-law.

He thought about Marguerite for the first time in years. How foolish he'd been not to recognize her type when they'd met. He'd fallen for her in a big way. Marguerite had been beautiful and sophisticated and very good at having fun. She'd often spoken about how much fun they'd have together.

Spending his money.

How gullible he'd been. No longer. He had agreed to the possibility of marriage to Haile as a way to connect the two families who had a strong mutual interest in oil. Now that was off the table, he could resume his solitary way of life. It would take another monumental deal to have him consider the institution again soon.

Lucky break, Haile's running away.

He wondered if his mother would ever see it that way. He'd have to be careful in what he conveyed to her this evening. She could accept things or constantly stir things up in her desire for answers.

How good an actress was Bethanne Sanders? Could he depend upon her? How ironic the woman he was looking to for help was the daughter of a man his family despised.

If she was anything like her father, he was playing a dangerous game.

He entered the villa a short time later and paused in the large foyer. The stairs leading up were to his left. The space to the right led to various rooms and eventually back to the kitchen. The evening breeze circulated, keeping the house cool and inviting. Why didn't he stay here more often? he wondered. His grandmother had left it to him when she died last summer. She'd bequeathed another dwelling and surrounding land on the other side of the city to his twin. Khalid had yet to take up residence. Both too busy.

Fatima started down the stairs, surprised to see him. "I didn't know you were here, Excellency," she said. She clung to the railing and looked back up. "I can tell her you have arrived."

"Please ask her to join me in the salon."

Rashid waited by one of the French doors. The entire estate was cooler than his flat in the city. He liked living closer to the action, but he had forgotten how much he'd enjoyed visiting when his grandmother was alive. Only a few minutes' drive from the heart of the capital, yet the estate was serene and lovely, and quite different from the glass and steel of the high-rise where he had his flat.

When he heard the rustle of silk, he turned and watched as Bethanne entered the room. She looked lovely in a rose-colored dress that was most demure. Her hair was done in a neat style, up and off her neck. She wore no jewelry, but her modest attire would please his mother.

"Good evening," she said with a bright smile. For a moment Rashid wished she meant the smile, that she was actually happy to see him. It was a foolish, fleeting thought.

"You look lovely," he said.

"Thank you—it's the dress." She turned slowly and

grinned. "I could get used to dresses like this. Most of the time I wear my uniform or shorts when hanging around at home."

He'd like to see her in shorts or a bathing suit. Or nothing at all.

Looking away quickly lest he give a hint of his errant thoughts, he walked to one of the chairs and gestured for her to sit in another.

She did so elegantly. What were the odds of having a suitable woman arrive just when Haile disappeared? One who seemed as at home here in his villa as she did behind the controls of the jet?

"So let the inquisition begin," he said whimsically.

She shrugged. "I looked you up on the Internet. There's quite a lot written about you and your brother. You have a lot of good press. Is that designed? Or are you genuine?"

"I'd like to say genuine. We are not given to excesses. We enjoy our work and do our best for it."

"Your brother is harder to find out about, but you are often in the press. But no special woman—hence the arrangement with Miss Haile, I suppose."

He kept his face without expression. At least the old press about his and Marguerite's disastrous breakup was old news, probably not in the top articles brought up when his name was entered in a search engine. He had his father to thank for that.

"So I know more about you than this morning. Enough to fool your mother? That I'm not sure. There's not much personal, like what your favorite food is or if you had a dog when you were a child."

He relaxed. She was not probing for intimate details, just basic facts.

"My favorite food is candied dates. My brother and I had a wonderful dog when we were children. I miss him to this day. But my life is too busy and hectic to have a pet."

She settled and began a litany of questions, firing them off as if on an invisible checklist—favorite book, movie, activity, color. Did he consider himself close to his family? Did he have special friends she should know about? A hobby that consumed him? How had he done in school? What did he like about his job and what did he wish to change? Who did he admire most in the world?

It was a novel experience to be so questioned. Not once did she ask about material things.

Finally she stopped. "Ready as I'll ever be," she said, looking as if she were about to jump to her feet.

Rashid looked at her. "My turn."

"I thought you had all you needed from the report Starcraft sent," she said, looking amused.

"Ah, but I didn't realize all the nuances of information necessary for an almost-engaged couple's knowledge bank. I do not know your favorites or your passions."

"Favorite color—blue. Food, anything with dark chocolate. Passions—flying. I have no boyfriend, which is lucky for you or we couldn't be doing this stupid charade. I am not close to my mother—nor the man she married after she divorced my father when I was little. I love traveling and seeing the world. I have experience shooting down other aircraft."

She looked adorable as she recited her list ending proudly with her startling fact. He was fascinated by the play of emotions across her face. Now sitting on the edge of her chair, her animation was a delight. Would his mother like her? What was not to like? As long as she didn't find out Bethanne's father's name.

"I hope there will be no need of the latter while you are in Quishari."

She laughed aloud. "I should hope never again, but it was training I received and just knowing I could do it improves my confidence. If I get into situations that make me uncomfortable, I remember I could shoot down a plane if needed and probably no one else in the room could."

"A strange way to improve confidence."

"It'll help when meeting your mother."

He laughed at that. This American woman was intriguing. He had even more reason to thank Haile for fleeing. If nothing else, Rashid planned to enjoy the next few days with Bethanne by his side. Without expectations on either part, they were free to enjoy the other's company without looking for hidden nuances or motives.

He rose. "Come, we'll be late if we don't leave soon. And tardiness is something my mother does not like."

"Tell me about her—I want her to be satisfied with the story we tell. Will she be hurt when the truth comes out?"

"Why should the truth ever come out?" he asked.

She looked at him in surprise. "Truth always comes out. You just make sure you put the right spin on it so she's not hurt by your deception."

"I would do nothing to hurt my mother."

"Good answer."

They were soon ensconced in the limo and on their way to the city.

"Where does your mother live?" Bethanne asked.

"In a penthouse apartment near the heart of the city, overlooking parts of the old section. She loves being in the center of things. It helps being close to friends since my father died."

"The soup is delicious," Bethanne said later, sipping the savory concoction. "So far I'm really enjoying the food here. I have a real sweet tooth and the candied walnuts really appeal. I shall have to buy a large package to take home when I leave."

Madame al Harum looked at her.

"And when do you leave?" she asked.

Bethanne smiled and glanced at Rashid. "Not for a long time, I hope."

She also hoped she was playing the role assigned her to his satisfaction. She'd been as gracious as she knew how when meeting his mother. She could tell at once that Madame al Harum did not like her. For one thing, she seemed to disapprove of tall, willowy blondes. She probably wanted a proper Arab woman for her son.

Then she expressed dismay that Bethanne was a pilot. It was too dangerous and too unseemly for a woman. Bethanne decided not to mention shooting down planes. She knew his mother would not appreciate that tidbit.

Dinner was easier. The food took some attention. She counted the minutes until they could finish and leave.

"And where is home for you?" the older woman asked.

"Galveston, Texas, right on the water. Galveston's an island that has been home all my life."

"What does your father do?"

"He's an antique dealer. But I have to say, history in Texas doesn't go back as far as here in Quishari. The old part of the capital city is thousands of years old. Texas has only been around for a few hundred years."

Rashid looked as if he were enjoying the meal. But Bethanne didn't think she was winning Brownie points with his mother.

"Tell me how you became interested in flying," Rashid said when the main course was served.

Grateful for the change of topic, Bethanne plunged right in.

"My father loved to fly and took me up in small planes almost as soon as I could sit up by myself." She smiled in memory. "It seemed logical when I got older that I, too, would love to fly. I actually learned when I was a teenager, to my mother's dismay. When I was accepted to the Academy, she really flipped. But I think Dad talked her in to letting me choose my own way. Anyway, I learned to fly a variety of air-crafts and here I am."

"So your father taught you to fly?" Rashid asked.

"No. That I had to do on my own. He was away more than home, actually. Probably why I'm following in his footsteps and seeing the world." She met his eye, holding it for a moment, silently refuting his ideas about her father.

"And that was your reason for choosing to attend a mili-tary academy?"

His mother's eyes grew large at that.

"Some of the recruitment material said join up and see the world. I knew I'd have the best education and pilot's training available. And I had a variety of aircraft to train on. I loved learning. And the service requirement enabled me to see Minot, North Dakota, in the dead of winter. Then a tour of Alaska. Can you imagine? I'm one who loves the sun and sea, and my two duty stations were the coldest in the U.S. I left the service when my commitment was up and landed a spot with Starcraft."

Rashid enjoyed watching Bethanne talk. He glanced at his mother. She had on that polite face she wore when tolerating others, but not connected to them. He felt a twinge of com-passion for her. She would have been so happy to have Haile sitting where Bethanne was sitting. She had met the woman on a trip to Morocco and had definitely approved of her.

He had seen pictures. She was a pretty woman. But not striking as Bethanne was. And he doubted she'd have shown much personality around his mother.

What would be his mother's reaction when he told her about Haile's fleeing? Nothing would bring her more happiness than to see one of her sons married—especially to a woman she liked. The fact he was the eldest—by seven minutes—made it seem as if the destiny of his family rested on his shoulders. One day he would have to marry—to father the next generation. He pushed aside the thought. As soon as the deal with al Benqura was finalized, he'd tell his mother Bethanne hadn't turned out to be the one for him after all. Maybe he'd even ask her help in finding him a suitable bride. Being a grandmother would delight her, he was sure.

"Tell me about North Dakota," he invited. "The only time I see snow is when we ski in Switzerland."

He was charmed by her storytelling skills. She made her experiences seem amusing while also revealing her reactions to different situations. She was skilled at entertaining and in giving him what he wanted—a devoted companion intent on meeting his needs. He hoped his mother saw her in that light. For a little while he could imagine what life would be like married to Bethanne. Never boring, of that he was sure.

She was having way too much fun, Bethanne thought at one point. This man was being polite in asking questions so she could talk, but she didn't need to give them her life's history—though Rashid did seem to be enjoying her rendition of her brief stint as an Air Force pilot. His mother looked rather horrified.

Glancing around, she could hardly believe she was sitting in an elegant penthouse overlooking the capital city. The furnishings were amazing. She wished her stepfather could see them. And surrounding the penthouse was a spacious terrace that had banks of pots with fragrant flowers. The doors were opened to allow the breeze to enter. It was delightful.

"You have a beautiful home," she said to her hostess. She had to find common ground or this dinner would end awkwardly.

Madame al Harum inclined her head regally. "I decorated

it for my husband. He loved to retreat from the world and find a place of beauty." She glanced at her son. "It's important that two people have much in common to make a happy marriage."

Bethanne also looked at Rashid. His mother wasn't buying their supposed commitment at all. Would he tell her now?

"Similar likes and dislikes, certainly," Rashid said. "But there is something to be said about learning about each other as the years go by, and have enough differences to be interesting."

His mother gave Bethanne a sour look and then nodded to her son. "That is important as well."

The rest of the meal processed without much comment. Bethanne was glad this was only a charade. She would not like being married into a family where the mother didn't like her. Or was it only because of her disappointment Haile hadn't come?

They did not stay long after dinner finished.

The ride back to the villa was completed in almost total silence. Bethanne knew Rashid had to be regretting his impetuous suggestion about their charade. Perhaps he'd end it tonight. The thought depressed her.

To her surprise, Rashid did not simply leave her at the door.

"It's early yet. If you are not tired, perhaps a few minutes on the veranda," he suggested.

"That would be nice. So do we change the charade now that we both know your mother doesn't like me?"

"My mother does not dictate my life. She is annoyed I didn't bring Haile tonight. She was instrumental in making that arrangement."

"It's more than that. She doesn't like me. Not just because I'm not Haile, but because of who I am," Bethanne said. She didn't need everyone in the world to like her, but she was a bit hurt Rashid's mother found her wanting.

"It's of no account," he said.

Of course not. This wasn't real. It was make-believe—

until he had his huge deal signed and sealed. Then she'd be on the next plane to Texas and his life would resume its normal course. Gossip would be quelled. He'd get his way and his mother would be very relieved.

"Her home was lovely," she said, looking for conversation. "Did you grow up there?"

"There and here and other places."

He looked out at the garden, visible now by the discreet lighting illuminating paths and special plants. He could hear the soft sound of the sea, noticeably different from faint traffic noise. "My flat today is not as pretty as this estate. It's downtown, not far from Mother's. I like living there yet I had almost forgotten how enjoyable this place is."

"Well, I appreciate being allowed to stay here. It's so much better than a hotel."

"I'm sure my grandmother would have been delighted to have visitors enjoy her home. She spent several months a year here. But had other property, as well."

Well, duh, Bethanne thought. His family probably had two dozen residences among them. She wondered idly if there were enough bedrooms among all the residences for him to sleep in a different one each night of the month. What must that feel like?

She had a sudden longing for her small apartment, with its familiar furnishings and photos. It might be fun to consider being Cinderella, but at the end of it all, wasn't she happier in her own home?

As Bethanne prepared for bed some time later, she thought about the evening. It would not have been better for Rashid's mother to welcome her into the family. She was not truly involved. And if the woman had liked her, she would have been disappointed when the charade was exposed.

Talking with Rashid on the veranda had given her a glimpse of what life married to him could be like. Only—there was no good-night kiss. She sighed softly. Was she going to be disappointed with no kiss before returning home? Yes. Yet she wasn't bold enough to kiss him.

Before turning off the lights, she opened the French doors to let the sea breeze sweep in. The light curtains billowed. The scents and fragrances from the garden were a delight. She slipped between cool sheets and lay down.

An hour later Bethanne was still wide awake. She'd tried lying on one side then the other, then flat on her back. Nothing worked. If she had a book or magazine to read, it might lead to sleep. She considered the situation, then sighed and got up. She had not brought a robe, thinking she'd be alone in a hotel room and not need one. Quietly she dressed in her slacks and shirt. Bare feet would be okay, she was sure. It was unlikely she'd run into anyone. It was after eleven. Surely all the staff had retired for the night.

She opened the door and stuck her head out, struck suddenly with the romantic-comedy picture that flashed into her mind. People sneaking from one room to another, peering into the hall to make sure the coast was clear. She planned nothing of the sort and stepped boldly out. She walked down the stairs, surprised when she reached the foyer to see a light coming from the library.

Silently she walked to the doorway. When she was within hearing distance she heard a phone. It was answered before the second ring.

The words were in Arabic, but she recognized Rashid's voice. She thought he had left long ago. When he'd bid her good-night, he said he had to pick up something from the library.

He was still here, and the phone call wasn't going well— not if the terse tone was anything to go by. She hesitated at the doorway, not wishing to interrupt, but still wanting something to read. She'd come this far; she'd wait for the conclusion of the call and then step in to find a book.

The conversation didn't take as long as she'd expected before a harsh word was sounded, then a string of them. She wondered what was going on. He sounded angry. Sudden silence ended the call.

When the silence had lasted several minutes, she took a breath and stepped closer, knocking slightly on the door frame. She saw him standing by open French doors. His back was ramrod straight. His body seemed to radiate strong emotion in contrast to the stillness with which he held himself.

He spun around, glaring at her for a second. Then he quickly adjusted his expression to reveal nothing.

"Something wrong?" he asked.

"I was going to ask you the same thing. I thought you left a while ago."

"I did. Then I remembered a file I had left and returned for it. I was about to leave when I got a phone call on my mobile phone." He still held it in his hand.

"I heard. Not that I understood a word, but it didn't sound like a very friendly call."

"It was from al Benqura. He found out about Haile. She contacted him. He was angry with me for not letting him know."

"How awkward that would have been."

Rashid sighed and walked back to the desk, leaning against it and nodding. "Awkward for him. He's threatening to end the deal. I told him in no uncertain terms that would not be acceptable unless he never wanted dealings with anyone in Quishari again."

Bethanne could empathize with the father whose daughter had run away and put him in a difficult situation. She watched as Rashid gradually relaxed. He was quick to anger, but also quick to regain his equilibrium. She saw when his curiosity was piqued by her arrival.

"What are you doing here?" His gaze dropped to her bare feet. His lips curved in a slight smile.

"I came for a book to read. I can't seem to sleep. You said you had some English books—I thought I'd get one of those."

He nodded and gestured to the shelving on the left. "English books on that wall. My grandmother used to entertain several friends from Great Britain. She has an assortment. The mysteries are on the lower shelves."

She crossed, conscious of his regard, and began to scan the titles. Finding a couple that sounded promising, she drew them from the shelf. Had Rashid read them? Could they discuss them after she finished?

Deciding to take both, she hugged them to her chest as she turned to face him.

"Now what?" she asked.

"You read them and fall asleep?" he asked.

"I mean with our charade. Did the phone call help or change things?"

"We continue. Whichever way the winds blow, we will adapt."

CHAPTER THREE

"I DON'T mean to intrude. But if you need someone to talk to, I could listen." She wished she'd had someone to listen to her when her father's disappearance became known. Her mother had long ago divorced herself from Hank Pendarvis—both legally and emotionally. She and Bethanne's stepfather had a loving and happy marriage from which Bethanne had often felt excluded. Plus, they never had a kind word to say about her father. Bethanne wished she could have him give her one of his bear hugs again. Did Haile's father feel that way?

"Did he hear from Haile?" she asked.

"He did. And is furious with her and with me."

"You're the injured party—why is he angry with you?"

"He believes I should have told him immediately. He could have taken steps. He overrates his power. By the time I found out, Haile had had hours to flee Morocco. She and her lover were married in Marseilles that very day. My telling him would not have prevented that."

"Will he tell others? Your minister?"

"Not if he wants this deal to go through."

He pushed away from the desk. "I have my folder. I won't keep you up any longer."

He looked at her slacks and T-shirt.

"Was sleeping attire not included in the clothes I ordered?"

"Yes, but no robe. I didn't know whom I might see if I came down for books."

"I shall remedy that in the morning."

"Please, I'm fine. Next time I'll take a book up with me. You've been more than generous. I don't need anything else."

"I thought all women loved beautiful things."

"I expect we do. But we don't have to own everything we see. Good night, Rashid."

Reaching her room a minute later, she softly closed the door and flung herself on the bed, the books falling on the mattress beside her. She had not expected to see him again tonight. He'd looked tired and somewhat discouraged. Not the best way to end a day. She hoped the deal would be signed soon. There was nothing else she could do but go along and hope in some small part she'd contribute to a satisfactory conclusion to their negotiations.

Trying to settle into a fictitious mystery when she had a real-life scenario in her own life was difficult. Murder was not involved in her case, but finding clues was. She tried to glean ideas from the book, but her mind turned time and time again to Rashid.

She knew he believed Hank to be a thief, but wouldn't he still want answers? Letting the book fall onto her chest, she gazed at the dark night beyond the billowing curtains. The man at the airport had said the son had no idea why her father took the plane. Didn't he want to know? She couldn't picture Rashid ignoring the situation. He'd push until he got answers.

Just before she fell asleep, she pictured herself with Rashid finding her father and finding the reason for the apparent theft. It could be explained away. Then Rashid would look at her with admiration and sweep her into his arms for a kiss....

She stopped herself—she had to stop fantasizing about his kisses!

Once again Minnah woke Bethanne the next morning, bringing a breakfast tray. The hot chocolate was as rich and satisfying as the previous day. The croissants were warm and buttery, melting in her mouth.

She debated going for a swim, but decided she had best set to searching for her father. She wanted to prove to Rashid his belief was misplaced.

"Pardon, I almost forgot," Minnah said after she opened the French doors and curtains to allow the sunshine to flood the room. "It is a letter from His Excellency. I will return for the tray in a while." She handed Bethanne an ivory-colored envelope with her name written in a bold script.

She opened it and read the brief note, her heart revving up. It had taken ages to fall asleep and then her dreams about Rashid had been exciting and most certainly not ones she wanted to share with anyone. The best favor she could do herself would be to remember always that this was merely make-believe.

A car will be at your disposal today. The driver will be waiting when you are ready to take you where you wish. He speaks English, and can translate if you wish to stop to shop or have coffee.

Disappointment warred with relief at the missive. What had she expected? A love note? An offer to spend the day with her?

The bold handwriting continued: *Saturday I have a polo match, I would like you to attend. Perhaps you'd care to see the horses before the game. If there is not a suitable dress for*

*you to wear, let the maid know and she'll relay the informa-
tion and something appropriate will be ordered.*

Bethanne was almost giddy with excitement. Trying not to
act like a schoolgirl with a major crush, she took a deep
breath. Of course someone being in a position of special guest
would want to attend the polo match. Mentally she reviewed
the new clothes. She wasn't entirely certain what was suitable
for a polo match, but didn't think any of the lovely dresses
were the right kind.

Still, the thought of his buying more clothes caused a pang.
He didn't need to spend so much on this charade.

"Get real," she said aloud. "He can afford it and the clothes
can go to some worthy cause when I leave."

Pushing the thought of leaving away, she quickly finished
breakfast, showered and dressed in a light tan linen skirt and
soft yellow cotton blouse. She planned to take advantage of
the driver the sheikh offered to see some of the sights of old
town this morning. She couldn't wait to see the ancient buildings, walk where generations past had walked. And maybe
find out more about her father.

Then, if time permitted, she'd take advantage of the beauty
of the Persian Gulf and laze on the beach until Rashid came
after work.

Bethanne was pleased to see the driver at her disposal
was the same one she'd asked about her father. She greeted
him and told him of her desire to see the old city, and where
Hank had lived.

When they arrived, he pulled into the curb and stopped.

"I cannot take the car any farther. The road becomes too
narrow. Down there two blocks." He handed her a sheet of
paper with Arabic writing. "I wrote his name and when he
lived there and where. Show it to people for information about

Hank. Many speak some English. If not, come get me to translate. I will wait with the car."

"Thank you."

"You will not get a good reception," he warned.

"Why not?" That thought had never crossed her mind.

"The old sheikh was well liked. It was not a good thing to steal his plane. Some speculate the pilot's betrayal caused the heart attack that killed him. The man had flown the sheikh for years. His treachery cut deep."

Bethanne recognized she was fighting an uphill battle to clear her father's name. He would not have treated his employer that way—she knew it. His letters and phone calls had been full of admiration and respect for his employer. But how to prove that, and find out what really happened?

When she climbed out of the car, she was instantly in a foreign world. The tall sandstone walls were built closer to each other than most American buildings. Rising fifteen to twenty feet in height, they seemed to encase the street. Archways, windows and doors opened directly onto the narrow sidewalks, most already shuttered against the day's rising heat.

Bethanne was almost giddy with delight. She'd longed to visit Quishari ever since her father had first spoken about it. He had loved it and she knew she would as well. Savoring every moment, she slowly walked along, imagining she heard the echo of a thousand years. The heat shimmered against the terra cotta–colored walls. Here and there bright colors popped from curtains blowing from windows, or painted shutters closed against the heat.

She got her bearings and headed in the direction indicated in the drawing. Where the street intersected another, she peered down the cross streets, seeing more of the same. Archways had decorative Arabic writings. Recessed doorways intrigued, beckoned. For the most part, however, the reddish-brown of sandstone was the same. How did anyone find their own place when they all looked alike? she wondered.

Reaching a square, she was pleased with the wide-open area, filled with colorful awnings sheltering stalls with everything imaginable for sale. There were booths of brass, of glass, of luscious and colorful material and polished wood carvings. Some stalls sold vegetables, others fruit or flowers. Women and children filled the aisles. The sounds of excited chattering rose and fell as she looked around. On the far side, tables at two outside cafés crowded the sidewalk. Men in traditional Arab dishdashahs with white gitrahs covering their hair sat drinking the strong coffee. Others wore European attire. Several women dressed all in black stood near the corner talking, their string bags ladened with fresh produce from the stands in the square. The air was almost festive as shoppers haggled for the best bargain and children ran and played.

Bethanne watched in awe. She was actually here. Looking around, she noticed she was garnering quite a bit of attention. Obviously a curiosity to the daily routine. She approached one of the women and showed her the paper. The woman began talking in Arabic and pointing to a building only a few steps away. Bethanne thanked her, hoped she was pointing out the apartment where her father had lived. She quickly crossed there. No one responded to her knock.

Turning, she explored the square, stopping to ask in several of the stalls if anyone had known Hank Pendarvis, showing the paper the driver had prepared. No success until she came to one of the small sidewalk cafés on the far side of the square. A waiter spoke broken English and indicated Hank had been a frequent customer, years ago. He had met with a friend often in the afternoons. The other man still came sometimes. She tried to find out more, but he had told her all he knew.

She had to make do with that. If she got the chance, she'd return another time, to see if her father's friend was there.

She asked if she could leave a note. When presented with a small piece of paper, she wrote only she was trying to find out information about Hank Pendarvis and would return in three days.

She dare not at this point mention her tenuous relationship to the sheikh. She did not want anyone trying to reach her at the villa. Until she knew more, she had to keep her secret.

Bethanne returned to the car then instructed the driver to take her to the best store in the city. She wanted to search for the perfect outfit to wear to a polo match. She did not need Rashid buying every stitch she wore.

When Bethanne returned to the villa late in the afternoon, the driver must have had some way to notify Fatima. The older woman met her in the lobby, her face disapproving, her tone annoyed as she said something Bethanne didn't understand. Probably chastising her for leaving her chaperone behind.

To her surprise, Rashid al Harum came from the library.

"Ah, the eternal pastime of women—shopping," he said, studying the two bags with the shop's name on the side.

"Your stores had some fabulous sales," she said. "Wait until you see the dress I bought for the polo match. I hope it's suitable—the saleswoman said it was." Conscious of the servants, she smiled brightly and hurried over to him, opening the bag a bit so he could peek in.

He did so and smiled. Glancing at the staff, he stood aside. "Perhaps you'd join me in the salon."

"Happy to," she said.

He spoke to Fatima and the woman came to take Bethanne's bags, then retreated.

"Is anything wrong?" Bethanne asked once the two of them were alone in the salon.

"Not at all. I have some spare time and came to see if you wanted to have lunch together. I have not forgotten you wanted to see some of my country. Where did you go this morning?"

"To a place in the old town. I walked around a square there, saw a small market. Then went shopping for the dress."

"I'd be delighted to show you more of the old town, and some of the countryside north of the city, if you'd like."

"Yes. I would. I probably won't get the chance to visit Quishari again after I leave." Especially if she didn't find her father, or convince Rashid he was innocent.

"And I remember you like exploring new places," he commented, studying her for a moment.

"I'll run upstairs and freshen up. I can be ready to leave in ten minutes."

"There's no rush."

She smiled again and dashed up to her room. She should have been better prepared for Rashid, but had not expected him to disregard work to spend time with her. She was delighted, and hoped they'd find mutual interests for conversation. She could, of course, simply stare at him all day—but that would look odd.

Rashid walked to the opened French doors. He gazed out at the gardens, but his thoughts centered on his American visitor. Bethanne fascinated him. Her profession was unusual for a woman. Yet whenever she was around him, she appeared very feminine. He liked looking at her with her fair skin, blue eyes and soft blond hair. Her casual manner could lead some to believe she was flighty—but he'd checked her record and it was spotless. He also found her enthusiasm refreshing after his own rather cynical outlook on life. Was that an American trait? Or her individual personality?

Rashid knew several American businessmen. Had dined with them and their wives over the years. Most of them cultivated the same aloof cosmopolitan air that was so lacking in Bethanne. Maybe it was that difference that had him intrigued.

His mother had called again that morning, bemoaning the fact Bethanne was visiting and that Haile had not come. When he'd told her he was just as well out of the deal, she'd appeared shocked. Questioning him further, she'd become angry when he'd said he wasn't sure the arrangement had been suitable in the long run. He didn't come out and tell her of firm plans with Bethanne, but let her believe there was a possibility.

He almost laughed when his mother had tentatively suggested Bethanne wasn't suitable and he should let her help him find the right bride. He knew he and Bethanne didn't make a suitable pair. Yet, if he thought about it, she would probably have beautiful children. She was young, healthy, obviously intelligent.

He stopped. It sounded as if he were seriously considering a relationship with her. He was not. His family would never overlook what her father had done. And after the aborted affair with Marguerite, he didn't fully trust women. He would do better to focus on finalizing the details of the agreement with al Benqura.

His mother had reminded him she expected a different guest, and so would others.

"Until they see Bethanne. Then they'd know why she's visiting," he'd said, hoping to fob her off. It would certainly give a shot in the arm to the gossip circulating. And, he hoped, throw off any hint of scandal the minister might try to expose. Animosity ran deep between them. Rashid would not give him anything to fuel their feud.

He'd already invited Bethanne to the polo match. Perhaps

a dinner date or two, escorting her to a reception, would give gossips something else to talk about. It would not be a hardship. And al Benqura was in a hurry to finish the deal, as Rashid had suspected. Once the papers were signed, Bethanne would be leaving. Life would return to normal and no one except he and she would know the full circumstances of the charade. The thought was disquieting. Maybe he wouldn't be in so much of a hurry to finalize everything.

Bethanne took care when freshening up. She brushed her hair until it shone. Tying it back so it wouldn't get in her face, she refreshed her makeup. She felt like she was on holiday—lazing around, visiting old town, now seeing more of the country. Spending time with a gorgeous man. What was not to like about Quishari?

She was practical enough to know she wasn't some femme fatale; she'd never wow the sheikh like some Arabian beauty would. Haile had had that sultry look with the fine features, wide chocolate-brown eyes and beautiful dark hair so many Arab women had. Next to them, she felt like a washed-out watercolor.

Leaving her room, she started down the stairs.

"Prompt as ever," he said from the bottom.

She glanced down at him, gripping the banister tightly in startled surprise. She could take in how fabulous he looked in a dark suit, white shirt and blue-and-silver tie. His black hair gleamed beneath the chandelier. His deep brown eyes were fixed on her. Taking a breath, she smiled and tried to glide down the stairs. Was this how Cinderella felt going to the ball? She didn't want midnight to come.

"You look lovely," he said.

Bethanne smiled at him. "Thank you, kind sir."

Once seated in the limo, Rashid gave directions to the driver. Bethanne settled back to enjoy being with him.

"So if I'm to watch a polo match on Saturday, maybe I should learn a bit of the finer points of the game," she said as they pulled away from the villa. "What should I watch for?"

Rashid gave her an overview of the game. Bethanne couldn't wait to see Rashid on one of the horses he spoke about. She knew he'd looked fabulous. She had to remind herself more than once on the ride—sheikhs didn't get involved with women from Galveston, Texas.

When they arrived at the restaurant, Bethanne was impressed. It was on the shore of the Gulf, with tall windows which gave an excellent view to the beautiful water. Their table was next to one of the windows, tinted to keep the glare out, making Bethanne feel as if she were sitting on the sand.

"This is fabulous," she murmured, captivated by the view.

"The food is good, as well," he said, sitting in the chair opposite.

The maître d' placed the menus before them with a flourish.

After one glance, Bethanne closed hers and looked back out the window. "Please order for me. I'm afraid I can't read Arabic."

"Do you like fish?"

"Love it."

"Then I'll order the same filet for us both and you'll see what delicious fish we get from the Gulf."

After their order had been taken, Bethanne looked at him. "Do you ever go snorkeling or scuba diving?"

"From time to time," he said. "Do you?"

She nodded. "It's almost mandatory if one grows up in Galveston. I've had some great vacations in the Florida Keys, snorkeling and exploring the colorful sea floor."

"We will have to try that before you go," he said politely.

She studied him for a moment. "I can go by myself, you

know. You don't have to take time away from your busy work schedule. It's not as if—"

His raised eyebrow had her stopping abruptly.

"What?"

"We do not know who can hear our conversation," he cautioned.

She glanced around. No one appeared to be paying the slightest bit of attention to them, but she knew it would only take a few words to cause the charade to collapse and that would undoubtedly cause Rashid a lot of trouble.

"So how goes the deal?" she asked, leaning a bit closer and lowering her voice.

"We should sign soon, if certain parties don't cause a glitch."

"The father?" she asked, feeling as if she were speaking in code.

"No, he'll come round. It's some of our own internal people who are against the proposed agreement who could still throw a wrench into the works."

"And your mother?"

Rashid leaned closer, covering one of her hands with his, lowering his voice. "My mother has no interest in politics or business. She only wants her sons married. Our personal lives have no interest to anyone, unless it causes a breach between me and al Benqura. That's what we are guarding against."

Bethanne knew to others in the restaurant, it must look as if he were whispering sweet nothings. Her hand tingled with his touch. For a moment she wished she dared turn it over and clasp his. The Quishari culture was more conservative than Americans and overt displays of affection were uncommon in public. Still, he had made the overture.

"Do not be concerned with my mother. She will not cause a problem."

"I wished she liked me," she murmured.

"Why? You'll hardly see her before you leave. She will be at the polo match and perhaps one or two events we attend, but her manners are excellent, as I expect yours to be."

Bethanne bristled. "I do know how to make nice in public," she said.

Amusement danced in his eyes. "I'm sure you do."

Their first course arrived and Bethanne was pleased to end the conversation and concentrate on eating and enjoying the view.

"This is delicious," she said after her first bite. The fish was tender and flavorful. The vegetables were perfect.

He nodded. "I hoped you would like it."

Conversation was sporadic while they ate. Bethanne didn't want to disturb the mellow mood she was in as she enjoyed the food. She glanced at Rashid once in a while, but for the most part kept looking at the sea.

When the sugared walnuts appeared for dessert, she smiled in delight. "I didn't know restaurants served these," she said, taking one and popping it into her mouth.

"I ordered them specially for you," he said.

"You did?" Amazing. She'd never had anyone pay such attention to details and then act on their knowledge. "Thank you very much. I love these."

She savored another then asked, "So what happened to your brother? Did he get the fire out?"

"He did. He heads a company that specializes in putting out oil fires as well as acting as consultants for wells around the world."

"Sounds dangerous."

"Putting out the fires can be, but the rest is consulting work."

"Isn't he part of the family business?"

"He is, but more a silent partner in the day-to-day operations. He prefers not to be stuck in an office, as he puts it."

She studied him, taking another walnut and savoring it as she put it in her mouth. "I don't see you as *stuck* in an office. I expect you love pitting your mind against others."

He smiled slightly. "One way to put it, I suppose. I find it satisfying to make deals to benefit the company. Pitting my wits against others in the field and continuing to expand the company beyond what my father did."

"How did your father die?" It was a bold question, given what she'd learned this morning, but she would never have a better opportunity.

"Heart attack. He was only sixty-three…far too young to die."

"I hope heart problems don't run in your family." Nothing said about what caused it. Maybe the timing was coincidental to the disappearance of her father and the plane. She hoped so. It was bad enough they thought her father a thief. Surely they didn't blame him for the old sheikh's death.

"No. He had rheumatic fever as a child and developed problems from that. The rest of us, including two of his older brothers, are fine."

More than fine, she thought, looking away lest she gave him insight into her thought process. Really, Bethanne, she admonished, you've seen other gorgeous men before. Just not so up close and interested in her—even if it was only pretend.

"Ready to leave? We can take the walnuts with us. I want Teaz to drive us up the coast. There are some beautiful spots along the way. And some ruins from ancient times."

Settled in the luxurious limousine a few moments later, Bethanne knew she could get used to such treatment in no time. And she could gain a bazillion pounds if she kept eating the sweets. Just one or two more and she'd stop. Until later.

Rashid gave a running commentary as they drove along one

of the major highways of Quishari. With the Persian Gulf on the right and huge family estates on the left, there was a sameness that gradually changed as they went farther from the city.

Soon they were surrounded by the desert, stretching from the sea to as far to the west as she could see.

"The ruins are best viewed walking through them," he said when Teaz stopped the car. The place was lonely, sandy and windswept, only outlines of the buildings that had once comprised a thriving village.

"Lonely," Bethanne said, staring west. Nothing but miles of empty land. And the memory of people now gone.

"Once it was a lively trading port. You can see a few of the pilings for the piers in the water. It's estimated these are more than two thousand years old."

"Makes America seem like a toddler. Most of our history goes back four hundred years—once the Europeans settled in. I'd like to see this from the air. Tell me more."

By the time the sun was sinking lower in the sky, they'd gone north almost to the border and turned to head for the villa. Bethanne enjoyed every moment. It was obvious that Rashid loved his country and enjoyed sharing his devotion with his guest. She learned more about the history of the area in their ride than she'd ever learned in school or from her father. Rashid had appeared surprised at the knowledge she did have.

"Tomorrow we can take the plane up again. Fly over the ruins and maybe west. There are a few oases that are large enough to support small communities."

"Did your family gather at the villa for holidays?" she asked.

"For some of them. Other times we met at my father's home. But the family loved the villa. In the summer, my parents often spent several weeks visiting my grandmother and enjoying the sea. My brother and I loved those times."

Rashid escorted her to the door when they arrived.

The butler met them, speaking rapidly to Rashid.

"We seem to have company," Rashid said to her in English. "My brother."

"Oh. Do you want me to go on upstairs?"

"No, come meet Khalid."

When they entered the salon, a man sitting on one of the chairs reading the newspaper rose. For a split second, Bethanne stared. He looked just like Rashid. Twins!

Then he turned to face them and the image was disturbed by the slash of burned skin going from just beneath his right eye, down to the collar of his shirt in a disfiguring swath. Bethanne caught her breath, trying not to imagine the pain and suffering that had resulted from such a burn.

"Bethanne, this is Khalid."

"How do you do. Rashid didn't tell me you two were twins."

Khalid nodded but stayed where he was, his eyes alert and suspicious.

"He told me about your plan to fool the world. Stupid idea," Khalid said.

She blinked at the hostility, then glanced at Rashid, who shrugged. "So you say. If it holds off the wolves until the deal is signed, I'm good with it. What brings you here?"

"I wanted to meet her," Khalid said.

Bethanne walked over and sat down. "Now you have. Questions?" She had spent her fair share dealing with obstreperous officers in the past. And some cranky clients. She could handle this.

"Do not cross the line," Rashid warned his brother.

"What do you expect from this?" Khalid said, ignoring his twin.

"A signed acceptance of the jet aircraft I delivered and a

few days exploring a country I have long wanted to see," Bethanne responded quickly.

Rashid watched his brother ask more questions than he should have. He was looking for a gold digger and that was not Rashid's assessment of Bethanne. She was more concerned with clearing her father's name than getting clothes or money from him. Not that Rashid had any intentions of providing his visitor anything more than was needed to attend the events where he'd show her off. Khalid was worried for naught.

"Did you get that oil fire out?" she asked at a pause in the interrogation.

Khalid nodded. "How do you know about that?"

"My dear friend Rashid tells me everything," she said sweetly.

Rashid laughed aloud. "Subtlety is not your strong suit. Leave her alone. I'm happy with the arrangement we have. No need to look for trouble where there is none."

Khalid studied her. Bethanne met his gaze with a considering one of her own.

"We are dining in this evening—would you care to join us?" Rashid asked.

He decided in that instance to stay for dinner. Maybe a few hours in Bethanne's company would end his brother's suspicions and gain his own cooperation in the situation.

CHAPTER FOUR

PROMPTLY at eight the next morning, Bethanne descended the stairs, dressed in her uniform. She was looking forward to another ride over Quishari. She and Rashid had discussed the trip last night. It would give one of his pilots a chance at the controls. She knew he would love the plane.

And she would spend more hours in Rashid's company. She was treasuring each, knowing the memory of their time would be all she'd have in the future. But for now, she relished every moment.

Fatima sat on one of the elegant chairs in the foyer. She rose when Bethanne reached the tiled floor. Saying something in Arabic, she smiled politely. Bethanne hadn't a clue what she said, but smiled in return.

The limo was in front and whisked them both away. Obviously today was a day that needed a chaperone. Was she going on the plane with them as well?

Bethanne had braided her hair in a single plait down the back to keep it out of the way. Her uniform was a far cry from the silk dresses she'd been wearing. Still, this was business. It would have been highly inappropriate for her to wear one of the dresses when flying the plane.

The jet gleamed in the sunlight when they arrived. Ground

crewmen stood nearby, but no one stood next to the plane. Once she and Fatima got out of the limo, the translator broke away from the group and headed their way.

"His Excellency and Alexes are already in the plane," he said with a slight bow.

Bethanne's heart skipped a beat and then began to race.

"I'll start the ground checklist," she said, ignoring her clamoring need to see Rashid again. She had her tasks to perform to carry everyone safely. "Ask Fatima if she wishes to accompany me or board now?"

A quick interchange, then he said, "She will remain by the stairs until you are ready to enter."

Bethanne took her time checking the aircraft then nodded to Fatima and climbed the steps to the plane. After the bright sunshine, it took a couple of seconds for her eyes to adjust. She saw an older man talking with Rashid in the back of the cabin. Starting back toward them, Bethanne watched as they studied the communication panel.

Rashid saw her and introduced the pilot. "We are looking at the various aspects of the aircraft. This one has more features than the one I've been using."

"But the one that was lost had some of these same capabilities," the pilot murmured, still looking at the dials and knobs.

The plane that was lost—was that the one her father had flown? The pilot was someone who might have known Hank. She hoped they had some time together on today's flight so she could ask him.

"If you are ready to depart, Alexes would like to sit in the cockpit to observe and then fly it once you give the go-ahead."

"I'm sure you'll be ready in no time," she said to the pilot. "For all the technology this baby carries, she's quick to respond and simple to fly."

The man didn't look convinced. Bethanne wondered if he was unsure of her own skills, or those of the plane.

"Fatima will accompany us," Rashid said. He handed Bethanne a topographical map. "I thought we could first fly over the ruins from yesterday, and then head west, toward one of the oases I spoke of."

"Sounds great. Did you already file the flight plan?"

"Alexes did."

"Then let's go."

The pilot bowed slightly to the sheikh and followed Bethanne into the cockpit. He slid into the copilot's seat and began scanning the dials and switches.

Bethanne smoothly taxied and took off, taking the route the pilot had filed with the ground control. She talked to the pilot the entire time about what she was doing and how the plane responded. His English was excellent and he quickly grasped the intricacies of the new jet.

When they reached their cruising altitude, she banked easily and headed north as the flight plan outlined. The sea was sparkling in the sunshine. The shoreline, irregular below them, gleamed. The vegetation edging the beach contrasted with the white sand and blue waters.

Even as she conversed with the other pilot, Bethanne scanned the land below, wondering if her father had flown this exact route. Her recall of the topographical map showed when they turned inland she would be flying almost directly west. Was that a routine flight for the old sheikh?

Rashid al Harum opened the cockpit door and looked in. "What do you think, Alexes?" he asked, resting one hand on the back of Bethanne's seat.

The pilot responded in Arabic and when Rashid spoke in the same language, the man looked abashed.

"My pardon. I told His Excellency that the plane handles like a dream. If I may take over for a while?"

Bethanne nodded and lifted her hands.

"Ahh, it does respond like a dream," Alexes said a moment later, approval in his voice.

"Below are the ruins," Rashid said, looking over her shoulder.

Bethanne looked out of the window, seeing the outlines of the structures they'd viewed yesterday. She kept her eyes on the ground when Alexes banked slightly so she could see the old piers marching out in the water. The crystal clarity of the Persian Gulf enabled her to clearly see each one. Her imagination was sparked by the picture below. Who had lived there? How had their lives been spent? What would they think of people soaring over them in planes they probably never even dreamed about?

Slowly the plane turned and the ruins were behind them. Below was only endless sand with hardy plants which could survive the harsh conditions. The scene became monotonous in the brown hues.

Bethanne looked over her shoulder at the sheikh. "How long to the oasis?" she asked.

"We'll be there in time to have lunch before returning. Once you're reassured Alexes knows what he's doing, perhaps you'd join me in the main compartment. Try out that sofa again."

She nodded, her heart skipping a beat. She didn't need to try out the sofa; she knew it was the height of luxury. She would love to spend a bit more time with Rashid, however. And demonstrate to the other pilot she trusted him with the plane.

The pilot seemed competent. He was murmuring softly, as if in love with the jet. She knew the feeling. It was her favorite model to fly. Still, she didn't leap at the chance to go back to the cabin. She had to focus on her primary responsibility, which was completing delivery of the aircraft—not spending time with the sheikh. She reviewed the various features of the cockpit, quoted fuel ratios, aeronautic facts and figures and answered all Alexes's questions.

When she was satisfied he could handle things, she turned over the controls and rose to head to the back. Fatima was dozing in one of the chairs near the rear.

Rashid looked up from a paper he was reading and watched as she crossed the small space and sat beside him on the long sofa.

"Alexes handling things well?" he asked.

"Of course. He said it was similar to another Starcraft plane he used to fly as backup. What happened to that one?"

"It was the one your father took—they both vanished," he said, putting aside his paper.

"It's hard to hide an airplane."

Just then the plane shuddered and began to dive. Bethanne took a split second to act. She was on her feet and heading for the cockpit when it veered suddenly to the right. She would have slammed into the side if Rashid had not caught her and pulled her along.

Opening the cockpit door a second later, she saw Alexes slumped over the controls. The earth rushed toward them at an alarming rate.

Rashid acted instantly, reaching to draw Alexes back. Bethanne slid into her seat and began to pull the plane from the dive. Rashid struggled to get Alexes out of the seat, but the man was unconscious and a dead weight. He called for Fatima and she hurried forward to help him, trying to guide the unconscious pilot's legs away from the controls as the sheikh pulled him from the copilot's seat. Once clear, she helped the sheikh carry him to the sofa while Bethanne regained control of the plane.

In only seconds the jet had resumed a normal flight pattern and once she verified the altitude, she resumed their approved flight track. Glancing around, she was relieved there were no other planes in sight.

"How is he?" she called back. The door separating the cockpit from the cabin had been propped open.

"Still unconscious…most likely a heart attack," Rashid called, loosening Alexes's collar.

"Oxygen is by the first-aid kit in the galley," she yelled back. She contacted ground control. Citing an emergency, she was directed to the nearest airport, in Quraim Wadi Samil, a few miles to the south of their original route.

Glancing over her shoulder, Bethanne could glimpse most of the cabin. Fatima held the portable oxygen tank while Rashid was still bent over the pilot. She shivered, hoping he was all right. What had happened?

In seconds Alexes's eyes flickered. He spoke in Arabic. Bethanne didn't understand him, but applauded Rashid's calm reply. In moments the sheikh had the older man take some aspirin and elevated his legs and feet. His color was pale, his speech slurred slightly.

"Might be a stroke," he called. "We'll head back immediately."

"They've directed me to an airport in Quraim Wadi Samil. It's closer and an ambulance will be standing by," she responded. She looked back again. "How's he doing?"

"Breathing hard. His color isn't good. How much longer?"

Contacting ground control, she requested emergency clearance for the airport and requested information on flight time remaining.

It came immediately. With new coordinates she altered course. In less than ten minutes she saw the small airport. In another ten, they were on the ground and the requested ambulance was already on its way to the hospital with Alexes. The sheikh conferred with the medical personnel before they left, then turned back to the two women standing at the bottom of the stairs.

"You handled that emergency well," Rashid said, his eyes rested on her.

"I was really scared to death. The plane responded well, however, and here we are. It's what I'm trained to do. What did the emergency medical technician say? Will he be all right?"

"Too early to tell. We'll follow to the hospital and see what we find out." He looked at the older woman and said something to her. She smiled and nodded, happiness shining from her face.

"What did you tell her?" Bethanne asked.

"That she was an asset in saving his life. It was providence that she was here and had Haile not left, things might have turned out differently."

"Helps with her guilt over Haile's defection, I'm sure," Bethanne said.

A cab drove up as he was speaking. The driver stopped near the plane and quickly got out, speaking to Rashid.

"Our transportation," he said.

"That was fast."

"I had one of the medical personnel radio for a cab. It'll take us to the hospital and I can decide our next move after I see how Alexes is doing."

"Will the plane be okay here?" Bethanne asked. They were on the far end of the airport tarmac. There were no personnel around and no fencing or other protection for the plane. Still, it was a small airport and so far off the beaten track, Bethanne couldn't imagine anyone wanting to harm the aircraft.

"It will be fine."

The cab was a standard sedan. Comfortable, but a far cry from the limo she'd been using. Oh, oh, she warned herself, don't be expecting that kind of luxury in the future.

* * *

When they arrived at the hospital, Alexes had already been cleared through the emergency room and was in a private room, with a nurse in constant attendance. Bethanne sat in the waiting room with Fatima while Rashid dealt with the paperwork. When he returned, she stood.

"Is he going to be all right?" she asked.

"Too early to tell, the doctor said." He looked worried. "I called the office to notify his family. If they wish to come here to be with him, I'll arrange for transportation."

Bethanne glanced around at the small facility. "Is this place equipped to deal with his situation?" she asked softly.

"It is not the latest in medical technology, but fortunately the doctors on staff are proficient. He will get good care here. Once he's stabilized, we can fly him back to Alkaahdar."

"And in the meantime?"

"We'll stay. Until we know something for certain."

He spoke to Fatima, who nodded.

"We'll find a hotel and check in. Then lunch. It's past one. Then you two can rest until we learn more about Alexes."

When they met for lunch on the small veranda of the hotel on the square, Bethanne wished she had something to wear besides her uniform. It still looked fresh and would have to do, but the warmth of the day had her wishing for one of the summer dresses in the closet at the villa. Something more feminine than a navy shirt and khaki pants.

Rashid sat at one of the tables. She joined him and he rose as she approached.

"Fatima decided to have lunch in her room. She wishes to lie down afterward," he said as he held the chair for Bethanne. "I think the excitement is catching up with her."

"I hope the situation didn't give her a fear of flying," she said.

"We're safe—that's what counts. I ordered already—a light

lunch since it is so late. We'll eat here tonight if we don't have definite word about Alexes before then."

Bethanne nodded. She hoped the other pilot would recover quickly, and be ready to fly again soon. For a moment she wondered what she'd do if she ever had to stop flying. She loved it so much, it would be a drastic change for her life.

The entire situation spooked her a bit. If Alexes had been flying solo, he could have crashed and no one would likely know why. Is that what happened to her father? A crash in some lonely location that no one had found?

"I hope he's going to be okay." She felt an immediate affinity to the older pilot. She hoped he recovered from whatever hit him and could continue flying.

Once they were served, Rashid asked if her room was to her liking.

"It's clean and neat and overlooks the square. Charming, actually."

"Not like the villa."

"Nice in its own way," she replied. "This changes your plans, doesn't it? You didn't expect to be away from the office all day."

"I can be reached by phone if there is an emergency. The staff is capable of handling things. Shall we explore the town after lunch?"

"I would love to."

When they started out, Rashid insisted on buying her a wide-brimmed hat to shelter her head from the sun.

"You aren't wearing one," she said as they left the gift shop.

"I'm used to the sun. Your skin is much fairer than mine and I don't want it burned."

She smiled, feeling cherished. No one had looked out for her in a long, long time.

They walked around the square, looking into the shops, but

when asked if she wanted to enter any, she declined. She wanted to see as much of the town as she could. The old buildings had ornate decorative carvings and bas-reliefs that intrigued her. The cobblestone streets showed wear but were still functioning centuries after they'd first been laid down.

"Tell me about this place. It's old, feels steeped in history. Is it a true representation of old Quishari?"

Rashid gave her a brief history of the town, telling her it had been on the trade routes, a favorite resting place because of the plentiful water.

As the afternoon grew warmer, she could feel heat radiating from the walls as they passed. Turning a corner and exploring some of the side streets put them in line with the breeze and it was pleasant.

"The air feels drier than the coast," she commented.

"Quite. There's a danger of dehydration. We'll stop soon and have something to drink."

Stopping after three o'clock for cold drinks at a small sidewalk café, she was glad the tables had umbrellas. Even with the hat, she was hot beneath the sun. Yet she relished the sights. She loved the sense of timelessness. This town had been here for a thousand years and would likely be around another thousand. If only the walls could talk.

"Will we be able to walk out on the desert a little?" she asked.

"We can ask the driver to take us as far out as you wish to go."

"Just enough to get the feel for it. It's amazing to me anyone can live in the desert."

"The old tribes knew the water spots which were crucial for survival. Caravans and nomads once roamed known trails. Now the routes are known to fewer and fewer people."

When they returned to the hotel, Rashid summoned the same cab. He spoke with the driver and before she knew it, she was sitting in the backseat with Rashid as the man drove crazily toward the west.

"So we ditch the town and take off," she murmured, feeling the delightful cool air from the air conditioner.

"For a while. It's best to see the desert with those interested, not those who wish they were elsewhere."

She laughed and settled down to enjoy the drive. To the right were rows of oil wells, the steady rising and fall of the pumpjacks timeless.

"I've seen those pumps in California," she commented. "In one place they are even painted to look like whimsical animals," she said, watching the monotonous up-and-down action of the machines.

"These kind of pumps are used all over the world. I had not thought about decorating them. They're functional, that's all."

"Is this an oil field that belongs to your company?"

"It is."

"Do you come here often?"

"No. Only once before, actually." He was silent for a moment, then said softly, "It was my father's special project. The wells don't produce as much as in other areas, but he insisted on keeping the field going, and on checking on it himself. I came with him once. It held special attraction for him, not so much for me. As long as there are no problems, I don't need to visit. Khalid comes occasionally."

"Must be nice for the local economy."

"One reason my father kept it going, I think. The discovery of oil helped revive the town and he felt an obligation to keep it going."

"And you do as well."

He shrugged. "I try. My father was a great man. I'm doing my best to do what I think would make him proud."

"Keep an open mind about mine," she said.

He looked at her, eyes narrowed. "What further is there to discuss?"

"We don't know what happened. But I know my father. And he was an honorable man. He would not have stolen your father's plane."

"My father was also an honorable man. The betrayal of his pilot and the disappearance of the plane caused such stress and anxiety he suffered a heart attack, which killed him. It isn't only the betrayal but the end result I find abhorrent."

Bethanne stared out across the desert as if she could search around and find a clue as to what happened to her father. She had only her belief in her dad to sustain her. "I have faith in my father just as you do in yours," she said slowly.

"It is not something we are going to agree on," he said.

"Tell me about being a twin," she said, turning to look at Rashid. It was a definite change of subject, but she wanted the afternoon to be special—not have them at odds because of the past. "I don't even have a sibling, much less a twin. It is true, you're so close you can read each other's mind?"

"Hardly. I can sense things when we are together—like if he's angry and hiding it. But we are two individuals. Growing up was fun. We delighted in playing tricks on our parents and tutors, switching identities, that sort of thing."

"Tell me," she invited.

He spoke of when he and Khalid were boys, visits to the villa to see their grandmother, trips to Europe and other countries around the Mediterranean Sea.

To Bethanne, it sounded glorious. So different from her childhood in Texas. She laughed at some of the antics he described, and felt a bit of sadness for their homesickness when sent to school in England for eight years when Rashid told her how much they'd missed their country.

When he spoke to the driver, he stopped. Rashid looked at

Bethanne. "When we get out, look in all directions. Nothing but desert."

She did so, stepping away from the car, seeking all she could from her senses. The air was dry, hot. The breeze was soft against her skin, carrying the scent of plants she didn't know. In the distance the land shimmered in heat waves, and she thought she saw water.

"A mirage," she breathed softly.

"There?" Rashid stood next to her at the rear of the cab, bending down so his head was next to hers so he could see what she saw. He pointed to the distant image and she nodded. "It does look like water, but we would never find it."

"I know. I have only seen one other mirage. This is fascinating. And quiet. If we don't speak, I think I can hear my heartbeat in the silence."

He didn't reply and for several long moments Bethanne absorbed everything, from the awesome, stark beauty of the desert to the heat from Rashid's body next to hers, his scent mingling with that on the wind. She never wanted to forget this special moment.

Turning, she was surprised how close he stood. "Thank you for bringing me," she said.

To her surprise, he put his palm beneath her chin and raised her face to his. "You constantly surprise me," he said before kissing her.

His lips were warm against hers, moving slowly as if savoring the touch. He pressed for a response and Bethanne gave it to him, sighing softly and stepping closer. His lips opened hers and his tongue teased her. She responded with her own and was drowned in sensation. Forgotten was the world; she was wrapped up in emotions and feelings and the exquisite touch of his mouth against hers. Only the wind was witness, only the sand reflected the heat of passion.

All too soon he ended the kiss and gazed down at her as she slowly opened her eyes. His dark gaze mesmerized. Her heart pounded, her blood sang through her body. If she could capture only one moment of her entire life to never forget, it would be this one.

"We should head back," he said.

The spell shattered. She stepped back and turned, trying to regain her composure so he would never know how much the kiss meant.

"I'm ready. Thank you for bringing me here. It is a special spot." And would forever remain so.

The drive back to Quraim Wadi Samil was silent. Bethanne hugged the sensation of his kiss to herself as the desert scenery whizzed by. Before long the roof lines of the buildings could be seen. They drew closer by the moment. As she and Rashid drew further apart. It had been a whim, an alignment of circumstances—the scare in the plane, the worry about the pilot, being away from home. It meant nothing beyond they were glad to be alive.

She wished it had meant something.

Dinner that evening was again on the terrace of the small hotel. Fatima joined them and the sheikh kept the conversation neutral, translating back and forth between the two women. Bethanne wasn't sure if she were glad Fatima was present or not. It kept things on an even keel, preventing her from reading more into the afternoon's outing than warranted. But it also meant she had to share the precious time with Rashid. And of course the topic of conversation remained focused on Alexes. The doctor had been cautiously optimistic.

Rashid had obtained the report upon their return to the hotel. It looked as if it was a small stroke.

"But he'll fully recover?" Bethanne asked when Rashid told Fatima.

"That's what the tests are assessing. I hope so. But I don't know if he'll ever fly again."

Bethanne nodded. "Or at least not as a solo pilot," she said. "If he were copilot, there'd be someone else in case of another emergency." Her heart hurt for the man. Flying was a way of life; how sad if it ended prematurely.

Rashid nodded. "However, I do not want my family or employees put in any danger if unnecessary. Alexes has served us well for many years. He will not be abandoned."

Sending up a quick prayer for his recovery, Bethanne asked if he would be released before they returned to Alkaahdar.

"Unlikely. We will return in the morning. He'll need care for several days."

Fatima spoke.

"She wonders when she will return home," Rashid said to Bethanne.

"She doesn't need to stay on my account," she replied.

"I believe my mother is more comfortable with her as your chaperone. Otherwise, you might have to stay with my mother."

Bethanne stared at him in dismay. "You can't be serious."

"If we are to continue the pretense, we need to be authentic. I would not have a woman in a home I owned without a proper chaperone—not if I were serious about making her my wife."

"That's totally old-fashioned."

"We are an old culture. We have certain standards and procedures that have served us well for generations. One is the sacredness of the marriage bond. And the high standards we hold for women we make our wives."

"So you might have a fling with someone in another country, but once in your own, it's old-world values all the way?"

He nodded, amusement showing at her indignation.

"I protect whom I'm interested in. There would be no gossip or scandal. The full authority of the al Harum family would be behind the woman I showed interest in—as it would for Khalid's chosen bride."

"Is he also getting married?"

"Not that I know of. He's not the older son."

Bethanne thought it over for a moment. In an odd way, it was interesting. Old-fashioned and a bit chauvinistic, but romantic at the same time. A woman who truly caught Rashid al Harum's interest and affection would be cherished, cosseted and treated like royalty at every turn.

Lucky girl!

The next morning Bethanne piloted the plane back to Alkaahdar. Rashid sat in the copilot's seat. Alexes had been declared out of danger, but the doctor in charge wanted him to remain a bit longer for observation to assess his reaction to medications. He would be transported home in another company plane in a few days' time.

As she flew back, Bethanne was lost in thought as she studied the landscape, so different viewed from the air than on the ground. There were endless miles of sand beneath them, no signs of life. Yet she'd felt the vibrancy of the desert when they'd stopped yesterday.

In a short time she saw the high-rises of the city on the horizon.

"I can't imagine living down there without the modern conveniences," she said.

"My brother likes the challenge. He goes to the desert a lot. I'm like you. I prefer modern conveniences—especially air-conditioning."

"Funny that twins would be so different."

"More a difference in circumstances. When Khalid was

burned so badly, he withdrew. I know the woman he thought to marry was horrified and did not stand by him. I thought he was better out of that arrangement, but it was still a bitter pill to swallow. It was after that he began seeking solitude in the desert."

"Can't the burned skin be fixed with plastic surgery?"

"He had some operations, decided against any more. He says he's satisfied."

Bethanne knew even with the badly burned slash of skin, Khalid was as dynamic and appealing as his brother. "Too bad."

"It could have been worse. He could have died."

Once they landed at the airport, the familiar limousine slid into place near the plane.

"I have work to do. Teaz will take you to the villa. I'll see you for dinner around seven?" Rashid said.

"I'll look forward to it," she said, disappointed they wouldn't spend this day together. "I'll double-check things on the plane before leaving."

Since Rashid would be tied up until later, she'd revisit the café in the square near where her father once lived to see if his friend had shown up. The longer she was around Rashid, the more she wanted to clear her father's name. It grew in importance as her feelings for the sheikh grew.

CHAPTER FIVE

SATURDAY Bethanne rose early. Today was the polo match, followed by a dinner dance in the evening. She hoped the dress she'd brought for the actual match was suitable. The light blue cotton had appealed to her the moment she'd first seen it. It was slightly more casual than the dresses Rashid had bought. Suitable for outdoors and easily cleaned if something spilled on it. She hoped she'd chosen well. The sparkle in her eyes and the blush of color on her cheeks showed how excited she was with the excursion.

The maid knocked on the door before nine and told her Rashid was waiting.

Grabbing her small purse and the wide-brimmed hat Rashid has bought in Quraim Wadi Samil, she hurried down to greet him.

He was waiting in the foyer, dressed in jodhpurs and a white shirt opened at the collar. He watched as she ran lightly down the stairs while she could hardly take her eyes off him. He looked fabulous.

"I'm ready," she said as she stepped onto the tile floor.

"A good trait in a woman, always being on time."

"Comes from pilot training, I expect," she said as they went outside.

A small sports car stood where the limousine normally parked.

"I will drive," Rashid said, escorting her to the passenger's side.

Bethanne loved riding in a convertible—especially beside Rashid.

Within twenty minutes, they had reached the polo field. The bustle of activity reminded Bethanne of horse races in Texas. Lots of people walking around, studying horses, reviewing printed programs, laughing and talking. Clothing varied from designer originals to the jodhpurs and white shirts that Rashid wore. Once in a while she spotted a man in more traditional robes, but for the most part she could be in England or France, or Texas.

Rashid parked near a stable and Bethanne went with him to one of the stalls where a groom already had a beautiful Arabian saddled.

"This is Morning Star," Rashid said with affection, patting the arched neck of the horse. His glossy chestnut coat gleamed. His mane and tail had been brushed until they looked silky soft.

"He's beautiful," she said, reaching out to pet him as well.

"He is one of four I have. Come, we'll look at the rest, all great animals. But Morning Star is the one I ride most often."

Bethanne loved the entire atmosphere of the event. She was introduced to other players. She petted a dozen or more beautiful horses. She watched as the grooms prepared horses for the event.

Khalid was also riding and they visited him shortly before Rashid escorted her to the viewing stands. His welcome wasn't exactly warm, but better than his mother's was likely to be, Bethanne thought.

"My mother is already in the royal box," Rashid said as they began to climb the stairs.

Bethanne's heart dropped. She had not known she'd be spending time with Madame al Harum. It was enough to put a damper on her enthusiasm. Still, with any luck, the woman would be so busy rooting for her sons, she would ignore the unwelcomed woman her one son was entertaining.

There were several guests in the al Harum box, and Rashid made sure everyone was introduced to Bethanne before he left.

"See you later," he said, with a special caress on her cheek.

She played the part of adoring girlfriend and told him to win for her.

Smiling at the others, she took a seat left for her on the front row and focused on the playing field and not the chatter around her. Not that she could understand it. Just before the match began, Madame al Harum sat in the seat next to her.

The game was exciting and Bethanne was glad Rashid had gone over the main points so she had a glimmer of an idea how it was played. Often she saw a blur of horses and riders when the players vied for the ball. Other times Rashid would break free and hit the ball down the field. Or Khalid. His horse was a dark bay. That wasn't the only way she could tell the men apart, but it helped. She seemed tuned in to Rashid and kept her eyes on him for most of the game.

When the match ended, Rashid's team had won by two points. The people in the box cheered and Bethanne joined right in.

"Come, we will meet them for celebration, then return home to change for tonight's fete," Madame al Harum said, touching Bethanne on the shoulder. The older woman walked proudly to the area where the winners were celebrating.

When Rashid saw them, he broke away and crossed swiftly to them, enveloping Bethanne in a hug. She hugged him right back, enthusiasm breaking out.

"It was wonderful! You looked like you were part of the

horse. And that one long drive…I thought the ball would never stop."

"Well done, Rashid," his mother said, watching in disapproval the animation on Bethanne's face.

Khalid came over, hugging his mother and standing with his arm around her shoulders as he greeted Bethanne again.

"Great match," she said with a smile.

He nodded.

"Don't you ever worry you'll get hit by the maillot?"

"It's happened. Glad you enjoyed it. Your first match?" he asked.

"Yes. I hope not my last," she said. Rashid had mimicked his brother with his arm around Bethanne's shoulders. She tried not to be self-conscious, but she knew his mother did not approve. She didn't care. She would not care. It's not as if they'd made a lifelong commitment to each other. The older woman would find out soon enough.

"Come to the dinner tonight," Madame al Harum said to Khalid.

"Not tonight. I have other plans." He gave her a kiss on her cheek, sketched a salute to Rashid and Bethanne and left, weaving his way through the crowd.

His mother watched with sad eyes.

"He never comes," she said.

"Let him find his own way, Mother," Rashid said gently.

After Rashid checked with the groom on the state of his horse, he escorted Bethanne to the sports car.

"So how often do you play? When do you find time to practice? Do you ever have games away from Alkaahdar?" she asked, fascinated by the sport.

He answered her questions as he skillfully drove through

the city traffic, giving Bethanne a fascinating insight to more of his life.

"I'll pick you up at six-thirty," he said when they arrived at the villa. "Dinner starts at seven. And the party will last until late."

"I'll be ready," she said.

Before she could get out of the car, however, he stopped her. "You did well today."

"I will do fine tonight as well," she replied gravely. "I'll be most adoring, now that you won the match."

He laughed at her sassy remark and watched as she entered the house.

Bethanne dressed with care for the dinner. She wore an ivory-white dress from the ones Rashid had bought. The one-shoulder gown fell in a gentle drape down to the floor, moving when she walked, caressing her skin with the softness of pure silk. Minnah came to ask if she could assist and Bethanne asked her to do her hair up in a fancy style.

The quiet woman nodded and set to work when Bethanne sat in front of the vanity.

"Could you also teach me some Arabic?" Bethanne asked.

"Like what?"

"Pleased to meet you. I am enjoying visiting your country. Just a few phrases?"

"It would be my pleasure," the maid said.

For the moments it took the maid to arrange her hair, she also taught Bethanne several phrases. With a skill for mimicking sounds, Bethanne hoped she was getting the correct intonation to the sounds she heard.

Minnah beamed with pleasure a few moments later. Bethanne gazed at herself in the mirror, very pleased with the simple, yet sophisticated style the maid had achieved.

"Thank you," she said in Arabic.

Minnah bowed slightly and smiled. "You pick up the words quickly."

"I'll be repeating them from now until we begin dinner," she said in English.

"His Excellency will be pleased with the effort you have made starting to learn our language. It is good for you to speak Arabic."

Bethanne didn't abuse her of the idea that she was being considered for Rashid's wife. Nothing like servants' gossip to spread like wildfire. That should suit him.

Bethanne was waiting in the salon when Rashid arrived. He wore a tuxedo. She loved the different facets of the man. From suave businessman to casual polo player to elegant sophisticate. She couldn't decide which appealed more.

"Ever prompt," he repeated when he stepped into the salon. "And you look lovely."

"Thank you," she said in Arabic, almost laughing at his look of surprise.

He said several words in that language which had her actually laughing aloud and holding up a hand.

"Please, I only learned a very few—such as please and thank you, nice to meet you and I am enjoying my visit."

"Very well done," he said.

His obvious approval warmed her.

"The dress is lovely, but missing something," he said.

She looked down. "I have a wrap on the chair," she said, moving to gather it.

"I was thinking of jewelry," he said, stepping closer. From his pocket he pulled out a beautiful necklace of sapphires and diamonds on a white gold chain.

Bethanne caught her breath. "It's beautiful." She took a step back. "But I can't wear that. What if it came undone and was lost?" She couldn't replace a fine piece of jewelry like that for years.

"It will not come undone and the stones match your eyes. It will complete the dress."

She looked at the necklace and then at Rashid.

"My intended bride would not come as a pauper to the wedding," he said.

Of course. It was for show. For a moment she was swamped with disappointment. What had she expected—that he'd really give her a lovely piece of jewelry like that?

"Very well, but it's on you if it gets lost."

She stepped forward and held out her hand, but he brushed it aside and reached around her neck to fasten it himself. She stared at his throat, her heart hammering in her chest. The touch of his warm fingers on her neck sent shivers down her spine. She could scarcely breathe.

Bethanne turned when he'd finished, seeking a mirror to see how it looked. There were none in the salon. "I want to see," she said.

"In the foyer, then we should leave."

Standing a moment later in front of the long mirror in the foyer, she gazed at her reflection. She looked totally different. It wasn't only the expensive clothing and jewelry, the sophisticated hairstyle. There was a glow about her, a special look in her eyes. She sought Rashid's in the reflection. He looked at her steadily.

"Thank you. I feel like Cinderella before the ball."

"It does not end at midnight," he said. "Shall we?"

The limo carried them the short distance to the luxury hotel where the dinner was being held. The huge portico accommodated half a dozen cars at a time and Bethanne had a chance to observe the other women getting out of cars and limousines who were wearing designer creations and enough jewelry to open a mega store.

Once inside, Bethanne was delighted with the sparkling chandeliers overhead that threw rainbows of color around the lavish room. Tables were set with starched white linen clothes, ornate silverware and fine crystal glassware. The room was large enough to accommodate hundreds, yet the space was not crowded.

Rashid placed her hand in the crook of his arm, pressing her arm against his side as they walked in. He greeted friends, introducing Bethanne to each. She smiled and gave her newly learned Arabic greeting. Many of the people seemed pleased, and then disappointed she hadn't yet learned more. They encouraged her to continue learning.

An older man stopped their progression. He spoke to Rashid, but his gaze never left Bethanne.

Rashid answered then spoke in English. "Bethanne, may I present Ibrahim ibn Saali, minister of finance for Quishari. He is a great polo fan. I've told him you are my special guest."

"Come to visit Quishari?" the minister asked.

Bethanne smiled brightly. "Indeed, and I'm charmed by what I've seen." She leaned slightly against Rashid, hoping she looked like a woman in love in the minister's eyes.

"I thought another was coming," the minister said.

She looked suitably surprised, then glanced at Rashid. "There had better not be another expected."

He shook his head, his hand covering hers on his arm. "Not in this lifetime," he said. To the minister he nodded once. "We are expected at my mother's table."

"Nice to have met you," Bethanne said in Arabic.

The older man merely nodded and stepped aside.

She could feel his gaze as they crossed to the table.

"He's the one, isn't he?" she asked.

"Indeed. But your acting skills were perfect." He glanced down at her and smiled. "If we keep him satisfied, the deal is as good as done."

When they reached their table, Madame al Harum was already seated. Next to her was an elderly man. He rose when Bethanne arrived and greeted her solemnly. Both expressed surprise at her Arabic response. For a moment she wondered if the older woman would thaw a bit. That thought was short-lived when Madame al Harum virtually ignored Bethanne and indicated that Rashid should sit next to her.

Despite not understanding the language, Bethanne enjoyed herself. The polo club was celebrating their victory and she could clap and cheer with them all. Several speakers were obviously from the club. Rashid leaned closer to give capsulated recaps of the speeches. At one point the speaker on the platform said something that had everyone turning to look at Rashid. He rose and bowed slightly to thunderous applause.

When he sat down and the speaker resumed, she leaned closer.

"What did he say?"

"Just thanks for funding the matches."

"Ah, so you're the sponsor?"

"One of several."

She knew he was wealthy, but to fund a sports team cost serious money. She was so out of her element. No matter how much she was growing attracted to her host, she had to remember in the great scheme of things, she was a lowly employee of a company selling him the jet she'd delivered. He was a wealthy man, gorgeous to boot. He had no need to look to the likes of her when any woman in the world would love to be in her position. How could Haile have chosen some-one else over Rashid?

* * *

When the after-dinner speeches were finally finished, a small musical ensemble set up and began playing dance music. Some of the older guests gathered their things to leave, but the younger ones began to drift to the dance floor.

Rashid held out his hand to Bethanne. "Will you dance with me?" he asked.

She nodded and rose.

He was conscious of the stares and some of the conversation that erupted when they reached the dance floor. Her blond hair and blue eyes stood out in this group of mostly dark-haired women. He enjoyed taking her into his arms for the slow dance. She was taller than most women he had dated and it was a novelty to not have to lean over to hear if she spoke. Or to kiss her.

He'd thought a lot about that kiss in Quraim Wadi Samil as they moved with the music. He tightened his hold slightly in remembrance. One kiss had him fantasizing days afterward. He'd kissed his share of women. He'd even thought he loved Marguerite. But Bethanne had him in a quandary. He knew this was an interlude that would end as soon as the contract with al Benqura was signed. Yet he found reasons to seek her out and spend time with her. He loved to hear her talk. She wasn't one to mince words, or be totally agreeable. He knew too many people who sought favor above friendship.

And while he tried to ignore the physical attraction, he couldn't do it. He longed to press her against him, kiss her, make love to her. Her skin was as soft as down. Her sparkling eyes held wit and humor and made him think of the blue of the Gulf on a sunny day. He wanted to thread his fingers through that silky blond hair and stroke it, feeling the softness, the warmth from Bethanne.

Comparing her to other women was unfair—to others. Unlike Marguerite, she was unpretentious and genuine. She did not show an innate desire to garner as much money as she could in a short time. He detected no subterfuge; had heard no hints about keeping the necklace she wore. He smiled slightly when he thought of her worry if it came undone. He would never expect her to repay the cost of the jewelry. When he'd asked his assistant to find something with blue stones, an array had been brought to the office. These sapphires had matched her eyes. He'd chosen it immediately.

How had he known they would match her eyes? He could not even remember what color Marguerite's eyes were. Glancing down, he studied his partner as they circled the room. She looked enchanted. And enchanting. Her gaze skimmed around the room, a slight smile showing her enjoyment. As if she could feel his attention, she looked up.

The blue startled him with its intensity. Her smile made him want to slip away from the crowd to a private place and kiss her again.

"Enjoying yourself?" he said, to hear her speak.

"Very much. This is even better than my senior prom, which was the last formal dance I attended, I think. Some of the gowns are spectacular. I'm trying to remember everything so I never forget."

"There will be others," he said, taking for granted the setting and the people—many of whom he'd known all his life. His polo team members had been friends for years.

"For you. Once you sign that contract, I'm heading back to Texas."

"Or you could stay a little longer," he suggested, wishing to find a way to keep her longer.

From the jump she gave, he'd surprised her with his suggestion.

"I may delay signing the papers until well after the deal is finalized," he said, half in jest. Far from being angry at Haile, he now thanked her for her defection. Otherwise he would not have known Bethanne. What a shame if he'd merely thanked her for delivering the jet and never seen her again.

"Now why would you do that?" she asked, leaning back a bit to smile up at him with a saucy grin.

It took all of Rashid's willpower to resist the temptation to kiss her right there on the ballroom floor. She was flirting with him. It had been years since someone had done that in fun. He knew she had no ulterior motives.

"Alexes might never fly again. Perhaps you could become my personal pilot." He hadn't thought about that before, but it would be a perfect solution. She'd remain in Quishari and he could see her whenever he wanted.

"My home is in Texas," she said slowly. "I don't speak the language here. I have family and friends in Galveston. I don't think it would work."

At least she sounded regretful.

"Think about it before deciding," he said.

"Would there be more dances like this?" she teased.

He laughed and spun her around. "Yes, as many as you wish to attend. I don't go often, except the ones with the polo team. But that could change. I receive dozens of invitations."

"I would imagine attending them all would prove tiring. And it would dim some of the splendor if you saw this kind of thing all the time. What makes it special is being rare."

"A wise woman."

The music ended. In a moment another song began. Rashid held her hand during the short break, rubbing his thumb lightly over the soft skin. The couple next to them smiled but said nothing, for which he was grateful. Even more grateful when the music began again and he could draw her back into his arms again. It had been a long time since he'd enjoyed spending time with anyone beyond his family.

The evening flew by. Bethanne focused on the offhand invitation to stay. She wasn't sure if he were serious or not. It was tempting. Maybe too much of a good thing. What would happen if she actually fell in love with the sheikh and he only wanted her as a pilot because Alexes was incapacitated? She gazed off, picturing him with other women—beautiful women with pots of money. He'd ask her to fly them to Cairo or even Rome on holiday. She'd be dutiful and resentful. She didn't want to fly him and some other woman anywhere. She wanted him for herself.

Startled at her thoughts, she glanced at him quickly, and found his gaze fixed on hers.

"If you are ready to leave, we can return to the villa," he said.

"I've had a lovely time, but it is getting late." Her heart pounded with the newly admitted discovery. She was in love with Rashid.

"Too late for a walk along the beach?"

To walk along the Persian Gulf in the moonlight—who could pass up such an opportunity?

"Never too late for that."

On the ride to the villa, he continued to hold her hand. Bethanne told herself it was merely a continuation of the evening. But she felt special. Would it ever be possible for a sheikh to fall for a woman from Texas? With no special attributes except the ability to fly planes? Undoubtedly when he chose a bride, he'd want a sophisticated woman who was as at home in the capital city as she would be anywhere in the world.

When they reached the villa, he helped her from the limo then bypassed the front door to head for the gardens. The pathways were discreetly lighted by soft lamps at foot level. Selective spotlights shone on a few of the topiary plants; the ambient glow felt magical. Fragrances blended delightfully with the salty tang of the sea. She heard the wavelets as they walked along.

"Should we change?" she asked, concerned for the lovely gown.

"More fun this way."

An unexpected side of Rashid. Every time she thought she had a grasp on his personality, he surprised her.

When they reached the beach, they sat on the chairs to take off their shoes. Rashid rolled his pant legs up and held out his hand for her when she rose. They ran to the water. Bethanne pulled her skirt to above her knees in an attempt to keep the beautiful silk from getting wet, holding it with one hand.

The water was warm. The moon was low on the horizon, painting a strip of white on the calm sea. Stars sprinkled the dark skies. In the distance a soft glow showed where the capital city lay. As if in one accord, they turned and began walking north.

"I can't believe you live in the city when you have this house," Bethanne said. "I'd walk along the beach every chance I got if I lived here."

"You seem to like simple pleasures," he said. Unlike other women he knew who loved new clothes, jewelry and being seen in all the right places.

"What's better? Maybe flying."

"Tell me why you like that so much."

"I'm not sure I can put it into words. There's a special feeling soaring high into the sky. The power of the plane at my command. The view of the earth, seeing the curvature, seeing the land as it is and not as man has rearranged it. I never tire of it."

"I see flying as an expedient way to get from one place to another in the shortest time."

"Then you need to fly in the cockpit more and give work a rest."

He laughed. "I would not be where I am today if I didn't pay attention to business."

"There's such a thing as balance."

"So you suggest I take more time off?"

"Take time to relax. Even in your time off you're busy. Do you ever just lie on the beach and listen to the waves?"

"No."

She danced in the water. "I do when I'm home. Galveston has some beautiful beaches and I like to just veg out and do nothing but stare at the water and let the rhythm of the surf relax me."

"Not often, I bet." She was too full of energy to be content to sit and do nothing for long.

"I guess not. That's why when I do, it's special."

He stopped and turned to face her. "You're special, Bethanne Sanders." He put his free hand around the back of her neck and drew her slowly closer, leaning over to kiss her.

The night was magical, the setting perfection, the woman with him fascinating and intriguing. The temporary nature gave an urgency to their time together. Too short to waste.

She kissed him back, slinging one arm around his neck, her other hand still holding her skirt.

For a long time Rashid forgot about responsibilities, about duties and about the pretense of their relationship. There was only Bethanne and the feel of her in his arms.

Both were breathing hard when he ended the kiss. They were alone on the beach, quite a distance from the villa. He was tempted to sweep her in his arms and find a secluded spot and make love all night long.

"We should return," he said. Duty over desire, hard to harness.

"Yes." She let go of his hand, gathered her skirt in both hands and began walking briskly back to the villa.

"Wait." He hurried to catch her. "Are you okay?" He tried to examine her expression in the faint light but she kept her head averted.

"I'm fine." She did not stop walking.

"Then the kiss upset you."

She stopped at that and turned to glare at him. "It did not upset me. What upsets me is that I don't know the rules of this game. We're pretending. But that kiss seemed real. You are solicitous in public playing the perfect gentleman who is showing someone around. It's all fake. Why the kisses?"

Rashid paused. "Because I can't resist," he answered, daring to reveal his feelings. It had been a long time since he'd let emotion make inroads. Would he regret the confession?

She blinked at that. "What?" It almost squeaked out.

"Why should that surprise you? I find you beautiful, fun, interesting, different. I want to be with you, touch you." He reached out his hand and trailed his fingertips down her bare arm, struck again by the warm softness of her skin. "I want to kiss you."

He could see her indecision. Finally she nodded once. "Okay, but unless we are really going somewhere with this relationship, no more than kisses."

Her words jerked him from the reverie he had of the two of them spending time together. He was not going anywhere with any relationship. He had tried love and failed. He had tried arranged marriage—and that didn't look like it was in the cards, either. Was it too much to ask just to enjoy being together for a while—as long as they both wanted?

"Then I'll just have to settle for kisses," he said, drawing her back into his embrace.

Bethanne awoke the next morning feeling grumpy and tired when Minnah entered with the usual breakfast fare. She refused to let her crankiness show and almost screamed with impatience while the maid fussed around before leaving. Bethanne had not had a good night's sleep and it was all Rashid's fault. She'd been a long time falling asleep thinking

of the kisses at the beach. And the words he had not spoken—
that their relationship had a future. That hurt the most.

She sipped her chocolate and wondered what she was doing.
Always one to face facts, she simply could not let herself imagine she was falling for the sheikh. She needed to visit the places
she wanted to, search for her father and remind herself constantly that Rashid's interests did not coincide with hers.

If she told herself a dozen times an hour, maybe she'd
listen. But her heart beat faster just thinking of Rashid and the
kisses they'd stolen in the night. His scent was permanently
affixed in her mind, his dark eyes so compelling when he
looked directly at her she could feel herself returning his
regard, wishing there were only the two of them. She had run
her hands through his hair, pulled him close and shown her
feelings while all he had wanted were a few kisses.

She frowned. Time to rise above the attraction that seemed
to grow by leaps and bounds and forget any flighty feelings
of love. She had her own quest that being here afforded. Today
she'd return to the square to see if the man her father had met
had returned. Yesterday the waiter who had spoken to her that
first day wasn't there. The one working had not understood
English. Maybe the other would be back today.

She'd focus on her search for her father and get over Rashid
before she saw him again!

Arriving at the square around ten, she went straight to the
sidewalk café, searching for the waiter she'd spoken with
before. Thankfully he was there. He came out of the interior
to greet her.

"I have a note for you," he said with great pride. With a
flourish, he withdrew it from his apron pocket and handed it
to her. "I knew you would return," he said.

"Thank you. I'll sit over here and have coffee, please." She
sat down at a side table and opened the folded paper.

"Hank was a friend of mine. A fellow American. I will stop by the café each day this week in hopes of seeing you." It was signed, Walt Hampstead.

Another American. That made it simple; at least she and he would speak the same language. She would have needed Teaz to translate if Hank's friend had been a native of Quishari.

"What time did the man come?" she asked the waiter when he delivered her coffee.

"Before lunch each day. He will be here soon." Setting the small cup and carafe on the table, he walked away.

Bethanne sipped the hot beverage while she waited until Walt showed up. She had a feeling things were speeding up and she needed to get any information she could before it was too late.

Sometime later a middle-aged man stopped at her table. She'd been writing a letter to a friend at home and looked up when he cast a shadow over the paper.

"Are you Hank's friend?" he asked. "No, that's not right. You're his daughter, Bethanne."

"Walt?" she asked, feeling emotion welling up inside her.

He nodded. Pulling out another chair, he sat down at the table. "He spoke of you often. I saw a picture once. You were younger. I'm Walt Hampstead. Pleased to finally meet you."

"You knew my father? He mentioned a professor at the university, but not by name. Is that you?"

He nodded. The waiter appeared and Walt gave an order for coffee.

"What happened to him? He's dead, isn't he?" Bethanne asked, hoping Walt would deny it all and tell her where Hank was.

But Walt nodded sadly. "I'm afraid so. I haven't heard from him in almost three years. He was a good friend. Not many Americans live in Alkaahdar. We'd meet and hash over how things were going at home. Expats sharing tales of home to fend off homesickness. And he'd tell me the amazing stories about his daughter."

"Have you lived here long?" Bethanne asked, trying to remember all she'd read and heard about his professor friend. She knew her father had liked the man, but always called him the prof.

"Yes, actually, longer than Hank. I teach English as a foreign language at one of the universities. I married a Quishari woman and we have made our home here."

"Tell me what you know about my father. It's been years since I've heard from him. Time just got away. I've been busy and I thought he was as well. But I can only find out the al Harum family thinks he stole a plane. He wouldn't have!"

The waiter returned with Walt's coffee. Once he'd left, Walt began to speak. "He told me two days before he left that he had a top-secret assignment, then laughed. Just like the movies, he said. I asked him what he was talking about, but he said he was sworn to secrecy, but maybe he'd give me some hints when he returned. He seemed in high spirits and I thought I'd hear from him soon after that. Only I never saw him again."

"I've heard he stole a plane and then vanished," Bethanne said, disheartened. This man had known and liked her father, but knew no more than she did on what had happened to him.

"There were stories going around. Then the head of Bashiri Oil died unexpectedly and the news was full of that and the stories of his twin sons. I never knew the official result of that secret mission," Walt said. He looked pensive for a moment. "Hank was a true friend. It was good to have someone from home to talk over things with. I miss him."

He sipped his coffee. "He flew the plane for the old sheikh, and often told me about where they went, what the different cities were like. Hank loved seeing the world and knew the job he had was great for that. He flew the sheikh to Europe, Egypt, even once to India. Most of the flights were around the Persian Gulf, though."

"Did the secret mission have something to do with the sheikh?"

"That I don't know. I could speculate it was because he worked almost exclusively for the man. But being a secret, I never heard any more. Your father did not steal a plane. He was too honorable for that."

Bethanne felt a wave of gratitude toward Walt for his comment. "I want to find out exactly what happened and let others know he wouldn't do such a thing." Especially let Rashid know. Every time he looked at her he had to remember his belief her father had caused the death of his. It was so unfair!

"Don't know how you'll find out. Do you speak the language?" he asked.

"No, except for pleased to meet you."

"This country is still very much a man's world. I bet they were surprised to discover you're a pilot," he said.

"At first. What happened to my dad's things?" she asked.

"I don't know. I went by his apartment once I realized he was probably dead. It had already been rented and the young woman who answered the door said it had been immaculately cleaned before she moved in. I guess the sheikh's people packed up. I don't know if they threw his things away or stored them."

"My mother tried to find out what happened to him—as his onetime wife. But no one told her anything. I guess if they had any of his things, they would have sent them to her." Bethanne gazed across the square, seeing the buildings her father would have seen every day. She missed him with a tangible pain.

"He spoke of you a lot. You were a bright spot in his life.

He talked about when you'd come to visit and what you two would see."

"We discussed it more than once. I longed to see Quishari, but not like this. It's a beautiful country and I've enjoyed everything I've seen. But I had hoped to see it with my dad."

Walt scribbled on a page of his notebook and tore it out. "Here's my phone number and address. Call me if you need anything. Or wish to visit. My wife would be delighted to meet you. She liked Hank, too. He came to dinner occasionally. Her English is not as fluent as it could be, so she enjoyed listening to our conversations and hearing English spoken by natives."

"Thank you." She took the paper and put it in her purse. "I don't know how you could contact me if you remember anything. I am staying at the sea villa of Sheikh Rashid al Harum. But I have no idea what the address is, or the phone number."

"Do you like him? Hank really respected his father."

"I do like him." Understatement, she thought. But she certainly didn't know this man well enough to even hint at more.

Walt rose. "I'll contact the sheikh if I think of anything else you might wish to know. Nice to have met Hank's daughter. He'd be proud of you. Do consider coming to meet my wife."

Bethanne rose as well and shook hands. "Thanks for coming each day until I was here."

Walt walked away, then stopped and turned. "I do have a photograph of him with me at home. Call me when you can come again and I'll bring it for you to see."

Bethanne nodded. Disappointment filled her and she smiled, blinking away tears. She had so hoped her father's friend would know more. What could a secret mission have been? One filled with danger that ended up costing him his life? How could the old sheikh have demanded that? Did Rashid know?

CHAPTER SIX

BETHANNE rode back to the villa wondering how she could find out more about that secret mission. The only one who had probably known was the old sheikh and he was dead. Would his wife have known anything? If she had, Bethanne would be the last person she'd tell.

Yet everyone seemed to think the plane was stolen. Even so, Hank would have had to file a flight plan. Someone must have known something more about the plane. But she wasn't sure if it were even possible to get a copy in Quishari, much less at this late date.

She could ask Rashid.

Mulling over the possibility of being rebuffed, she weighed it with the possibility of annoying Rashid. But she hadn't a clue where else to go.

When she reached the villa, Fatima was in the foyer, her suitcase beside her. Minnah was there as well and smiled when she saw Bethanne.

"Fatima leaves for the airport. She is returning home," the maid said in English.

Bethanne nodded. "Please tell her I'm sorry for the inconvenience of remaining here when she must have wished to return home immediately."

Minnah relayed the comment, then listened to a rapid burst of speech from Fatima.

"It is she who is grateful for you and whatever arrangement you made with the sheikh that she does not fear returning home. Her charge put her in a very awkward situation and if not for the compassion of the sheikh, she'd not wish to return home. She spoke with her family and there is no retribution awaiting."

"I should hope not," Bethanne said. "She couldn't help—" She paused. Hopefully Fatima had been circumspect in her complaints. Remembering the charade, she finished. "She couldn't help the situation. Tell her I wish her a pleasant journey home."

Once Fatima left, Bethanne went into the library again, wandering around, studying the various books on the shelves. She stopped at the desk and looked at the computer, considering. Turning it on, she sat down and began to search the Internet on any information she could get about Quishari and flight plans and Rashid's father.

Losing track of time, she was surprised when Minnah knocked on the opened door. "Miss, you haven't come for lunch. It is on the terrace. Are you not hungry?"

Bethanne nodded, reluctant to leave her search, but suddenly feeling ravenous.

She was glad she took the break a few moments later when Rashid arrived. She felt almost guilty using the computer to find out more about his father. If her need hadn't been so strong, she would not have done more than a cursory look to learn a bit more about him. Rashid loved his father and wanted to be like him.

She loved her father, and wanted to clear his name.

"Late lunch," Rashid said, drawing out a chair and sitting at the small table.

"I had coffee at a square in the old town midmorning, so wasn't ready to eat until now," she explained. "What are you doing here? Is the workday over?" She knew he devoted many hours to business; was something special going on to have him leave so early?

"I thought we could take the jet up again, fly over the wells to the south and see how things are going. Khalid said the well that was burning has been capped. I'd still like to see how much damage was done. There's an airport nearby and I'll have a car waiting so we can drive to the docks, and then go to the derricks themselves."

"I'm at your command," she said, taking another drink of the iced lemonade she enjoyed so much. This was unexpected, but she relished a chance to see more of what he dealt with daily. She was soaking up as much as she could about Rashid. Down the years, she'd have plenty of memories.

"No rush. Finish your lunch. Where in old town did you go?" he asked.

Bethanne looked at her salad, hoping hearing about her morning wouldn't make him angry. "I went for coffee at the square near where my dad lived. I met another American—a friend of Hank's," she said.

"Anyone I know?" he asked.

"A professor of English at the university. Walt Hampstead. He was pleased to see me. My dad had spoken of me to him. He said he's lived here for more than twenty years. Even married a local girl and they have two children."

Rashid appeared unconcerned by the revelation. "Did you visit the shops?"

"No, I enjoyed the architecture and got a feel for the place. The older section really draws me. I love it. If we are going soon, I'll run up and change."

When they reached the airport an hour later, Bethanne went to the air traffic control office to file a flight plan. The service was quick. As she was turning to leave, she asked if there were archived flight plans for the past five years. The clerk was instantly curious as to why she wanted to know. She shrugged it off as mere curiosity and left. The reports would be in Arabic undoubtedly. No help there—unless Walt could translate them for her.

Rashid had remained with the plane and she did her visual inspection before boarding. He was already in the cockpit and for a moment, the intensity of her wish that things had been different floored her. What would it have been like if she and he had met under different circumstances? If he did not think her father a thief and he was seriously interested in her? That they were going off for a day of fun, just the two of them.

She couldn't help her own excitement at seeing him. Try as she might, it was difficult to remember it was all a charade. Especially after his kisses.

Once soaring over the Persian Gulf, she leveled out the plane and watched the earth below. There were large container ships on the sea, white beaches lining the shore. As they approached the oil rigs several hundred yards offshore, she circled slowly. The fire was out. There was a huge oil tanker anchored on the seaward side of one of the high platforms.

"Taking in oil?" she asked, pointing to the ship.

"Yes. Then it goes to a refinery. That's one of our ships. Another branch of the company," Rashid said. "My uncle runs that. Set us down and we'll head out to the rigs."

They landed on the runway that ran beside the sea. After Bethanne taxied the plane to a sheltered area as directed, she shut down the engines. A dark car drove over and a man jumped out of the driver's side. In only moments they were driving toward the docks.

The launch that took them to the rigs was small and rode low on the water. Bethanne studied the huge platforms that rose on pilings from the sea floor. When they arrived, they had to climb a hundred steps to get to the main platform. The noise surprised her as machinery hummed and clanked as it pumped the crude from beneath the sea.

Khalid was there and strode over to greet them. His manner was reserved and more formal than Rashid's. A difference in the twins. Even though they looked alike, they didn't behave alike.

A moment later Rashid excused himself, saying he had to confer with Khalid on a private matter.

Bethanne walked away, toward the activity near the ship. There were lots of men working in a choreographed way that showed they all knew their respective jobs well.

After watching for a while, she saw a man walk over to say something to her.

"Sorry, I only speak English," she said.

"I speak it," he replied with a heavy accent. "You fly jet that landed at airport?"

"Yes," she replied.

"I used to work planes for the old sheikh." He shrugged. "After he die, I come to oil—" He gestured around them. "Sheikh Rashid don't travel like father did."

"The old sheikh traveled a lot?" she asked, suddenly wondering if this man had known her father.

"More than son." He looked at the activity, studying it a moment as if assessing the efficiency.

"Did you know Hank Pendarvis?" she asked.

He looked back at her and nodded.

"Someone asked me to look him up if I got to Quishari. I think maybe he died several years ago."

The man nodded. "Bad time. Caused old sheikh's death."

"What happened?"

"Flight in west, something special." He paused a moment as if searching for the English word. "Sandstorm crash plane. All die."

"I heard he stole the plane, took an illegal flight." Her heart pounded. This man said her father had crashed. She knew something kept him from contacting her. Still, maybe all hadn't died. Maybe it was even a different plane.

"No. Job for old sheikh."

Bethanne's interest became intense. "Did you tell anyone? Why does everyone believe he stole a plane?"

"Those need to know do."

"Where did he crash?"

"West."

"Who knows about this?"

He shrugged.

Either he knew no more or wasn't going to give her specifics.

"And he is buried out west, too?"

He shrugged. He peered at her closely, searching her face and eyes. "In a town called Quraim Wadi Samil."

Bethanne gave an involuntary start of surprise. "We were just there," she said.

The man shrugged. "Perhaps you go again."

"Why didn't you tell someone at the time? Sheikh al Harum believes he stole the plane."

"No, I tell the sheikh." He looked at where Rashid stood talking with the other men.

A helicopter approached, its blades whipping the air around the platform. It set down near the far edge.

Someone on the platform called the man and he waved. "I go." He loped across the platform and climbed aboard the helicopter with two other workers.

Bethanne stared at the helicopter until it was out of sight. It had not remained on the rig for more than a few minutes. Where was it taking the maintenance worker? She had to have answers. According to him, he had told Rashid.

That didn't make sense. If Rashid knew, why not tell her? He didn't pull punches accusing her father of being a thief, why not say if he were dead? If Rashid knew about the sandstorm and the plane crash, why not tell her?

"Makes you wonder, doesn't it?" a male voice asked to her right.

Turning, she saw Khalid had joined her, staring at the damaged oil rig.

"What?"

"Why men put themselves in danger just to pump oil from beneath the sea," he said.

"Was anyone injured in the fire?"

"One man was killed. Another burned."

"I'm sorry."

"As were we. Mohammad was a good man."

"You were burned once, yet you still fight the fires."

"I do not want fire to win. Why are you here?"

"Rashid brought me."

"I mean, why still in Quishari. You delivered the plane. You did not deliver Haile. Yet you stay."

"Ask your brother."

"I did. He said to stop rumors flying that would damage the negotiations with Benqura. I say forget it. Rashid has little to offer for you to stay—unless you hope to cash in somewhere down the line. A story for a tabloid? A bit of blackmail for your silence?"

She turned to him, affronted at his comment. "I have no intentions of blackmail or talking to a tabloid. Maybe I feel a bit responsible I didn't make sure Haile was on board when we took off. What's not to like about a few days in this lovely country? The villa is exquisite. The staff makes me welcomed. Your brother has shown me places I would not otherwise have seen. I would not repay such hospitality with anything you suggest. I stay because he asked me to." She wasn't going to dwell on the attraction she felt any time she was near Rashid. That was her secret alone.

Khalid studied her for a moment, his eyes assessing. "Maybe. But I don't buy it. Not from an American woman in this day. There has to be something for you in it."

"You're cynical. Maybe I'm enjoying a mini vacation."

"Yet you still fly."

She laughed. "That's for fun."

Rashid walked over. "Khalid." He acknowledged his brother. Rashid looked at Bethanne and then Khalid. "Problems?"

"Just questioning your guest as to why she's here. Watch your back, brother."

"I know what I'm doing," Rashid said with a steely note.

"Maybe it's time for me to leave," she said.

Rashid shook his head, his gaze still locked with his brother.

"No one helps out a stranger by pretending so much without something in return," Khalid warned.

Obviously Rashid had not shared all he knew about Bethanne to Khalid. She wanted to confront him about the information she'd learned from the older man. But not with Khalid standing there. How soon could she get back to Quraim Wadi Samil?

Rashid reached out to take her hand, pulling her closer to his side. "Give me an update on the estimated repair time, if you would. Then we'll be going." He was making a definite statement for his twin.

Khalid shrugged and began speaking in rapid Arabic. Bethanne could feel the tension from Rashid as his hand held hers. She let her mind wander since she couldn't understand a word. Why had Rashid asked her to stay—actually almost coerced her? The longer she knew him, the more attached she became. For a few moments, she'd let herself imagine he'd fall in love with her. He'd be as attracted to her as she was to him. Which could lead to happiness beyond belief.

But the reality was more like heartache the size of Texas. She wondered if she dare hint that her feelings were engaged. He'd given her no indication he wanted anything more than a buffer with the minister to buy him some time. And he had not told her the truth about her father.

Yet those kisses had been magical. Had he felt any of the pull she had? With all the women he could date with a snap of his fingers, the fact he spent so much time with her had to mean more than just subterfuge for the minister's sake. Or not. He was so focused on work.

"Is there anything else you wish to see?" Rashid asked her. Bethanne looked at him. Khalid was already some distance away, walking to a group of men near one of the large machines.

"A quick tour would be great. I'll probably never be on an oil rig again." Chafing with impatience to find out more about her father, she refrained from asking him while others could hear. And a quick tour might give her time to figure out how to formulate her question so he'd answer.

"I thought Hasid might have explained some things to you."

"Who?"

"The man you spoke with earlier."

"No." So much for waiting. "Rashid—he said my father's plane crashed near Quraim Wadi Samil. He said you knew."

Rashid stared at her, glancing briefly to the sky where the helicopter had flown. "I do not know what happened to your father. Why would he say that? He never told me. Why does he think that?"

She stared back. Had the other man lied? Why would he? Yet, she couldn't believe Rashid would lie about it. It didn't make sense.

"I'll speak to him. Maybe you misunderstood him. While he speaks some English, he is not fluent. He would have come forward when the plane was lost if he knew anything."

"He says he spoke to you."

"He did not."

She broke her gaze and looked across the water. What to believe? She wished she could return to Quraim Wadi Samil and search for the grave herself. What if he was there? Who could she trust? Who to believe?

The flight home was conducted in almost total silence. Bethanne was trying to figure out how to find out for sure if her father had crashed. Rashid seemed to have dismissed the other man's revelation without a care. Would he if it were true?

Or would he try to stop her if she suggested another visit to Quraim Wadi Samil?

After lunch at the villa, Rashid invited her to go swimming. Bethanne's first response was a yes! She'd love to spend more time with him. But the situation with her father loomed between them.

"I'd like that. I'd also like to learn more about my father."

"Very well. Today we swim. I'll have someone contact Hasid and ask for details. I think you misunderstood him. We have no knowledge of where your father is, or the plane. Do you think a plane crash could be hidden?"

Put that way, she doubted it possible. Still, she had understood what the man said. There was no denying he said he spoke to Rashid.

There was nothing more to be done today. If she didn't get a satisfactory answer from Rashid's questioning, she'd see if she could get back to the oil rig and speak with him again.

* * *

The small boat Rashid drove to was larger than a runabout yet easily handled by one. The marina not far from the villa, it didn't take long to be on their way.

Once out on the water, Bethanne seated in the seat next to his, he turned south. The homes along the shore were varied, from tall and austere, to low with lush gardens and fountains sparkling in the sunlight. Some were set back from the water, some bordered the beach. The farther south they went, the more space grew between homes. Finally he nodded to the thick foliage. "Can you see the villa?"

She caught a glimpse of the roof and a tiny corner of the veranda.

"That's where we eat," she said. It looked smaller from this vantage point. She sighed in pleasure. "It's as pretty from the water as the view is from balcony."

"My grandmother loved beautiful things. This is only one of her homes. They all had gardens that gave her such pleasure."

"My grandmother loves roses. She's a longtime member of the rose society in Galveston and wins prizes for her blossoms year after year."

"Yet another thing we have in common," Rashid said, cutting the engine and letting the boat drift. "Care to swim?"

"I'd love it." She quickly shed the cover-up and reached into the pocket for a band to hold her hair back. Tying it into a ponytail, she waited while Rashid went into the small cabin to change. "Ready when you are," she called.

Rashid stepped out a moment later, clad only in swim trunks. Bethanne almost caught her breath at the masculine beauty. His shoulders were broad; that she already knew. His chest was muscular and toned, not a spare ounce of flesh anywhere. His skin was bronzed by the sun. Masculine perfection. She could sit and stare at the man for hours.

She just hoped she didn't look liked a stunned star-struck groupie. Get your mind on swimming and nothing else, she admonished herself.

Rashid tossed two towels on one of the seats and brought a small ladder from one of the storage compartments. Hooking it to the side, he stood aside, gesturing with one hand.

"After you."

She took a breath, passed close enough to feel the radiant heat from his body, before taking a quick vault over the side. The water closed over her head a moment later, cooling her off in an instant. She felt the percussion of his hitting the water, then rose, blinking in the bright sunshine.

"It's heavenly," she said, turning to swim slowly parallel to the beach. She didn't want to get too far from the boat. The water felt like soft silk against her skin. Its temperature enough to cool, yet warm enough to caress. After a few minutes of swimming, Bethanne stopped and began to tread water. Rashid was right beside her.

"This is fabulous," she said, shaking water from her face, and spraying him with the water from her ponytail.

He laughed and splashed her. In only seconds a full-fledge water fight was under way. Finally Bethanne cried to stop. She was laughing so hard she was swallowing water.

She began to cough and Rashid was there in an instant, supporting her in the water, pounding on her back.

"I'm okay," she gasped a minute later. "I shouldn't be laughing when I'm being deluged by tidal waves."

"I haven't played like that in a long time," Rashid said as they began slowly swimming back toward the boat.

"You should. I think you work too hard."

"Ah, maybe it's the company I'm keeping. Makes it more fun."

She glowed with the compliment. From a rocky beginning, it looked as if things were changing.

"I could say the same. I've enjoyed being here."

"It won't be much longer."

She felt her heart drop. "How close are you to completing your deal?" she asked, almost fearing the answer.

"Close enough to expect to sign the papers this week."

Bethanne felt the disappointment like an anchor in her chest. She actually faltered a moment in swimming. What had she expected—that it would take years to sign the contracts?

"I hope you won't dash off the instant the ink hits the paper," Rashid said.

They reached the boat. He steadied the ladder while she climbed. Once she was on board, he swiftly followed.

"I need to return to Texas," she said slowly. She could stay a few days, maybe, yet to what end? She could go sightseeing on her own, but it wouldn't be the same as with Rashid. And he had to believe her father had taken the plane, no matter what the man on the platform had said. He'd mentioned it often enough. Had she misunderstood Hasid?

"I could stay for a little longer." Was that breathless voice hers? Those foolish dreams lingering?

"Because?" he pressed.

"Because I want to."

Rashid smiled in satisfaction, then pulled her gently into his arms to kiss her.

His warm body pressed against hers as the boat bobbed on the sea, his arms holding her so she didn't lose her balance. Her own arms soon went around his neck as she savored every inch of contact. She was in love with the most exciting man she'd ever known. And he hadn't a clue.

* * *

They dined together on the veranda. As twilight fell, Bethanne felt as if she couldn't hold so much happiness. The conversation was lively and fun. She wondered who else saw this side of the man.

"How come you aren't married?" she asked at one point, wondering why some smart woman hadn't latched on to him years ago.

The atmosphere changed in an instant. His demeanor hardened. "The woman I planned to marry ran off, remember?"

"Come on, you're too dynamic and sexy to not have your share of women interested. How did no one capture your fancy?"

He was silent for so long Bethanne wondered what she'd said to cause the change. Wasn't it all right to question his single state?

"I was engaged a long time ago," he said slowly.

Oh, oh, she hadn't seen that coming. "What happened?" No matter what, it couldn't have a happy ending. She was bubbling with so much happiness, she wanted him to share. Now her stupid comment had changed the evening. She wished she could recapture her words.

"She loved my money."

"Ouch."

"I should have seen it coming." He looked at her. "All her conversation centered on things and trips. I was the gold at the end of her rainbow."

"She might have loved you as well?" she offered.

He shook his head. "When my father bought her off, she left like a fire exploding at the rigs. I haven't heard from her since."

Bethanne didn't know what to say. Her heart hurt for the pain of betrayal he must have felt.

"How about you? You're not married," he said a moment later.

"I'm footloose and fancy free. I don't see settling down

when there is the entire world to see. Working with Starcraft, I get the chance to explore places I haven't been." Besides, I have never fallen in love before, she thought, watching him. And I don't expect to find another like you.

"You don't see yourself settling down, making a family?" he asked.

"If I meet the right guy, I guess I would," she said. "If he loved me in return." For too long she'd considered herself like her father—too interested in the wide world to settle for one spot. Now that she met Rashid, she sure didn't feel that way. She'd traveled to every continent on the globe. Made friends in various places. Yet nothing drew her like Rashid. Maybe that was the difference falling in love made.

Rashid nodded, wondering why he cared if she settled down or not. He was not interested in marriage. He'd agreed to the scheme with Haile as a business move. Her defection saved him. He would be grateful to her on two counts—keeping him single, and introducing Bethanne into his life.

She was different from women he knew. That was the novelty of being around her. Soon the novelty would fade and he'd move on. He didn't want to think like a cynic, but he had no expectations of falling in love. He wanted Bethanne, liked being with her. But surely there was more to love than that.

She was a refreshing break from the routine of his life. One he didn't want to end too soon. It didn't hurt that she was so pretty. He enjoyed watching her. Or taking her to events. She looked relaxed and pleased with life in the blue dress she wore. He would love to adorn her with jewels, but she'd carefully returned the sapphire necklace once they returned to the villa after the polo dinner. He'd offered for her to keep the necklace, but she'd refused.

He should have told Khalid that. Maybe knowing Bethanne better, he'd realize his assessment was off. She wanted nothing personal from this charade. She was almost too good to be true. But he'd seen no sign of avarice in her.

He stared out across the garden, wondering about Hasid's comments to her. The old man couldn't know more about Hank than he did. Hank had worked for his father. In the morning he'd have his assistant find out more about the wild story the man had told Bethanne.

"I need to fly to Morocco on Friday to sign the contract."

She sipped her coffee before nodding. "Then I'll ask for a few more days of vacation so I can stay a bit longer," she replied.

He was pleased she agreed to stay. Maybe he'd take time from work and spend it all with Bethanne before she left for good.

The thought of her departure weighed heavily. Yet he knew better than she that there was no long-term future for them together. His family would never accept the daughter of a thief—moreover the one whose actions contributed to his father's death. She didn't speak his language. He didn't want a wife. And he would not dishonor her by having an affair. Time together, memories made, then goodbye.

His gaze shifted to her as she sipped the hot tea. She loved flying. And he couldn't see asking her to stop. It was a novelty to have her fly his plane. Maybe he could hire her to fly for him—his private pilot. That way she'd always be around. And when he needed to travel, Bethanne would travel with him.

"After Morocco we could fly on to Paris, if you like," he said. He knew women around the world loved Paris.

"That would be nice."

"You don't sound as excited as I thought you'd be."

"I haven't seen Paris with you. That would make it special," she said slowly. "I enjoyed our excursion into the western part of your country. Maybe another trip there?"

"Quraim Wadi Samil? It's hardly a hot spot. Not a place we would have gone had Alexes not needed immediate medical attention."

She faced him. "It hardly matters where we go, if we're together, don't you think?"

He wanted her as he had wanted no other woman. Not even Marguerite. But caution held him back.

"It doesn't matter, as long as we're together," he said, already regretting the day they would say goodbye.

CHAPTER SEVEN

RASHID answered the phone the next morning when his assistant told him it was Khalid.

"So the deal is done. You've both signed?" his brother asked without amenities.

"I'm flying to Morocco on Friday to sign with Benqura. Then it is done. And a better deal than expected, thanks to his daughter's flight. He needs to save face and I've assured him I will handle things on this end."

"And how to explain to the minister that your special friend Bethanne left?"

"I don't have to explain anytime soon."

"Because?"

"I've asked her to stay. I may offer her a pilot's job. Alexes will not be able to fly again. Another stroke could happen at any time."

"There are other pilots who work for us."

"I choose who will fly my planes."

"Fly your planes and warm your bed."

"Hardly that. Bethanne and I are not involved to that extent," Rashid said coldly. Not for lack of desire on his part. Bethanne was special, and he would treat her so. For as long as it suited him. And her.

"She wants something. Mark my words."

"And what does it take to prove you wrong—her friendship and loyalty for fifty years?" He knew what Bethanne wanted. It was impossible to give it to her. Beyond that, she cared for nothing he had to offer.

"That's a start."

Rashid laughed. "Give it up, Khalid. She is not like the others."

A groan sounded. "You are too far gone. All women are alike."

"Cynic. Is that why you called—just to warn me again about her?"

"No, I'm going to open Grandmother's other house. I can't decide whether to live there or sell it. So I thought if I stayed there a few weeks, I'd know what I want to do. It's strange to go there without her."

"She wanted you to have it, Khalid. She loved that house because it was her father's that he gave to her when she married."

"My flat suits me. I'm not in it long enough to feel closed in."

"Give it a fair chance. You don't have to rush into selling."

When Rashid hung up, he thought about his brother. Life had treated them so differently. Both had the same advantages until the fire had destroyed part of his brother. It wasn't only the scar. There were wounds that went deeper. Were the al Harum men doomed to stay single? Not leave heirs on the earth?

How would he fare if he took that step? What if he considered marriage with someone like Bethanne? Their children would be beautiful. She'd be full of surprises for a long time. Would they agree on how to focus their lives, or always want something different?

Not liking the way his thoughts were going, he picked up a report and refused to think about her for the rest of the morning.

Easier said than done, he admitted a few moments later. He

didn't believe Khalid. His brother had not been around Bethanne long enough to know her. Yet that shadow of doubt wouldn't fade. Marguerite had seemed devoted, until offered a sum of money. Would Bethanne prove as shallow?

Restless, he checked his calendar. There was nothing pressing. Telling his assistant he was going to take the rest of the day off, he headed for the villa. He wanted to see her, spend time with her. Assuage the doubt and prove once and for all she was different.

Prove to Khalid that Bethanne was unique.

When Rashid reached the villa it was to find Bethanne had gone out.

"Where?" he asked the maid. Maybe he should have kept Fatima to watch her.

But Bethanne wasn't a prisoner. She was free to go where she wished.

"She received a note and then asked if Teaz could drive her to the city," Minnah said. "I don't know when she will return."

Rashid nodded and went into the study. Using his mobile phone, he called the driver.

"Where are you?" he asked when Teaz answered.

Hearing they were in old town, Rashid arranged for Teaz to stay there until he arrived. He'd enjoy showing Bethanne some of the history of the capital city. She'd enjoyed Quraim Wadi Samil; he was sure she'd enjoy the architecture of the Romula district.

When Rashid pulled in behind his limo, driving his own small sports car, Teaz climbed out and came to open his door.

"Where is she?"

"I stop here. She walks to the square," Teaz said.

"You're dismissed. I'll bring her back to the villa."

The chauffeur bowed and returned to the limo.

Rashid walked toward the square. It brought back memories. Hank Pendarvis had lived in this area of town. He remembered that. His father had thought so highly of him. His assistant had not yet contacted Hasid. What if there was some truth to the old man's story? Could Hank have crashed? It still did not explain why he stole the plane.

When Rashid reached the square he paused for a moment, searching. Her blond head was quickly found. She sat at a table with an older man. From the way they were talking, Rashid knew they weren't strangers. Who was he?

The spurt of jealousy that hit him surprised him. He didn't want to admit he had stronger feelings for her. But seeing her laugh at something her companion said jarred him. He wanted her laughter and her smiles. He wanted her.

Walking around the square, his gaze never left them. They were so caught up in their conversation, neither looked up until he stopped at the table.

Bethanne's eyes widened when she saw him. For a moment anger burned. He realized he was used to seeing a spurt of happiness when he came near. Now she looked startled—guilty? He kept his anger under control. The first rule—find out the facts before acting. Nothing so far condemned her.

"Hi, Rashid. I didn't expect to see you here," she said with a quick glance at her companion.

"Probably not." He looked at the other man.

"This is Walt Hampstead. He teaches English at the university," Bethanne said quickly. "Walt, this is my host, Sheikh Rashid al Harum."

Host? They were pretending more than that. To everyone.

The man rose and extended his hand. "Sheikh al Harum. It's a pleasure to meet you."

Rashid shook hands and then looked at Bethanne. "The man who knew your father?"

She nodded. "Do join us. We were talking about mutual friends." She gathered the photographs displayed in front of her and stacked them, handing them back to Walt. He put them in an envelope before Rashid could see them.

"I was showing her pictures of my family. It's good to talk to Hank's daughter. I don't see many Americans in Quishari, you know," he said easily, tapping the envelope against his leg.

"You have lived here long?" Rashid asked.

"Almost twenty years. Married a local girl. We have two children—teenagers now." He glanced at Bethanne. "I hope to see you again soon. Thanks for the update."

Bethanne smiled and nodded, her glance flicking to Rashid.

"I did not mean to run you off," he said.

"I need to be going. Classes soon." Walt nodded once and quickly walked across the square and down one of the side roads.

Rashid pulled out a chair and sat. The waiter hurried over and asked if he wanted anything.

"I'll have a coffee," he said, leaning back. His curiosity rose. "What was really going on?"

Bethanne looked at him, her eyes wide. "He knew my father. He doesn't believe my father stole a plane, either."

When his coffee was delivered, he took a sip of the hot beverage. Bethanne fidgeted with her own coffee cup, now nearly empty.

"What are you doing here?" she asked at last.

"I thought I'd take you up on your offer to take some time off. I expected to find you at the villa."

"I still want to see as much as Alkaahdar as I can. Wander around town. This is a nice café."

"We can wander around old town if you like. I sent Teaz away. I drove."

"Lovely. The architecture is similar to that in Quraim Wadi Samil, don't you think?"

"It's from the same age."

They finished their coffee and started out. The stalls selling food were crowded. The others had vendors calling out, enticing people with special sales. Bethanne smiled and walked at his side. When they reached a cross street, he waited to see what she'd do. She appeared to be studying the architecture as if she were genuinely interested. Rashid watched her. He was still bothered by the encounter with the other man. She was tenacious in searching for Hank. She was not one to give up quickly. He wondered how she'd found the man who had known Hank.

A woman came from an apartment building. Rashid stepped aside to allow her to pass on the narrow sidewalk. When she saw Rashid's gesture, she smiled as she walked past—stopping suddenly when she saw Bethanne.

"Were you coming to see me?" she said in Arabic.

"No. Should I be?" Rashid asked, wondering who she was.

"The woman was here in the street a few days ago searching for the man who had the flat before me. She was told I knew nothing about him. I thought maybe you were coming to seek more information. I have nothing else to add."

Bethanne watched, her eyes darting from Rashid to the woman back to him.

He looked at her.

"You were looking for more information about your father?" he asked in English.

Bethanne nodded. "I was hoping he'd left something behind that might tell me where he'd gone and why. She wasn't home last time I was here. But Walt said he came by when he hadn't seen my dad for a while and was told the apartment had been cleared before being rented again. The man on the oil rig told me he crashed. Walt said he spoke of a secret assignment, a special flight. There had to be more to it than he appropriated a plane and I want to know what. I want to know the truth. I want you to admit the truth."

He stared at her. "I would tell you if I knew more. Do you think I like knowing your father was a thief? Especially after years of service with my family? What else might he have stolen? What other harm might he have done?"

"None. He was not like that. He loved working here. We often spoke about his finding his ideal job. He planned to show me the country, introduce me to his friends. He went on some secret mission for your father. If you don't know what it is, come with me to find out what it was."

"Come with you where?"

"Quraim Wadi Samil. Isn't that where the answers lie?"

"There are no answers."

"Only questions? Like why people think he is a thief? I need to find out what happened to him."

"Everyone wants something—Khalid was right. I thought we had something developing between us. But you only see me as a way to prove the unprovable."

"We might have something growing between us. Just because the reasons I agreed to stay haven't changed doesn't mean my feelings aren't genuine or aren't involved. I...love you, Rashid."

"No!"

"If I do?"

"Impossible." He glared at her. "Please give me some credit. Women say words like that hoping to bend men to their will."

"We're talking two different things here, Rashid. First I want to prove to you my dad is not what you think. And second, why wouldn't I fall for someone like you? You're—"

"Enough! We have an agreement, nothing beyond the charade until the negotiations are complete and the contract signed. What do you hope…that I'll fall for you? Maybe see you as my wife? I would not dishonor my family by marrying a woman whose father was a thief. Who caused the death of my father."

Rashid resumed walking, at a quicker pace. He clamped down on his emotions. Khalid had been right; he should have sent her back the first day. How dare she say she loved him? He knew better—he was a means to an end. Find out about her father. Hadn't they tried that three years ago? The sooner he got her to the villa, the sooner he could be rid of her.

Except for the flight to Morocco, he thought. Should he consider using another pilot?

"Wait." She hurried to catch up. "Rashid, this doesn't change anything."

"It changes everything. Here's my car. Get in."

Ignoring his manners, he strode to the driver's side and got in just as she jumped in the passenger's side.

Starting the engine, he pulled away from the curb at a pace faster than safe. For a moment anger ruled. Then he deliberately slowed down. He would not take his anger out on others.

How dare she suggest she was in love with him? They had not known each other long enough for emotions to grow. It was a ploy, just as Khalid suggested. He was furious for letting his own emotions grow concerning her. He'd been so confident he could enjoy her company and then say farewell. She turned out to be like all others.

"What did Hampstead tell you?" he bit out.

"That the last time he saw Hank, my dad spoke about a secret mission. Walt thought he was pumped up about it, like a thriller or something. He wouldn't tell Walt any more than that. But Walt thought it more a lark than a dangerous mission. He was obviously wrong since it seems likely my dad ended up dead. The man at the derrick said Hank's buried in Quraim Wadi Samil. It would be worth checking out. Did you question him?"

"My assistant is handling that." And it sounded like Rashid needed to make sure it was done immediately. "The reason he was pumped up was probably considering stealing a multimillion-dollar jet plane."

Bethanne refused to respond.

Rashid stopped in front of the villa a short time later. She scurried out of the car before he could come around to her door. Running up the shallow steps, she turned and looked at him. "I shall leave the villa, of course. I understand you wouldn't want me here. I'll call a taxi to take me to a hotel."

"Stay here until we leave."

"We?" she asked.

"I still need to fly to Morocco tomorrow."

"And Quraim Wadi Samil?"

"Once we return, you'll have to find your own way there."

She glared at him. "Don't worry, I shall!" She turned to enter the villa.

Rashid stood standing beside his car. The door closed. She was gone.

For endless minutes he stood staring at the door, feeling numb. One moment she says she loves him. The next she's talking about leaving. The images of them together over the last few days danced in his mind. He could almost hear her laughter, see the sparkle in her eyes. For the first time since Marguerite he'd let himself consider— No, he was not going there.

He clenched a fist and hit the top of the car. He'd been thinking of ways to keep her in Quishari, and she'd been playing him. At least she had no idea he'd been halfway falling in love with her.

It was a small solace.

* * *

Bethanne reached her bedroom and shut the door. Sinking on her bed, she blinked her eyes. She would not cry. But the heartbreak she'd feared was closing in. Rashid had been so annoyed. Why? It wasn't as if he hadn't known from the beginning she was searching for her father. She should not have confessed her feelings. He hadn't wanted any emotional entanglements. He was probably laughing all the way back to the city about her claim. Her throat ached with keeping back the tears.

His reaction was unexpected. How could he feel so strongly about his own family and not recognize the same bond she had for hers?

She loved him. She hadn't meant to tell him, not without some indication he might be feeling something for her. But she had blurted it out. And he threw it back in her face. She did not want to go to Morocco or ever be around him again. How embarrassing that would be. Oh, if only she could go back in time a few hours and change everything.

She jumped up and began to pace the spacious area between her bed and the French doors. Rubbing her chest, she tried to erase the ache that was growing in her heart. She had warned herself repeatedly. But no matter—she'd fallen in love with a man who had never given any hint he returned her feelings. If he thought she was as dishonorable as he thought her father, he never would. Despite the kisses they'd shared.

Her father had been an honorable man. She resented the fact people thought he'd stolen a valuable plane and disappeared. She wanted the world to know the truth.

And she wanted Rashid to fall in love with her—daughter of a thief or not.

She might as well wish for the moon.

* * *

Minnah came into the room some time later with a message the sheikh had moved up the departure for Morocco to the next morning. They would depart at six.

Bethanne accepted her visit to Quishari was over. She'd fly the sheikh to sign his important contract, return to Quishari and be on the next commercial flight to the United States.

Packing, she took only those clothes she'd brought. She fingered the beautiful dresses that hung in the closet. She had felt like a princess wearing them. Who would wear them next? Would he donate to a charity or dump in the trash?

Taking advantage of her last afternoon, she went to the beach. Walking eased some of her distress. She was still trying to figure out a way to get to Quraim Wadi Samil when she looked up and saw Rashid.

Her traitorous heart gave a leap of happiness when she saw him, even though his face was grave. When would she get over this feeling of delight in his presence?

"Is something wrong?" she asked when he got closer.

"My mother is having a small dinner party tonight and insists we attend." The muscles in his cheeks clenched with anger.

Bethanne hadn't expected that. She searched his face for a clue he also wanted to attend. He glared at her. No hope there.

"Surely you can tell her about the charade. She wouldn't expect us to attend after finding out about that," she said.

"The minister and his wife will be there. The contracts are not yet signed. I will do nothing to jeopardize this deal. Not having come this far."

"Of course. The deal. No matter what."

"Nothing's changed. Except my perception of your cooperation. If you do anything tonight to enlighten anyone, you'll be sorry."

"Gee, what will you do? Send me back to the U.S.? Banish me from the country I'm leaving anyway?" An imp of mischief goaded her. She wanted him to want her. As she'd thought his kisses had indicated. So be it that he had not fallen in love with her as she had with him. She would not go off like some quiet, docile child. He was a wonderful man. Her love was not returned, but it didn't make it wrong, just sad that the one man she'd found she'd want to build a life with had no similar feelings for her.

"Don't push me, Bethanne."

"You have something I want. I have something you want. Let's make a deal."

"You have nothing I want."

"My silence. My continued acting like a love-struck woman clinging to your every word—especially if the minister is present."

He looked out to the sea.

"And in return, I want a plane ride to Quraim Wadi Samil. We swap."

He was silent for so long she knew he was going to refuse. She had no other leverage. She would have to find the grave herself—if in fact it was there.

"Deal."

His answer surprised her. Before he could change his mind, she held out her hand, but when he turned back, it was to grab her shoulders and draw her close enough to kiss. It wasn't a sweet kiss, but one full of anger. His mouth pressed hard against hers. His fingers gripped tightly. She scarcely caught a breath before he released her a second later. No matter, her heart pounded.

"Consider the deal sealed," he said and turned to head toward the villa.

"I'll pick you up at six-thirty," he called over his shoulder.

She brushed her fingertips across her lips. Tears filled her eyes. She wanted kisses, but not punishing ones. Could she ever forget the passionate ones they'd shared? She was afraid she never would. All men in the future would come short when compared with Sheikh Rashid al Harum.

"I hope your deal brings you joy. Nothing else seems to," she said to the empty beach.

Bethanne took extra care getting ready for her farewell performance, as she termed it. She had Minnah style her hair and selected the prettiest of the gowns hanging in the closet. It was a deep burgundy, long and sleek. Her makeup was donned for impact, making her eyes look larger and mysterious. She matched the gown color with lipstick and studied the dramatic effect in the mirror.

"Eat your heart out, Rashid," she whispered.

She went downstairs to await her escort. When he arrived, she met him at the door. "I'm ready," she said, walking past, head held high. She planned to deliver exactly what he wanted: a woman infatuated with him—when in public.

Teaz stood at the back door of the limo. Once she was seated, Rashid joined her on the bench seat. The ride was conducted in total silence.

Once at his mother's, Rashid morphed into a charming host. He greeted the other guests, introducing Bethanne to those she hadn't met before. She was gracious and friendly. She was never going to give him a single reason to think of her as less than professional in all her dealings. Her greeting to Madame al Harum was warm, as she felt suitable to a prospective mother-in-law. The older woman did not thaw at her overtures. Bethanne merely smiled. She would never please her. And tonight she had no reason to even pretend.

She greeted the minister again. Tonight she met his wife. The woman did not speak English, so Rashid translated. When they moved on, she breathed a sigh of relief. So far so good.

Conversation was a mixture of Arabic, French and English. She had a nice chat with a young diplomatic couple, on their way to a post in Egypt. The minister of finance was no more friendly than he'd been at the polo event. She wondered if he were perpetually grumpy. She wished Walt had been invited. It would have been nice to have one friendly face in the group.

Dinner was traditional Arabic fare—from an avocado appetizer to the delicious lamb to the sweets at the conclusion. Bethanne enjoyed every bite. She especially liked the sugared walnuts that Rashid insisted be brought for her enjoyment. She smiled her appreciation, wishing he'd meant the gesture for more than show to the people present. To the rest of them, she was sure they looked like a couple who enjoyed each other's company. Maybe were in love.

Only the two of them knew the lie behind the facade. It was bittersweet to have him so attentive, when she knew by the look in his eyes how false it was. She met him gaze for gaze, tilting her chin up to convey she had no qualms of standing up for herself. Or defending her stance. He'd asked her to stay to foil the attempts of the opposition to bring an end to negotiations. She'd done just that. He had not asked for more. It was her own foolish heart that betrayed her—not him.

The company moved to the salon and terrace after dinner. Soft music played in the background. The view from the terrace was beautiful; the entire city of Alkaahdar spread out before them, lighted in the darkness. In the distance, the Persian Gulf, where a lone ship gleamed with lights as it slid silently along on the horizon.

She would miss this place, she realized. In the short time she'd been here, she'd fallen in love with Quishari and one very special person. Her father had loved this country and she felt the same.

She realized she was alone on the terrace when Madame al Harum came to stand beside her.

"You are leaving," she said.

"Yes. We fly to Morocco tomorrow. When we return to Quishari, I will fly home."

"It is good."

"I'm sure you think so. What if Rashid loved me? Do you think a broken heart is good?" she asked.

"He would never be so foolish to marry someone so unsuitable. It's obvious you have fallen for him, but my son knows his duty. He will marry to suit his family. It is the duty of children to honor their parents."

"It is a bit old-fashioned," Bethanne said gently. "We honor our parents, but don't marry to please them."

"We are a traditional country. We have the modern conveniences necessary to enjoy life, but our values are time-honored. My son does not need you."

Bethanne nodded, the thought piercing. "You are right. I'm leaving and you will be happier for it, right?"

The older woman stared at her for a long time, then looked out toward the sea. "I will be content. It is what I want."

Bethanne longed to ask her if she missed her husband. Hadn't they been love? If not when first married, had love come? No matter what the custom, it had to be awkward to marry if not in love. Yet the union had produced two dynamic men. Had she longed for a daughter? For grandchildren?

Bethanne had once thought she'd never marry. She'd been fooling herself. If Rashid asked her, she'd say yes in a heartbeat. Her declarations of independence had been made before falling in love. The world changed when that happened.

Even if the ending wasn't happy.

"Mother, one of your guests is leaving," Rashid said from the doorway.

She turned and smiled politely at Bethanne. "If I do not see you again, have a pleasant flight home."

"Goodbye, Madame," Bethanne replied.

Rashid stepped onto the terrace. "Are you ready to leave?"

"Anytime. Your mother can't wait for me to be gone. I'm glad this pretense will end soon. I'm thinking it never should have begun."

But then she would not have spent but ten minutes with Rashid while he signed the papers for the new jet. She'd have missed these days which, despite the circumstances, would remain some of the happiest of her life.

"The past can never be changed," Rashid said.

The future could. But she refused to cling to false hope.

Bethanne arrived at the airport before the sheikh the next morning. She checked with the ground crew and had visually inspected the aircraft before he arrived. Her flight bag was already stowed. Teaz loaded a small suitcase for Rashid and then drove away. Rashid brought a briefcase and was soon seated on the sofa, papers already pulled out to review.

"The weather outlook is good the entire way," she said. "We'll have a refueling stop in Cairo."

He nodded and Bethanne went to the cockpit to begin her preflight checklist. They were soon airborne. She watched as the land moved beneath her. She was not familiar enough with it to recognize landmarks. Somewhere below them soon would be the oasis in the desert where her father lay. She was not going home without stopping there. Maybe she'd ask Khalid to find out from Hasid where exactly her father was buried. If he knew she were leaving, he might be amenable to helping her.

As the hours slipped by, the topography changed. The hills and valleys gave way to mountains. Crossing over a while later, the blue of the Mediterranean Sea could be seen in the distance.

It was late afternoon Morocco time when she approached the runway of Menara Airport, serving Marrakech.

It had been a long day. They'd refueled in Cairo where Bethanne had stretched her legs for a while. The flight had not brought the usual delight. She dwelled on the vanished hope the two of them might come to mean more to each other. It was also a bit lonely without someone to share the cockpit with. She would love to talk about the beauty of the earth below or the freedom flying usually gave her.

Rashid remained in the cabin. He'd declined to get off in Cairo. She had hoped for some kind of truce, but he obviously wasn't of the same mind.

She followed the directions from the tower and pulled the jet to a stop near a private hangar on the edge of the vast airport. Cutting the engines, she leaned back in her seat and closed her eyes for a moment. She was tired—not just from the long flight but from the emotional toll of the last two days.

Garnering what energy she could, she finished her checklist, signed it and left the clipboard on the copilot's seat. Going to the door, she opened it and stood aside, waiting for Rashid to leave.

He carried his briefcase and headed down the stairs, where there was already a chauffeured limousine for his use. She wondered how all the details of such precision were conveyed. She knew his staff was efficient, but this seemed almost miraculous.

When the uniformed chauffeur saw him into the back of the car, he came to the plane to retrieve the sheikh's suitcase. He nodded briefly to Bethanne, but didn't say a word. She stood back and watched as the limo pulled away.

If she had not told him about her feelings, or if he had believed her, she would be going with him, meeting the man whose daughter caused the charade. There was no need to keep up the pretense here where no one from his country could see. Once the contracts were signed, it would no longer matter.

She sighed and turned to check the cabin. It was as neat and tidy as if she'd flown it empty.

A maintenance worker came aboard, saying something in Arabic.

She replied in English. He shook his head, so she tried French. That he understood and explained he'd come to clean the interior. She told him to go ahead, but she'd wait until he was done. In fact, Bethanne wasn't sure what she would do. Stay with the plane was her inclination. She had no hotel reservations, hadn't a clue how to get a cab to this isolated area of the airport, didn't know how to find a place to stay since she couldn't speak the language. She could sleep on the sofa. Food and beverages stocked the refrigerator.

"And as the ranking crew member present on the plane, what I say goes," she murmured. When the maintenance worker left, she activated the door, retracting the steps and closing it. Cocooned in the aircraft, she hunted up a magazine and went to flop down on the sofa. In less than ten minutes she was asleep.

Rashid registered at the hotel, paid for a second room for Bethanne's use and sent the limo driver back to get her. It was petty to leave her like that, but he was still angry—more with himself than her. She had things to do when a plane landed, so the timing would probably be perfect.

He checked out his suite, found it satisfactory. Truth be told it could have been a hovel and he wouldn't have cared. Leaving it behind, he went to find a decent restaurant for an early dinner and to finalize his strategy for tomorrow's meeting.

When Rashid returned to the hotel, it was after ten. He'd had a leisurely meal, then gone to a small coffeehouse to work on the final details of the deal he and al Benqura would sign the next day. Walking back to the hotel, he enjoyed the atmosphere of Marrakech. He'd visited as a younger man on holiday one summer. The walk brought back memories.

He crossed the lobby heading for the elevators when the desk clerk called him.

"Yes?"

"Message for you, sir," he said.

Rashid went to the counter and took the folded paper. Scanning it as he started for the elevators, he stopped.

"When was this delivered?" he asked, turning back.

"A bit before six. It's written on the back."

He murmured an expletive. The note explained Bethanne had not been at the plane when the chauffeur arrived. The door was closed and no one had seen her since the arrival. Crossing to the house phone discreetly located in a quiet corner, Rashid dialed the number on the note. The car service was closed for the day. Crushing the paper in his hand, he went outside and asked the doorman to hail a cab.

CHAPTER EIGHT

WHERE could she have gone? She didn't know anyone in Marrakech. Not that he knew of. Of course she had a life apart from the few days she'd spent in Quishari. Maybe she had a host of friends here.

But she'd said nothing about that when they'd first discussed the flight.

The cabdriver was reluctant to go to the section of the airport Rashid directed. An extra handful of coins changed his mind. The hangar had a light on inside, scarcely enough illumination to see the door. The jet was parked nearby, where it had been that afternoon. It was dark inside. The door was closed. How had she managed that from the ground?

A lone guard came out of a small office, alert with hand poised on a gun worn at his side.

"Sir? This is private property," he said when Rashid got out of the cab.

"This is my jet. I am Sheikh Rashid al Harum. I arrived this afternoon."

"What are you doing here now, sir?" the man asked, still suspicious.

"I'm looking for my pilot."

The man looked surprised. He glanced around. "There's no

one here but me. The maintenance workers come back in the morning. I haven't seen a pilot."

"I need to know where she went," Rashid said.

"She? The pilot is a woman?" the man exclaimed in surprise.

"Yes. Who do you call if there is a problem?"

"What problem?"

"Like a missing pilot," Rashid said, leaning closer. The guard took a step back.

"I will call."

Rashid followed him to the small office. In a few moments he was talking to one of the men who worked the special planes. He had not serviced the private jet but knew who had. He'd call him to find out if he knew where the pilot was.

Rashid had his answer in less than five minutes.

"Open the door," he instructed the guard, walking back to the jet.

"I do not know how," he said, following along.

Rashid cupped his hands and yelled for Bethanne. He heard only the background noise from the busy part of the airport. This was futile. The jet was insulated; she couldn't hear a call.

"Bring a ramp."

"A ramp?"

Rashid was getting frustrated with the echoing by the guard.

"Yes, I want to open that door from the outside. I'm not tall enough standing on the tarmac." He was losing his patience trying to determine if Bethanne was indeed on board the jet.

Beckoning the cabdriver, the three men pushed a ramp in place, ramming it into the side of the jet as they tried to line it up next to the door, so as not to interfere with the steps coming down if he was successful in opening it.

He started up the steps but before he reached the top platform, the door to the jet opened, the stairs slowly unfolding. Bethanne stood in the opening.

"Rashid, what in the world are you doing?"

"Trying to find you. I sent the limo back for you but the fool driver didn't see you so left. What are you doing here?"

"I was asleep." She frowned as she looked at the ramp and the two men at the foot of it. "Your crashing into the side of the plane woke me. I hope you haven't scratched or dented it."

"Doesn't matter. It's my plane. Come on. The taxi is waiting."

"Come on where?" she asked warily.

"I booked you a room at the hotel I'm using."

He walked back down the ramp and thanked the two men who had helped him, giving each of them a folded bill. From the look of surprise on one and gratification on the other, he was satisfied they'd been amply rewarded for their help.

Bethanne still stood in the doorway, indecision evident in her expression.

Rashid hoped he wouldn't have to use stronger measures to get her to the cab. But he was not leaving her to spend the night in the jet. Unless he stayed with her.

She ducked back inside and a moment later tossed her bag over the railing of the movable ramp. Stepping over herself, she reached back and initiated the mechanism that closed the jet's door. When the plane was secure, she picked up her bag and walked slowly down the stairs.

"I'm guarding the plane," the guard said when she reached the tarmac. "No one will get on it tonight."

She looked at Rashid with a question in her eyes.

He translated for her and she smiled at the guard, saying in her newly learned Arabic, "Thank you."

Rashid took her bag and handed it to the cabdriver. Taking her hand, he helped her into the back of the cab and climbed in next to her.

"You can't have thought I would leave you to fend for yourself in a country where you don't speak the language," he said gruffly as the driver started the engine and they pulled away from the maintenance hangar.

"You're angry at me. Why not?"

He looked at her. "Bethanne, anger or not, I wouldn't do such a thing."

She nodded. He was not reassured.

"It is quite a few hours after you left," she said.

"I went to dinner. When I returned to the hotel, I learned you had not checked in. It's taken me all this time to find you."

"I appreciate it, but I was fine in the jet. It has all the conveniences of home."

When they arrived at the hotel, Rashid accompanied her to her room. Once he'd checked it out, he went to the door. "I'm in suite 1735. Call me if you need anything."

"Thank you for the room. What time do we leave tomorrow?"

"My meeting with al Benqura is at ten. I expect to be finished before noon. Perhaps you'd care to explore Marrakech before we leave."

"I'll do that in the morning, and be at the plane by noon," she said, standing near the window.

As if putting as much distance between them, he thought. "I meant, explore together. I was here about twelve years ago. I wouldn't mind seeing some of the souks and the Medina again."

"With me?" Her surprise was exaggerated.

He debated arguing with her, but decided against it.

"I'll meet you here at the hotel at noon." He left before she could protest.

Bethanne watched the door shut behind Rashid. She didn't know what to make of his coming to find her. She would have been okay all night on the jet. She'd slept in worse places. And she did not want to feel special because of the determination he'd displayed in locating her. But it touched her heart. She blinked back tears. She'd so love to have him always look after her. To know she was special to him in a unique way.

Taking a quick shower, she went to bed. It was more comfortable than the sofa for a night's sleep, she thought as she drifted off.

The next morning she ordered room service. She sat at the table next to the window, wishing she had a balcony and a sea breeze. Which would be hard to do in Marrakech, which was located far from the sea. She gazed out her window at the newer buildings, anticipating the afternoon tour of the old section, the Medina.

Bethanne went down to the lobby shortly before noon. She sat on one of the plush sofas and people-watched. It was a favorite activity. She wished she spoke the languages she heard. There were a variety, from Arabic to French to German and Spanish.

She saw Rashid the instant he entered through the revolving doors. He strode directly toward the elevators and she wondered if she should call him or let him deposit the briefcase and then let him know she was here. As if she had spoken, however, he looked directly at her. He walked over.

"So did you get it signed?" she asked as she stood.

"I did." The quiet satisfaction showed her more than anything that he was pleased with the deal.

"Good."

His eyes stared into hers. For a second, Bethanne felt the surroundings fade. There was only Rashid in her sight. Then sanity returned and she blinked, looking away.

"I know you want to ditch the briefcase. I'll wait here."

"I can send it up to the room," he said. "Ready to go?"

"Yes."

He gave the briefcase to the bell captain with instructions to deliver to his suite. Then he offered his arm to Bethanne.

The gesture surprised her. It was almost as if he were continuing their pretense.

She glanced down at the uniform she wore and slowly shook her head.

He reached for her hand and drew it through the crook of her arm.

"I'm hardly dressed like a woman going out with someone," she said.

"You look fine. Al Benqura has invited us to dine with him tonight. I said I had to make sure you wanted to do so."

"Do you want to?" she asked, surprised by the invitation.

"It would be a nice gesture to wind up the negotiations and the signed deal. But if you say no, I'll decline."

"I have nothing to wear."

He laughed sardonically. "Classic woman's response."

Bethanne looked at him. "Am I missing something? You were so angry the other day I thought you'd have a fit. Now you're like Mr. Nice Guy. What's going on?"

He didn't reply until they were in the back of the limousine she'd seen yesterday.

"I'm afraid I let the pretense go further than it should," he said cryptically. "You did your part. There was never anything more I could have expected. So today is about exploring Marrakech and seeing the sights. Tomorrow we'll return to Quishari and you'll be free to return home."

"So today we celebrate success," she said, disappointed at his explanation. She wanted more. She wanted him to say he couldn't let her go. That he'd fallen in love with her as she had with him. That he believed in her no matter what.

Only, today was merely a reward for a pretense well done. Some of the sparkle and anticipation dimmed.

Still—if today was all she had, she'd take it. Make more memories to treasure down through the years. Maybe she could pretend for just a few hours that they still enjoyed the camaraderie they had before. They were both away from home, no one to see or hear. She would be herself and hope he'd at least come to realize she had not lied or been dishonorable in any way. She wanted him to remember her well even if he couldn't love her.

First Rashid had the driver crisscross through town, pointing out places of interest, telling her a little about when he'd visited before.

They stopped at a hotel with a renowned restaurant on top where they had lunch. Then it was to the old fortified section of town, the Medina. Because of the crowd, Rashid took her hand firmly in his as they walked along the narrow streets. The souk was also crowded with vendors and tourists and shoppers. The wares were far more varied than the ones at the square in Rumola near where her father had lived. Bethanne stopped to look at brass and some of the beautiful rugs. She ran her hands over the bolts of silks and linens for sale. Whenever Rashid suggested she buy something, she merely smiled and shook her head.

Late in the afternoon they ended up in the large square of Djemaa el Fna.

"This is said to be the largest open-air market in north Africa," Rashid said.

There were stalls selling orange juice and water. Food and flowers. Acrobats performed on colorful mats. A snake charmer caught her eye and she watched for several moments as he mesmerized crowds with his ability. The atmosphere was festive.

"Is it a holiday or something?" she asked.

"No, it's always like this. It was when I was here last."

They walked around, ending up in a sidewalk café on a side street that was just a bit less noisy and hectic. Ordering cold drinks, they sat in companionable silence for several moments.

"Thank you," she said.

"For?"

"For today."

For a moment she feared she'd shattered the mood, but he quickly looked away and she wasn't sure she'd seen a flash of anger in his eyes.

"Today has been enjoyable. Tonight we dine with al Benqura."

"I still don't have a dress," she said, sipping her iced drink.

"One will be at the hotel when we return."

She gazed across the amazing square. "It must be nice."

"What?"

"To wave your hand and have things taken care of. You live a charmed life, Rashid."

He stared at her for a long moment. "No, Bethanne. You see only the surface. I live a life like others, maybe not the majority of the world, but others of my station. We have heart-aches and disappointments like any other men."

"Like what?"

He hesitated, took a sip of his own drink and then put the glass down.

"I thought I was in love when I was in my early twenties. Marguerite was beautiful, sophisticated and fun to be with. We shared so much—or so I thought. I told you before that my father bought her off. That taught me forever that love is an illusion. I cannot depend on it."

"Wrong. You may have loved her. She didn't love you. But that doesn't negate love. You are the better person for having loved her. I know it must have hurt when she left. But would you trade those feelings for money? Would you pretend to care for someone and be only out for money?"

"People can pretend and be out for other things."

She nodded. "Or maybe they don't pretend. Maybe things

become real. Love is not rationed. It is available for all. And I don't believe there is only one love in all the world for each of us. I think we have the possibility of falling in love with the wrong person as well as the right person."

"So how does one know who is the right person?"

She shrugged. "I can't say. It's just there." She knew Rashid was her right person. She wished she was his.

"Never in love?" he asked.

"Only once. For me it was the right person," she replied slowly.

"What happened?"

"He doesn't love me back," she said, her gaze on her glass. "But I wouldn't trade a moment of being together. I can't make someone love me. I will always have memories of happy hours spent together. And just maybe, because I loved once, I will love again and be happy."

After a long silent moment, he said slowly, "I wish that for you."

She nodded, blinking lest the tears that threatened spilled over. She'd told the truth. She loved him and would have happily spent the rest of her life with Rashid. But if that was not meant to be, she hoped some day in the future she'd find another man to love.

Though she wondered if it would ever be the same.

True to his word, a lovely dress awaited her when they returned to the hotel. It was white, shot through with gold. A golden necklace and golden slippers were part of the package. She felt like a princess in the lovely clothes. No matter what, she'd go with her head held high. She really wanted to meet the father of the woman Rashid might have married. Would there be any mention of that tonight?

The dinner surprised her. She expected only another couple

or two, but there were thirty couples. The dinner was a lavish affair with servants scurrying to carry in the dishes, remove dirty plates and make sure everything went smoothly.

Because she could not speak Arabic, Bethanne sat next to Rashid. But she noticed other couples were separated to mingle with the other guests.

"I'm content to eat and watch. You don't have to translate everything for me," she said softly after about ten minutes of his commenting on what others said.

"You'll be left out."

She looked at him in exasperation. "Rashid, I would never fit in here. I'm delighted to taste some more dishes and watch the other women in their finery. But I don't expect to become friends with anyone. Enjoy yourself. Truly, I'm happy enough."

Sheikh al Benqura was not like Bethanne's image. To her he looked like a father who had been disappointed in his only child. His gray hair was worn a bit long. His wife looked sad—especially every time her gaze landed on Rashid. Bethanne knew they had both wanted the marriage. Still, they were doing their best now to smooth things over. Rashid had told them he and Bethanne had a special friendship. It was true to a certain degree, but not to the level they suspected. Clever use of words, she thought.

After dinner, they stayed for only a short time, claiming an early departure time in the morning as a reason to be the first to leave.

"That went better than I expected," Rashid said as they settled in the limo for the ride back to the hotel.

"Did it?"

"Yes. You played the part perfectly. Madame al Benqura wished me happiness in our marriage."

"Which you denied."

"Of course, but in such a way she didn't believe me. I wonder why."

"Because she's also embarrassed by her daughter's running off. And I think she believed your heart might be involved. So she would be relieved if you were involved with someone else. No matter how unsuitable."

"You are not unsuitable," he replied.

Bethanne didn't respond. He still thought her the daughter of a thief. She was tired and wanted to go to bed. Tomorrow they'd return to Quishari and the goodbyes that waited.

"You are a kind man, Rashid. It was good of you to save face for them. It will make the working relations run more smoothly in the future."

The next morning they took off early, leaving Marrakech just awakening in the dawn. Once again the plane was refueled in Cairo. Then began the final leg of the trip. It was growing dark as they flew over the Quishari western border. Before long scattered lights speckled the landscape below them. The skies were full of stars, so much clearer at this elevation. Bethanne loved flying at night. There was something special about rocketing through the darkness with only the stars as a guide.

She checked her coordinates and contemplated her next move. If Rashid wasn't going to help, she'd have to do it herself.

Rashid rested his head on the sofa cushions. He was tired. The dealing with his new associate had been long and more difficult because of Haile's actions. To pretend things were fine when they weren't went against his grain. He was all for openness and honesty—where it didn't hurt anyone. Having Bethanne along, pretending he was involved with her, had given his host a way to save face. The deal was too important to end up contentious because of a willful woman's actions. But the strain of being with her and yet not wore on him.

The airplane shifted slightly. Rashid opened his eyes. Glancing at his watch, he saw it was too early to be landing in Alkaahdar. Yet it definitely felt as if the plane was descending. Was there a problem?

He rose and walked to the cockpit just as Bethanne spoke into the microphone, "Fasten up."

"Is there a problem?" he asked.

She shook her head, concentrating on the task at hand. "You need to sit down and fasten your seat belt," she said.

"Why are we descending?"

"We're landing."

He slipped into the copilot's seat and looked out. The blackness below went on for miles, with only a speck of light here and there and a small glow in front of them. Ahead was an array of lights—a runway.

"Where are we?"

"Buckle up, Rashid. We're going to land in about five minutes and if it's bumpy, you don't want to be tossed around."

He snapped on the belt and reached out to take her arm.

"Where are we?"

"Airborne over Quishari, soon landing in Quraim Wadi Samil."

"No."

"Oh, yes," she said softly.

He heard the determination in her tone. Unless he knew how to take control of the plane, there was nothing he could do.

"I'll call your office and have you fired."

"Go for it." She flicked him a glance. "I came to Quishari with two purposes. To deliver the plane and to find my father. I'm not going home when I'm so close. Now, I would like to concentrate on the landing, so kindly keep quiet."

Rashid was struck by the novelty of having someone telling him to shut up. Did she know who he was?

Of course she did, and was not a bit intimidated by the fact. She claimed to love him. Yet she had not repeated that statement once he'd shown her he couldn't be persuaded. Had it been a gambit?

With a resignation that the truth was probably she had tried that to get his cooperation, he settled back and watched her bring the jet in with a perfect landing.

It was not so late the airport wasn't still functioning. But late enough they were probably the last plane to land this evening. Quraim Wadi Samil didn't qualify as a hot spot in the world of travel.

She taxied where directed and shut down the engines.

"We're here," she said.

"Do you plan to go to the cemetery in the dark?"

She shook her head. "I plan to find a room somewhere, sleep until morning and then go. After you get the location from your assistant. If you want me to, I'll take you to Alkaahdar before leaving for Texas."

"And if I call your home office to have you dismissed?"

"As I said, go for it. I may never get this chance again. I need to know for absolute certain." She rose and went to get her small suitcase and open the door. Walking down the steps, she turned toward the terminal.

Rashid was tempted to call her bluff. She had openly defied him. He sat down in the seat and considered his options.

He knew why she had landed here. If it had been his father, wouldn't he do all he could to find out the truth? To learn what happened?

He reached in his pocket for the cell phone and called his assistant at home. It was late, but he needed answers now.

Rashid checked into the hotel they'd used when last in

Quraim Wadi Samil. He verified Bethanne was already there before heading up to his room. He had a lot of thinking to do.

The next morning, he waited in the lobby until she came down. Crossing to her, he took her arm and pulled her aside.

"I've ordered a car to take us to the cemetery near the older part of town. I know where your father is buried."

She looked at him in astonishment. "You're kidding. Have you always known?"

"I learned of it last night. Come, we have time before the car comes to have breakfast. Have you eaten?"

She shook her head.

They sat in the sunshine in the small courtyard off the main restaurant adjacent to the hotel. Once their orders had been given and the waiter left, Rashid began.

"I called my assistant last night. He had talked with Hasid. Then I called Khalid."

"Khalid?" Bethanne said, puzzled.

"He is the sheikh Hasid spoke with, not me."

Of course, both the twins were sheikhs. Hasid had nodded toward where Rashid and Khalid had been speaking. In his mind he probably thought she knew who he meant.

"And?"

Rashid looked around, as if assuring himself they would not be overheard.

"I owe you an apology, Bethanne. Your father's friend was correct. Hank was doing a special favor for my father—a secret assignment, as said. He came here to Quraim Wadi Samil to pick up someone special. The flight was cut short with a freak sandstorm shortly after they departed the airport. They were blown off course, or flew wide trying to avoid the sand. But the plane crashed. Everyone on board died."

Bethanne stared at him. Rashid tried to gauge her feelings, but her expression was wooden. "What was the secret?"

He didn't want to tell her. He didn't want to believe it, but his brother had made it clear it was the truth. After accusing her father—he owed her the truth.

"A daughter my father had with a woman not his wife. He wanted to see her before sending her to finishing school in Switzerland. Hearing of her death triggered his heart attack and he died. Khalid has known, and chose not to reveal it to anyone. Until I forced it out of him last night."

She still didn't say anything.

"My apologies for accusing your father. Had I known the truth from the beginning, I would never have said such a thing."

"So you know where he's buried?" she asked.

"I have directions."

She nodded and then stared around the courtyard as if she didn't know where she was.

"I'm sorry, Bethanne."

She nodded again. "Does your mother know?" she asked.

"No. Khalid's rationale was no one needed to know. He never expected Hank's daughter to show up. When I told him who you were, he finally agreed to tell me everything. He was protecting my mother."

"And you," she said slowly.

He nodded. "It's hard to discover the honorable man I revered my entire life had cheated on his wife and had another child. One, moreover, he spent a great deal of time with. I thought his reasons for keeping the oil fields operational and under such close observation was he wanted the best for the people of Quraim Wadi Samil. Turns out it was a cover for visiting his mistress and child."

"Now I'm the one who's sorry. That has to be hard to learn at this late date."

"I can deal with it. It's my mother who continues to need protecting. Fortunately he was circumspect and few people knew of the situation. Now that the daughter is dead, and my father, the story is unlikely to come out."

The waiter reappeared with their breakfast. Conversation ended while they ate. Rashid wished Bethanne would say something. But he couldn't have said what. She had a lot to forgive with his family. If he'd told Khalid sooner, would he have told Bethanne the truth immediately? Before he had a chance to know her, to grow to care for her?

After they finished eating, they summoned a hired car. Rashid gave directions to the cemetery and when they reached it instructed the driver to wait. The graveyard was dusty and brown. Few scraggly plants grew, no grass. The tombstones were lined up in rows. The main path cut the grounds in half.

Bethanne looked at the tombstones as they walked through one section. Her heart was heavy. Tears threatened. She had known for a long time her dad was dead. He would not have ignored her this long had he not been. But she had clung to hope as long as she didn't know for sure. Now that hope was gone.

As if he knew exactly where he was going, Rashid led her across a series of sections and stopped in front of a newer stone. Hank's name was in English. Other words were carved in Arabic. She hadn't a clue what they said.

"What does the inscription say?" she asked, staring at the foreign script.

"It says, 'Here rests a true friend, loyal to the end.'"

"Probably not the words that would be used if he were a thief," she murmured. She wished the words had been in English.

"Hi, Dad. I found you," she said softly. She knelt on the ground, reached out and touched the stone. It was already warm from the sun. Memories flashed through her mind. She loved her father. Felt curiously happy to find him, even though he had died three years ago. She had known it all along, just denied it. He would not have ignored her for so long had he been on earth. The cards and letters had came sporadically, but the phone calls had been as regular as the sunrise.

She wouldn't have been a pilot if he hadn't fostered the love of flying in her. She wouldn't have seen as much of the world as she had. And he wouldn't be lying here now at age fifty-two if he hadn't been who he was. Wild and free, only touching down when he had to. Otherwise the skies were his home.

Would she end up like he had? Alone, far from her native land? Having lived life the way she wanted?

She glanced at Rashid. One thing she wanted she wasn't going to get.

"How did you know right where he was buried?" she asked.

Rashid was silent for a moment, staring at the headstone. "Khalid told me. And where our half sister lies. I want to see that stone as well. I didn't know I had a sister until last night."

"The mechanics at the airport said Hank stole the plane and vanished. That the sheikh's son didn't know anything. Hasid said he'd told you."

"No. I didn't know. But Khalid did. He was the one who discovered what happened when they didn't arrive as planned. She was to go to college in Europe and my father wanted to see her before she left."

"How was he planning to do that without your mother's knowledge?"

"I have no idea. But she doesn't know. She would be so hurt. She herself always wanted a daughter."

Bethanne looked at the graves marching away from her father. "And where is her place?"

"Come, Khalid told me. It was he who arranged the stones.

He who took care of everything, careful to keep our father's name out of it."

Bethanne rose and touched the stone again. She would in all likelihood never be here again. She'd found her father, only to have to say softly, "Goodbye, Dad."

Rashid led the way down several rows. Soon they stood before a stone engraved completely in Arabic.

"The place next to it is saved for her mother. She loved my father and he loved her. When they met—when he came to start the oil fields—he was already married with two sons. According to Khalid, the arranged marriage with my mother was important in a business sense. Yet he wanted to end it. My mother would not without causing a scandal and pulling out the money that would have sunk the business back then. In the end he stayed married to her. He told Khalid this as he was dying. He visited Quraim Wadi Samil as often as he could, enjoying his daughter and spending time with the woman he loved. He swore to Khalid our mother never knew.

"The plane crash and his daughter's death caused his own heart attack and death. Khalid never made the facts known. It would do nothing for those who died. He said he'd rather have the living content with life as they knew it. What point to shatter that?"

"I'm so sorry, Rashid," she said simply. She had no idea of the circumstances. Yet she was glad he had not known and not told her. She was glad her father had been helping someone when he died. It sounded more like him than being a thief.

"You once said truth always comes out. This is one I hope doesn't," he said.

"I understand. Thank you for telling me. And restoring my faith in my father. I never believed what you thought."

"Ironic, isn't it?" he said.

"What?"

"Hank was a loyal employee of our company and a loyal friend to my father. A man trusted to carry his most precious daughter. A man of integrity. It was a tragedy to end as it did."

She looked around the cemetery, imprinting it on her mind. She'd remember the words on the stone. Remember he'd died trying to help a friend.

"Instead, it was my father who was less than honorable. I'm sorry, Bethanne, for doubting your father."

"I'm ready to leave now," she said, turning away lest he see the tears in her eyes. She'd never hug her robust father again. Never get a card or letter. Never be able to tell him how much he'd meant to her—even though they rarely saw each other. She knew he'd known, but the plans they'd made—for some-day—would be carried out solo now. She had his memory and his love of flying. It would have to be enough.

"Thank you for bringing me. I will honor the secret. I would do nothing to hurt your mother," she said as they walked slowly back through the cemetery.

"Her behavior could be better toward you."

"She doesn't like me. That's okay. She doesn't need to." Bethanne stopped at the gate, the hired car only a few yards away. "Truth always comes out. I'm glad you found out before I left. And told me. If I hadn't been able to wrangle the flight to deliver the plane, I would never have gotten to know you, and that would have been my loss. I'm grateful for all you've done for me. I wish you the best life has to offer, Rashid."

He studied her for a moment. This was the time for him to say something, if there was anything to say. He merely in-clined his head.

"And you, Bethanne."

Bethanne summoned a smile and turned, walking swiftly to the car. There was nothing left to say.

* * *

When the jet landed in Alkaahdar, she finalized all the details for leaving the plane near the private hangar. Taking her bag, she saw Rashid had already disembarked. She carefully withdrew the beautiful dress from her case, along with the shoes and golden necklace. Putting them on the sofa, she was sure they wouldn't be overlooked. Glancing around once more, she smiled. This jet was the best Starcraft had to offer. She knew Rashid would get years of service from it. She'd think about him from time to time, imagining him flying high in the plane. And she'd remember the times they'd flown together.

"Bless this aircraft and all who fly it," she murmured before leaving.

When she reached the tarmac, she looked around for a conveyance to take her to the main terminal. She had a flight to Texas to catch.

CHAPTER NINE

"So THE deal is signed," Khalid said.

"It is. We begin to implement next week," Rashid returned. He looked up from his desk. "What are you doing here?"

"Came to say goodbye for a while. I'm heading inland on another consultation job for a new field opening up. I'll be gone a few weeks, probably."

"The Hari fields?"

Khalid nodded, walking around the office. He touched one of the statues on the bookcase, then went to the window.

"Where's your pilot?"

"She's not my pilot."

Khalid turned at that. "You could have fooled me. You seemed as besotted with her as you were with Marguerite."

"Then that should have told you something."

"Only I don't think Miss Bethanne Sanders is anything like Marguerite."

"Don't bet the oil field on it," Rashid said.

Khalid raised an eyebrow in silent question.

Rashid hesitated, but Khalid was his twin.

"She wanted something from me after all."

"Money?"

He shrugged. Hesitating a moment, he looked up. "She said she loved me. Once."

Khalid stopped and stared at his twin.

"And that's a problem because?"

"She was trying to get info on Hank."

"That must have hit her hard, when she learned you thought he'd stolen the plane."

Sighing at the inevitability, Rashid related the entire story to his brother.

"I wanted you to remember our father with love. How honorable was it for him to have another family?" Khalid said. "I never expected anyone from Hank's family to show up. Was she hurt when she discovered his death?"

He shook his head. "I believe she'd known all along, just kept hoping. I'm the one in the wrong, accusing her father of theft when it was ours who acted dishonorably. Did you ever meet her? Our sister? What was she like?"

"I didn't know about her until after her death," Khalid said. "Father had pictures of her. He loved her mother and her. I have the photos. You can look at them if you wish."

"So there is love in the world," Rashid said.

"Which doesn't always bring happiness. Do you think any of them were happy?"

"Maybe the daughter, cherished by both her parents."

"At least he went after the love he wanted. Ever think you should have gone after Marguerite?"

Rashid shook his head. "But I'm thinking of going after Bethanne."

"Why not?" Khalid asked.

"You're suggesting that I should? I thought you didn't like her."

"I like her fine. I was worried she was after something else. But if she wanted closure about her father, that's different."

"She doesn't care about me—she only wanted to find out about her father."

"There were other ways to do that than pretend to be involved with you. To say she was in love."

"You thought she was after something and she was."

"Family. Not money. There's a big difference," Khalid said.

Rashid nodded. "She wished me a good life." He remembered how he'd fought to resist taking her into his arms when she'd said that. He had let her go without telling her he wanted her more than anything—even his next breath.

"She's gone?"

Rashid shook his head. "I still haven't signed off on the new jet. She can't leave before then. That's as important to her as finding her father was."

"Then I suggest you decide if you want to end up like our father, or maybe grab for the gold ring first time round," Khalid said.

Rashid drove to the villa as soon as Khalid left. Entering, he called for Bethanne. Minnah came into the foyer.

"Excellency, she is not here. She took you to Morocco. Did she not fly you back?"

"She did, earlier this morning. She didn't return here?"

"No. I have not seen her."

He turned and went back to the car. Where would she be? He never knew what to expect with her. Was she still at the plane like in Marrakech? Rashid headed for the airport, feeling a sense of déjà vu.

A quick cursory inspection upon arrival showed the jet empty—except for the dress he'd bought her in Marrakech. She truly had wanted nothing from him except to find her father. A woman more unlike Marguerite he'd never find.

He pulled out his cell phone and called his office, setting every assistant he had with the task of finding Bethanne Sanders. He also instructed them to let him know the minute the Starcraft office opened in Texas. He had to find her and he was calling in all markers to do so.

Impatiently Rashid drove back to his office. He would find out more from there than running around town. Walking in, he began to fire questions at his assistant.

"Did you check the local hotels? How about car rental companies? Car hire companies. She has to be somewhere."

The assistant nodded. "We've been checking every place in the capital city, Excellency."

"I have a confirmation," one of the clerks said, looking worried.

"And?" Rashid snapped.

"She departed the airport at eleven on a flight to Rome."

Rashid couldn't believe she'd left.

He went into his office and closed the door.

Bethanne watched as the smoggy air of Rome seemed to encase the airliner as it descended into Leonardo Da Vinci Airport. She had several hours to wait for a connecting flight to New York. Time enough to visit a few of the highlights of the city. She couldn't muster much enthusiasm for that, however. Still, who knew if she'd ever be in Rome again? And it beat the other choice—sit and brood.

When they landed, she waited until more impatient passengers had deplaned, then followed. Finding a locker, she stowed her flight bag and went to find a cab to drive her around the city. Her flight did not depart until ten that evening. She had time to see some of Rome and get a fabulous dinner before heading for the United States.

Despite her best efforts, Bethanne couldn't help comparing what she saw in the city with the buildings and architecture she'd loved in Quishari. Both countries were old, both rich in history. She was fascinated by all she saw and wished she could share it with Rashid.

How long would it be until she no longer felt his loss like a part of her had been cut out? She knew she would survive, but wasn't sure she wanted to. She *ached* with longing to see him again. Touch him. Share a warm kiss. Go sailing or flying. Or just spend the evening on the veranda listening to the waves of the sea.

Hours later, after finishing her dinner, she took another taxi back to the airport. The city gleamed with lights, looking beautiful in the soft illumination. But Bethanne was blind to it all. It was all she could do to keep from bursting into tears.

She probably had no job. Would be hard-pressed to find another one as perfect as this one had been. She had walked away from the only man she'd ever loved, which had been the hardest thing she'd ever done. Harder than acknowledging finally that her beloved father was gone. Raw emotions had her so confused. She wanted to go home, crawl into bed and weep for a week.

Her future was uncertain, except for the ache in her heart. She pressed a hand against her chest, trying to ease the pain.

She'd found her father, but would have traded that for another few days with Rashid al Harum. Pretending they were falling in love.

Or not pretending, falling for real.

She retrieved her flight bag when she reached the airport. Shopping at one of the kiosks there, she couldn't find any books in English. She'd do better to sleep on the flight, but was too keyed up. Finding a couple of magazines she could look at, she headed for her gate.

"Bethanne."

Turning, she stared at Sheikh Rashid al Harum. Or a man

who looked a lot like him. She shut her eyes tightly, then opened them. He still stood in front of her.

"Rashid?" she asked tentatively.

"You constantly surprise me. Makes for an interesting relationship."

"What are you doing here?"

"I'm flying to the United States on a flight that leaves at ten. You?"

She licked her lips. "I'm leaving on that flight, too. Why are you going to the United States?"

"To spend time with you, of course."

"Of course? There's no of course. You made your feelings perfectly well known to me."

"Perhaps we have a minor misunderstanding."

"Rashid, what's going on?"

"I didn't expect you to leave like that. I guess I expected more Yankee tenacity."

"What are you talking about? You practically ordered me to leave. I don't understand."

He glanced at his watch, stepped out of the way of a porter with a trolley of bags. Taking her arm, he pulled her to the side of the concourse. "It's not often I admit to making mistakes. I try not to make them to begin with. But I made a monumental one with you."

"Pretending to be involved?" That hurt.

"Not admitting when the pretense ended."

"When you signed the contract in Marrakech," she said.

"No, when it changed to love."

Bethanne's eyes widened. "If you're throwing that up to me—"

"What I'm trying to say is that I love you."

Rashid smiled at her look of astonishment, dropping his briefcase and pulling her into his embrace, kissing her on the mouth.

"Rashid!" she exclaimed when she pulled back. "This is a public place."

"So? I want the world to know I love you. What better place to start than here?"

"Here?"

"Everyone is greeting someone or bidding them farewell. Kisses are not out of the ordinary. Though I prefer our kisses to be in private. I don't wish to share."

"Did you say you loved me?" she asked.

"I did. I'll say it again. I love you, Bethanne Sanders. I fought against it. I didn't want to fall in love—my experience with that emotion has not been good. But foolish thought, that I can control emotions. You are all I have ever sought for in a partner. Beautiful, smart, talented in ways I can't compete, and interesting enough to keep me enthralled for decades."

She laughed, throwing her arms around his neck. "I am so unsuitable to be the wife of Arabian royalty. I'm much too casual in dress and manner to impress your associates. I want to fly whenever I can and I really don't think your mother is going to be at all happy with this. But I love you! I've been in the biggest funk ever since I left Alkaahdar. I thought I'd never see you again."

"I couldn't believe you left." He hugged her tightly, as if he'd never let her go. "So does this mean you will marry me? Live with me in Quishari? Spend our nights together, maybe even have a few kids to round things out? I love you, my dearest Bethanne. Will you marry me?"

She stared at him, faces so close she could not see anything around them. Her heart pounded. He'd asked her to marry him. Dare she risk it?

Dare she refuse?

"I would be so honored, but you must know what you're doing first."

"Oh, I know exactly what our life will be like. We'll live at the villa. My grandmother loved that house. We can raise our children to love the sea and the air. Will you insist on their learning to fly?"

"Perhaps not insist. But if they love it, we can't stand in their way. Are you serious? About everything? Marriage, children? You and me?"

"I love you. Why wouldn't I want to spend the rest of my life with you? I thought a lot about my father and his love and daughter in Quraim Wadi Samil. His happiness could not be complete because he never severed the legal bonds that kept him from staying with the woman he loved. I don't want to be dying and regret a single moment we spent apart."

"I never thought I'd get married. I wanted the life my father had—flying around the world. But he found his spot in Quishari. He lived there the longest of any place after he was an adult. And I know why. I love what I've discovered about Quishari. I think I would be happy living there. And flying wherever the mood takes us."

"I have just the plane for that."

The announcement for their flight was made.

He hugged her and then released her. "So, do we go on to the U.S. or back to Quishari?"

"Whichever you choose," she said.

"Ah, the perfect answer for a perfect wife-to-be." He dropped a quick kiss on her lips.

"This time. I'm not planning to become a yes person," she warned, warmth in her voice.

He laughed, clasping her hand in his and retrieving his briefcase. "I never expected that. I'll take it when I can get it. Let's go to Texas so I can meet your parents and tell them of our plans."

"My mother is going to be astonished." And, she bet her

mother would be thrilled to know her daughter was marrying a sheikh.

"I believe my mother will be as well," he said wryly.

"I told you, I value truth. Your mother's honest. Maybe she'll come around one day, or maybe not. It will never change how I feel about you. I love you. I always will."

"That I'll hold you to." He lifted her hand to kiss it. "I will always love you," he vowed. "Come what may, we'll always have to look for clear skies and smooth flights."

"Always."

The future beckoned bright with happy promise.

* * * * *

The Correttis

Introducing the Correttis, Sicily's most scandalous family!

On sale 3rd May

On sale 7th June

On sale 5th July

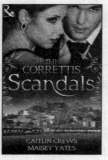

On sale 2nd August

Mills & Boon® Modern™ invites you to step over the threshold and enter the Correttis' dark and dazzling world…

Find the collection at
www.millsandboon.co.uk/specialreleases

Visit us Online

0513/MB415